Praise For Hilary Green

'Epic' *Sunday Express*

'An unforgettable saga of love and loss in wartime'
Good Book Guide

'Compelling' *Publishing News*

'A delightful and heady mix of romantic ingredients – spies, high-kicking dancers, forbidden love and friendship in the face of death. Who could ask for anything more?'
Lancashire Evening Post

'Leaves you holding your breath for the next instalment'
Historical Novel Society

Also by the same author

We'll Meet Again
Never Say Goodbye

The Follies Series
Now is the Hour
They Also Serve
Theatre of War

About the author

Hilary Green is a trained actress and spent many years teaching drama and running a youth theatre company. She has also written scripts for BBC Radio and won the Kythira short story prize. Hilary is now a full-time writer.

HILARY GREEN

The Final Act

First published in Great Britain in 2009 by Hodder & Stoughton
An Hachette Livre UK company

4

A Hodder Paperback

A CIP catalogue record for this title is available from the British Library

ISBN 978 0 340 93267 4

Typeset in Plantin Light by Hewer Text UK Ltd, Edinburgh
Printed and bound by Clays Ltd, St Ives plc

Hodder & Stoughton policy is to use papers that are natural, renewable and recyclable products and made from wood grown in sustainable forests. The logging and manufacturing processes are expected to conform to the environmental regulations of the country of origin.

Hodder & Stoughton Ltd
338 Euston Road
London NW1 3BH

www.hodder.co.uk

This book is dedicated to all those who entertained us during World War Two, helping to maintain the morale of both troops and civilians and lightening a very dark period in our history.

I should like to express my thanks to Silvano Valiensi who fought with the partisans in the Garfagnana and was kind enough to give up his time to make sure that my facts were correct and to provide me with many fascinating details. As always I am grateful for the help and encouragement of Vivien Green, my agent and Alex Bonham, my editor at Hodder and to my husband David for proofreading.

I

England in March – specifically, the village of Wimborne in Dorset. A still, quiet evening under a sky of unsullied duck-egg blue, save where a line of purple cloud lay like a bruise along the western horizon. Rose Taylor put down her suitcase at the garden gate and eased her aching back. Under the fruit trees in the cottage garden daffodils glimmered in the fading light and a blackbird dropped the notes of its evening song like pearls into a still pool. The garden smelled of rich, moist earth and the green odour of new grass. Rose breathed it in, relishing it after the astringent saltiness of the sea, trying to shut out of her mind the memory of other, less recent smells, the smells of mud and blood and decay. She picked up her case, pushed open the gate and walked up the path.

Her mother answered the door in her apron. 'Rose! Oh, Rose, love! You're here! Why didn't you let us know when to expect you?'

Rose hugged her, smelling a mixture of soap and freshly baked cakes. 'Hello, Mum. How are you?'

'Me? I'm fine. What about you? Let's have a look at you.' She held her off and gazed at her. 'My goodness, aren't you brown!'

Rose laughed. 'I know. Madame would be furious, wouldn't she? But you can't help getting a tan where I've been.'

'You look well, really well. Never mind what Dolly Prince would say. Come in, come in! I'll put the kettle on. You've never walked all the way from the station!'

'There weren't any taxis.'

Rose followed her mother into the kitchen. Obviously Mrs Taylor had just finished her tea. There was an eggcup containing an empty shell on the table, together with the remains of a loaf and a pot of home-made jam. The table was laid for one.

Mrs Taylor went on. 'Why on earth didn't you phone? Jack Willis would have come and picked you up. We weren't expecting you till tomorrow, earliest.'

'I know.' Rose smiled at her. 'The ship docked earlier than we expected, in the middle of last night, but I didn't ring you from Liverpool because I had no idea how long it was going to take me to get here. You know what the trains are like. And I did try ringing the Willises from the station, but there was no reply. I expect they're both outside working.'

'Yes, that would be it,' her mother agreed. 'It's a busy time of the year for people with a market garden.'

'You don't have to tell me. I remember,' Rose said with a laugh.

''Course you do!' Mrs Taylor was putting the kettle on. 'Only it seems so long since you were here. Nearly a year, and then it was only for a couple of weeks. Oh, it is good to have you home again!'

'It's good to be here, Mum,' Rose told her. 'Coming up the lane just now I suddenly felt really homesick. Silly that, isn't it? I mean, it's not as if I grew up here, but somehow when I think of home I think of here, not Lambeth.' She paused and looked round the kitchen. 'Where are Bet and the boys?'

On the long journey from Liverpool she had been imagining her homecoming and her mental picture had always included her sister and the two boys. She had presents for all of them in her case. It was good to see her mother again, but without the noise and excitement the boys would have created it felt a bit flat.

'They're up at the farm,' Mrs Taylor said, briefly. 'Now, I bet you're hungry. How about a boiled egg? Enid Willis gave me half a dozen this morning – strictly off the ration, of course – but I've been helping out in the market garden. Want one?'

'A real fresh egg? Oh, yes, rather! I can't remember when I last had a fresh boiled egg! Bet's still working up at the farm, then? I thought it was mornings only.'

Mrs Taylor put a pan on the stove for the egg and then turned and sat down opposite Rose. Her expression was solemn and Rose felt a sudden twinge of anxiety.

'She is all right – Bet, I mean? I felt awful, having to leave so soon after Reg was killed. And her letters have been a bit – I don't know – odd, somehow. Not like Bet. Has she got over it?'

Mrs Taylor drew a breath and compressed her lips. Then she said, 'Yes, she's got over it.' She leaned across the table and put her hand over Rose's. 'Rose, love, I've got a bit of news and it'll be a shock to you. Bet's married again.'

'*Married!*' Rose stared at her mother. 'Married again! Why on earth didn't you write and tell me? Who's she married to?'

In her mind a succession of faces flipped past like the riffled pages of a book. Who did they know in Wimborne? Most of the men were either too old or too young. All the rest were away in the services. Perhaps it was a serviceman, someone stationed at the nearby airbase, maybe. The thoughts raced through her mind as she stared back into her mother's serious eyes.

Mrs Taylor said, 'We thought it would be best to wait until you came home. Didn't want to upset you, while you were overseas.'

'Upset me?' Rose frowned. 'Why should I be upset because Bet's married? Good luck to her, I say.'

Her mother's hand tightened a little on her own. 'She's married Matthew, Rose. Just after Christmas.'

Rose gazed at her in silence. *Bet was married to Matthew!* Matthew, who had proposed marriage to Rose herself. Who had announced their engagement without warning on that ill-fated New Year's Eve when Richard had arrived out of the blue, just when she had given up hope of ever seeing him again. Matthew, who, more than a year later, had hinted that the offer was still open. Matthew was now married to Bet.

Her mother was saying, 'I'm sorry. You had to be told. Do you mind very much?'

'I don't know,' Rose replied breathlessly. It was true. She simply did not know whether to be hurt, or angry, or relieved. 'I suppose . . . I suppose, as long as they're both happy, it's none of my business, is it?'

'Of course it's your business,' her mother said gently. 'No one's forgotten that he asked you first. It hasn't been easy for Bet, either – being second best. But over this last year they've got to know each other. Bet's really taken to the work at the farm. You'd never think she was brought up in Lambeth! And, of course, the boys love it up there.'

'How do they get on with Matthew?'

'Like a house on fire! Better than they did with their own dad in the last few months before he was killed. Things weren't right between them for a long time, you know.'

'Yes, I remember,' Rose murmured. Now that the first shock had passed she was beginning to realise that her main emotion was one of relief. Now she need not worry about Bet and the boys, and she could meet Matthew without feeling guilty. She looked up and smiled at her mother. 'It's for the best, isn't it? Bet's much more suited to that life than I am. She needs a good home and a good man to help her bring up the boys and Matt is a good man. They deserve each other. I'd have got itchy feet after a few months and wanted to go back to the theatre. This is better all round.'

Her mother gave a sigh of relief. 'I'm so glad you see it like that! It's been a weight on my mind, I can tell you. When you've had your tea will you go up and see them? I know Bet will be relieved to know everything's all right.'

'Of course I will,' Rose said. 'I'm dying to see her, and the boys. I bet they've grown!'

'You won't recognise Billy, hardly,' her mother prophesied. 'Quite a young man now, he is!'

She set the egg in front of Rose and cut a doorstep of freshly baked bread. Then she seated herself opposite her again and poured them both another cup of tea.

'So, what about you, love? How is everything with you?'

'Fine!' Rose said, with just a little too much emphasis. 'I love the job and the girls in the troupe are great. Oh, we have our ups and downs and some of them can be a bit temperamental, but you can't blame them for that. It's been tough in Italy and the conditions are pretty awful sometimes. But it's so rewarding! You should see the faces of some of the soldiers we perform for. Some of them haven't seen a woman for months and they're living in the most appalling conditions and suddenly we bring a bit of glamour, a bit of life and colour into that miserable existence.'

'Sounds a bit dangerous to me,' her mother said dubiously. 'A few young girls among all those lonely men.'

'It's not, Mum,' Rose said earnestly. 'At least, the danger is not from our soldiers. They always behave perfectly. Oh, they whistle and catcall and ogle the girls during the performances, but afterwards they just want a chance to be near us, to talk about their wives and girlfriends back home. I've seen men in tears, Mum. Grown men crying just because we remind them of what they've left behind.'

Mrs Taylor frowned. 'It's bad, then? Everyone thought once the Italians surrendered it was going to be a doddle.'

Rose swallowed. She knew that it was part of her duty not to spread alarm and despondency among the civilian population but there was a hard knot of anger in her stomach when she thought about the suffering she had seen.

'Mum, you've no idea. People think Italy's all sunshine and . . . and pretty girls treading grapes under a blue sky. Well, it's not. The ordinary peasants are desperately poor. They live on dry bread and onions and a bit of olive oil and plough the fields with oxen as if they were still living in the Dark Ages. This winter's been awful. The rain has just gone on and on and up in the mountains it's bitterly cold. Our men are up to their knees in mud and they often don't see a hot meal for days on end. The casualties are horrific, but they don't seem to be able to move. The Germans are in such strong positions we can't shift them. Some of the men are what we call "bomb happy" – it's like shell shock. They just can't take it any more and they have to be sent back to special rest camps. We've played some of the camps and it's pathetic to see the state they're in.'

Rose paused and looked at her mother's face. She had said much more than she had intended but she had needed to speak out, to somehow puncture the bland complacency of civilian life. Now she was afraid that she had upset her mother, but Mrs Taylor merely compressed her lips and nodded.

'It's bad, then,' she repeated. But Rose knew that her message had gone home. There was a pause. Then her mother went on. 'Did you see Merry before you left?'

'Yes, he came to the docks in Naples to see us off.'

'How is he?'

'He's fine. Now that we know Felix wasn't killed when his plane crashed after all, he's as happy as . . .' Rose checked herself. She had never been sure how much her mother guessed, but she suspected that she would be deeply shocked if she knew the true nature of the relationship between the two men. Now she was afraid that she had said too much again. Her mother simply nodded, however, and finished the sentence for her.

'Happy as Larry. Fancy Felix turning up like that, out of the blue. Must have seemed like a miracle.'

'Yes, it did,' Rose agreed. She was trying to think of some way of changing the subject, because any explanation of Felix's sudden reappearance would involve a mention of Richard's part in it, and she had no wish to bring his name into the conversation. She finished her egg. 'That was absolutely delicious, Mum. Thanks.'

'Don't thank me, thank Enid Willis,' her mother responded. 'More tea?'

'Please. How arc the Willises? Has Babe been home lately?'

'She was home for Christmas, with her husband.'

'What's he like?'

'Oh, very nice. Good looking, good manners – like all these Yanks. But that doesn't make it any easier for Enid.'

'He's a Canadian, Mum, not a Yank.'

Mrs Taylor sniffed. 'Same difference.' There was a pause. Rose felt herself tense. She knew what was coming next. 'How's that young man of yours? You still writing to each other?'

'He's not *my young man*, Mum. He's just a . . . a man I happen to be friendly with. Yes, we're still writing. He's fine. Well, he was last time I heard.'

She thought of Beau, with his fresh-faced good looks and his old-fashioned, courtly manners. He was still talking about taking her home to meet his 'folks', as if it was a foregone conclusion, and she had still not had the courage – or was it hardness of heart? – to disabuse him. One look at her mother's shut face told her that her greatest fear was that she might follow the same path as Barbara Willis and marry a man who would remove her to the other side of the globe. She got up and moved round behind her mother's chair to give her a hug.

'Don't worry, Mum. I'm not going to marry Beau and leave you.'

Her mother did not respond to the gesture. 'You must do what your heart tells you. Never mind me. I'll survive.'

'I am doing what my heart tells me,' Rose said, and for the first time she was quite sure that it was the truth. 'I'm not in love with Beau and I'm not going to marry him.'

'Is there someone else, then?' her mother asked, tilting her head to look up.

'No, there's no one else,' Rose assured her.

Mrs Taylor did not look reassured. 'What you going to do with yourself then, girl? This war's not going to go on for ever, please God. You don't want to end up a bitter old maid.'

Rose drew back. 'Oh, really, Mum! Just because I'm not prepared to marry any man who asks me, that doesn't mean I'm going to end up an old maid. And even if I do, I shan't be bitter.' She resumed her seat on the opposite side of the table. 'I've got a good job, a job I love. It's great being in charge of all the dancers in a show, and being able to choreograph all the numbers. And I'm good at it, Mum! I don't see why I shouldn't go on doing it after the war. I might get a job in one of the big London theatres – or I could end up like Madame, with my own show somewhere.'

A smile forced its way through the cloud of anxiety on Mrs Taylor's broad face. 'Can't see you as an old tartar like Dolly Prince. You haven't got it in you.'

'Well, no, not quite like her,' Rose agreed, grinning back. She leaned forward and put her hand over her mother's. 'Don't worry about me, Mum. One thing I've learned in the last year or two. I can manage on my own. I don't have to have a fellow to rely on. There are lots of girls like me, who've made the same discovery. Girls who've found out they can do men's jobs, driving lorries, working in factories, even flying planes. Things are going to be different after the war. Women are going to want more than just a home and kids, and they won't be ashamed of not being married. For one thing, there won't be enough men to go round. I shan't be the only "old maid" – if that's the way things turn out.'

Mrs Taylor sighed and got up. 'Well, as long as you're happy. But just don't go turning your nose up too quickly. You might live to regret it.'

'I'm not "turning my nose up"!' Rose began to exclaim in exasperation. Then she stopped. She knew from experience that it was no good trying to talk her mother out of an entrenched idea, but at least she had scotched the immediate worry over her relationship with Beau. She got up from the table and began to clear the dishes.

'You leave that,' her mother commanded. 'You've had a long day. If you've got any energy left, go up and see your sister at the farm. She'll be on tenterhooks till she knows how you feel – and so will Matthew.'

Half an hour later Rose pedalled her mother's bike up the country lane towards the farm. As she passed the Willises' smallholding she was tempted to stop and call in, but she knew that if she did it would be an hour before she could get away, and Bet would never forgive her for visiting someone else before going to see her. As she pedalled onwards she was swept by a sudden feeling of intense nostalgia. She had ridden this way so often, on her way to work at the farm. Now she had the strange impression that the intervening time had been wiped out, that she had merely been away for a short holiday and she would find the farm, and Matthew, exactly as she had left them. No, not as she had left them, but as they had been in those early months, before Matthew proposed to her. At a gateway into a field she dismounted. Cows were grazing the lush spring grass and she gazed from one to another, trying to recognise individual animals. At one time she had known each one by name, but now she could not be sure if they were even the same cows. After all, it had been more than three years.

Three years! Not just a short holiday. So much had happened since she last cycled up this lane. Those terrible months at the farm in Shropshire, which had ended with the illness that had come close to killing her. The weeks that had followed of recuperation and then the long struggle to get fit again and to relearn her dancing technique and the soul-destroying disappointment of failed auditions. And then the time she had spent touring with Monty Prince and his little ENSA company. Good old Monty! She must try to see him when she got back to town, if he was around. She remembered the grimy industrial cities, the performances in factory canteens, the dismal digs. There was that nice man who gave up his room so she could have a bed – in Coventry, wasn't it? What was his name? Then memory returned like a blow to the stomach. He had gone on the night shift so as to leave the room vacant for her and had been killed when the factory was bombed. *And she couldn't even remember his name!*

Rose remounted and put her weight on the pedals, so that she swept into the farmyard scattering chickens and ducks in all directions.

Getting off the bike, she found that her heart was thudding with more than the effort. She had no idea what she was going to say to Bet – or to Matthew. It was the two boys who smoothed over the difficulty. As Rose stood hesitating, the door of the farm kitchen crashed open and Billy and Sam hurled themselves through it.

'Auntie Rose! Auntie Rose! When did you get back? Have you brought me a present?' Sam flung himself against her with a force that almost toppled both her and the bike. She hugged him with her frec arm, laughing.

'Hallo, Sammy! How are you? A present? Oh, now, I don't know. I'll have to see what I can find, won't I?' She looked beyond him to his brother. Her mother had been right. She would scarcely have recognised him as the same pale-faced, scrawny kid she had known in Lambeth. At fourteen he was half a head taller than herself, brown faced and with a man's shoulders and the beginning of a moustache shadowing his upper lip. He had checked his headlong rush and now stood, suddenly shy, a few feet away. Rose reached out a hand over Sammy's shoulder. 'Hello, Billy. My goodness, I wouldn't have known you. You're so grown-up!'

He smiled, still shy, and came close enough for her to give him a peck on the cheek. Looking past him, she saw Bet standing in the doorway with Matthew behind her, her expression a complex mixture of defiance and appeal.

'Hold my bike a minute, Billy,' Rose commanded, and as he took it she ran forward. There was no time to compose suitable words. She flung her arms round her sister, exclaiming, 'Oh, Bet! I am glad to see you! Congratulations! I'm so happy for you. For both of you!' She drew back and looked at Matthew, reading in his face the same mingling of pride and embarrassment and apology. Rose moved to him and held out her hand. 'Congratulations, Matthew. You picked the right girl in the end.'

He blushed and ducked his head to kiss her on the cheek. 'Welcome home, Rose. It's good to see you.' Then, turning to put his arm round his wife's ample waist, 'Yes, I do believe I did, in the end.'

2

Captain Guy Merryweather edged his jeep through the crowded streets of Naples, en route to his office at the headquarters of the Combined Services Entertainments Pool. He was feeling jaded and depressed and the sight of the city around him only added to his gloom. When he had arrived in Naples in the last glow of autumn he had thought nothing, not even the malicious depredations of the departing Nazis, could ruin the beauty of the place. Now, in the cold light of a reluctant spring and under the seemingly unceasing rain, he saw it for the slum it was. Its people were on the verge of starvation, in spite of the shiploads of supplies from America that were unloaded daily at the docks and which, nightly, seemed to disappear from under the eyes of the guards, to resurface on the black market. Mingling with the locals were the hordes of servicemen – British, American, Italian, Free French, Poles – who were on leave or recovering from wounds. He saw three of them on a street corner, chatting to an Italian girl who had once, you could just see, been ripely beautiful but was now gaunt and garish, flaunting her wares even at this early hour. Naples was becoming such a hotbed of venereal disease that the authorities were considering putting the city off limits to all military personnel not actually employed there.

Meanwhile, the Allied armies were still bogged down along the Gustav Line, unable to break through the German defences, and the Americans, under General Mark Clark, had failed to capitalise on their initial advantage and were now penned into the Anzio beachhead. The expected triumphant progress through the territory of an enemy recently turned ally had become a miserable war of attrition.

Merry had his own reasons for depression. All through North Africa and to a large extent in Sicily he had operated as a free agent, keeping up with the front-line troops and off-loading his piano to give impromptu concerts wherever it seemed appropriate. When he had been summoned to Italy to help run the Combined Pool he had been given to understand that a large part of his job would still be up at the front, still actively engaged in performing or directing. Instead he found himself chained to a desk, and the enormous success of the Gala Performance in the Opera House last Christmas only seemed to have confirmed the idea in the minds of the top brass that his place was here in Naples.

As he parked the jeep and made his way through the corridors of the hotel that they had requisitioned as HQ, Merry was sufficiently self-aware for an inward, ironic smile. He was fed up, 'browned off' in the current parlance, but simply being able to experience the sensation showed how far he had come from the numb despair of a few months earlier. Felix was alive. Beside that fact, nothing else really mattered.

Merry's efficient secretary had already sorted the mail and laid it out on his desk. On top of the pile was a letter whose provenance he immediately recognised. Presumably she had recognised it too, which was why it was on top. He picked it up with a tremor of anxiety. He was not expecting a letter from Felix, since he had not yet had time to reply to the last one. They had parted two months ago, in Cairo, after a fortnight's leave, every moment of which was stored away in Merry's memory to be retrieved and relived in the quiet of his own room, between sleeping and waking. Felix had been posted back to London, where, as he had predicted, he was 'flying a desk' at the Air Ministry. That was fine by Merry, who found the possibility that he might be wounded by a random bomb easier to live with than the thought of him risking his life in the skies over Europe. He knew Felix well enough, however, to understand that he would not rest until he had persuaded the 'penguins' at the ministry to let him get back in the air. And now this letter . . . ? His hand shook slightly as he tore open the envelope.

My dear Merry,

This is just a hasty note to tell you that my father has been killed. Apparently he was on his way back from the States and the plane he was in was shot down over the Atlantic. There were no survivors.

My mother contacted the Air Ministry to find out where I was and I got the news via my CO this morning. I have been given five days' compassionate leave and am bidden home for the memorial service! Though God knows what role I have been cast in – black sheep or Prodigal Son?

No time to write further now, as I have to catch a train within the hour. I'll let you know how things go as soon as I get back.

Yours ever,

Ned

PS. Wish you were coming with me!

Merry folded the letter and sat gazing at it abstractedly while he tried to work out the implications of the news. So the Hon. Edward Mountjoy – aka Felix Lamont, one-time magician and *illusioniste extraordinaire* – was about to return to the family home from which he had been banished – what? – ten years ago. What sort of reception could he expect? Was it possible that his mother had been so shocked by the death of her husband that she had decided to put her moral scruples aside and be reconciled to her errant son? Recalling his one encounter with Lady Malpas, Merry thought it was unlikely. Perhaps she felt that, whatever his misdemeanours, Felix (Merry could never think of him by any other name) could not be denied the right to mourn his father with the rest of the family. Or was it simply that it would 'look bad' to the neighbours if he failed to show up at the memorial service? That, Merry decided cynically, was probably the most likely explanation. But, in that case, at least the proprieties would be observed. No one outside the immediate family must be allowed to guess that the younger son of the Mountjoys had disgraced his name. Merry clenched his teeth to suppress the sudden upsurge of anger. It did not matter to him that society made men of their persuasion outcasts. He had learned to live with it long ago, and besides, he had no family left to be distressed or disgraced. But he knew, although they had never spoken of it, that his parents' attitude was a wound in Felix's soul that still festered, like a piece of shrapnel embedded too close to a nerve to be removed.

There was nothing he could do to help at this range, however, so he wrote a brief note asking Felix to give his condolences to his mother and expressing the hope that the visit would turn out better than he expected. He added that he would be thinking of him and looked forward to hearing further from him as soon as he had a chance to write.

The next day Merry left Naples for a brief tour of the battlefields, to see for himself the conditions under which his artistes were performing. On his return his vague sense of depression had been replaced by two much stronger and mutually contradictory emotions. One was anger at the incompetence of the High Command that had allowed the Allied forces to get into their current position. The other was admiration for the way those forces were conducting themselves in the face of constant bombardment and the obstacles thrown in their way by a combination of the enemy, the weather and the local terrain. He had particular sympathy for the men of the tank regiments, with whom he had crossed the desert the previous year. That had been a bitter and bloody struggle in extreme conditions, but at least there had been space in which the tanks could be deployed effectively and, towards the end at least, an exhilarating sense of forward movement. Here in Italy it was very different. The route to the north was regularly bisected by mountain spurs running down from the Apennines and between them were deep ravines carved by rivers swollen to torrents by the endless rain. The Germans had blown every bridge and mined every culvert and each river crossing required a long and costly battle. The Americans had lost hundreds of men in the attempt to cross the Rapido alone. In the towns and villages things were no better. The tanks were reduced to crawling single file through the narrow streets where every building presented a possible vantage point for a sniper. And everywhere there was mud, in which the convoys of supply vehicles constantly became bogged down.

For the men whose job it was to lift the spirits of the troops and provide some respite from the stress of battle by offering an hour or two of entertainment, conditions were no easier. And not only men, now. Merry was also responsible for the well-being of the ENSA troupes sent out from England, which included women, and even some extremely well-known and glamorous female stars, although their activities were largely confined to the rest stations and hospitals behind the lines. Nevertheless, all had to travel the roads pitted by shell holes and churned up by tank tracks and cross ravines on hastily constructed bridges which were frequent targets for enemy bombing. As for the Stars in Battledress, the serving soldiers who had been pulled out of the front line to entertain their comrades and who were Merry's prime concern, he found them performing in roofless village schools or tents in the middle of fields churned to liquid mud or in the open air, where the music was often drowned out by the sound of incoming shells. Driving back into Naples, Merry reflected grimly that he had failed to appreciate his own good fortune in being confined to his snug hotel and his efficiently organised office.

Another letter from Felix awaited him on his desk, and a rapid calculation told Merry that it must have been written immediately on his return from Malpas, if not before.

My dear Merry,

God, I wish you were here! I have just experienced the most ghastly forty-eight hours of my life – and I am not excepting coming round in hospital after my first crash. Only the aftermath of the Cambridge business compares.

It seemed initially as if it was going to be all right. I was received pleasantly enough, not exactly with enthusiasm but with the sort of courtesy one extends to a visitor whom one has felt obliged to invite. (Dear God! Merry thought. This is his mother he's talking about!) *Brother Anthony was there, having been flown back from somewhere in mid-Atlantic, and was quite affable to start with. I got there on the day before the service and everything was OK until dinner. It was when I realised that the rector and his wife had been invited to dine with us that I knew I was for it. This same 'man of God' was largely responsible for all the trouble last time, I believe. Even so, we got along swimmingly to begin with. I was congratulated on the gong and there was tactful appreciation of Archie McIndoe's handiwork and relief was expressed that the rumours of my death had been so greatly exaggerated – to coin a phrase. Then he got closer to what he was really there for. The war, of course, was a terrible business, but it had had one good outcome. It had turned a lot of boys, who might otherwise have wasted their lives in the pursuit of pleasure, into men! I pointed out, as politely as I could, that it had also turned a lot of them into corpses. That did not go down well! He came closer to home then. It had to be admitted that as a youth I had tended to be 'somewhat frivolous'. (Nice phrase, that. Never heard it expressed that way before.) He quoted St Paul – when I was a child I thought as a child, etc. – and hoped that I had now put away childish things and proposed, in the words of the Prayer Book, to lead a 'sober, righteous and Godly life' from here on. I tried to lighten the tone a bit by remarking that as a serving officer in the RAF it was a bit difficult to lead on entirely sober life, but that was not well received either. The wretched man was not to be deflected. I was, he suggested, trying to avoid the real question. The point was that, in my youth, I had made some rather undesirable relationships and what my mother wished to be assured of was that this had now ceased. I was tempted to enquire why my mother could not ask the question herself, since she was sitting there at the table with us, but I'd had enough by this point. I mustered all the dignity I had left and said that yes, I admitted some of my friendships in the early days had been unwise, but that that was a thing of the past. (You should have seen how their faces brightened.) I had now, I went on, formed an honourable relationship with someone I love and respect and which I hope will last for the rest of my life. And at that point I excused myself and left the room.*

Merry lowered the paper and gazed blindly into space. He could sense, as if he felt it himself, the quivering distress which that calm exterior concealed and hear the clear, steady voice declaring 'an honourable relationship with someone I love and respect'. And he could read no further because his eyes were full of tears.

When he had himself under control again he unfolded the letter and read on.

I went down to the pub in the village, where I must say I got a very different reception. It seems I've become a bit of a local hero. They even have all the press cuttings about my DFC and the crash, both crashes, and my supposed death and subsequent 'resurrection' pinned up on a board behind the bar. The publican took them down and insisted on my signing them. After that, of course, I had to buy drinks all round and we had quite a jolly evening. I hung about until I thought everyone would have gone to bed, but no such luck! Brother Anthony – now, of course, Lord Malpas, though I find that very difficult to accept – was waiting up for me to read me a lecture on how much I had added to our mother's distress, etc., etc. I told him pretty sharply that if they hadn't set the rector on me the whole miserable scene could have been avoided. I added that it hadn't been my idea to come home and that, after tomorrow, I should probably never set foot in the place again. And that if he didn't want a punch on the nose we had better leave it at that.

I stayed for the service and the funeral baked meats next day (today, in fact) and made myself reasonably pleasant to assorted aunts and cousins and then made the excuse that I had to be back on duty the next day and buggered off back to town. I've got two days' leave left, so I think I shall go and look up a few old mates at (here the censor had obliterated a location with his blue pencil) *and get thoroughly drunk.*

I wish to God you weren't such a long way away! We could get plastered together! Write as soon as you can.

Yours as always,

Ned

Merry's hands were shaking as he put the letter back in the envelope. How could members of a family treat each other like that? How could a priest be so mercilessly sanctimonious? Then, as the first shock passed, he became aware of other emotions. There was an anxiety, which at first he found difficult to identify. Then it came to him. Those words, obliterated by the censor's pencil, had been a reminder that the letter had been read by a third party – as, of course, Felix would have known it would be. All servicemen's letters were automatically censored and Merry had had to read enough of his subordinates' mail to be aware of the intimate secrets which the censor could not avoid sharing. For this reason he and Felix had always been very circumspect in their correspondence. It was why, for a start, he always addressed Felix by his proper name – or at least the diminutive of it – and why the replies were signed in the same way. It avoided the need for explanations.

Now, however, in the white heat of emotion, Felix had forgotten to be cautious.

Merry took out the letter and reread it carefully. As he did so his alarm abated slightly. It would be obvious to anyone that there had been a family rift and that Felix had in some way disgraced himself but there was nothing that would indicate the nature of his misdemeanour. The reference to 'the Cambridge business' and phrases such as 'undesirable relationships' and 'unwise friendships' might suggest forays into homosexuality but could not be used to prove them. Likewise, his admission of 'an honourable relationship' in which he was now engaged could refer to a liaison with a woman, though perhaps not a woman of whom his family would approve. Merry drew a deep breath. Felix had not been as incautious as he had at first thought. The letter might have raised doubts in the mind of a senior officer – doubts which, if passed on, could possibly have an adverse effect on his prospects of promotion – but nothing worse. Meanwhile, for Merry the message was reassuringly clear. Faced with the choice between his family and his lover, Felix had bravely proclaimed their 'honourable relationship . . . which he hoped would last for the rest of his life'. Once again he folded the letter and tucked it into the breast pocket of his tunic, where it seemed to glow with talismanic warmth.

3

Rose stayed in Wimborne for ten days but returned to spend the last few days of her leave at her old flat in Lambeth. There were several old friends she wanted to look up, for one thing, but, far more importantly, she needed to see Beau. He had wanted to come down to Wimborne but she had struggled to think up excuses to put him off and had been relieved when it had turned out that he could not get leave. It seemed to her that giving him the opportunity to meet her 'folks' would simply reinforce his assumption that their relationship was going to be permanent. She had resolved to meet him in London and to clear up the misunderstanding once and for all. He managed to get an overnight pass and they arranged that he would pick her up at the flat on her first evening in town.

He arrived, as always, punctual to the minute in an immaculately pressed uniform and carrying an enormous box of chocolates, the like of which had not been seen in England since the outbreak of war. Rose, struck by guilt at the thought of what she intended to say, protested that he should not have been so extravagant.

'Why not?' he cried. 'Nothing's too good for my best girl!' He caught hold of her hands and held her at arms' length. 'Let me look at you. Gee, honey, you look great! I'd almost forgotten how gorgeous you are.'

She tried to look modestly self-deprecating, but the fact was that she had had her hair freshly permed and had spent longer than usual over her make-up. He whirled her round, laughing with pleasure, and then pulled her to him and kissed her, briefly and quite chastely, on the lips.

'Gee, honey, I've missed you! It's been one hell of a long time.'

She had forgotten how very good looking he was, and how infectious his sheer high spirits could be. She had been trying to decide whether to have things out with him straight away or whether it would be kinder to wait until the end of the evening. Now she decided to wait. After all, they might as well enjoy themselves while they could.

He took her to the Trocadero and as soon as they stepped on to the dance floor Rose was swept away by the pure exhilaration of dancing with a partner whose style so perfectly matched her own. They tangoed and quickstepped and jitterbugged all evening, and she was aware that very soon the other dancers were making space for them so as not to cramp their style. Once or twice the applause at the end of a number was just as much for them as for the band. When the time came to head for home she was hot and tired but her nerves were still humming with excitement like high-tension cables. In the taxi – Beau seemed to have a magical ability to conjure up taxis even in central London in the blackout – he put his arm round her and kissed her, a passionate, lover's kiss, and she felt her body respond. All her senses were crying out for her to let go, to give herself up to the pleasure of the moment. Only somewhere, at the back of her mind, a small, merciless voice kept reminding her that she had a different, much harder, task to perform.

When the taxi stopped he accompanied her, as always, to

her front door. It was a move dictated by his punctilious good manners, not by any desire to pressure her into asking him in. When she suggested that he might like to come up for a cup of coffee she saw him go pale and then flush, and before she could stop him he had turned away and paid off the taxi.

Inside the front door he swept her into his arms again, whispering in her ear, 'Oh, Rose, sweetheart! It's so good to have you back again. You don't know how much I've missed you.'

She struggled free and managed to say, 'Beau, come upstairs. We've got to talk.'

'Sure, honey. I guess there's a lot we've got to say to each other.'

He followed her meekly into the living room and sat down beside her on the settee. She took his hand in both her own and held it tightly.

He laughed. 'Hey, lighten up, sweetheart. I'm not going to take advantage of you.'

'I know that,' she said. Her chest felt constricted and it was difficult to draw enough breath to speak. 'Beau, I'm sorry. I've let you get entirely the wrong impression. I haven't asked you in for the reason you think.'

'Don't worry! I know you're not that sort of girl. I've waited over a year. I can wait a bit longer, I guess.'

She shook her head. 'That's the whole point, Beau. All this time, while I've been away, I've let you go on . . . waiting . . . and thinking . . . thinking . . . Oh, this is so difficult! You seem to have got the idea that we've got some sort of *understanding*.'

'Well, we have, haven't we? I think we understand each other pretty well.'

'No, that's what I'm trying to say. You *don't* understand.

I'm trying to tell you – some of the things you seem to take for granted just aren't going to happen.'

'Such as?' He looked puzzled, a little concerned, but not really worried.

She squeezed his hand hard to give herself courage. 'I don't want to come to America with you, Beau.'

'You don't?' He absorbed the information in silence for a moment, frowing with the concentration of a chess player caught by an unexpected move. 'Well, in that case, I guess I'll have to look at the possibilities of staying here, but I don't know . . .'

'*No, you still don't understand!*' She was getting desperate. Suppose she was the one who had got hold of the wrong end of the stick and his intentions were not at all what she imagined. She made up her mind that, right or wrong, she had to press on. 'Beau, you've made all these plans, but you've never even asked me to marry you.'

'I haven't?' He looked first confused, then apologetic. 'Gee whiz, Rose! No more I have! What an idiot! You've got every right to feel mad at me. Every woman deserves to get a proper, romantic proposal. There just never seemed to be the right time, or the right place. I've always imagined it'd be back home, on the front porch after my folks have gone to bed, with a big, yellow moon coming up and the scent of gardenias in the air. But I guess here and now will do just as well.' Before she could stop him he slid from the settee on to one knee, her hand still clasped in his. 'Rose, honey, will you do me the honour of becoming my wife?'

She looked at him. His big, handsome, country-boy's face shone with innocent confidence and there was no mistaking the love in his eyes. For a brief moment she pictured herself, sitting on that front porch, waiting for him to come home at the end of the working day. She never doubted for a moment that if she said 'yes' she would be secure in his unquestioning love for the rest of her life. Slowly, with an effort, she withdrew her hand from his.

'Beau, I'm sorry. I can't marry you. That's what I'm trying to tell you.'

He gazed up at her, his lips moving soundlessly as if she had spoken in a foreign language and he was trying to translate. 'You can't?'

'No. I'm sorry.'

'Are you trying to tell me you're married already?'

'No. I'm not married.'

'But there's someone else?'

'No.' For a moment she was tempted to say yes, but after all it would have been a lie. There was no one else – not any more.

'Then why can't you marry me?'

'Because I'm not in love with you. I like you very much. You're a lovely man. You're kind and generous and good looking and some other girl is going to be very, very lucky when you find her. But I'm not the right girl.'

'You are, as far as I'm concerned!'

'No, I'm not! Or you're not the right boy for me. I'm sorry, Beau, truly, truly sorry. But that's the way it is. I should have made it all clear much sooner but I felt I ought to wait until I could tell you face to face, rather than putting it in a letter.'

For a moment he was completely still and silent. Then he rose slowly to his feet.

'In that case, ma'am, I guess I'd better be moving along.' He spoke tonelessly, his face set in a mask of formal courtesy.

Rose jumped up. 'Beau, please! Don't take it like that. We can still be friends, can't we? We can still enjoy each other's company. Look what a good time we had this evening. We could go on doing that, couldn't we?'

He looked at her as if she had suggested that he take part in some strange foreign ritual. 'No, ma'am. I guess not.'

He picked up his cap from the chair where he had dropped it and headed for the door. Rose followed him downstairs to the street, reduced to a numb silence by the dignity of his pain.

At the door she tried again. 'Please, Beau! We can't part like this. I didn't mean to hurt you, but you had to know the truth. You just jumped to conclusions . . .'

He turned, bending his head towards her. 'Thanks for a very pleasant evening, ma'am. I guess I took too much for granted. I apologise. Goodnight.'

He opened the door and was gone, closing it behind him in one swift, decisive movement. For a moment she stood still, tempted to run after him. Then she turned and trudged slowly up the stairs. At the top she suddenly remembered that he had dismissed the taxi. Even Beau would not find a taxi in Lambeth at that time of night and she had no idea whether he could find his way around on the Underground. She sat down on the settee and began to weep silently.

The following morning she had arranged to meet her old friend Sally Castle. They had written to each other intermittently ever since they parted company after the last performance of the Fairbourne Follies and usually managed to meet up when Rose was in London. A couple of months earlier Sally had written to say that she had given up her job at the Windmill Theatre, where she had worked as a dancer almost since the outbreak of war. She gave no reason, except that she 'couldn't stand it any more'. Instead, under the government's Direction of Labour powers, she had found herself working in the Royal Ordnance factory at Greenwich. Rose found it difficult to imagine the flighty, pleasure-loving Sally working at a factory bench – but then, she would never have envisaged herself milking cows a few years ago.

Sally was working a late shift, so they had agreed to meet for morning coffee at their usual rendezvous, the Lyons Corner House at Piccadilly Circus. Rose had been looking forward to it, but now she was not in the mood for Sally's brittle banter. She had passed a miserable night, constantly replaying in her mind the scene with Beau and asking herself how she could have handled it better. She had acted with the best intentions but she could not escape a sense that she was responsible for his anguish. Somehow, at some point, she must have given him the impression that she saw the future as he did, a future they would spend together. She should have realised what was happening and nipped it in the bud. Perhaps she had just been enjoying herself too much. She had been selfish and insensitive and now Beau was suffering the consequences. She agonised over the question of what to do next. Was it better to leave things as they were, to make a clean break and hope that Beau would soon find someone else? Or should she try to heal the wounds she had caused last night? Perhaps that would simply prolong the agony. She was haunted by the thought that tonight he would be flying again, facing the ever-present threat of enemy action in the dark skies over Germany. She resolved to write to him that afternoon and try once more to explain herself.

Meanwhile, she had to meet Sally. She was tempted to forget the whole idea but there was no way she could get in touch with her and it was unthinkable simply to fail to turn up. So she combed her hair and did her make-up, and as she put on her ENSA uniform it occurred to her that there was an advantage, after all, in the less-than-glamorous serge suit. At least she would not have to compete with Sally, who, in spite of shortages and clothing coupons, always seemed to have a new dress and a chic little hat to match.

She was a few minutes late entering the Corner House but she thought for a moment that Sally had not arrived. Most of the tables were occupied, mainly by men and women in uniform. There were a few smart civilian hats but none of them belonged to Sally. Even when she realised that someone was waving to her from a corner table it was a moment before she recognised the woman in the shabby navy coat with her hair tied up in a scarf. Not that headscarves were unusual these days. In the egalitarian mood of making do, of 'bare legs for patriotism' and beetroot juice instead of lipstick, even the two princesses were to be seen wearing scarves instead of hats. But Sally Castle had never been one for making do.

As Rose advanced towards the table she began to see that it was not just the clothes that had prevented her from recognising her friend. The face beneath the headscarf was different too; the eyes deeply shadowed, the cheeks gaunt, the pallor only emphasised by the brave, scarlet slash of the mouth.

Rose caught her breath, swallowed and forced a smile. 'Sally, darling! It's lovely to see you.'

Sally accepted her kiss with a bitter, ironic grin. 'It's OK, you don't have to pretend. Go on, say it.'

Rose sat down opposite her. 'What's happened, Sally? Have you been ill?'

Sally's lips twisted. 'You could put it like that. Courtesy of an RAF flight sergeant who had the bad manners to go and get himself killed the next night.'

'Oh, Sally!' Rose murmured, momentarily stunned. 'You mean he . . . ?'

'Got me up the duff? Put a bun in my oven? Yeah, the bastard!'

'But didn't you take precautions?'

''Course we did! There must have been a hole in it, or something.'

'So, what . . . what did you do?' Two years ago Rose would have been acutely embarrassed by this conversation, but she had heard too many like it since then.

'What do you think? But I couldn't afford one of those expensive Harley Street jobs and I guess the slimy little character I went to didn't keep his instruments as clean as he should have done. I bloody nearly died.'

'Oh, Sally, I'm so sorry!'

A waitress appeared at the table and Rose ordered tea and toasted teacakes. Sally lit a cigarette.

'Doesn't matter now. Water under the bridge.'

'I wish you'd let me know. I would have tried to help. Wasn't there anyone you could go to, to borrow the money? What happened to that nice Canadian bloke you were going out with?'

'Bill? Oh, he's long gone.'

'Killed?'

'Not as far as I know. We parted company, that's all.'

'What about Lucy? Wouldn't she have helped out?'

'Lucy? She's the last person I'd turn to.'

'Sally! Your own sister? You were always so close.'

'Yeah, until she went into the ATS and took up with her officer feller.'

'What officer feller?'

'Didn't I tell you? Our Lucy's married a captain in the Royal Artillery. Ten years older than she is and frightfully posh! Oh, she's quite the officer's lady now. Too good for the likes of me.'

'I can't believe that,' Rose protested, but in her heart she could imagine that it might be true. Before the war Lucy had lived in her sister's shadow. It had always been Sally who took the first pick of the available men. Lucy tagged along with whoever was left over. Joining the ATS had been her break for freedom, and Rose could imagine her delight at having hooked such a good catch. All the same, she could not believe that she would have refused to help her sister. It was Sally's pride that had prevented her from asking.

'You and this flight sergeant,' Rose said, changing tack, 'were you . . . did you love him?'

'God, no!' Sally stubbed out her cigarette and removed a thread of tobacco from the tip of her tongue. 'He was lonely, so was I. It was just one of those things. A one-night stand.' She looked at Rose. 'And before you put on that holier-than-thou look just tell me this. Would you let a bloke go back to face almost certain death without the comfort of one night in someone's arms?' Rose felt her throat close up and was unable to answer. Sally stared at her more closely. 'You bloody would, wouldn't you! Anything rather than give up your precious virginity.' She turned away. 'Well, it's no good expecting you to understand, is it.'

The waitress brought the tea and Rose tried in vain to turn the conversation to other things. Questions about Sally's job brought the snapped retort that she had not worked since that 'sodding so-called doctor messed me up'. She was living on the dole, in a single room near the docks. She clearly had no interest in what Rose had been doing and little bits of information about Barbara Willis and the other girls in the Follies dance troupe were received with indifferent shrugs.

Eventually Rose leaned forward and put her hand on Sally's. 'Look, if there's anything I can do . . . Why don't you come and stay with me in Lambeth for a bit? I don't know how long I'll be in London, but you'd be welcome to stay in the flat until you get yourself back on your feet again.'

Sally looked at her and for the first time the defensive shield of irony left her face. 'You're a good kid, Rose. A bit old fashioned, but your heart's in the right place. I'm sorry about what I said earlier. But it wouldn't work. You'd get fed up with my slovenly ways and I'd get browned off with you being so neat and organised. I'm OK where I am. Don't worry about me.'

'I wish there was something I could do,' Rose murmured.

'Tell you what, you can pay for the tea. That make you feel any better?'

And that was all Sally would allow her to do. They parted soon after, and as Rose watched her walk away she saw, suddenly, a trace of the old, self-confident, sexy swagger, and a soldier passing in the opposite direction paused and turned his head. Rose drew a breath. Perhaps, after all, what Sally had said was right. Perhaps she would be OK.

Back at the flat she sat down with a pad of notepaper and tried to compose a letter to Beau. After several attempts, she gave up. There seemed to be nothing meaningful that she could say. She had no intention of changing her mind and agreeing to marry him, so what, exactly, was she trying to suggest? The idea that they could go on meeting as before, she now realised, was pure selfishness on her part. How could she expect Beau to spend his money and lavish his gifts on her? Far better to remain silent and let him find someone else. With his looks and charm, and the apparently limitless resources of the USAF behind him, it could not take more than a few days.

She took up the pad again and wrote instead to Merry in

Naples, a long, chatty letter telling him about Bet's marriage and giving him news of the boys and of the Willis family. She told him about Sally, too, but she did not mention Beau.

Two days later Rose reported for duty at the Drury Lane Theatre, which had been the headquarters of ENSA from the outbreak of war. Clifford Wallace was waiting for her and, after a few brief pleasantries, got down to business.

'I want you to start auditioning dancers for a new show. Only six girls, this time. We're not planning another big musical extravaganza like the one you took to North Africa. This has to be something much smaller and more mobile. A show that can be packed into a couple of trucks ready to move quickly when necessary.'

'Move? Where to?' Rose asked unwisely, and received the tart rejoinder, 'You'll find out when you get there.'

His discretion had no effect. The theatre was buzzing with rumour. The Second Front, so long promised, was going to be opened soon. Troops were gathering all along the south coast. It could mean only one thing. The Allies were about to invade Nazi-occupied France.

4

Some hundreds of miles north of Naples, Major Richard Stevens, aka Ricardo Benedetti, stretched his hands to the brazier and stamped his feet to try to bring some feeling into them. High up in the Alpi Apuane spring had scarcely made itself felt. The peaks were still snow-covered and, although the snow had melted from the pastures of the valley where he stood, the pre-dawn air was bitter. Beside him, Armando, the leader of the partisan band, and Gianni, his lieutenant, stamped and shuffled too, and spread out at strategic points along the valley bottom little groups of their men huddled into their sheepskin coats and blew on their numb fingers. Richard looked up. Above the mountain the sky was paling and the stars had disappeared. It would be a long time before the sun rose high enough to warm the valley floor, but up there it was already morning and the sky, thank God, was clear. A perfect day for an airborne supply drop.

He had had considerable difficulty persuading his superiors to let him return to Italy. After delivering his maps and observations and attending debriefing sessions with a variety of senior officers in Algiers he had been told that he was to be flown back to England, where his information would be of value to the High Command. He was, as his CO pointed out, due for 'a spot of leave'. They had been most put out when he had refused the offer and begged to be returned to the field. He had been confused, himself, about his motives. He knew that he should go back to London and sort things out with Priscilla. Her letter, demanding a divorce, had been a shock but, on reflection, he knew he should have seen it coming. His last home leave had not been a success and he had heard from Victor, his former Conducting Officer and now a friend, that she was probably having an affair. It was distressing, in an abstract way, but his main reaction was that it was an unwelcome distraction from the more important work awaiting him in Italy.

He had made a commitment to Armando and he was determined to honour it. Over the past months, helping them to fight the Nazi occupiers, he had felt for the first time that he was making a genuine contribution and was no longer a helpless pawn in a game he barely understood. He pointed out to Dodds Parker, his CO, that he had given Armando his word that he would return and that the British could scarcely expect the partisans to cooperate if they could not be relied on to keep their promises. Eventually his tenacity had been rewarded and he had been dropped back into the mountains at the beginning of January.

This time it had been easier. He was still terrified, almost to the point of paralysis, before the jump, but it had been a comfort to see below him the prearranged pattern of fires that marked the landing ground and to know that he was dropping to friends. The enthusiastic embraces of Armando and his lieutenants had been his reward. Even Nick Macdonald, his radio operator, reverted to the manners of his Italian mother and hugged him.

The supplies that had dropped with him that night had been the last they were to receive before the weather closed in and the valley they had chosen as a dropping ground was cut off by snow. A fresh drop was urgently needed. They were running out of ammunition and the radio had begun to behave temperamentally and needed a new set of batteries. In addition they were hoping for more weapons and boots and warm socks for some of the recruits. Richard also secretly hoped that the packages would contain a few home comforts, such as coffee and jam or chocolate. After three months of living on the sparse peasant diet of bread made from chestnut flour and pasta and root vegetables he was desperate for something sweet.

Beside them the shepherd boy, Giancarlo, lifted his head and froze like a pointer dog.

'What?' Armando asked.

'Plane,' the boy replied succinctly.

Richard strained his ears. 'Ours or theirs?'

A brief hesitation. Then, 'English. Four engines.'

Richard exchanged looks of triumphant relief with Armando. The promised supplies would be with them in a few minutes. Armando turned to look along the valley. The others had heard it, too, and were alert, looking towards him. A moment later the Wellington hove into view, just clearing the pine trees on the col at the head of the valley, and a signal light winked from its belly. The Morse letter D. As Richard returned the agreed code letter with his torch Armando signalled to his men and fires sprang up along the valley bottom. The plane overflew them, banked into a steep turn and came back so low that they could see the pale faces of the two dispatchers as they heaved the packages out of the cargo door. Parachutes blossomed in the still air, catching the early sun for a moment before descending into the shadows. Men raced forward as each one hit the ground, bundling up the parachutes and manhandling the containers on to the backs of waiting mules for the journey down to the farmhouse. Richard waved to the departing aircraft and raised his thumb. Someone must have seen, because the plane waggled its wings in response before disappearing over the mountain.

Back at the farm there was a brief period of frantic activity as containers were opened and their contents dispersed to caches around the neighbourhood. Some items that would be required for immediate use were hidden behind hay bales in the loft above a stable. If the need arose the farmer's bull, an animal of very uncertain temper, could be shut in there to deter any unwelcome visitor from attempting to climb up to it. Others were stored behind ancient wine casks in the cellar. The rest went on muleback or in packs carried by the men to caves in the hills or remote woodcutters' huts. The parachutes and containers were buried, at Richard's insistence, though the local women would have risked their immortal souls for the parachute silk. Within an hour all trace of the drop had been eradicated. Only then was Richard able to attend to the items that had been separately packed in a container addressed to him. There was, as he had hoped, coffee and chocolate and cigarettes, which he shared round among Armando and his closest colleagues, who were living in the farmhouse. There was a tin of delousing powder – a regrettable necessity in this remote rural community where water for washing or bathing had to be drawn from the well and there was no spare fuel for heating it. There was also a packet of letters from home. There were three from his mother, one from Victor, one from Sir Lionel Grey, Priscilla's uncle and erstwhile guardian, and one from Priscilla. He opened that one first. A single sheet of flimsy airmail paper.

Dear Richard,

I know that letters only reach you erratically, wherever you are, but I feel sure that you must have had my last one by this time. I need an answer. As I told you, Jean-Claude wants us to be married as soon as possible. He can't explain why, for security reasons, but I get the impression that he hopes to be going back to France soon and wants the wedding before that happens.

I'm sure you will do the gentlemanly thing and arrange to give me grounds for divorce. It can't be too difficult to arrange. There's no point in pretending that our marriage was ever going to work out, so we might as well cut our losses, don't you think? Then you will be free to run your life as you see fit, without me interfering. I'm sorry it's turned out like this, but the sooner we get it over with the better. I'm sure you will agree.

Richard's first reaction was one of incredulous anger, not at Priscilla's infidelity but at her easy assumption that he was in a position to go to a hotel with some prostitute in order to give her grounds for divorce. 'Where the hell does she think I am?' he demanded inwardly. The answer, of course, was that she had no way of knowing. As far as his family was concerned he was still stuck behind a desk in Algiers, working for the Inter-Services Liaison Bureau. But Priscilla knew more than that. It was her position with the FANY, the First Aid Nursing Yeomanry, whose members were often employed by SOE to look after and entertain agents waiting to be sent abroad, which had brought them together in the first place. She must guess, although she could not know, that he was engaged in some dangerous operation behind enemy lines. But it was typical of her, he thought, to banish all such recognition from her mind if it stood in the way of achieving her immediate desires. From her childhood Priscilla had been brought up to expect that her every whim would be satisfied as soon as it was expressed. This was why Richard's refusal to accept the secondment to a safe position with the Council for the Encouragement of Music and the Arts had so enraged her. She wanted him in England, pursuing his own career as a singer so that she could bask in the position of the woman behind one of the rising operatic stars of his generation, and as soon as he refused to cooperate in the project she had lost interest.

His thoughts were interrupted by the hasty entrance of Armando.

'Trouble!' he said brusquely. 'They are signalling from the village.'

Richard swept the letters into a pile and stuffed them inside his battledress tunic. Then he followed Armando out into the farmyard. From here it was possible to see across the valley to the village perched on the shoulder of the adjacent hill. From an upper window of one of the houses a crimson blanket was hung, as if to air. Richard brought up the field glasses that he invariably carried hung round his neck and scanned the narrow ribbon of road leading into the village. At first he could see nothing. Then they appeared. Two motorcycle outriders first, then a staff car, then three armoured vehicles and a truck crammed with men.

Richard swore quietly and handed the glasses to Armando. 'They must have seen the parachutes coming down and decided to conduct a *rastrellamento*.'

'God help our friends over there in the village,' Armando murmured.

They were both silent for a few seconds. It was well known that the Germans had carried out brutal reprisals against villages suspected of sheltering or aiding the partisans. But it was also a vital element in the survival strategy of the partisans themselves that one did not confront the enemy when they appeared in strength. They both knew what must be done, and without further comment Armando turned away and began issuing orders. Within minutes runners had been dispatched to warn the various groups that had dispersed to hide the supplies, while the rest of the men began slipping away from the farm in ones and twos. Some carried saws and axes and headed for the forest that clothed both sides of the valley. If encountered by a German patrol they would be nothing more sinister than a pair of woodcutters plying their trade. Others headed for the pastures where the sheep grazed, carrying shepherds' crooks, or burdened themselves with bundles of firewood destined for remote farms higher up the valley. Only Nick remained, hidden with his precious radio set in the loft above a very angry bull. It was too heavy to be easily carried away and he refused to be parted from it.

Richard and Armando were the last to leave, as the German troops began to fan out from the village. Towards evening they reached their goal, a large cave set high on the steep side of the valley, almost level with the pass above which the aircraft had disappeared a few hours earlier. The snow was still deep at this altitude but the approach to the cave was via a rocky slope, swept clean by the wind, which showed no trace of footprints.

Inside the cave they found eight of the others already assembled. A fire had been lit, well back from the entrance, fed carefully with the dry wood they had stored there the previous autumn so that it created very little smoke. Armando looked around and made a rapid tally of those present.

'Where's Gianni?'

The answer was shrugs and shaken heads. Someone said, 'He went with the men taking the guns to Pietro's place.'

'I know,' Armando replied, with unusual sharpness. 'I sent him. But Franco should have caught up with them and warned them. He moves fast and he wasn't carrying anything.'

'Perhaps he's holed up somewhere for the night,' Richard suggested. 'He knows the area. Are any of his group here?'

There was no answer.

During the last hours of daylight a few others arrived, having made their way by circuitous routes and in various disguises. Someone had had the forethought to grab one of Richard's bags of coffee, though Armando reprimanded him on the grounds that he would have been hard put to it to explain where he got it from if the Germans had stopped and searched him. They boiled some water and consoled themselves with the thin, sugarless brew. Coffee was too great a luxury to be used all at once. The cave had been provisioned before the winter snows came in anticipation of just this situation, but tinned goods were almost unobtainable so they had had to content themselves with dried hams and sausages and some hard-tack biscuits that had been dropped by one of the supply planes. As darkness fell, they wrapped themselves in the sheepskins they had stored with the provisions and huddled together against the cold to snatch a few hours' sleep.

The following day they heard the rumble of engines and Richard and Armando crawled out of the cave to a vantage point from which they could see down the valley. Below them three armoured vehicles were grinding up the track through the forest, flanked by two files of foot soldiers with automatic weapons at the ready. They exchanged glances, the same thought in both their minds. Had someone down in the village cracked? Only their own men knew of the plan to use the cave as a hideout but everyone in the village knew of its existence. They watched tensely as the tanks came closer. Almost directly below their hiding place the track came to an end. From that point there was only a steep and rocky path, which was used by shepherds looking for lost sheep or the occasional villager heading for a farm in the next valley. It was impassable for any form of wheeled or tracked vehicle. The tanks came to a stop and the men stood around, obviously waiting for orders. After a moment an officer emerged from the leading tank and led a party of them up the path. Again Richard and Armando looked at each other. The almost invisible track that led to the cave diverged from the path about halfway up. Richard eased himself back a fraction in preparation for a rapid move and loosened his revolver in its holster. But the small group of men pressed straight on until they reached the top of the pass. Here the officer paused and scanned the area through his glasses. Richard and Armando ducked behind a rock and remained frozen until they heard the scraping of boots on rock going back down towards the tanks. A few minutes later the engines started up again and the vehicles turned themselves laboriously and headed back downhill.

Later they heard distant voices and looked out to see dark figures outlined against the snow on the opposite side of the valley, fanning out in a systematic search.

Armando gritted his teeth. 'They're not going to give up easily. Today that side, tomorrow this? Who knows? If they search like that over here they're bound to spot the cave.'

Richard woke in the middle of the night to a new sound. At first he thought it was aircraft, or the tanks heading their way again. Then he realised that it was the wind. By morning a blizzard was blowing, obliterating everything farther away than ten yards.

'God is on our side after all!' Armando said, grinning.

All day they huddled in the cave, keeping close together for warmth. There was little conversation. They were all too preoccupied with what might be happening in the valley below. Most of the group came from farther afield. Some, like Armando, were from towns down on the coast. Others had deserted from the Italian army when it was disarmed by the Nazis after the armistice and had found their way to the first point of organised resistance that presented itself. There were three ex-prisoners-of-war who had been let out by the Italians and were now seeking to evade recapture by the Germans. Of these, one was Russian and two were Polish. But there were a few locals, young men evading call-up or forced labour under the Germans, and older ones who had joined the partisans out of political or religious conviction. Although the band belonged officially to the Fiamme Verde, the Green Flames, the right-wing Christian Democrat group, Richard found a reason for optimism in the fact that it also contained at least two committed communists. Now, however, those of all persuasions were united in their anxiety over the fate of the villagers, and no one was feeling optimistic.

At some point Richard remembered his letters, which were still inside his battledress tunic. He pulled them out and opened the first one from his mother. Like the two subsequent ones, it was full of local gossip, mainly about people he did not know or could not remember, with the occasional irksome reference to men who had been his contemporaries at school. Mrs So-and-So's son had been involved in an important naval engagement and had been promoted; someone else was fighting with his unit in Italy and had been mentioned in dispatches. Richard knew that it was a comfort in one way to his mother to believe that he was safely occupied in a desk job but on the other hand she would also have liked to have something to brag about to her friends. Every time he received a letter from her he felt an increasingly sharp stab of regret that he could never tell her about his successes or the dangers he faced every day.

This time, however, it was the letter from Sir Lionel Grey that really made him angry. Priscilla's guardian wrote:

Eleanor and I are most distressed to learn that you and Priscilla are contemplating divorce. As you know, I had some doubts when you first asked my permission for your marriage but I subsequently became convinced that you and she were ideally suited to each other. Apparently I was mistaken, and it hurts me deeply to think that you have made her so unhappy. Of course, your prolonged absence has made matters worse. I appreciate that this has been due to the exigencies of war and your duties as an officer, but perhaps if you had availed yourself of the opportunity which presented itself for secondment to the Council for the Encouragement of Music and the Arts things would have been very different. I am sure you realise that both Priscilla and I went to considerable lengths to obtain that offer and we were both deeply disappointed when you turned it down.

However, I feel sure that it is not too late to put things right between you. You have so much in common, after all. I suggest that you apply for leave immediately – I think I can say with some certainty that the application will not be refused. Once you are home again you and Priss will be able to pick up where you left off.

I think I should make one thing clear at this point. During your time in this country we made various plans for your career after the war. My backing for all these is, naturally, conditional upon the continuation of your marriage to Priscilla. Her happiness is the overriding consideration in all these matters.

I expect to hear from you shortly.

Richard clamped his teeth together to suppress an oath. Bloody man! The arrogance of assuming that his money and influence could bend everyone to his will. Well, he would wait a long time for a reply to his letter. Though he was able to receive mail through occasional drops like the last one, there was no way he could get letters out. Any communications that his wife or family received would be in the form of pre-written, non-committal postcards, sent off at intervals by one of the small group of men who were running his operation and others like it from the base in Algiers.

When his anger subsided Richard realised that there was another sensation, more lasting and significant, beneath it. This was the end of more than his marriage. It was farewell to all his hopes and plans for the future. There would be no useful introductions to eminent conductors or BBC producers; no touring opera company. He would be back where he started in 1939. It occurred to him briefly that, instead of shivering in a cave waiting for the blizzard to clear so that the Nazis could seek him out, he might have been in England giving concerts of light operatic arias to workers in factories. He knew that CEMA was doing wonderful work, raising morale and opening up new horizons for thousands of people, creating a new audience for all sorts of music, ballet and opera. He could have been part of it. He looked at Armando, huddled in his coat a few feet away. He had given up a flourishing law practice to take to the mountains, just as Gianni had given up his studies in medicine. The sight of his friend strengthened Richard's conviction that this was where he belonged, and as for the future – it was quite possible that for him the future could be measured in days or weeks rather than years.

Towards dusk on the third evening the blizzard stopped and day four dawned still and clear. By then the strain of being cooped up together in the spartan conditions of the cave was beginning to tell. They posted scouts to watch all the approaches and waited tensely for the sound of engines. At midday they were all brought to their feet, weapons at the ready, by a sudden burst of shouting. Richard made his way to the entrance of the cave, keeping well back against the rocky wall with Armando close behind him. Feet scrabbled on the rock, there was a sound of harsh panting and then a voice called the password. A moment later Giancarlo, who had been posted as one of the sentries, came hastily into the cave accompanied by a small, gnarled man with skin like leather and a shock of grey hair, whom Richard recognised as a local shepherd. He was panting from the climb but at the same time cackling with inarticulate mirth at some private joke. They sat him down and gave him a tin mug of the sharp, thin red wine of the area and eventually he began to make sense.

'The Germans?' Armando asked urgently. 'Where are the Germans?'

'Who knows?' chortled the old man. 'Back in their billets – some of them. Not all. We led them a merry dance, I can tell you.'

'You did? How?' Richard demanded.

The story came out at last. The villagers, too, had been prepared for the German *rastrellamento* and had prepared a plan. When the tanks arrived the mayor had greeted the officer in charge with effusive protestations of loyalty. Yes, they thought there might be partisans in the area. Yes, they too had seen the parachutes coming down but they were afraid to go up into the hills and tackle these dangerous men themselves. Did they know where they were hiding? Well, that was a tricky question. There were a number of possibilities. He would consult some of the outlying farmers and the men who worked in the forest. They were bound to have seen something. It would take a day or two. Meanwhile, if the Herr Major would permit, he and his men would be their honoured guests.

For two days the German patrols had followed a variety of wild-goose chases. Then had come the blizzard, and when it was at its height the mayor had announced that at last he had definite information. A local shepherd knew where the partisans were hiding, but it was a place inaccessible to any form of wheeled transport. Not to worry! As soon as the blizzard abated he would find mules and guides who would lead the Germans to their quarry.

The weather, of course, began to improve down in the valley long before the mountain peaks were clear, but the German officer was eager to set off and the mayor was as good as his word. With the officer mounted on a mule and the men trudging behind, they filed out of the village, guided by four local men, and ascended a path leading diametrically away from the cave where Armando and his band were sheltering. As they climbed the snow grew deeper and the visibility deteriorated until they were enveloped in cloud. Then the four guides came to a standstill. The cave where the partisans were hiding was just ahead, round the corner of that bluff, but they were afraid to go farther. They were, after all, unarmed.

From here it was for the soldiers to take the lead – but it would have to be on foot. The ground was too steep and treacherous for the mule.

As soon as the German troops had disappeared into the mist the four 'guides' had rapidly made themselves scarce. They knew a different and much faster route back to the valley and were home before darkness fell. Meanwhile, the clouds and the last flurries of snow had served to obscure the tracks left by the advancing troops. Some of them had stumbled back into the village the next morning but neither the officer nor the NCOs had appeared. After some consultation among themselves the survivors had climbed into their vehicles and headed back towards their base. They would find, the little man added as an afterthought, that their radios were useless. Enzo, who knew about such things, had seen to that.

Asked how he knew all this in such detail, the shepherd admitted that he had been one of the four who had led the enemy troops astray. Armando shook his hand and assured him that his patriotism would not be forgotten, and Richard handed over one of his precious packets of cigarettes. Then they prepared to leave the cave, departing as they had arrived, one or two at a time.

When Richard and Armando reached the farmhouse they were relieved to discover that both Nick and their supplies were intact. The Germans had searched but no one had been tempted to enter the stable where the bull was stamping and fretting at the loss of his liberty.

'Has anyone seen Gianni?' Armando asked urgently.

No one had, nor was there any sign of the men who had gone with him, or of Franco, who had been sent to warn them. Armando dispatched two of his fittest men, Lorenzo and the boy Giancarlo, to see if they were still at the disused farmhouse, known locally as Pietro's after its last owner.

The other members of the group drifted in a few at a time, and by early evening a roll-call showed that everyone was accounted for except Gianni and his party. Richard and Armando were about to sit down to their first hot meal in days when they heard a hasty challenge from the sentry posted outside and the door burst open to admit Giancarlo.

The boy was gasping for breath and almost on the point of collapse, and in answer to Armando's questions he could only blurt out, 'Pietro's! You must go! Go and see what they have done!' Then he burst into tears.

Without asking further questions Richard took his Sten gun off the hook on the wall beside him. Armando was giving rapid instructions.

'Giuseppe, Marco, you come with us. Federico, you're in charge here until we get back. Somebody, look after the boy.'

With that they left the house and headed up into the hills again. It was hard going after four days of little food and fitful sleep, but Richard was constantly surprised at what his body was now capable of in terms of speed and endurance. Nevertheless, by the time they reached the ruined farm buildings on a tiny plateau high above the village they were all at the point of exhaustion. Lorenzo was sitting on a log in what had once been the farmyard, his face the same colour as the trampled snow around him. He got up as they arrived and jerked his head without speaking towards the door of the house. Armando and Richard exchanged brief looks and Armando turned to the other two and ordered curtly, 'Wait here.'

Coming into the dimness of the low-ceilinged room after the snow glare outside, Richard could at first make out only huddled shapes. Then he began to see details. Gianni and the five men who had been with him were all there. Two lay on the floor. Gianni and the other three were tied to chairs. Each of them had a neat bullet hole in the temple, but it was what had been done to them before they died which made Armando turn away and blunder back to the door, gasping and retching. Richard stood quite still, except that his fingers loosened their grip on his gun, allowing it to clatter to the stone floor. He felt a terrible chill that seemed to begin somewhere in the middle of his stomach and spread outwards, yet at the same time his skin crawled with sweat. He had been warned at Beaulieu during his training of what the Nazis were prepared to do to obtain information. He had even been given a very mild taste of it – how mild he only now truly understood.

Armando regained control and came back to stand beside him.

'They didn't talk,' Richard said, his lips numb.

Armando nodded and made an inarticulate sound of assent. After a moment Richard went on, 'The others mustn't see this.'

'Giancarlo will have told them.'

'Telling is one thing. Seeing is different.'

There was a silence. Then Armando said, 'The ground is too hard here for us to bury them.'

Richard nodded and thought. At the far end of the room there was a pile of dry firewood, laid in by Pietro before his death. He said, 'Were they religious? I don't know the right prayers.'

Armando swallowed. 'I know them.' He hesitated and added, 'Antonia!'

An image of a strong-faced, handsome girl in nurse's

uniform flashed across Richard's memory. Armando's sister had been engaged to Gianni.

'Tell her he died a hero's death. But don't tell her how.'

When darkness fell the villagers in the valley below looked up and saw a wavering point of light on the hillside. Somebody said, 'Looks like a fire.'

'Must be old Pietro's place,' his companion returned. 'Some idiot's been sheltering there and thrown a lighted cigarette end away.'

5

Rose closed her eyes. With all the blinds down in the bus there was nothing much to do except doze. Outside, the early summer sun was shining. There would be fields of young wheat, or hills with sheep grazing, perhaps the sparkle of sunlight on waves. Inside the bus there was only a dim, artificial light. Even the driver's compartment was screened off so that the passengers were denied any glimpse of the surroundings or the route being taken. No one was unduly troubled by this. Indeed, there was a certain amount of light-hearted speculation about where they were going to end up tonight, and bets were being laid by some of the more affluent, or less cautious, members of the party. Most of them were thoroughly familiar with all the resorts along the south coast, having played them before the war, and it was not too difficult to work out distance and direction from their base in a small hotel just outside the town of Lewes.

The bus made a sharp left turn and came to a standstill. Outside, a voice called a challenge and the driver answered. The disembodied voice gave instructions and the bus lurched forward again, bouncing over uneven ground. At length they came to a stop and someone opened the door. Climbing out, stiff and half blinded by the sudden sunlight, Rose saw that they were parked behind a large marquee, painted in camouflage colours. On either side of them stretched long rows of khaki tents and men in army uniform moved between them, or lounged on the grass in their shade. Jeeps buzzed busily back and forth. Rose raised her eyes. Beyond the tents the rounded ridges of the South Downs faded little by little into the summer haze. And wasn't that circle of trees Chanctonbury Ring? She turned, and there in the distance was the sea. What was the point of these blacked-out bus rides? If she had been a spy, she could have pinpointed this camp on a map without the slightest difficulty. The same was true of the one they had visited last night, and the night before.

The whole of the south of England was one vast armed camp. Rose was not sufficiently familiar with regimental insignia to know exactly which units were quartered where, but it was clear that huge numbers of soldiers were now assembled along the coast. There were English, Americans, Canadians, Australians, New Zealanders and Free French, and probably others she could not name. If she had been a spy, of course, she would have been able to identify them all. That was why only those with official passes were now allowed within ten miles of the coast from the Wash to Land's End – and why the ENSA entertainers were not supposed to know where they were performing each night. Everyone knew what was coming. The 'big push', the Second Front, the invasion of Fortress Europe. But no one knew when it was going to start, or where it was going to be directed.

A voice called, 'Come on, girls! Don't just stand there, get stuck in!'

The men in the company were already beginning to unload the equipment from the bus and Rose and her six girls turned to, lifting and lugging with the rest. It was wartime, and chivalry was dead. They had been touring the camps for three weeks already and the routine was well established.

Hampers of costumes, musical instruments, lights, dimmer boards, microphones and reels of cable were dragged out of the bus and carried into the mess tent. Within an hour the lights had been coupled to an army generator, the sound equipment tested, the costumes ironed, and they were ready. There was no time and no need for rehearsal.

The show was well received, as always. With all leave cancelled and everyone confined to barracks, all ranks were glad of any entertainment they were offered. But that night Rose sensed something different in the atmosphere. The laughter was a little too hilarious, the clapping and whistling and foot-stamping a bit too uninhibited. The sense of nerves stretched almost to breaking point was palpable.

After the performance they were invited to return to the mess for drinks, but made their excuses. The equipment had to be repacked and loaded, and then it was 'all aboard the mystery coach tour' as they headed back to Lewes. It was well after midnight by the time they reached their hotel.

Next morning Rose found a letter by her place at the breakfast table. Her pulse quickened as she recognised the handwriting. It was Beau's. It was almost two months since he had walked out of her Lambeth flat and she had missed him, she had to confess as much. Although she had worried about his intentions and felt guilty for encouraging his hopes, she had looked forward to his letters, and the evenings they had spent together in various dance halls had been some of the most enjoyable she could remember. As she opened the envelope two conflicting explanations whirled through her head. One was that the letter was a final farewell, informing her that he had found a new girlfriend; the other that it was a last desperate plea for reconciliation. She knew that she should wish it was the former but a small, hastily suppressed voice somewhere in her mind was hoping for the latter.

My darling Rose (she read),

I want you to have this letter so you will know how very much I love you. I guess I'm not very good at saying these things out loud so the best I can do is put it on paper.

I want you to understand what it has meant to me to have you as my girlfriend. We're all a long way from home here and most of us get pretty lonesome at times. Of course, all the guys in the squadron make out to be very laid back, easy come, easy go sort of fellows, and we all pretend that the bad things, like getting shot down, are never going to happen to us. But I guess we're all scared every time we take off. I know I am. If I hadn't had the thought of you and all the good times we've had together I guess I might have fallen apart long ago. I fill all my spare moments with dreams of the future and the life we're going to have when this war is over and I can take you back to meet my folks.

Rose stared at the page. He was writing as if their last conversation had never happened, and yet surely the letter had not been chasing her for that long. She looked at the postmark. It had been redirected a couple of times but had started out on its journey only ten days earlier. Had he not believed what she had told him? Or was he attempting a kind of moral blackmail? She turned the page and read on:

If you ever get to read this letter, it will be because I am dead or missing. I have promised myself that if I survive I will say all this to you personally on the day I ask you to marry me. But, in case something goes wrong, I am giving this to Mike, a good buddy, to send on to you so that you will know what I would have said.

Don't forget me, Rose, or the good times we had – but don't let the memory get in the way of you marrying someone else. You're far too lovely to waste your life on a memory.

With all my love, always,

Beau

There was a second page in another hand.

Dear Miss Taylor,

Beauregard gave me this letter a couple of months back and asked me to send it to you if anything happened to him. Lately he hasn't spoken of you so much and I have wondered if something has gone wrong between you, but he never asked for his letter back so I guess he would want you to have it. Of course, I haven't read it but I know he loved you very much and set great store by the plans he had made for your future together.

I am sorry to have to tell you that last night Beau failed to return from a bombing mission. His plane was shot down somewhere over Germany and the other men in the squadron say it is very unlikely that there were any survivors.

He was a great guy, a splendid pilot and a good friend. We shall all miss him very much. Whatever has happened with you and him, I know you will be distressed to learn of his death.

With my sincere condolences,

Michael T. Weinstock

Rose folded the letter carefully and put it back in the envelope. Then she got up from the table, ignoring the concerned enquiries from her colleagues, and headed for the door. Somehow she managed to reach the room that she shared with two other girls before the tidal wave of sobbing engulfed her, flinging her helpless across her bed.

Half an hour later Violet tapped gently on the door and tiptoed in. Rose was sitting at the dressing table, doing her make-up. Yes, she admitted, it had been bad news – a good friend killed on a bombing mission. But no, they had not been engaged and she had not been in love with him. It was very, very sad but that was just the way things were at the moment. Thousands of others were suffering just the same every day. Chin up, stiff upper lip – and all that.

Violet and Alice were the only girls left from Rose's original troupe. When auditions started for the new show, Peggy had telephoned to say that her elderly father was too infirm to be left alone, so she was staying at home to look after him. And May, to everyone's surprise, had conducted a whirlwind romance with a young corporal, who had been allotted to them as a driver in Italy, and was now married and pregnant. Violet was still an inveterate flirt, but she had a good heart and Rose was fond of her. Even so, she felt unable to confide in her. All the girls were tired and stressed. It was up to her to put on a brave face. The guilt and anguish she was feeling were something for her to deal with in private.

By the time the company was ready to board the bus for that evening's engagement Rose was able to tell herself that she was in control. The journey that day was longer and they had been warned in advance that they would be spending the night at their next venue and moving on again the next morning. When the bus pulled up they found themselves in the middle of another army camp, almost identical to the previous one except that this one was located on level pastures beside a river instead of on top of the downs. When they had unloaded and set up for the performance they were shown to their accommodation – a Nissen hut with a curtain across the middle to divide the men from the women. The ablutions facility was fifty yards away and the latrines were simply a row of seats above a deep trench, shielded by canvas screens. One or two of the older members of the company were heard objecting vociferously, while the girls giggled and screwed up their noses. Rose did what had to be done without comment. What right had she to complain about minor discomforts? She had sent a fine, brave, loving man to his death with a broken heart.

Before the show they were entertained as usual in the sergeants' mess. Rose forced herself to be bright and chatty. These men, too, were about to face death, and the least they might expect from her was a little light relief for one evening. Unusually for her, she accepted a second gin and orange and then a third. As she talked and laughed she became aware of someone watching her. A young man with a thin face and a bad case of acne was following her every move and at length he plucked up enough courage to come over.

Rose smiled at him. 'Hello. I'm Rose. What's your name?'

She saw the blush start at his collar and rise till it suffused his whole face. 'P . . . p . . . Peter.'

'Hello, Peter. How long have you been in the army?'

'Couple of years.'

'Are you looking forward to the show?'

'Y. . . yes. I suppose so. I mean . . .'

He ran his fingers round the inside of his collar as if the coarse khaki tunic were throttling him. Rose thought she had never seen anyone so painfully shy. She set herself to draw him out and learned that he came from Solihull and had been apprenticed to a printer before his call-up. Other men were trying to attract her attention and it was hard work getting the boy to talk, but she persisted until it was time to get ready for the show.

After the performance there was no reason not to accept the usual invitation to return to the mess, and as soon as she entered Rose found Peter at her side. Inevitably, within minutes someone had put a record on the gramophone and the men were queuing up to ask the girls to dance. Apart from Rose and her six dancers there were two other women in the company: Valerie, a plump comedienne in her mid-thirties who was married to a petty officer in the navy, and Ann Dwyer, who sang duets with her husband Leighton. They were all used by now to being the only women in a camp full of men and shared their favours as evenly as possible, while smilingly resisting the half-serious invitations to step outside for a 'breath of fresh air'.

As soon as the music started Peter seemed to take it for granted that Rose would dance with him. He was not a good dancer, lacking any sense of rhythm, and he held her a little too close with hands that were hot and clammy. After two dances she released herself gently, pointing out that it was only fair to let the others have a chance. He gave way without argument, but all the time she was dancing with someone else she was aware of his eyes following her, like those of a dog waiting to be taken for a walk.

As soon as he saw an opportunity he was back at her side again, whispering urgently in her ear, 'Please, I need to talk to you. Come outside with me for a minute. I've got to talk to someone. Please, Rose!'

Normally she would have refused, but there was something about the desperation in his eyes that found an echo in her own deep sense of guilt. The least she could do was listen to him, though she knew that eyebrows would be raised at the sight of her slipping out of the tent.

Outside, the evening was still and warm, not yet completely dark although it was almost eleven o'clock. Rose looked around at the rows of tents and was oppressed by the sense of watchers in the shadows. Beside her Peter slipped a hot hand into hers and she was afraid he was going to kiss her. To distract him she said, 'Let's stroll down to the river, shall we?'

The river was low after several weeks without rain, running almost soundlessly in its sandy bed, and a grassy shelf overhung the half-empty channel.

He said, 'Let's sit down here, shall we?'

They sat and Rose said, in her most matter-of-fact manner, 'Now, what was it you wanted to talk to me about?'

He gripped his hands between his knees and did not look at her. 'I've never had a girlfriend.'

Poor boy, she thought, *I can see why*. Aloud she said, 'Well, you've got plenty of time. After all, you're only young. How old are you?'

'I'll be twenty next week. And I haven't got time. I could be dead by then.'

'Peter,' she said earnestly, 'you mustn't think like that. Who knows what's going to happen? It could be all over before you get near a battlefield.'

His only response to that was a slight shrug and a grunt. He went on, 'All the other blokes I know have girls. I get fed up with hearing them bragging about what they get up to.'

'Most of it probably isn't true,' Rose pointed out.

'Half the time I don't know what they're talking about, even,' the boy said miserably.

'Have you tried asking girls out?' she enquired, not knowing what else to say.

''Course I have! They always turn me down. And then I hear them laughing about it afterwards. The lads laugh at me, too.'

Rose could imagine it all only too vividly. The Saturday night hop, the girls permed and powdered, the boys scrubbed and brilliantined, Peter with his hot hands and his erupting skin – and the casual cruelty of the refusals, the giggling disgust. No wonder he had that hangdog look.

Peter went on, 'You're different. You're kind.'

'I'm just a bit . . . older,' she murmured.

'That's just it!' he said eagerly. 'You're older. You're . . . a woman of the world. Please, Rose! I don't want to die without ever knowing what it's like to be with a girl. *Please!*'

She turned her face towards him in the fading light. 'Peter, what are you asking me to do?'

'You know what! Just once, just for tonight. No strings attached. I can't go over there not knowing how it feels.'

Her first instinct was to jump to her feet and run back to the others but simple humanity prevented her. She said, 'Peter, it would be all wrong. For one thing, I'm so much older than you. You need a young girl, your own age. And it shouldn't be just for one night. Wait until you meet a nice girl and fall in love. It will happen, one day.' She knew as she was speaking that these were storybook platitudes, the romantic ideals with which she had grown up and which had been swept away by the war.

He said urgently, 'No! I can't wait! And I don't want a young girl. I want someone like you, someone kind and . . . and experienced.'

She gazed at him helplessly. In the twilight the spots on his face were less visible and the eyes that stared back into hers were deep wells of longing. She found herself remembering Sally Castle's bitter taunt. 'Would you let a bloke go back to face almost certain death without the comfort of one night in someone's arms? You bloody would, wouldn't you! Anything rather than give up your precious virginity.' And she had. She had let Beau go to his death uncomforted. She had an opportunity now to make amends.

She leaned towards the boy, her voice thick in her throat. 'You're wrong, Peter. I'm not . . . experienced. But if it's what you really want . . .'

She had so often imagined what it would be like, but always in the context of the honeymoon night, in a soft bed in a nice hotel, in the arms of . . . she blotted the image from her mind. Instead there was this undignified struggling with buttons and shedding undergarments, a stone digging into her back and Peter's hot breath on her facc, a desperate fumbling and then a sudden sharp pain. Afterwards he wept and thanked her and wanted to kiss her but she pulled on her knickers and straightened her clothes and somehow managed to persuade him that it would be better if she went back to the Nissen hut on her own.

Rose woke the next morning with immediate total recall of the events of the previous night. She lay very still, listening to the breathing of the other women and the snores from the far side of the blanket, and probed her emotions. So that was it, then. That was the goal towards which all the heroines of the romantic novels she had once read so avidly were striving. No wonder the authors always drew a tactful veil over the final consummation! It occurred to her that Peter was probably even now bragging about his conquest. 'I had her, you know –

that dark-haired one – down by the river last night. Well, she's getting on a bit. D'you know she was still a bloody virgin? Poor old thing probably thought it was her last chance!' She knew how men talked. Or did she? What did she know of men, or sex? Only what she had read in books, or heard as gossip. And Peter had wept and thanked her afterwards. As for what had happened last night . . . at least she had not turned him away unsatisfied to face whatever lay ahead. Beyond that, and a nagging soreness between her legs, she felt nothing at all.

It was not until they were on the bus and she was assailed by a sudden queasiness that the possible repercussions struck her. They had taken no precautions! She thought back, forcing herself to recall exactly what had happened, details that her mind had sought to blank out even at the time. Surely Peter had not been so foolish, so thoughtless! He must have used a rubber. But no, though she tried hard to persuade herself that he had, memory told her that he had not. Had he imagined that she was protected in some way? The stupid little idiot! Her own sense of justice stopped her short at this point. She was the older woman. She knew what the risks were. If she had not given it any thought, how could she blame him? Feverishly she calculated the date of her next period. It would be two weeks before she knew whether she was safe. The spectre of Sally Castle's gaunt face rose up before her mind's eye and she longed to bury her head in her arms and weep.

Three days later, on 4 June, they were informed at breakfast that all their future engagements had been cancelled. They were to remain at their base in Lewes and await further instructions. On the same day Rose received a letter from her mother. Bet was pregnant. The baby was due just before Christmas.

6

At nine o'clock on the evening of 5 June Squadron Leader the Hon. Edward Mountjoy, DFC, was summoned, along with the rest of his squadron, to the briefing tent alongside the temporary airstrip near Bognor to which they had been posted the previous week. The men took their seats, silent and expectant. For two days they had been confined to the airfield and all operations had been cancelled while the aircraft were painted in a special livery of black and white stripes. They had been puzzled by the move to Bognor, having spent the previous month stationed at Biggin Hill, patrolling the Pas de Calais and shooting up anything that moved, presumably in preparation for the invasion. The sudden relocation westward seemed to make no sense.

When everyone was settled the wing commander looked around at them and said, with a broad grin, 'Well, chaps, this is it! D-Day tomorrow.'

The murmur of mingled relief and excitement faded as he began to unfold and spread out maps of the Normandy coast, pointing out the beachheads where the invasion was to take place and explaining the disposition of the troops of the various nations taking part – British, American and Canadian. Now the move made sense. The operations in the Calais area had been part of an elaborate deception.

'Your job, lads, is to fly escort duties to the convoys and

make sure they're not bothered by the Luftwaffe. You will come to readiness before dawn tomorrow.'

Lying in his camp bed, too much on edge to sleep, Felix wondered whether he should have written a last letter to Merry. Not one of their normal cryptic communications, designed to be read by the censor, but an open affirmation of love to be sealed and handed to a colleague for safe delivery if anything happened. Then he told himself he was being melodramatic. He had been in far greater danger on Malta and it had never occurred to him to do anything so final. The very idea suggested that he was expecting to be killed and his reason told him that there was no greater probability of that tomorrow than on any day since he had persuaded the 'penguins' at the Air Ministry to let him return to active duty. Since the Americans had entered the war, Allied air superiority had been so well established that the life expectancy of a fighter pilot, so short in the desperate summer of 1940, was now vastly increased. Nevertheless, every week brought its casualties. He himself had been brought in to command this squadron after it had lost two previous COs in the space of as many months. Over the last weeks they had flown many missions as escorts to the bomber formations that were, daily and nightly, reducing German factories and railways and shipyards to rubble. In between, they had embarked on 'Ranger' missions, flying low over occupied France, shooting up airfields, trains and army convoys. It was exciting work, sending the adrenalin throbbing through the veins, but Felix found that he was tiring more quickly, and instead of relishing his victories he was left only with a sickening sense of waste. He had had nearly five years of war and very few of the men he had started out with had survived. He knew he had been lucky and now he just wanted to stay alive until the end.

With an effort he collected his wandering thoughts. This was no time for morbid introspection. Tomorrow might be the 'big day' for the land forces but for him and his men it would be business as usual. The important thing was to be fully alert, and for that he needed to sleep. He willed himself to relax and empty his mind.

He was woken by his batman at 3.30 a.m. from the very deepest level of sleep. The air in the tent was chill and his clothes felt clammy as he struggled into them. Outside the tent he shivered in the brisk westerly breeze blowing across the field. After weeks of summer heat the weather had broken three days ago, with gale-force winds and low cloud. Today was a slight improvement but according to the Met reports the outlook was far from settled. Felix looked up. The sky was opaque and colourless, banded with streaks of ragged cloud. It was not yet dawn but there was enough light for him to make out the shapes of the aircraft at dispersal and the figures of the fitters moving around them. To either side of him the bulky shapes of his fellow pilots in their flying suits plodded, zombie-like, towards the planes. Voices exchanged brief greetings, but they spoke in husky half-whispers, as though the sound might reach the ears of the enemy across the Channel and alert him to his danger.

Felix greeted the mechanic who looked after his aircraft and hoisted himself into the cockpit. He put on his helmet and checked that the oxygen mask fitted snugly to his face, then tested the flow of gas. A few deep breaths dispelled his drowsiness. He ran through his pre-flight checks: oil pressure, fuel, glycol, engine temperature. He pressed the button of his RT and called up the control tower.

'Control, this is Firefly Leader. Are you receiving me? Over.'

'Firefly Leader, this is Control. Receiving you loud and clear. Nothing yet. Stand by.'

Felix took off his helmet again and looked around him. His cockpit cover was still open and above him the sky had changed to the most delicate shade of turquoise and, as he watched, the trees at the end of the runway were suddenly flooded with golden light, like a stage set caught in a spotlight. Somewhere, far overhead, a skylark loosed a cascade of silver notes into the clear air. Felix looked at his watch. Just after four. Perhaps it was worth being woken up so early, just to catch a dawn like this. Then the sun went behind a cloud and the spotlight was switched off as abruptly as it had appeared.

The minutes dragged by. Then, at about 4.20, the controller's voice came over his radio.

'Firefly Squadron scramble! Scramble, scramble!'

Felix looked at his fitter and gave him a thumbs-up. The man wished him luck and pushed the canopy shut. All round the airfield engines roared into life, sending flocks of pigeons exploding from their roosting places in the trees along the perimeter. Felix pushed the throttle open gradually, checking the revs, until the plane quivered against the chocks like a living creature, then throttled back, signalled 'chocks away' and taxied out across the airfield to his take-off position. He looked to his right and saw that his wingman, Charlie Henson, was in position, then to his left, to where the other two planes that would make up the 'finger four' formation were also in place. He waved a gloved hand in a forward direction and opened the throttle. The four planes surged forward in line abreast and lifted into the air.

They circled above the airfield until the rest of the squadron joined them and then Felix led the whole formation off on a vector that would take them almost due south towards the Normandy coast. Within minutes they were over the Channel, but there was unbroken cloud below them and they could see nothing except a brilliant snowfield of white mist. Felix stared to his right, beyond his wingman, his gaze sweeping the sky from twelve o'clock to six o'clock, above and below, in search of enemy aircraft. Charlie would be doing the same for him. Away in the distance, a thousand feet lower, he saw a large formation of Lancaster bombers, heading back towards their base in England. Behind them was another and over to his left a third. The German defences had certainly been getting a pasting during the night.

A mile or two off the French coast, following instructions from Control, Felix put his plane into a shallow dive and led the squadron down through the cloud cover.

Suddenly a voice crackled in his ear. 'Christ! Look below us, Skip!'

He looked down. The sea was covered with a mass of vessels, stretching to either side until they were lost to view, and back behind him almost, it seemed, to the English coast. He could make out the grey bulk of battleships, standing out in mid-Channel, and the slimmer shapes of destroyers surging forward with a white curl of foam around their bows. Between them were hundreds of other craft, troop transports and merchant ships, low in the water with their cargoes of tanks and men. There were tankers and tugs towing what looked like huge, floating blocks of concrete. He tried to make a rapid estimate of how many ships there were. Three thousand, four? No, more, far more. And above the ships, a few hundred feet below Felix's position, was another, aerial armada – flight after flight of heavy transport planes, many of them towing gliders. Airborne assault troops, heading inland to drop behind the German lines.

Felix raised his eyes towards the coast. It was half-tide and between the ships and the sandy beaches was a stretch of gleaming shingle studded with a fearsome collection of obstacles – steel posts welded together like giant starfish, jagged concrete teeth connected by steel cables, even obsolete tanks half buried in the sand. How in heaven's name, he wondered, were the landing craft supposed to get through that lot? Beyond the tideline, the beach was defended by row after row of barbed wire, and beyond that were concrete bunkers and anti-tank ditches, all part of Hitler's famous Atlantic Wall. As Felix watched, puffs of smoke issued from the battleships on the horizon and a few seconds later he saw the plumes of sand and earth rise into the air from where the shells had landed. The assault had begun.

He pressed the button on his RT. 'This is Firefly Leader. OK, chaps, this is the big one and those fellows down there are going to bear the brunt of it. Let's give them all the protection we can. Keep your eyes skinned. The Luftwaffe aren't going to let us have it all our own way.'

Amazingly, it seemed that he was wrong. They patrolled up and down the coast, expecting at any minute to encounter a squadron of Me 109s, but the German air force was apparently under orders to stay out of trouble. Below them they could see the flashes of gunfire and the impact of shells falling on the defensive lines, while a series of incredible monsters trundled off the landing craft to tackle the obstacles along the beach. Felix took his flight down low to see what was going on and was lost in admiration for the ingenuity and planning that had gone into the assault. There were tanks equipped with flails to set off mines and others that unrolled long strips of what looked like carpet across areas of soft sand or dropped bundles of logs to fill up holes. There were armoured bulldozers and 'swimming' tanks that ploughed through the water and came up the beaches already firing. The first landing craft had reached the shore now and men could be seen pouring down the ramps. Many of them fell under the hail of bullets from the machine-gun nests above the beach but the rest pressed forward, firing as they ran.

Felix was jolted rudely out of his contemplation by a sudden violent crash. Looking up he saw that a star-shaped crack had appeared in the cockpit canopy, while all around him streamed the glowing red 'golf balls' of light anti-aircraft fire. He had led his flight straight into the jaws of a German ack-ack battery! He dragged the stick back and the Spit clawed upwards, struggling for height. When he was safely above the flak he levelled out and looked around him and was thankful to see Charlie moving up into his usual position. Thank God for Charlie – steady as a rock and always on the ball! He searched the sky to his other side and found it empty. He felt sick. If he had lost two good men through his own stupidity . . .

A voice crackled in his headset. 'Red Leader, this is Red Three. Are you OK, Skip?'

'Red Three this is Red Leader. I'm fine. Where are you?'

'Three hundred feet below you and astern. Thought I'd keep an eye on your tail in case you'd blacked out or something.'

'Red Three, resume your position. Red Four, do you read me?'

'Red Four here, Skip. Had to take evasive action but I'm coming up on you fast.'

Felix called up the rest of the squadron and maintained his course until all the planes were in formation. Then he banked and turned north and led them home. He had committed the unforgivable sin. He had allowed himself to be distracted and a moment of such inattention could have resulted in his own death or the death of one of his men. It occurred to him that in a few months he would be thirty and he remembered the dictum – 'There are bold pilots and there are old pilots, but there are no old, bold pilots'.

They were sent up again in the early afternoon, this time with instructions to interdict any movement of German reinforcements heading for the coast. They spotted a convoy moving towards Arromanches and Felix led a strafing attack and had the satisfaction of seeing several lorries explode as bullets hit their petrol tanks. There was a third, largely uneventful sortie in the evening, and by the time they landed the sun was going down. Too tired to eat, or even drink, Felix staggered to his tent and fell asleep fully clothed on his camp bed.

They were allowed to lie in the next morning, but were airborne again by midday on a mission to destroy a viaduct carrying a railway line. For the next two weeks the routine followed a similar pattern of two or three sorties a day, except when the weather, which was still unsettled, prevented them from flying. The wireless broadcasts carried news that the Allied beachhead had been successfully established and their observations from the air confirmed that, day by day, the armies were clawing their way forward, but painfully slowly, fighting for every yard of ground.

Felix and his squadron expected daily to receive the order to relocate to an airstrip in Normandy. Instead, to their great surprise and Felix's secret relief, they were withdrawn from operations and sent to an airfield near Southend for a week's rest. At the end of that time they were posted back to Biggin Hill to take up a role defending London against the attack from Hitler's latest 'secret weapon', the V1. The first of these unmanned flying bombs had landed on 13 June, while Felix and his men were too busy over France to pay much attention, but since then they had become familiar with the menacing drone of their engines, quite unlike an ordinary aero-engine. At night they could be identified by a long tail of orange flame, but what alarmed people most was that this new form of destruction could suddenly materialise without warning in broad daylight. Already Kent and Sussex were becoming known as 'Bomb Alley' as those V1s that fell short of their target in London inevitably dropped there. People were queuing to buy the new 'Morrison' shelters, steel structures that could take the place of a table by day and provide a barrier against falling masonry during raids. There was talk of a second evacuation of children from London.

Before taking up their duties the squadron were given forty-eight hours' leave. Felix smilingly rejected suggestions that he should go up to town with some of the others to 'do a show and see if we can pick up a couple of popsies', implying with a wink that he had better fish to fry. Instead he climbed into his old Lagonda and headed for Seaford, for the modest brick-and-flint cottage where Merry had grown up and where, at widely spaced and all too brief intervals over the past four years, he, Felix, had spent some of the happiest hours of his life. He had first returned to the house when he was posted back to London in January and had found it permeated with the musty odour of neglect. A woman from the village came up once a week to open a few windows and check for burst pipes but the place had not been lived in for eighteen months, and then only briefly. Everything was damp and the garden, on which Felix had once spent so much time and care, was overrun with weeds. Little by little, going down every time he had a day off from his desk at the Air Ministry, he had got it back into order. He had had the chimneys swept and lit fires in all the rooms and, as the spring advanced, he had worked at clearing the garden, revealing clusters of snowdrops and leggy daffodils. He had even sown some quick-growing vegetables – lettuce and beetroot and runner beans. When he had returned to active duty and been posted to Biggin Hill he had been delighted, since this meant that he was able to get over to Seaford even more frequently.

With the move to Bognor and the prospect of being sent to France he had assumed that he would never get the chance to harvest his crops. Now it seemed he might. He had Merry's key in his pocket and as he put it into the lock he found himself framing the words 'home again'. For a moment he paused to reflect that it was strange that he should feel that way about this modest house where he spent no more than a few scattered weeks, rather than the imposing half-timbered manor house in Cheshire where he had grown up. Then he recalled his last visit there and decided it was not strange at all. He pushed open the door and went inside.

On 13 June, one week after D-Day, Rose and her company were given their embarkation orders. No one told them where they were going but they were in no doubt that they were headed for France. The following day they put out from Weymouth on board a cross-Channel ferry converted for the duration into a troopship, as part of a convoy carrying reinforcements to the front. The sea was still rough and the ships pitched and wallowed in the choppy water. Rose, who had never been a good sailor, spent the voyage hanging over the side swept by wave after wave of nausea.

They docked at one of the Mulberry harbours, extraordinary constructions of steel and concrete that had been towed piece by piece across the Channel and assembled off the

Normandy coast to provide a haven for the ships of the invasion force. Driving inland, they passed through shattered villages where scarcely a house remained intact. The roads were pitted with shell craters and churned into ruts by the tracks of tanks, and the bus bounced and jolted as it negotiated them. The remaining inhabitants stared in amazement at the convoy, and Rose could understand why. They must make a bizarre spectacle. First came a motorcycle outrider, then what appeared to be a London bus painted in camouflage colours and emblazoned with the letters ENSA and the words 'STAND EASY!', then a truck and finally an officer in a jeep. Three miles back from the front line, with German snipers still holding out in every village, ENSA was here! It seemed hardly credible.

As soon as the bus stopped at a temporary rest camp in an apple orchard the company swung into its well-rehearsed routine, unloading and setting up for the performance. Rose worked with a frantic determination, lifting and carrying the heaviest loads her muscles could manage. Some of the men in the company protested and tried to take the heavier items from her, but she refused all offers of help. The weather had changed again and the sun was shining. The girls who had never left England before were complaining about the heat. Rose chivvied them on, scoffing, 'You should have been in Tangier with me! You don't know what hot is.' Nevertheless, as they worked she could feel the sweat trickling between her breasts and staining the underarms of her shirt. She had a headache and a dragging pain in her lower abdomen and she longed, above everything else, for a bath.

Before the show, socialising in an improvised mess tent with some of the NCOs, she was more animated than usual, laughing and chattering, fuelled by a far larger intake of gin than she had ever consumed before. When the time came to perform she danced like one possessed, throwing herself into high kicks and splits as if she had suddenly shed ten years. Then, when the final bows were over and the audience were still clapping and stamping and shouting for more, she quietly fainted into the arms of Leighton Dwyer and had to be carried to her tent.

It was Violet who noticed the bloodstain on her tights and shooed the men away.

7

It was four months after receiving it that Richard forced himself to sit down and reply to Priscilla's letter. To begin with there had been no way of communicating with her, but Allied advances over the spring had meant that a courier service of a fashion could now operate through the mountains; but still he had been putting it off. The torture and death of Gianni and the others had a bad effect on morale and he had been fully occupied devising activities, in cooperation with Armando, to keep the men occupied and give them a much-needed sense of wreaking revenge on the enemy. In comparison to all this, his personal affairs seemed trivial.

There was Antonia to consider, too. Richard was not present when Armando broke the news of her fiancé's death to her, though he knew that all he told her was that Gianni had been shot by a German patrol while guarding a cache of armaments. He had refused to leave his post and died a hero's death. It was her reaction – a fierce, wild-eyed determination to give up her job and throw in her lot with the partisans – which caused Armando to call him in. It took the two of them an hour to persuade her that she was far more use to them where she was. As a nurse in the hospital at Castelnuovo, she had access to vital drugs and dressings, which had already saved lives among the band. Also, she could get petrol for her little car and the necessary permits to allow her to travel around the valley. There was a further advantage, which Richard pressed home in his efforts to calm her. He had realised early on that she and her fellow nurses were admirably placed to collect information. They saw German units moving through the valley, which formed one of the vital connecting routes between central Italy and occupied Europe. They could count and chat to casualties, and men were less on their guard in conversation with them. In this way, Nick Macdonald's radio set had been able to convey much essential information back to their superiors at Special Force 1, who could pass it on to the High Command.

Richard had great admiration and affection for Armando's sister. It was she who had taken the risk of introducing him to the partisans, before he had revealed his identity and his connection to the British forces. Without that leap of faith, he might never have made that vital contact. He knew that she ran greater risks than he did, working day to day among the enemy who occupied the area, and without the support of an armed band or the protection of a weapon.

After that initial tragedy, it had been a good summer so far for the partisans. Most importantly, they were no longer working in isolation. In the spring they had received a visit from a man who called himself Ferrucio, accompanied by a British officer, Major Michael Newman. They brought the news that partisan bands all over the country were being brought under central control and formed into organised brigades. The communist-led Garibaldini formed the largest group, but the Partito d'Azione and the Fiamme Verde had constituted themselves into brigades as well, and all had agreed to accept the authority of the Committee of National Liberation in Milan. Armando's group now worked in conjunction with other bands in adjacent valleys, and Richard was in regular contact with other British liaison officers who had been dropped to them.

The news that the Allies had broken through the Gustav Line and were advancing lifted morale, and their triumphal entry into Rome on 4 June was an excuse for a celebration that went on most of the night. Since then there had been a steady trickle of recruits from surrounding towns and villages, who saw that the partisans were likely to be fighting on the winning side. There had been further reinforcements in July, after a disastrous attempt by partisans in the Emilia region to create a diversion to coincide with the Allied attack on the 'Gothic Line'. The result had been defeat at the battle of Montefiorino, and some of the survivors had found their way into the Garfagnana. Armando's band now constituted a useful fighting force.

On 25 July the BBC's Radio Italia had broadcast a message from General Alexander asking the partisans to redouble their attacks on German lines of communication. They had mined bridges and railway tracks and mounted frequent ambushes. As a result, the Germans found themselves losing control of all but the main roads, and it seemed that soon they might be routed from the Garfagnana altogether. Once that happened, there would be no need for Richard to remain. It was time to set his affairs in order.

It was not an easy letter to write and he had already made several attempts. He reread the final version.

Dear Priscilla,

I am sorry that it has taken so long for me to answer your letter, but I am sure you will understand the reason. I hope the delay has not caused you too much inconvenience.

It's sad that our marriage has to end like this, but I am

aware that things have not turned out the way you expected. I know that you put in a lot of effort on my behalf and were disappointed when I was unable to follow up the openings you created for me. Perhaps if the war had not come between us things might have been very different, but there it is. I had to do what I felt was my duty and it seems our lives were destined to take different directions.

I enclose a signed affidavit from the owner of a hotel in Naples, certifying that I spent a night there last December with a young woman by the name of Gina. I hope this will suffice as evidence of my infidelity in the divorce court.

(The document was a forgery, of course, drawn up by Armando, who was after all a lawyer in civilian life, and signed by one of his men. Richard felt that it was unlikely, in the middle of a war, that the English court would want to investigate too closely.)

I suppose when I eventually get back to England you will have moved to France. I shall miss you. After all, we did have so much in common and I have very happy memories of our brief time together. I hope that, when the war is over, we shall be able to meet as friends. Meanwhile, I wish you every happiness.

He struggled for a while to find suitable words to sign off and settled in the end for –

Affectionately yours,
Richard

After that he wrote a letter to his parents, which was almost more difficult, trying to explain the breakdown of his marriage. He could imagine his mother's lips closing in that tight, disapproving line and hear her remark that she had always known that '*that Priscilla*', for all her money and her airs and graces, was not to be trusted. His father would remark in return that he'd have been better off marrying a sensible lass from his own class. The news had to be broken somehow, however, before they read about it in the papers.

Finally, he set himself the task of writing to Priscilla's guardian.

Dear Sir Lionel,

It is with great regret that I have acceded to Priscilla's request for a divorce. I know that for you, as for me, her happiness is the paramount consideration and I do not wish to stand in her way. I only hope that she will find that happiness in her new relationship. I can assure you that I would never willingly have caused her distress and if the war had not come between us I believe we could have been very happy. I am very sorry that I was unable to fulfil the hopes and ambitions that she had for me but I am sure that you will understand that I had to do my duty as I saw it.

When the war is over I hope, still, to forge the sort of career that I so often discussed with Priscilla, and with you and Lady Vance. I shall always be grateful for your interest and encouragement, which meant a great deal to me. I should like to think that, in spite of the ending of my marriage, I can still rely on your friendship, and I hope you will allow me to visit you on my next leave.

With my best wishes to you and to Lady Vance,
Yours sincerely,
Richard Stevens

When he was finally satisfied with all three letters he sealed them and addressed the envelopes, then enclosed them all in a larger packet with a note asking that they be forwarded to England at the earliest opportunity. Then he took them out into the yard and handed them over to a lean, agile man in the dress of a shepherd. He was one of the Montagnards who knew every goat path along the ranges of the Apennines and were prepared, for a fee, to carry messages or conduct escaping POWs through enemy lines.

Richard gave him the required sum of money and watched him leave. Then he turned to look round the yard. It was Sunday and there was a temporary lull in operations. Armando had gone to mass in the village church, along with all the rest of the men who were not on duty. The local priest had thrown in his lot with the partisans some months earlier and was said to carry an automatic pistol under his robes, even while celebrating the Holy Eucharist. As one of the few non-Catholics in the group, Richard had excused himself from attendance at services and was usually glad to have an hour or two to himself, but today it meant that there was no one in whom he could confide. Finding that there was nothing requiring his immediate attention, and feeling the need for exercise, he picked up his Sten gun and set off to check on the sentries guarding the approaches to the farm and its surrounding buildings.

As he strode up the mountain path, Richard brooded over the finality of the letters he had just written. True, it would take some time yet before the divorce came through but today, to all intents and purposes, marked the end of his marriage. Where had it all gone wrong? Was it just because he had refused to accept the secondment to a safe, cushy position with the Council for the Encouragement of Music and the Arts? Why had he turned it down? After all, he had always maintained that he was a soldier only by accident, that he hated the futility and savagery of war. It was music which mattered to him, above all else. And yet he had turned the posting down, without hesitation. Why? Because, while men like Pat O'Leary (or whatever his real name was) languished in a German concentration camp, and Armando and Antonia risked their lives every day, he could not sit at home and devote himself to giving concerts in village halls and factories. But if Priscilla had really loved him, surely she would have understood that. Had she loved him? Or had she just been in love with the idea of marriage to an up-and-coming star? Had he loved her? Perhaps they had both been deluding themselves. He pushed the thought to the back of his mind, telling himself that there were more important things to worry about, but it lurked at the fringes of his consciousness, casting a chill shadow over the sunlit landscape.

He found the first two men on his round alert, but they had nothing of consequence to report. The same was true at the other sentry posts. It was a glorious summer day and all the surrounding area seemed to be at peace. For weeks the Germans had stuck to the main road through the valley and there had been no reports of patrols venturing up into the hills. Relishing the temporary sense of freedom, he decided to walk farther. At this altitude the heat of the sun was moderated. The air was thin, but after eight months he was acclimatised and the constant physical activity had toned his muscles to a peak of fitness he had never experienced before. The mere action of swinging along the path, which here followed the crest of the ridge, produced a sense of physical well-being that also soothed his mind. It was good to be out on his own, away from the constant demands and the nagging anxieties of his position.

He came to a spot he had visited several times before but

which always took his breath away. Monte Forato meant, literally, the mountain with the hole. Here a gigantic rock arch surmounted the ridge, visible from miles away as a hole in the top of the mountain. Richard paused to take in the view. Behind him the land fell away in steep, wooded slopes to the twisting valleys that led down to the River Serchio. In front was a sheer drop to the pastures and little villages of the coastal plain. He found a flat-topped rock and sat down and laid his Sten gun on the grass beside him. He unhooked his water bottle and drank and wished he had brought something to eat with him.

He found the notes of one of his favourite operatic pieces running through his mind, Phillip II's aria from Verdi's *Don Carlos*. It was the aria he had chosen to sing during his mock interrogation at Beaulieu – was it only three years ago? It felt like half a lifetime. *Ella giammai m'amo* . . . The heartbroken cry of the betrayed king. *She has never loved me!* How apposite the words seemed now! He sang the recitative through softly. *Ella giammai m'amo . . . amor per me non ha, amor per me non ha* . . . Then he heard in his head the yearning notes of the orchestral introduction to the aria proper and the measured, dignified despair of the king's voice. *Dormiro sol sul manto mio regal . . . I shall sleep alone in my royal robes* . . . It was a long time since he had sung – *really* sung. Not since that impromptu appearance in Merry's concert last Christmas. He straightened himself, opened his shoulders, filled his lungs and gave himself up to the music, finding in it the expression for the unacknowledged pain in his own heart.

He knew that sound carried in the mountains, but what of it? All Italians sang. It pleased him to think that, down in the valley below him, a farmer might call to the ox that drew his plough to stop for a moment, or a woman might pause in the act of drawing water from the well and smile. What he was not prepared for, when he came to the end of the piece, was the sound of a single pair of hands applauding and a voice with a strong German accent calling, 'Bravo! Bravo!'

Richard froze. His first instinct was to reach for the Sten gun on the ground beside him but his training told him that if another weapon was already aimed at him any such movement would mean instant death. He thanked heaven that he was not in uniform. Officially, he was supposed to wear it at all times, as his only protection against being shot as a spy should he be picked up. In practice, he felt a good deal safer and less conspicuous dressed in the simple clothes of a local peasant. The fact that he had not shaved for three days and that the only barbering his hair had received in months was the occasional rough trim from one of Armando's men lent verisimilitude to the disguise. He turned slowly and looked behind him.

A short distance away and slightly above him, a man in the uniform of a German major stood on a rocky outcrop. He was a few years older than Richard, tall and rather gangling, his arms and legs seeming too long for the rest of his body. He carried a pair of field glasses round his neck and wore a holstered pistol on his hip, but apart from that he was unarmed. He was also, as far as Richard could tell, alone. Richard glanced down. The Sten, to his relief, was concealed from the newcomer by the rock on which he was sitting. He produced an ingenous smile and said, in an accent he hoped was a close enough approximation to the local speech to fool a foreigner. 'You startled me, signor.'

'I'm sorry,' the man replied, in passable Italian. 'That's a fine voice you have. It's a shame to waste it on the goats.'

'Ah, signor,' Richard said, smiling more broadly, 'the

goats do not boo or hiss. There is no *claque* here in the mountains.'

The German laughed. 'You sound as if you speak from experience.'

He moved as if to come down and join him. Richard saw instantly that if he did so he would inevitably see the Sten. He jumped to his feet. 'Take care, signor! The rocks just there are treacherous. Wait, I will come to you.'

In a couple of bounds he had scaled the rocky outcrop and stood beside the German on a little grassy plateau. Close to, he could see that the other man was slightly built and was, moreover, breathing heavily from the climb. *Not fit!* his training said. *I can take him from here, if I have to*. The German smiled in a friendly manner.

'So, tell me. Where did you learn to sing like that?'

'In Milano, signor,' Richard replied. His mind was racing, constantly assessing the situation. There was no point in trying to pretend that his voice was completely untrained. 'I was lucky. The schoolmaster at my village school saw that I had some talent. He spoke to a professor from the Conservatoire and they arranged a scholarship for me.'

'Then what are you doing here, serenading the goats, instead of singing in La Scala?'

Richard lifted his shoulders expressively. 'The war, signor. I was called up.'

The German looked away from him, out towards the sea. 'Ah, the war,' he murmured sadly. 'It ruined a good many young lives, I am afraid.' He sat down on a rock near by and Richard hunkered down beside him, balanced, ready to spring if the need presented itself. 'You came home, when your people . . . capitulated?'

'Oh, before that, signor. I was wounded in the leg and

invalided out, quite early on.' It was a story that had served him well before and he saw no reason not to use it again, though it occurred to him that it would have been better if he had not shinned up those rocks quite so rapidly. He had no wish to be arrested as a deserter or called up for forced labour in Germany.

'Ah.' The other man nodded wistfully. 'You were lucky, my friend. I envy you the peace of your mountains.'

It struck Richard abruptly that here was a man who felt the same as he did about the war, a man with whom he might have become friends, in different circumstances.

'You like the mountains, signor?' he enquired.

'I love all wild places – and the creatures that inhabit them. Before the war I was studying ornithology at the University of Heidelberg.'

'Then you have come here to look at birds?' Richard said.

'Yes, vultures, specifically. I was told that there are vultures in these parts. Is that so?'

Richard vaguely recalled that one of Armando's men had once pointed out some dark shapes circling above them and said that they were vultures, but he could not have identified one if he saw it. He said, 'Oh yes, certainly. But not exactly here. I've not seen them around here for a long time.'

'Where, then?' the other man asked eagerly. 'Can you tell me where to find them?'

Richard thought quickly. The last thing he wanted was this earnest German poking round the area of the farm, or up at the head of the valley where they had marked out their dropping zone for supplies. He pointed towards the next ridge. 'Over there, beyond those mountains. That is where they nest.'

'So far away? Then I have been directed to the wrong area. A pity.'

'You have transport, signor? You could drive over there in two hours.'

The German sighed. 'Sadly that is not possible. My unit is stationed down there on the plain. I have snatched an hour or two to come up here but I cannot be away for long.'

Richard's brain was still engaged in busy calculations. The man was apparently alone, seemed harmless enough. But could that be taken on trust? Was he as innocent and unsuspecting as he seemed? Perhaps birdwatching was simply a cover for spying out the area, looking for signs of partisan activity. Had he already seen enough to arouse his suspicions? The German had taken up his field glasses again and was absorbed in scanning the sky. Richard offered up a passing prayer that there were not, in fact, any vultures in the area, to prove him a liar. He decided that, if the German was engaged in some form of covert activity, he would not risk sitting as he was with his back half turned, apparently completely relaxed. On the other hand, he was an enemy. Was it best to dispose of him now, while he was off guard?

Looking at him, Richard knew that he could reach him in one spring. There would be no need for a weapon. He could break his neck before he had time to reach for his pistol or utter a cry. Equally, he recognised that he was psychologically incapable of an unprovoked attack on this pleasant, unsuspecting man. He found a ready excuse. If the officer did not return to his unit by nightfall the whole lot of them would be up here at dawn, searching for him, and that was the last thing he wanted.

Aloud he said, 'I didn't think German officers had time for birdwatching.'

The other man lowered his glasses and smiled his engaging smile. 'Even German officers get time off occasionally.'

'I could ask my cousin if he knows where to see vultures,' Richard offered. 'He knows more about birds than I do. Will you be in the area for long?'

'That depends. We have been sent to flush out the partisans, but so far we have seen no sign of them.'

Richard met his eyes and spread his hands in a gesture of innocence. 'Partisans, signor? Not around these parts. Our mayor is a supporter of Il Duce. He would not put up with any nonsense from partisans in this area.'

The German nodded slowly. 'Good. I am glad to hear that. Unfortunately, not all your compatriots are so sensible.' He got up. 'What is the name of that village down there?'

'Down on the plain? That is Stazzema, signor.'

'Is that where you live?'

'Me? No, signor. I live back there.' He nodded vaguely towards the valley behind them.

The other man looked at him for a moment and nodded again. 'Good. That is good.' He picked up the rucksack that lay on the rock beside him. 'I must get back. I am glad to have met you. One day, when all this is over, I shall hear you sing at La Scala. *Arrivederci*.'

'*Buon giorno, signor*,' Richard responded automatically, as the German turned away and began to scramble back down the path that led to the valley. He sat where he was, watching the receding figure, until it disappeared round the shoulder of a hill, and then he still sat on, making sure that the man did not intend to turn back and follow him. Eventually he saw him far below, still descending the winding path. Satisfied, he retrieved his gun and set off back towards the farm.

As he came down the last slope he saw a familiar figure climbing to meet him – a girl in nurse's uniform. He paused by a gateway where someone in the past had hollowed out a rough seat from a fallen tree trunk and waited for her. When she reached him he took her hands and kissed her on both cheeks.

'*Ciao, Tonia! Come sta?*'

'*Ciao, Ricardo*. I'm well, thank you.'

But studying her, he saw that she had lost weight. Well, there was no surprise in that. They had all lost weight. Food was in short supply. Her face was thinner, emphasising the strong bone structure that made her brother Armando such a strikingly handsome man but robbed her of the softness conventionally required for feminine beauty. There were deep shadows under her eyes, and the eyes themselves had lost the glint and sparkle he remembered from their first encounters.

Richard said, 'I'm sorry I wasn't there when you arrived. Have you been waiting long?'

She shook her head. 'Not long. It doesn't matter, but we were beginning to worry about you. You shouldn't go off on your own like that.'

Richard acknowledged the rebuke with a grimace. It was exactly what he would have said to any of the others. 'I know. But I needed a bit of time to myself.'

'Is something wrong?'

'No, not here. It's to do with me, my life in England. I seem to have come to a sort of crossroads.'

Antonia frowned. '*Caro*, you're not thinking of leaving us, are you?'

'Of course not. Nothing would get me away from here except a direct order from HQ – and even then they would have to repeat it two or three times before I was sure I was decoding it correctly! No, it's just personal stuff.'

'Do you want to tell me about it?'

He looked around, then took her hand and said, 'Shall we sit here for a bit?'

They sat side by side on the fallen log, her hand cool and firm in his. He went on, 'You remember, the first time you brought me up here, I told you I was married?'

'Of course.'

'Well, it seems that now I'm not – or I soon shan't be.'

'Your wife . . .' She hesitated. 'Your wife is ill?'

'No, no. Not as far as I know. But she wants a divorce and I don't see any reason to stand in her way.'

'A divorce!' Antonia's voice expressed the shock of a girl brought up in a Catholic society where such a thing was almost unheard of.

Richard smiled briefly. 'It's not such an uncommon thing in England, especially these days.'

'But when did you hear about this?'

'I got a letter some time ago, when I was in Algiers. But I haven't got round to answering it until now.'

'And you have said nothing about this before. Why?'

'I didn't see any point in burdening you with it. There was nothing anyone could do.'

'But why does she want a divorce?'

'Apparently she's met someone else, someone she feels will make her happier than I can.'

'But why do you not fight for her? Why let this other man take her away from you?'

'I think it's too late for that.'

'She has been unfaithful to you?'

'I believe so.'

Antonia's nostrils flared and some of the old fire returned to her eyes. 'What sort of woman cheats on her husband when he is away fighting for his country?'

He sighed. 'Well, it can't be much fun for a girl like Priscilla, having a husband you haven't seen for over a year.

And of course I can't tell her where I am or what I'm doing.'

'But she must have some idea, surely?'

'Oh, she could make a fairly good guess,' Richard agreed.

'And yet she cheats on you with another man? You are right to let her go, *caro*.'

Richard said, 'You mustn't think too badly of her. I think I have been a serious disappointment to her. She had grand plans for us both and I wasn't able to go along with them.'

'She is a very foolish woman,' Antonia pronounced. 'If I were in her place I should forget all my grand plans and be proud to wait for you to return.'

Richard looked at her. Her dark eyes were still glowing and her lips had a fine, contemptuous curl. He found himself remembering Priscilla's face, so pretty and alluring when things were going well, so petulant when she could not get her own way. The woman beside him now was a different breed altogether.

Voices below them cut across his thoughts. A small group of men were crossing the farmyard. Someone shouted and waved. Richard got up and drew Antonia up with him.

'There's Armando – and there's someone with him.' He turned to her and smiled. 'Don't worry about me, Tonia. It was all over between me and Priscilla a long time ago. I'm not breaking my heart over it. Let's go down, shall we?'

The newcomer with Armando was Leandro, the leader of the partisan group based at Alpe di San Antonio, a few miles farther south. As soon as Richard was close enough to see his expression he knew that it meant bad news. Armando led them into the farmhouse kitchen and closed the door.

'What's happened, Leandro?'

'It's bad. Someone must have told the Nazis where we are. Two nights ago a patrol approached our camp. One of the sentries lost his head and shot the officer leading it. The patrol withdrew, but they know now where to find us.'

Armando shook his head. 'They won't leave it at that. There will be reprisals.'

'I know,' Leandro said. 'They've decided that we are too much of a nuisance to be ignored. They'll be back in force before long.'

'They already are,' Richard said. He told them about his encounter with the German major.

'Then we don't have much time,' Leandro said. 'I've come to ask for your help. Will you stand with us, when they attack?'

They were sitting together the following morning, drawing up their plans for the defence of Alpe, when there was a sudden outbreak of shouting outside. Armando strode to the door and threw it open.

'What's going on?'

Three of his men were surrounding a boy of around twelve years old, who was pushing a battered bicycle and panting for breath. Richard recognised him as the son of the local mayor.

'What is it, Gino?' Armando asked.

'My father sent me. He had a telephone call from the mayor of Stazzema. Two days ago the Nazis discovered three partisans hiding out in the padre's house. Now there is a German column advancing in their direction. He is afraid they are coming to take reprisals.'

'Stazzema?' Richard exclaimed.

The boy nodded and Richard turned away, gritting his teeth. The German officer had tried to warn him! He had specifically asked the name of the village and had hinted that partisans had been discovered. 'You idiot!' he berated himself. 'If you had not been so wrapped up in your own affairs you would have spotted that.'

Armando swung round, barking orders. Antonia led the boy inside as men came running from every part of the farm and the surrounding buildings, grabbing their weapons as they came. Within minutes they were all streaming out of the farmyard, scrambling for places in the motley collection of vehicles, the spoils of ambushes and raids over the past months.

Stazzema was on the other side of the mountain and there was no direct route by road. They were forced to leave their vehicles in the tiny village of Palagnana and complete the journey on foot. As they crossed the ridge Armando, in the lead, came to a sudden halt.

'Look!'

Below them they could see the rooftops of the village and the road leading into it. A column of grey-painted troop carriers, led by an officer in a jeep, had just reached the first buildings.

'Come on!' Armando started forward, but Richard caught his arm.

'Wait! We're outnumbered and outgunned. If we rush in we could run straight into a trap.'

Armando surveyed the slope between them and the village. 'We have to do something, we'll follow the stream down. That will give us some cover.'

Slipping and sliding on the loose rocks, they led their men down the ravine carved out by the water until they came within a hundred yards of the village square. Lying flat behind a low wall, Richard studied the scene. The German soldiers were going from house to house, ordering all the inhabitants out. The men and the older boys were lined up on one side of the square, while the women and children huddled together on the other. When they were all assembled the officer in charge stood up in his jeep and shouted an order. With a wrench at the pit of his stomach Richard recognised the officer he had talked to the previous day.

In response to the command the soldiers began herding the men and boys into the troop carriers. 'Bastards!' Armando hissed. 'Where are they taking them?'

'Forced labour, probably,' Richard responded grimly.

'We can't let them. We must do something!' Armando gazed around him, gesturing his men forward.

'No!' Richard grabbed his arm. 'It's hopeless. Can't you see that? There are too many of them. If we attack we shall just end up with the other men – those of us who are still alive.'

'But we must do something! Can't we create a diversion? Hold them up somehow? How about ambushing the convoy as they leave?'

'That way we risk killing our own people as well,' Richard said. 'Maybe we could draw some of the soldiers off and then we might have a chance against the remainder.'

He turned to the men behind him and whispered rapid orders. Six of the youngest and fittest detached themselves and began to work their way back up the hill. 'When they start firing there's a chance some of the Nazis will go after them. They're all good runners. They should be able to lead them quite a dance and give the rest of us time to attack the convoy.'

All the men from the village were in the trucks now and the soldiers began shepherding the women and children towards the church. Their protests and pleas were met with blows and curses.

'Now what?' Armando asked.

Once all the women were inside there was a flurry of activity around the doors and the sound of hammering. 'They are nailing planks across the doors!' Armando exclaimed.

'I imagine they are shutting them in so they can't run for help,' Richard said. 'It's a good job we're here to let them out again.'

The vehicles were started up, filling the square with the roar of their engines.

'What's happened to the men you sent to cause the diversion?' Armando demanded. 'It will be too late in a minute.'

As he spoke gunfire crackled in the hills above them. Richard saw several of the Germans turn to scan the hillside, but just as he began to hope that his tactic had worked the officer in charge shouted an order and they returned to their vehicles, which began to manoeuvre into line facing the narrow street. Beside him Armando was swearing under his breath. Then a sudden movement near the church caught their attention. Something bright flashed in the air and disappeared, followed by the crash of breaking glass. A second object followed the first.

'They're breaking the windows, vandals!' someone exclaimed behind Richard.

Then the first curl of smoke appeared, spiralling lazily upwards from the rose window above the west door.

'Christ!' Richard yelled. 'They've fired the church!'

The last vehicles were still edging into the narrow street as he and Armando led their men in a reckless charge across the square, but either the men in them were not looking back, or they had orders not to react. But the incendiary devices had done their work and already flames were licking up out of the windows. More windows smashed, showering them with broken glass, and they heard the sound of splintering wood as a beam gave way, and above all that rose the screams of women and children. With bleeding hands Richard and the others dragged at the planks that had been nailed across the doors, but without tools it was impossible to shift them. Someone found a sledgehammer in a nearby barn and began beating at the doors, trying to smash a hole in the ancient oak. Richard left them and ran round the church looking for another way in, but when he found another door it too had been nailed shut. He hurled himself against it again and again, oblivious to the crushing pain in his shoulder, but it was useless.

With a rending crash part of the church roof gave way, showering them all with sparks and glowing embers. Men were throwing buckets of water from the village well through the windows but they made no more impression than spit in a bonfire. The screaming had diminished now, and then the smell reached him, the nauseatingly sickly stench of burning flesh. Richard staggered away, retching, and clung to the wall of a nearby building for support while he vomited until he thought he would spew up his own guts. When the spasms subsided he sank down in a crouch and wrapped his arms round his head to shut out the noise. Among all the horror, one thought predominated. He could have prevented this. If he had paid proper attention to what the German officer was trying to tell him, the villagers could have been warned. The Germans would have had to wreak their revenge on an empty shell. He could not forget that yesterday he had had the man who had ordered this atrocity at his mercy. Yet even now it was hard to believe that such a man could commit an act so evil. Or had he been as sickened by his orders as Richard was by their effects? Was it possible that a gentle ornithologist from the University of Heidelberg could have ordered this massacre? If so, could anyone in the world be trusted, or were all human beings corruptible? And if he, Richard, had acted on his training and killed the man, would it have prevented the tragedy? Was he, ultimately, to blame?

He became aware of a voice near by. One of Armando's men was on his knees, murmuring the prayer for the dead. Richard wanted to shout at him, to tell him that prayer was useless, worse than useless. What sort of God could allow this to happen? What was the point of churches if they could be put to this use?

Armando was giving orders. The glowing ruins of the church were still too hot to enter. The village was searched but there were no survivors. More prayers were said. Richard sat where he was and let them get on with it. Suddenly he felt exhausted. He had been in the field too long, and for the first time he desperately wanted to go home. At length he raised his head and saw winged shapes circling above him, black against the sky.

'Vultures!' he muttered. Then, seized with something between tears and hysterical laughter, he screamed in the direction of the departing Germans, 'Vultures! You wanted vultures, you bastard! Now you've bloody well got them!'

8

Around the middle of August Merry was summoned to the office of his CO. Slessor greeted him with a smile. 'Got some news for you, old chap. You're going home. George wants you back.'

'Home? When? Why?' Merry asked in sudden alarm. His first thought was that he must somehow have transgressed, to be recalled so abruptly.

'Soon as we can find a flight that can accommodate you,' Slessor responded. 'As to why – I've been given no reason, of course. But I can make a guess. I imagine George wants some help with organising the Stars in Battledress effort in France and is looking for someone with experience of working at the "sharp end". I'll be sorry to lose you, Merry. You've done a bloody good job here. But presumably that's why George wants you back.'

'I'll be sorry to go, too,' Merry murmured. It was true. He felt a responsibility towards the men he had been working with, many of them making use of talents they had only half suspected they had before the war. Added to that was the new mood of optimism that had swept through both the civilian population and the invading forces. Everyone was convinced that by the end of the summer the Allies would have swept the Germans out of Italy. It seemed the wrong time to be leaving.

But along with the regret came a new thought, almost too

tantalising to be real. Felix was in England. Merry knew from his recent letters that he was back on active service. He could not, of course, say where he was stationed, but each of his letters contained a reference to 'popping over to the house to keep an eye on things' or to working in the garden, so Merry knew that he must be somewhere near the south coast. If George Black's summons meant he would be based in London they would be able to spend time together.

'You'd better go back to your hotel and pack,' Slessor said. 'There's no telling when a flight might become available.'

Before leaving the building Merry made his way to the office of the signals officer and persuaded him to send a message to Felix via a contact in the Air Ministry, to let him know that he was on his way home. He had to wait two days for a flight to Gibraltar and then another twenty-four hours for a seat on a plane bound for Portreath in Cornwall. From there he took the night train to London and arrived crumpled, weary and in need of a bath. He checked into the Strand Palace Hotel, spruced himself up and reported to George Black at the Central Pool of Artistes headquarters in Grosvenor Street.

Black came round his desk and welcomed him with his usual geniality. 'Merry! Good to see you! You're looking fit. Darn sight better than you looked last time we met.'

Merry recalled their last interview. He could picture himself, pale and thin, hands still unsteady after three weeks without alcohol. He had begged George to send him out to North Africa, to give him a chance to redeem himself. That was the way he had presented it, but they had both known that what he was really seeking was a more or less honourable death. He gave the senior officer his slow, self-deprecating smile.

'Yes, I'm pretty well, thanks. And thanks for trusting me out there.'

'Never regretted it for a minute!' Black said robustly. 'You've done us proud, old chap. I'm delighted to see you looking so well.' He returned to his seat behind the desk and looked up with a complicit smile. 'I was glad to hear that Squadron Leader Mountjoy made it after all. The papers here were full of it. Amazing story!'

'Yes, it was, wasn't it,' Merry agreed, and held the other man's eyes for a moment. His relationship with Felix had never been openly discussed but it was well understood between them.

'Right, down to business,' Black said. 'Have a seat, old boy. I expect you've guessed why I sent for you. We've got a big SIB operation in Normandy already and it's going to get bigger as we advance. I need someone out there who's had experience of running this sort of show, so that's where you come in. You'll be based in Caen for the time being and move forward as and when the need arises.'

'When do I leave?' Merry asked, afraid that he might be required to set off for France immediately.

'Not for a week or two yet,' Black reassured him. 'I think you're probably due for some leave, aren't you? When did you last have some time off?'

Merry thought. 'Christmas,' he said.

'Right. Take two weeks, as from today. When you get back we'll discuss the details of what you're going to do over there. Meanwhile, have a good rest. You won't get much chance in France.'

Merry was about to leave when Black added, 'Oh, nearly forgot! There was a message for you. Mountjoy phoned. Said to tell you he's at Biggin Hill and ask you to call when you got here.'

'Thanks,' Merry said.

'Tell you what,' Black added. 'My old dad's got a new revue on at the Palladium – "If It's Laughter You're After". Damn fine cast – Tommy Trinder, Jewell and Warris, lots of good supporting acts. If you and Felix fancy a night out just let me know. I'll get them to put aside a couple of tickets for you.'

Merry thanked him again and made his way to the office that had once been his and begged the use of the telephone from its current occupant. After some delay he got through to the aerodrome at Biggin Hill and asked if it was possible to speak to Squadron Leader Mountjoy.

'I'm sorry, sir,' responded the businesslike female voice on the other end of the line, 'I'm afraid the squadron leader is not available at the moment.'

Merry was disappointed but unsurprised. Felix was presumably up on a mission. 'Well, in that case, can you give him a message for me when he comes down?' he asked.

'I'm sorry, sir,' the woman repeated. 'I'm afraid I can't guarantee to do that.'

Bloody service red tape! Merry thought. Aloud he said, 'Well, look. If you see him just tell him that Merry called and I'll be at the house this evening. OK?'

He put the phone down while the woman was still burbling about not being able to take messages.

He reached the house in Seaford in the late afternoon. Pausing at the garden gate he scanned the windows but there was no waiting figure behind them. He glanced at his watch. Too early for Felix to be off duty yet, but from the look of the garden he had obviously been here recently. He let himself in through the front door and called, 'Felix?' – just in case. The house smelt of warm wood and furniture polish. Merry dropped his case and went into the sitting room. The baby grand piano, which had been Felix's present to him for his birthday two – no, three – years ago stood in the bay window. He crossed and opened the lid and ran his fingers over the keys. It had been recently tuned. Smiling to himself he returned to the hall, picked up his case and carried it upstairs.

Inside the room, which he still thought of as the spare room but which he and Felix had always shared, he stood quite still. The room smelt of Felix, of that subtle blend of soap and hair oil and body odour that he would have recognised among the most exotic perfumes in the world. The bed had been made, but had obviously been slept in. *Soon*, he told himself, *soon!*

Then he saw the piece of paper on the pillow. He picked it up, smiling. A welcome home note!

My dear Merry,

Life's a sod, isn't it? I've just had a phone call recalling me to the station because we're being sent overseas – taking off at first light. I'm so sorry! I've been counting the hours ever since I got your message and now this! I know you will be as cut up about it as I am. Of course, no one will say where we're being sent, but I assume it's France. I'll write as soon as I can and let you know what's happening. Meanwhile, keep your pecker up and try to have a good leave.

Love, as always,
Felix

Merry's first impulse was to drum his heels and shout 'It's not fair! It's not fair!' like a child having a tantrum. He controlled it, but the pleasure had drained out of the day and he was overcome by a listless gloom that was all too familiar. For the rest of the evening he moped round the house, unable even to summon up the energy to cook a proper meal.

For the next two days he pottered around, going for walks and dropping in on the pubs that he and Felix had frequented on earlier leaves, playing the piano or sitting in the garden reading. He heard on the news that the American tanks had broken through the German lines at St-Lô, allowing them to escape from the defensive containment that had prevented significant advances since D-Day. He wondered how close to the action Felix was.

On the third morning he roused himself to do some work in the garden. He was mowing the front lawn when the telegraph boy appeared at the gate. It was such an exact re-enactment of what had happened two years earlier that for a moment he thought he was suffering from some sort of flashback. He wanted to say, 'No, you've got it all wrong. That's all in the past, and anyway it wasn't true.' But the boy was real enough, and so was the telegram. He tipped him automatically and walked back into the house. For perhaps ten minutes he sat at the kitchen table and stared at the unopened envelope. *It can't happen*, he told himself. *This sort of thing doesn't repeat itself. Fate can't be that cruel!* But he knew that it could. The thought came to him that he was not going to endure again what he had been through last time. If this news was what he suspected it must be, his service revolver was upstairs. This time he would use it.

That thought gave him the strength to open the telegram. He unfolded the flimsy paper and read:

Anthony killed stop (Anthony? Who the hell was Anthony? Some fool had got the names muddled.) *Returning London soonest stop Will telephone stop Felix.*

It was several seconds before his brain managed to unscramble what he was reading. *Anthony!* Anthony was Felix's elder brother, who had inherited the title of Lord Malpas only a few months earlier. It was not Felix who had been killed. The telegram was from Felix and he was coming back to England – was probably on his way even now. Merry threw back his head and let out a long, tremulous sound that was half sob, half a cry of exultation.

He realised that his hands were shaking and got up to put the kettle on the gas. Over a mug of strong tea that used up the last of his ration he tried to think through the implications of the telegram. If Anthony was dead, then Felix was presumably now Lord Malpas. Black sheep or Prodigal Son? He recalled Felix's description of his last visit home. What sort of reception could he expect this time? He gave a passing thought to Felix's mother, who had suffered the loss of a husband and her elder son in the space of a few months, but found it impossible to summon up a great deal of sympathy for that glacial woman. He recognised, in a vague, abstract way, that this new development was going to have a big impact on their future lives but could not focus his mind on the details. All he could think of was that he would see Felix soon. He tried to calculate when the telegram might have been sent and how long it might take Felix to get back to London but there were too many imponderables.

The telephone call came just before five that afternoon.

'Hello, Merry? It's me.'

'Felix! It's so good to hear you! How are you?'

'I'm OK – a bit stunned, I suppose.'

'Not surprising, in the circumstances. Where are you?'

'London. A chum's lent me his flat in Maida Vale. Can you come up?'

'Of course. I'll be there in a couple of hours. Give me the address.'

It was around eight o'clock when Merry rang the bell of the

flat in an anonymous mansion block. Felix answered so quickly that it was obvious he had been waiting. Merry stepped inside, dropped his case, kicked the door to behind him and took Felix in his arms. For a long time they stood still, not speaking or kissing, but just holding each other.

At length Felix drew back a fraction and murmured, 'I'm so glad you're here!'

'So am I,' Merry replied, scanning his face. He looked very tired and, beneath the tan acquired after a year with the partisans in Italy, the faint scars left by Archie McIndoe's plastic surgery showed up as fine white lines, as they always did when he was under strain. 'How are you?' Merry asked again.

'I'm OK. Still a bit shocked.'

'Of course.' He hesitated and added, 'I'm so sorry, Felix, about Anthony.'

Felix lifted his shoulders slightly. 'You know Anthony and I were never very close, and we parted last time on particularly bad terms. I can't pretend it's a great personal tragedy.'

'How did it happen?'

'His ship was torpedoed on convoy duty in the Atlantic. They picked him out of the drink, apparently, but he was dead. No possibility of a mistake.'

'Have you spoken to your mother?'

'I rang just before I spoke to you.'

'How is she?'

'Bearing up – in full control. She's a tough old bird.'

There was a pause. Merry said, 'So now you're Lord Malpas.'

'So it seems. Rum, isn't it?' Felix drew back. 'I expect you could do with a drink. There's some beer, or would you rather have a Scotch? The chap who owns this place told me to help myself.'

Merry opted for a beer and followed Felix into the kitchen. 'Should I be calling you my lord?' he enquired, trying for a lighter tone.

'Only if you want a poke in the eye,' Felix returned, with a glimmer of a smile. 'Have you eaten?'

'Not since lunchtime.'

'Me neither. There's nothing in the flat. We'll have to go out later and see what we can find.'

They carried the beer into the sitting room and sat on the settee. Merry said, 'What next?'

'I have to go up to Cheshire tomorrow. I imagine there will be legal formalities to complete and a memorial service of some sort. God knows what sort of reception I'll get.' He stretched his arm along the back of the settee and laid his hand on Merry's shoulder. 'I'm just thankful I shan't have to go through it alone, this time.'

Merry stared at him. 'Felix, you surely aren't suggesting that I should come with you!'

Felix looked disconcerted. 'Well, of course, I know it's an imposition, taking up your precious leave and all that, but . . .'

'Don't be an idiot,' Merry chided him. 'You know I don't mean that. I just don't want to make things more difficult. Don't you think your mother will regard it as an act of extreme provocation? She'll probably throw me out.'

He was remembering his one encounter with Lady Malpas. He had never told Felix about it, feeling that it could only be hurtful. It occurred to him that he ought to mention it but now did not seem to be the right time.

Felix's face had set mutinously. 'She can't throw you out. The estate is entailed, so Malpas is mine now, whether she likes it or not. And I'll bloody well invite whoever I want.'

'I see that,' Merry murmured, 'but we ought to consider her feelings just now, don't you think?'

Felix's expression softened. 'Look, I'm not proposing to introduce you under your true colours, as it were. God knows I'd like to. I'd like to be able to stand up and acknowledge you in front of the whole world. But the law won't let me. So I shall just introduce you to my mother as an old friend who has very kindly offered to give up his leave to keep me company.'

'Will she believe that?'

'It won't matter whether she does or not. She's one of the old school. *Noblesse oblige – pas devant les domestiques*, etc. Whatever happens, you must never make a scene or create a scandal. She'll realise that if she tries to chuck you out there will be an almighty row and that's the last thing she wants, under the circumstances. So she will either believe that you are exactly what I say you are, or she will pretend to. It's all a matter of saving face, you see.'

'I suppose so,' Merry agreed dubiously.

Felix rubbed a hand up the back of his neck. 'Don't worry. I promise you won't have to contend with any unpleasantness. You'll be a guest, and as such you'll be treated with due courtesy.'

'It's not myself I'm thinking of,' Merry insisted.

'I know,' Felix responded. 'Please come, Merry. I honestly don't think I can face it without you.'

Merry leaned closer to him. 'Then I'll be there, of course. You know I'd rather spend a week in hell with you than eternity in paradise on my own.'

Some time later they went out and found a restaurant, which served them with the toughest steak Merry had ever eaten. Felix insisted it was horse meat. In spite of that, their mood lightened as they talked, catching up with each other's news, and they returned to the flat feeling more relaxed.

'I'm sorry I've messed up your leave,' Felix said, unbuttoning his tunic. 'I could have howled when that call came through telling me we were being sent overseas. Were you devastated when you read my note?'

'Utterly,' Merry told him, adding as an afterthought, 'but not as completely as I was when the telegram arrived.'

'The telegram?' Felix repeated. 'Why?'

'Oh, not when I'd read it. When the boy brought it. It was so exactly like what happened when I got the other one, saying you'd been killed – almost exactly to the day.'

Felix was aghast. 'Oh God, Merry! I'm so sorry!' He dropped his tunic on the back of a chair and came to lay his hands on Merry's shoulders. 'I never thought. I just wanted to make sure you got the message, in case you were planning to go off somewhere else.'

'Well, why should you,' Merry returned. 'After all, you weren't there when the first one came and I don't think I ever told you about it.'

Felix nodded. 'Oh yes, you did. I remember it now. You said it arrived on your birthday. Your birthday! It's not, is it . . . No, not yet. Can't be.'

'No, not till next Friday,' Merry reassured him. He could feel the warmth of Felix's skin beneath his hands, through the fabric of his shirt.

'We'll celebrate,' Felix promised.

'We shan't be able to. We shall be in Cheshire and celebrations will be out of order.'

'We'll find a way,' Felix said, slipping his arms round Merry's neck. 'Why don't we start now?'

* * *

In the middle of the night Merry woke suddenly, aware that Felix was awake and tense beside him.

'What is it?' he asked.

'Listen,' Felix said.

Merry became aware of a throbbing drone. A second or two later the siren sounded. 'Air raid,' he concluded.

'Doodlebug,' Felix corrected.

'What?'

'V1. Hitler's latest weapon. No pilot, just a bomb with wings and an engine.'

'It's stopped,' Merry said.

'Yes,' Felix responded tautly. 'That means it's on its way down. It's OK. They say if it's overhead when the engine cuts out it won't drop on you. It's the poor buggers who never heard it coming who cop it.'

A moment later there was a distant crump and the curtains at the open window billowed in the shock wave.

'See what I mean?' Felix said.

'My God!' Merry exclaimed. 'Do you get many of those?'

'Far too many.'

'Can't the RAF do anything about them?'

'Not so far. They're too damn fast and they come over singly, not in formations. By the time we know there's one on its way it's too late. Our best hope is to bomb the launching sites but they're well dug in and buried under tons of concrete.'

Merry eased himself back on to his pillow. 'Well, all I can say is I'm glad we're leaving London tomorrow!'

The following morning, in the taxi on the way to the station, Merry addressed the question that had been hovering at the back of his mind since he received the telegram.

'I suppose all this is going to make a big difference to your plans for the future.'

'Inevitably,' Felix agreed. 'But to be quite honest with you I haven't really got to grips with that yet. Obviously, from now on I take over responsibility for the house and the estate, and the people who work on it – though Mother will have to carry on running things for the time being.'

'But when the war's over, you'll settle down to being a country landowner?'

'I suppose so.'

'Do you think you'll enjoy that?'

'Oddly enough, I think I shall.'

Merry digested this idea in silence for a while. The first, disturbing questions about the future were stirring in his mind. How would their relationship fit in with Felix's new role? If he was going to return to the conventional society in which he had grown up, would he also feel it necessary to conform to the moral rules of that society – the breaking of which had once resulted in his banishment? He felt disloyal, even to consider such things. Felix had given him ample proof of his commitment. But the thoughts would not be suppressed.

Felix said slyly, 'Anyway, I think you'll prefer that to my earlier plans.'

'What do you mean?'

'I was thinking of staying on in the RAF. You know I love flying, and there are some revolutionary new engines coming along. They'll need experienced pilots to test them.'

'*Felix!*' Merry protested. 'Don't you think I've spent enough years worrying about what's happening to you up there?'

'Well, soon you won't have to,' Felix said.

Merry remarked, 'I can't see you settling down to the country life. What will you do for entertainment?'

'Oh, the usual things, I suppose. Shoot a bit, ride to hounds . . .'

'You can't ride,' Merry said with certainty.

Felix looked at him with an incredulous grin. 'Merry, I was brought up as a scion of the landed aristocracy. Of course I can ride! I was put on a pony almost before I could walk.'

'I've never seen you on a horse,' Merry persisted.

'No,' Felix agreed. 'I rather gave all that up when I . . . when I left home. It was all part of the old life, if you see what I mean. But it's like riding a bicycle. You never forget how. And I used to love it.'

Merry looked at him. He remembered his last conversation with Harriet Forsyth, and the picture she had painted of the young Edward Mountjoy, tackling big fences on a horse too large for him. This was a Felix he had never known. 'You'll be bored out of your mind within a month,' he predicted bleakly.

All through the journey the thought nagged at Merry that he must tell Felix about his earlier meeting with his mother. It was highly likely that she would recognise him and the result would be embarrassment all round, if nothing worse. But the train was crowded and there was no opportunity for private speech. It was late afternoon when they alighted at the small country station and there was not a taxi to be seen.

Felix said, 'I could telephone the house and get them to send a car, but it's only a couple of miles and it's a nice evening. I fancy stretching my legs. Do you mind?'

'Not at all,' Merry agreed. He knew that they were both putting off the moment of confronting Lady Malpas, but at least it gave him a chance to say his piece.

As they strolled along the country road Felix pointed out landmarks from his childhood – a tree where he and friends had built a tree house; the fence where he had fallen on his first day out hunting; the orchard where he had been caught scrumping apples. The day had been hot but as the sun dropped lower the air became fresh and sweet with the scent of cow parsley. Farmers were hard at work harvesting the ripe wheat, many of them driving the new combine harvesters provided by a government desperate to feed the embattled population. It was not long before Merry began to sneeze.

'Oh God, your allergies!' Felix said remorsefully. 'I shouldn't have dragged you up here. I hope it isn't going to bring on your asthma.'

'I don't get asthma any more,' Merry snuffled into his handkerchief. 'And anyway, there's just as much dust and grass pollen down in Sussex.' When the bout of sneezing was over he knew that this might be his last chance to embark on his confession. 'Felix, there's something I've got to tell you before we arrive.'

'Oh?'

'I have actually met your mother.'

'Met her? When? You never mentioned it.'

'It was back in 1940, soon after we . . . soon after that first week in Seaford. Do you remember I had to come north to give some concerts in Manchester and Liverpool?'

'Ycs, but it was Richard's mother you ran into on that trip, wasn't it?'

'Yes, I met her but that was an accident. I called on your mother deliberately.'

'Called on her? Here?'

'Yes. I had the loan of a car to get to Liverpool and a day to spare, so I thought I'd make a small detour. I wanted to tell her face to face what you'd been through and try to persuade her at least to write to you.'

Felix stopped walking and faced him. 'What happened?'

'I was shown the door. She thought I was a friend of Anthony's to start with. When she realised her mistake she said . . .' He floundered for a moment. 'She said she didn't want to hear anything about you.' He gazed apologetically at Felix. 'I'm sorry. I thought I was acting for the best.'

'Why didn't you tell me?'

'I didn't see any point in hurting you.'

'You didn't tell her – about us?'

'Oh God, no! I'm not that much of a fool.'

Felix turned and walked on. After a moment he said, 'It won't make any difference. You didn't actually have a blazing row?'

'Oh no. It was all quite civilised.'

'Well, if she remembers you it will only be as a friend who called. What I said last night still holds good. She'll have to receive you. She doesn't have any choice in the matter.' He looked at Merry and smiled suddenly. 'Stop looking like Eeyore. I know you meant well.'

They reached the gates at the end of the drive leading up to the Hall and Merry found himself vividly recalling his bitter mood as he drove out through them all those years ago. He looked at Felix and saw that his face was set and tense. Felix glanced round, gave him a crooked smile and said, 'Oh well, over the top!'

The door was opened by the same woman who had admitted Merry four years earlier but this time, instead of an apron and hands covered in flour, she was neat and clean in a black coat and skirt. Felix took off his cap and said easily, 'Good evening, Mrs Barrett.'

To Merry's consternation the woman bobbed a curtsy, took the cap and replied formally, 'Good evening, my lord. Welcome home.'

He glanced at Felix, who appeared to accept the title without a tremor and said, 'This is Captain Merryweather, an old friend. I'd like you to put him in the room next to mine.'

'Good evening, sir.' The housekeeper took Merry's cap and added, 'Her ladyship is in the small drawing room, my lord. She told me to ask you to go straight in.'

'How is she, Mrs Barrett?' Felix asked.

'Bearing up very well, sir, under the circumstances.'

'Right!' Felix squared his shoulders. 'I'll go to her now.' He moved away across a broad hall, then paused and looked back. 'Come on, Merry.'

Merry hesitated, inclined to demur, then gave in and moved to join him. The housekeeper tapped on a door and announced, 'His lordship, my lady, and Captain Merryweather.'

Lady Malpas was seated at a small writing desk with sheets of notepaper in front of her. She was dressed in black and Merry saw that the fair hair, which had been so much like her son's when he first met her, was now faded and streaked with silver, and the lines and shadows in the fine skin were much more pronounced. However, she rose to her feet to greet them with perfect control,

'Good evening, Edward.' Her voice was steady and without emotion, her face expressionless.

Felix moved to her and, after an almost undetectable hesitation, took her hand and stooped his head to kiss her cheek. 'How are you, Mother?'

'As well as can be expected. Thank you for coming home so quickly.'

'I'm glad I was able to get here.' Again a fractional hesitation and then, 'I'm so sorry about Anthony.'

'It's a great tragedy,' she agreed, her voice as distant as if she were speaking of a casual acquaintance. 'A terrible loss to all of us. But there are thousands of others suffering similar losses. We have to resign ourselves to the will of God.'

For a moment Merry thought that Felix was going to argue that Anthony's death had more to do with the will of Hitler than of the Almighty but he refrained, turning instead to him. 'Mother, this is Guy Merryweather, an old friend who happened to be on leave and very kindly agreed to come and keep me company.'

Merry tensed himself for the reaction. Lady Malpas's eyes moved from her son to his face and he saw recognition but her expression did not change. She said, 'I believe we have met before, Captain Merryweather.'

'Several years ago, Lady Malpas,' he replied, taking the hand she extended. 'May I offer my condolences on your tragic loss?'

'Thank you. It's good of you to give up your leave to support Edward.'

'I'm only too happy to do anything I can to help.'

His hostess turned back to her chair. 'Do sit down, both of you. Did you find a taxi at the station?'

'No,' Felix said, 'we walked.'

'You should have telephoned. I would have sent the Daimler for you.'

'I know, but we enjoyed the walk after sitting in the train all day.'

Merry looked from mother to son. They were speaking as if Felix were a neighbour paying a casual call.

Lady Malpas went on, 'In that case I expect you're both thirsty. Dinner will be in about an hour. Would you like tea, or would you prefer a glass of beer, or a whisky? I believe we still have some.'

They opted for beer and she rang the bell and gave

instructions to Mrs Barrett. Then she said, 'I have arranged for a memorial service on Wednesday morning – the day after tomorrow. I hope that is agreeable to you, Edward. I felt it was necessary to go ahead with the arrangements, since you only have a short time.'

'That seems perfectly all right to me,' Felix agreed.

'The rector is calling tomorrow at eleven to discuss the form of service. And Mr Callender is coming in the afternoon to read the will and deal with any legal matters.'

'Fine.'

She reached for a sheet of paper on her desk. 'I've drawn up a list of people I feel should be invited but, of course, the final choice is up to you. I have already telephoned close relatives.'

Felix barely glanced at the list and handed it back. 'I'm sure you know best, Mother. I leave that to you.'

The beer arrived. Lady Malpas said, 'I understand you were in Francc when you got my message, Edward. I won't ask you where, because I know you can't tell me. Are you close to the front line?'

'Close enough,' Felix said. 'But things are pretty quiet in the air. It's the ground forces who are bearing the brunt.'

For a few minutes they discussed the war in general terms and then Lady Malpas rose to her feet.

'If you'll excuse me, Captain Merryweather, I should like to rest before dinner. Edward will show you to your room when you've finished your drink. We'll meet again later.'

Both men rose and Felix moved swiftly to open the door. In the doorway his mother turned. 'We shan't dress for dinner.'

Dear God! Merry thought. *In the middle of all this tragedy and upheaval she can think about dressing for dinner!* He was unsure whether his principal reaction was anger or admiration.

Felix downed the remainder of his beer. 'Come on, I'll show you where you're sleeping.'

As they ascended the broad staircase to a galleried landing Felix said, 'I hope you don't mind being banished to the top floor.'

They passed down a corridor and climbed a second, narrower staircase and then went through a dividing door into another passageway. Felix said, 'This used to be the nursery wing when Anthony and I were babies. Day nursery there, night nursery there, bedroom and sitting room for Nanny at the end. When we started school and Nanny left, Anthony took over the day nursery as his room and I had the night nursery. Anthony was promoted to the floor below, with the grown-ups, when he left school, but I elected to stay up here. I liked the idea, even then, of having my own little private suite, as it were.'

He opened a door and led the way into a room. 'This is mine – was mine.'

Merry looked round. It was a pleasant room, set partly into the eaves, with a sloping ceiling and windows looking out over the gardens, and it could not have been touched since Felix was banished at the age of nineteen. On one wall was suspended an autographed cricket bat, with a photograph below it of a cricket team. There was a bookcase against another and on top of that a photo of Felix in full hunting kit astride a nervy-looking chestnut horse. Balsa-wood models of aeroplanes hung from the ceiling, evidence of an early obsession with flight.

Felix sighed. 'I suppose I ought to clear this lot out, like you did with your room at Seaford. A rite of passage, sort of thing.'

'Time enough for that,' Merry said, sensing that what he needed now was continuity, not disruption.

Felix crossed the room and threw open a connecting door. 'Your room,' he said, then added softly as Merry passed him, 'our room.'

The room was comfortably, if anonymously, furnished with curtains and a bedspread of flowered chintz. The main feature was a double bed.

Felix said, 'It was being removed from one of the downstairs bedrooms, when I was about sixteen. I persuaded Mother to let me have it up here, in case I ever wanted friends to stay. Of course, I had other hopes for it at the time.' He looked Merry in the eyes. 'I hasten to say that it has never been slept in by more than one person – until tonight.'

Merry said uneasily, 'Felix, do you think we dare?'

'Why not?' Felix demanded. 'Do you really imagine my mother is going to come creeping up in the middle of the night to check up? Or do you think she's going to set Mrs Barrett to spy on us?'

'No, of course not.'

'Well then. Merry, we can't waste five whole nights together!'

Merry put his arms round him. 'No, we can't, can we. As long as Mrs B's not going to bring up morning tea . . .'

'Up two flights of stairs?' Felix grinned. 'Once maybe, when we had plenty of staff. Not these days.'

Merry was relieved to find that there were only the three of them for dinner. Lady Malpas had obviously decided not to risk another encounter between Felix and the rector. Nevertheless, it was not an easy occasion. Conversation was stilted and Merry had a feeling that both mother and son were glad to have a third party to ease it along. Inevitably before long he found himself subject to an inquisition, and having to explain the function of the Central Pool of Artistes and its offshoot, Stars in Battledress. For once he did not see the familiar look of indifference, verging on contempt for the non-combatant, which he so often encountered. Instead Lady Malpas said, 'How very interesting. You play the piano, you say?'

'Yes.'

'Brilliantly,' added Felix.

'Perhaps after dinner you would play for us, if you're not too tired.'

'I'd be happy to, Lady Malpas,' Merry agreed, 'if you think it appropriate.'

'I cannot see anything inappropriate in a little classical music. I presume you do play the classics?'

Merry sensed that his hostess was glad to be relieved of the need to make conversation and did not demur any further. After the meal she led the way to the principal drawing room where there was a Beckstein grand in perfect condition. He hesitated for a moment, choosing a suitable piece, and opted for a Chopin nocturne, followed by a couple of Mendelssohn's 'Songs without Words'. Soon after he had finished Lady Malpas rose and bade them goodnight.

Felix finished his glass of brandy and said, 'Thanks for that. I knew I was right to bring you with me.'

'Just to provide the entertainment?' Merry said.

'Depends on what you mean by entertainment,' Felix responded. He rose. 'I think we've had a hard enough day to warrant an early night, don't you?'

9

Rose woke with a start as the old bus jolted to a sudden halt. She was sitting on the top deck, along with the rest of the company, the lower deck being reserved for baskets containing props and costumes. They were on a narrow road in the middle of a forest and the trees arching overhead blocked out much of the sunlight. Around her, some of the others were craning out of the windows, looking for an answer to a barrage of querulous questions. They had been on the road all day, constantly having to change their route as first one road then another turned out to be impassable. Even here in the shade it was uncomfortably hot and tempers were getting frayed. Rose stretched and felt the shirt sticking to her back.

'I'd give anything for a bath, Violet,' she said to the girl sitting next to her.

'You and me both,' her companion replied. 'Why have we stopped? Not another bloomin' puncture!'

'It's not that.' Ronnie, who played trumpet and clarinet in the little band, pulled his head in from the window. 'There's a tree down across the road. The lieutenant and the two motor-cycle chappies are trying to shift it. God knows what . . .'

The window he had just left exploded in a shower of glass and he was hurled bodily across the bus. Amid the screams and shouts Rose heard a sound she had become all too familiar with in the past weeks – the rattle of gunfire. She grabbed Violet and dragged her down on to the floor between the seats.

'Get down! Get down!' The voice of Lieutenant Jamieson, who was in charge of the party, cut through the din, and Rose heard him running up the stairs. 'It's an ambush! Stay down!'

More windows were breaking and Rose could hear bullets thudding into the body of the bus and whining as they ricocheted. Someone was shouting, 'Bloody fools! Bloody fools! Don't they know what ENSA stands for?' Ronnie was groaning and clasping his arm, with blood dripping down his fingers, and somewhere near by a girl was screaming. Jamieson knelt on the seat above Rose's head and she heard him fire his revolver. Then he drew back.

'Someone give me something white. We're outnumbered. We'll have to surrender. Come on, anything will do.'

Rose started to unbutton her shirt. It was grubby and stained but white enough for the purpose, she reckoned. A jumble of thoughts raced through her mind. What would it be like to be taken prisoner? Would the Germans regard them as combatants – or might they be mistaken for spies?

Someone called, 'Quiet a minute! Listen!'

In the brief hush Rose realised that, although she could still hear gunfire, the bullets were no longer hitting the bus. There was shouting now from outside, and the voices were French.

Jamieson said, 'Hold on! We've got company. Thank God for the Resistance!'

A moment later the floor vibrated as someone leapt into the bus.

''Ello, Inglish! It's all right, *mes amis*, you can get up now. The enemy 'ave run away.'

Rose clambered to her feet, rebuttoning her blouse, and peered down the stairs. At the door of the bus stood a young man in a torn khaki tunic, a beret perched rakishly on unkempt dark hair, a rifle slung on his shoulder.

The lieutenant ran down to him. 'Look, I don't know who you are or where you sprung from, but you've saved us from a very nasty situation. Thanks.'

'*De rien, mon ami*,' the young man said with a grin. 'My name is Jean-Paul. I lead this group of *maquis*. It's lucky for you one of my men heard the tree being felled, but I'm sorry we could not get here soon enough to stop the attack.'

'Never mind that. You seem to have got rid of them – for the moment anyway.' The lieutenant looked ahead. 'Are they likely to come back with reinforcements?'

Jean-Paul shook his head. 'Oh no. They were just a small group, a few snipers left behind as a rearguard.' He looked round the bus. 'But you are not soldiers. There are women with you. What are you doing here?'

'We're ENSA.' Jack Holmes, their plump stage manager, was poised on the stairs. 'We're here to entertain the troops.'

'Entertainers?' Jean-Paul's face expressed a mixture of scepticism and admiration. '*Mon dieu!* You English! In the middle of the battlefield, you sing and dance?'

'Not usually in the middle,' the lieutenant explained. 'I think we may have wandered off course a bit.'

'*Eh bien!*' Jean Paul stepped back. 'Come and meet my *copains*. Perhaps we have a sing-song right here, no? Don't worry, it is quite safe now.'

Rose followed the others down the stairs. Her legs were shaking and her throat was parched. She wanted above all to sit somewhere cool and quiet, with a large glass of cold water. Surrounding the bus was a group of about twenty men, all as ragged and unkempt as Jean-Paul, but all with the same devil-may-care laughter in their faces.

'What did he say they were?' Violet whispered to Rose.

'*Maquis.*'

'What's that when it's at home?'

'Resistance. Freedom fighters.'

'Ooh! How romantic! Wait till I tell the girls back home that I've been in an ambush and been rescued by freedom fighters!'

Rose looked at her and suddenly found herself laughing. They had all been close to death, but to Violet it was just a romantic adventure.

'Trust you, Violet!' she said.

There was a shout from one of the motorcycle outriders who accompanied the convoy and Rose looked towards him. Her laughter froze in her throat. Beside the tree that blocked their path lay a still figure in khaki uniform. It was the second dispatch rider. Jamieson ran towards him, with Jean-Paul close behind, and the three men bent over the prostrate body. Rose saw the lieutenant place his fingers on the man's throat, then stoop closer. After a moment, he looked up and shook his head. Rose's legs gave way and she sank down on the step of the bus. Jamieson looked around and beckoned Jack Holmes. They spoke together quietly and then Jack turned away and nodded to one of the other men in the band. The two of them went to the truck that carried the scenery and the band instruments and came back a moment later with the roll of velvet they used as an improvised curtain. Rose saw them wrap the dead man in it, then, helped by the other motorcyclist, they carried him back to the truck and laid him inside.

A voice above her head said, '*Tenez!* Drink. It will help.'

One of Jean-Paul's men stood beside her, holding out a flask. She took a mouthful and swallowed, then gasped as the spirit seared her throat.

Her companion grinned. 'Good, *n'est-ce pas*? Calvados. My grandfather makes it himself.'

Rose tried to thank him but her throat seemed to have closed up and her eyes were full of tears that had nothing to do with the situation. All the same, the potent spirit steadied her nerves. She stood up and looked around. Alice was sitting with her head in her hands, weeping. One of the new girls, Maisie, had blood running down on to her collar from a cut on her face, and Valerie, the comedienne, was kneeling by Angela, the youngest girl, examining a long cut on her leg. Rose felt a stab of shame. She should be doing that, instead of sitting there like a dying duck in a thunderstorm! She got up and went over to put her arm round Alice.

'Are you hurt?'

Alice shook her head but Rose could feel that she was shaking. 'I don't think so.'

'Come on, then, love.' Rose gave her a hug. 'Pull yourself together. There are others who are, so see if you can help them.'

She left her and went to Maisie. 'Come and sit down, and let me have a look at that cut.'

The lieutenant's voice cut across the babble of conversation. 'Any more casualties?'

Someone called, 'Ronnie's got a nasty gash in his arm.'

Valerie got up. 'Let me have a look – see how much I can remember from my days as a Girl Guide.'

It seemed that, apart from the motorcycle outrider, Ronnie had been the only serious casualty, though a number of the company had suffered cuts from flying glass. There was a first-aid case in the bus and Rose busied herself dressing wounds and encouraging the other girls.

'You were lucky,' Jamieson said. 'Because the snipers were

lying low, hiding in the undergrowth, and you were all on the top deck, most of the shots were at too sharp an angle to touch anyone crouching on the floor.'

Ronnie, it turned out, had suffered only a flesh wound in the upper arm, but Valerie insisted that it needed stitching. 'He's losing blood,' she said. 'We need to get him to a hospital or a dressing station as soon as possible.'

Jamieson turned to Jean-Paul. 'Can you ask some of your men to help us get this tree trunk shifted? Then we can get on our way.'

'Not that way!' Jean-Paul said with a wry grin. 'The Boches are dug in in the next village. If they had not stopped you here, you would have driven straight into them. You should say thank you!'

'Which way, then?' Jamieson asked.

The Frenchman shrugged. 'Back the way you came. There is no other way.'

'Right!' Rose saw the lieutenant straighten his shoulders and realised that he was almost as tired as she was. 'Back on the bus, everyone. We'll have to try a different route.' He turned and held out his hand to Jean-Paul. 'We owe you our lives, or at least our liberty. I'll make sure they hear about it back at HQ. Thank you.'

'*Il n'y a pas de quoi, mon ami,*' the Frenchman replied. 'You are here to liberate La France, and for that we thank you.' He laughed. 'Even if you come to do it with songs and dances. *Bonne chance, tout le monde! Et vive l'entente cordiale!*'

There were handshakes and embraces all round and then Rose and her companions climbed back on to the bus. It was impossible to turn round in the narrow road, so there was nothing for it but to reverse until they came to a wider point. It took a laborious and nerve-stretching quarter of an hour before they finally reached a clearing and the drivers were able to manoeuvre the vehicles to face the right way. After that, they made faster progress, but they were all grimly aware that they were just retracing ground they had covered an hour ago and although it was high summer, the sun was already quite low in the sky.

'I don't fancy being stuck in the middle of this forest when it gets dark,' Violet murmured. 'Who knows how many other Germans there may be lurking around.'

'We must get out into open country soon,' Rose said. 'I don't remember it taking this long on the way in.'

Eventually, the trees came to an end and they were driving through a landscape of small fields, broken by thick hedges – the Normandy bocage, which had provided such excellent cover for the German forces during the early days of the invasion. There were shell craters in the fields, and they could see where the hedges had been torn up by tanks. There was a sickly-sweet stench that forced them to close all the windows.

'What is it?' Alice asked, her hand over her mouth.

Violet half stood and peered out of the window. 'Dead cows,' she said, dropping back into her seat.

Behind her, Rose heard Ann Dwyer asking petulantly, 'How much longer is this going on?' and Valerie responded grimly, 'Not too much longer, I hope. This man needs proper attention before he loses too much more blood.'

'We need to get back to base,' Ann's husband, Leighton, said. 'To hell with the next performance. None of us are in a fit state. And apart from poor old Ronnie there's . . .'

He broke off as Valerie shushed him, but Rose, craning round, had seen him jerk his head towards the following truck. She shuddered. She had almost forgotten the dead man lying wrapped in a curtain among their scenery.

'Look! There's traffic up ahead!' Violet exclaimed. 'We're coming to another road.'

'Thank God for that!' someone said.

Very soon they reached the crossroads, and their momentary optimism evaporated. The other road was jammed in both directions. On one side was a solid rank of tanks and trucks and armoured troop carriers, grinding their way forward against the oncoming flow on the opposite side. This consisted mainly of refugees, some in vehicles or on trailers drawn by tractors, some in carts pulled by horses, but the majority on foot, carrying their possessions with them. In among them were ambulances and staff cars, with motorcycle outriders struggling to clear a path for them. It was the kind of chaos that had driven them off the main routes earlier in the day, and now they were back in the middle of it. With great difficulty Jamieson nosed the jeep into the throng of refugees and Rose realised with relief that he had given up trying to get them nearer to the front, which had been the original intention. He was heading back towards the field hospitals in the rear. Jack nudged the bus forward, but inevitably they became separated from the jeep, wedged between a farm tractor and a cart piled high with furniture.

Peering ahead, Rose saw that beyond the cart was a vehicle with a red cross painted on its roof. She got up and made her way along the aisle to where Valerie was crouching beside Ronnie, who was lying on the back seat.

'There's an ambulance just up ahead. Do you think we could get them to look after Ronnie?'

'It's worth a try, if we can attract their attention,' Valerie agreed. 'But it's difficult when we're going along.'

'This lot will all grind to a halt soon, take my word for it,' said Pete Walton, the double bass player. 'When it does,

I'll nip along and see if I can persuade someone to take a look.'

His prediction proved correct in the next few minutes and he clattered down the stairs. Rose saw him run up alongside the convoy and bang on the driver's door of the ambulance. There was a brief conversation and then a woman got out on the passenger side, carrying a medical bag, and they both came back to the bus. The woman was young, only about her own age, Rose guessed, and in a uniform that she did not recognise, but she had a capable manner that instilled confidence. Valerie explained what had happened and, after a brief examination, the woman straightened up.

'Yes, you're quite right. This needs proper attention. We'd better get him into the ambulance.'

'Can't you do something here?' Ronnie pleaded. 'I don't want to leave my mates.'

'Sorry,' was the brisk response. 'You need a doctor. I'm not qualified to stitch a wound like this. Now, can you walk? We need to get going before the convoy starts moving again.'

Rose was curious. The woman's voice was definitely upper class, what she would once have called lah-di-dah, and although she was so young her manner was authoritative, as if she was used to giving orders.

'You're not a doctor, then?' she ventured, as Ronnie was helped to his feet.

The woman flashed her a quick smile. 'No, no. FANY.'

Rose swallowed. 'Sorry, what?'

'First Aid Nursing Yeomanry. The FANYs. We're volunteer ambulance drivers.'

If she was aware of the stifled giggles and the hastily straightened faces, she gave no sign of it. Between them, she and Pete got Ronnie down the stairs, where they were met by Jack. Rose saw them exchange a few words, then Jack nodded to Pete and the two of them walked back to the scenery truck. The FANY woman helped Ronnie towards the ambulance and a moment later Jack and Pete appeared carrying a burden wrapped in the stage curtain. They disappeared from sight behind the cart, and came back a moment later empty handed. Barney, the remaining member of the band, was peering over her shoulder.

'Oh well,' he muttered. 'I guess it's curtains for that poor bastard.' And there was a ripple of hysterical laughter, hastily suppressed.

They watched as the ambulance pulled out of the line on to the grass verge, bouncing and swaying over the uneven surface, until it disappeared beyond the other vehicles. The bus edged forward again and Rose went back to her seat at the front and closed her eyes. In the six weeks since their arrival in France the relief of discovering that she was not pregnant had been overtaken by a spirit of weary endurance. It was partly the unrelenting routine of travelling on the overcrowded roads and sleeping in whatever empty building they could find that still had a more-or-less intact roof. But she had endured all that, and worse, in Italy the year before. This malaise went deeper. The nearest she could come to describing it to herself was 'disappointment'. After all these years, all her romantic dreams – after her refusal of Richard's proposal, her aborted engagement to Matthew, her rejection of Beau – it had come down to an undignified, loveless scuffle in an open field. Was that what she had saved herself for, for so long?

She knew that the girls had seen a change in her. She tried to be her old self, to recapture the pride and pleasure she had had in choreographing the dances and seeing their reception by their audiences. She tried to be as caring and supportive as before. But she no longer had the energy, or the will.

Loud voices roused her. The farm cart had somehow vanished and they were now following an army truck. The canvas flaps at the back were open and in the gap she could see a group of soldiers, some standing, others perched on the tailboard. Many of them had bandages round their heads or their arms in slings and all were covered in mud and soot, but in their filthy faces their teeth showed white as they grinned and waved. It took Rose a moment to realise that they had spotted her and the other girls and were trying to attract their attention. She looked at the others. Maisie was still dabbing at the cut on her face, Alice had her head on Angela's shoulder, Liz was curled in a ball and apparently asleep. Even Violet was oblivious to the masculine attentions on offer. And every one of them was tousle haired and without make-up. She felt suddenly angry. What right had these men to expect them to be always on show, always ready to entertain?

A louder voice cut across the general din. 'Come on, girls! Give us a smile!'

She could see the speaker. One arm was strapped tightly across his body and there was blood on the side of his face. Yet the grin was indomitable. Rose sat up. What right had she to claim exhaustion as an excuse, when her suffering could not come near what these men had endured? She reached for her handbag and rummaged in it for her powder compact and a comb.

'Come on, all of you! Pull yourselves together. Don't let these chaps see you down.'

Unwillingly the other girls straightened up and began to repair their faces. Rose put the final touches to her lipstick, closed her bag and waved cheerfully to the men in front. A cheer went up. Soon the rest of the girls were crowding to the front of the bus, waving and blowing kisses, and Rose thought, with sudden amusement, how contrary all this was to the way she had been brought up.

A few minutes later the line of traffic slowed to another unexplained halt and immediately some of the men in the truck vaulted over the tailboard and headed towards the bus. Others followed, the less able helped down by their comrades. Rose got up.

'I'm going down. Anyone coming?'

They clattered down the stairs and jumped down into a welcoming crowd. 'What are you doing here, girls?' 'Where are you going next?' 'When's the next show, then?'

The man whose shout had roused her held out his hand. 'I'm Joe.'

'I'm Rose.'

'Pleased to meet you, Rose.'

'What do you girls do?' someone asked.

'We're dancers,' Violet told him.

'Dancers? What sort of dances?'

'Oh, a bit of everything. Tap, ballet – all sorts.'

'Bet you don't do the can-can!'

'Oh yes we do.'

'Get away! All those high kicks and that?'

'Yes, of course.'

'Go on, then. Show us!'

'What, here?'

'Yeah! Why not? Don't suppose we'll ever get to see the show properly. Most of us'll be shipped back to Blighty.'

Rose looked at the others. 'What about it, kids? Shall we give them a taster?'

Alice backed away, shaking her head, and Angela pointed to

her bandaged leg, but Violet moved to stand by Rose. 'Yes, why not? Come on, you three.'

Giggling, the others joined them and the men fell back to give them space. The five girls linked hands behind each other's backs and Rose counted softly, 'One, two three, and . . .' And they were off, kicking in unison, breathlessly humming the Offenbach tune. Within seconds, it was taken up with raucous enthusiasm by the men and then, from behind them, Barney's accordion joined in. Men from other trucks crowded round, or climbed on to the roofs to watch, and when the dance came to an end the cheers were deafening.

'Look out!' someone shouted. 'We're on the move again!'

The men broke away, running to catch up with the truck and hauling each other up over the tailboard. Joe paused briefly and winked at Rose. 'Thanks for that! Cheered us all up no end.'

He ran after the others and Rose scrambled back on to the bus. As she regained her seat there were calls of approval and encouragement from the rest of the company, except from Ann Dwyer, who sniffed and said, 'Well, I don't know! Whatever next?'

Rose dropped into her seat, panting, and realised that her incipient headache had gone and she felt more cheerful than she had for days. *Whatever next?* Well, that remained to be seen.

10

Lady Malpas did not appear at breakfast on the morning after Merry and Felix arrived in Cheshire, and after they had eaten, Felix looked at his watch and remarked, 'We've got a couple of hours before I have to meet the rector. I'll show you round, if you like.'

They explored the house, much of which dated from the seventeenth century, and then wandered out on to the terrace. Felix sighed at the sight of what had obviously once been a broad expanse of lawn and which was now entirely planted with potatoes.

'Adolf Hitler's got a lot to answer for! It's going to take years to get this place back to rights after all this "dig for victory" stuff. I hope to God they've left the rose garden alone!'

They followed a path between the plots of potatoes and passed through an archway into a walled garden, formally planted with beds of roses. It was another beautiful summer day but not yet hot, and the scent of the roses drifted on the air, as elusive as a half-remembered melody. Felix took a deep breath and said, 'I always loved this spot.'

Merry said with a smile, 'I can see where you get your interest in horticulture from. My little patch must seem very small beer compared to this.'

'I have a great affection for your little patch, as you call it,' Felix replied. 'Not least because I can actually do what I want there. I never dared lay a finger on anything here without consulting old Alf Watts, our head gardener, first.'

They passed through another archway into the stable yard, where two horses looked out over the doors of their loose boxes. Felix said, 'Ah, the heart of the whole establishment! I loved the gardens as a kid but this is where I spent most of my time.'

A lanky boy appeared from one of the boxes with a barrow of manure and stopped dead, obviously embarrassed. Felix called, 'Hello there. I don't think we've met. What's your name?'

'Peter,' the boy said, eyeing him doubtfully. Then his glance travelled to Merry. 'Hey, I know you! You're that secret service bloke what came here years ago.'

'Of course!' Merry exclaimed, avoiding Felix's quizzical look. 'I remember you now. You were evacuated here at the beginning of the war.' He turned to Felix. 'The day I called here, your mother was working in the farm office and Mrs Barrett asked Peter to show me the way.'

The boy gazed from Merry to Felix. 'Oh, cripes! You're . . . Sorry, sir – your lordship. I didn't recognise you, like.'

'Why should you?' Felix said. 'Don't worry – and sir will do very well.'

'What happened to the other children?' Merry asked.

'Went back to London, sir, soon as the Blitz ended.'

'But not you? I thought you didn't like the country.'

'I didn't much, to start with. But then old Mr Fletcher let me start helping with the horses.' He looked over his shoulder to the stables. 'I love them.'

'So you decided to stay on when the others left?'

'Well, my dad bought it at Dunkirk, like, and my mum and my aunt copped a direct hit during the Blitz, so I thought I might as well.' He looked at Felix. 'Her ladyship's been real good to me, sir. When I finished at school she offered me a job here in the stables.'

'I'm delighted to hear it,' Felix said. 'Is Alan Fletcher still here?'

'No, sir. He had to give up 'cos of his arthritis. I looks after them on me own now.'

'Well, they certainly look in good condition,' Felix said, moving to caress the nose of a big bay horse. 'This is old Nutmeg, my father's hunter, isn't it?'

'Yes, sir. He's a fine old chap, in't he?'

'I don't suppose you ever came across a chestnut gelding called Ginger, did you?' Felix asked, adding with a smile to Merry, 'One of my mother's little conceits, calling them all after different spices. That's Cinnamon over there, her mare.'

'Can't say I ever knew a Ginger,' the boy said.

'No,' Felix said wistfully, 'I expect they got rid of him after I left.' He smiled at Peter. 'Does anyone ride Nutmeg these days?'

'Her ladyship takes him out sometimes, but she hasn't got time for two horses really.'

'I might try to get out for an hour or two while I'm here. You wouldn't mind, Merry?'

'Of course not.'

As they moved away Felix said, 'Secret service? Where did he get that idea from?'

'My fault, I'm afraid,' Merry admitted sheepishly. 'He wanted to know what unit I was with and I said SIB. He jumped to the conclusion that it stood for Secret Intelligence Bureau. I didn't like to disillusion him.'

'Quite right,' Felix agreed. 'He's probably been bragging about meeting you to his chums ever since.' He looked at his watch. 'We'd better get back. I don't want to keep the rector waiting.'

Merry hung about on the terrace, reading the paper, until he heard Felix's voice in the hall. Looking in, he saw him shaking hands with a large, florid man in a dog collar and was relieved to see that the two were parting in an apparently amicable manner.

Felix joined him, wiping imaginary sweat from his brow. 'Phew! Well, thank God that's over.'

'Everything OK?'

'Absolutely tickety-boo. Not a cross word spoken and no probing questions about the state of my immortal soul. It's amazing what inheriting a title does for one's moral standing!'

Merry was left to himself for most of the afternoon but he was happy enough to sit in the rose garden with a book. When he eventually rejoined Felix and his mother for tea on the terrace he was relieved to see that they both looked a good deal more relaxed. The discussion with the family solicitor had not apparently produced any surprises and the necessary legal formalities had been completed. All that remained was to finalise the arrangements for entertaining their guests the following day.

As they smartened themselves up for dinner Felix said, 'By the way, just so as you don't get a shock tomorrow, I ought to mention that Harry Forsyth will be one of the guests.'

'Lady Harriet? How come?'

'Well, she's at home, apparently. You do know that her family are our neighbours?'

Once again, Merry remembered his conversation with Harriet, when they both thought Felix was dead, but he felt disinclined to go into the details at that moment. Instead he said non-commitally, 'Oh, are they?'

'Oh yes. We grew up together – went to the same parties, competed in the same gymkhanas, rode to hounds . . . She's a brilliant horsewoman. You know she's now an accredited war photographer?'

'Yes, I've seen some of her pictures.'

'It seems she's home on leave, so she'll be there tomorrow, with her mother.'

Merry left it at that, but the occasional reappearance of Harriet Forsyth on Felix's horizon always disturbed him.

The next morning Merry was given the job of collecting the guests from the station in the Daimler and ferrying them to the church, which kept him occupied until about ten minutes before the service was due to begin. Lingering at the church door in case of late arrivals he saw Harriet Forsyth coming up the path with an elegant woman who was obviously her mother, the countess. Harriet was in the uniform of a captain in the ATS, but she made it look as chic as the latest creation from Balenciaga. The countess paused to speak to an acquaintance but Harriet came on and held out her hand in greeting.

'Merry, it's so good to see you again after all this time.'

He shook hands and forced a smile. 'How do you do, Lady Harriet?'

'Oh, please!' she exclaimed. 'It's Harry, or just plain Harriet if you prefer. Let's not be formal. I'm so glad you are able to be here. It must be such a comfort to Felix.'

The remark sounded absolutely genuine and her eyes met his without wavering. He said, a little more gently, 'I'm sure he'll be pleased to see you, too.'

'Oh, that's quite a different thing,' she said. 'How is he?'

'He's tired and under a lot of strain, but he's coping. Things seem to be working out all right. Better than we might have expected, actually.'

'That's a relief,' she said, lowering her voice. 'And Lady Malpas?'

'She's very brave. She seems to be . . . reconciled to the situation.'

'Thank goodness!' She looked round. The countess was coming up the path. 'I must go in. I'll see you later, up at the Hall.'

Merry took a last look round. The church had filled up, partly with family and friends but to a large extent with workers from the estate and their families. Others from the village had gathered at the lychgate to watch the arrivals. He went inside and took a seat modestly towards the back of the church, but at the end of a pew so that Felix could catch his eye easily if necessary. A few moments later he heard a murmur from the crowd which heralded the arrival of the chief mourners, and Lady Malpas entered the church, leaning on her son's arm.

Merry thought, as he watched them move down the aisle, that if Harriet had had her camera she might have taken their picture as the perfect symbols of the national spirit after five years of war; the dignified, erect woman in deepest mourning, her face hidden behind a black veil, and beside her the young warrior in his uniform, tense but composed, the scars that seamed the handsome face serving as a testament to courage and endurance.

The service took its course. Felix read the lesson, choosing the passage from St John's Gospel, 'greater love hath no man than this, that a man lay down his life for his friends'. His voice was clearly audible right to the back of the church, solemn without being sentimental, controlled but not unfeeling.

Afterwards Merry heard two ladies from the congregation surmising that it was his experience and training as an officer which gave him the confidence. He wondered what they would think if he were to tell them that it was, in all probability, more the result of several years learning to hold an audience while performing conjuring tricks.

Back at the Hall, Merry occupied himself passing plates and pouring drinks. Busy with the role of unobtrusive friend, he watched with growing admiration as Felix circulated among his guests, pitching his manner perfectly according to the age and personality of each. He was respectful to the older men, gallant to the ladies, comradely to those of his own age, deferential to his mother. All this without appearing conscious of the fact that, in terms of the social hierarchy, he now outranked the majority of the guests; yet always, effortlessly it seemed, the host, the master of the house. What pleased Merry less to observe was the fact that Harriet was frequently by his side and that many of the others seemed to take it for granted that they were in some way 'a pair'. He even overheard one lady murmuring something to the effect that they made a lovely couple but, of course, it was sensible to wait until the war was over.

By mid-afternoon all those who were not staying overnight began to drift away and he was glad to see that the countess and her daughter were preparing to take their leave too. Felix accompanied them to the door and for a moment he and Merry stood together with Harriet. She held out her hand to each of them in turn, kissed Felix on the cheek and then gave Merry a broad wink.

'No extra charge for the camouflage!'

Merry looked at Felix as the two women went down the steps to their car. 'Did she mean what I think she meant?'

Felix grinned. 'Oh yes, I'm sure she did. Good old Harry!'

After that only the house guests remained. The ladies retired to their rooms to rest and the men settled in the library with cigars and the daily papers. That left Felix's cousins, Eric and Melinda. Eric was a lieutenant in the Royal Tank Regiment and had been wounded in the D-Day landings and sent home to convalesce. Melinda, whom Merry judged to be about twenty years old, was helping out as a teacher in her local village school, but obviously felt her true vocation was as an adjunct to an eligible male. Felix's attentions having been, apparently, taken up by Lady Harriet, Merry was uncomfortably aware that he was seen as being the next best prospect.

'Well,' said Melinda, looking at her three companions, 'I don't know about anybody else but I'm dying for a breath of fresh air.'

'Good idea,' said Eric.

'Let's all go for a walk,' the girl suggested. She batted her eyelids at Merry. 'I'm sure you'd like to stretch your legs, wouldn't you, Captain Merryweather?'

'Well, that depends,' Merry responded cautiously.

Felix came to his rescue. 'I think I ought to stay around, just in case I'm needed. You and Eric go. Merry can stay and keep me company.'

That left the two cousins with little option but to set off together. When they had gone Merry looked at Felix. 'You look done up,' he said. 'Let's go and sit in the garden, shall we?'

They strolled down to the rose garden and found a bench underneath an arbour almost hidden beneath a tangle of unpruned honeysuckle and clematis. Merry settled himself at one end and Felix swung his feet over the other and lay back with his head on Merry's lap. Merry looked down at him, seeing once again the pallor beneath the tan and the shadows under his eyes. He touched his brow with delicate fingertips, smoothing back the hair from the temple.

'You did terribly well this morning,' he said. 'I was proud of you.'

Felix's lips twitched into a grin. 'Really? I'm touched.'

'I'm sorry,' Merry said quickly. 'That sounded unbearably pompous. I mean to say I was very impressed.'

Felix closed his eyes. 'I'll settle for proud.'

'I've been wondering,' Merry went on. 'All these relatives who you haven't seen for so many years – where do they think you've been? Before the war, I mean.'

'South Africa, apparently. It seems the family decided that the best explanation for my sudden disappearance was that I had decided to do the classic younger-son thing and seek my fortune in the colonies. Mmm, that feels good. Don't stop.'

A bee hummed in the honeysuckle overhead and in a rose bed near by a blackbird chuntered softly to himself as he turned over leaves. Within a couple of minutes Felix was asleep.

Dinner that night was a livelier affair than might have been expected. The party was gripped by the urge towards almost hysterical frivolity that comes after occasions of great solemnity. Inevitably the conversation turned to the war. Eric was asked for his account of the D-Day landings, which was necessarily brief since he had received a bullet in the shoulder in the first desperate scramble for the beach and had been removed to a hospital ship offshore. Felix contributed his description of the sight of the great armada from the air and was quizzed about his experiences with the partisans in Italy. Then it was Merry's turn, and it was no surprise that it was Melinda, seated on his left, who fixed him with wide brown eyes and asked, 'What about you, Merry? Where have you been serving?'

'In Italy, until recently,' Merry replied. 'I'm about to be redeployed to France.'

'Doing what?' Melinda asked.

It was Lady Malpas who supplied the answer. 'Captain Merryweather has a most interesting role. He is a musician by training and a very talented pianist. His job is to bring a little relief and spiritual uplift to the poor boys in the trenches. I do feel that it is so vital not to lose sight of the more lasting values. Don't you agree, Andrew?'

Colonel Weatherby, who was married to Lady Malpas's sister and who, as far as Merry could make out, had spent his war behind a desk in Whitehall, cleared his throat. 'Morale!' he pronounced. 'Vital, as you say.'

His wife smiled at Merry. 'I see you are wearing the ribbon of the DSO, Captain Merryweather. I'm sure you didn't get that playing the piano.'

'Oh, that.' Merry glanced down briefly at the ribbon on the breast of his tunic. 'That was years ago, in North Africa. Pure chance, I assure you.'

'Pay no attention to him,' Felix said crisply. 'He took out an enemy machine-gun nest single handed, although he was wounded, and got his entire company back to safety after they were ambushed.'

'You were in the desert?' Eric asked. 'I went right through that campaign with Monty. When did this happen?'

'During the retreat from Gazala,' Merry said.

'Ah, the Gazala gallop! So I suppose you didn't see the final advance, after Alamein, if you were wounded.'

'I went back the following year,' Merry said. 'After that I went right through to Tunis.'

'It must have been very exciting . . .' Melinda began, but she was interrupted by a sudden exclamation from Eric.

'My God, I knew I'd seen you somewhere before!' Then, in response to a reproving look from his mother, 'Sorry. But I've just realised who this chap is. You're the phantom pianist, aren't you?' There was a ripple of amused surprise around the table. 'It is you, isn't it?' Eric persisted.

Merry murmured, 'I believe I was known as that in some quarters.'

'This man,' declared Eric, 'used to drive around the battle-fields all on his own in a soft-skinned truck with an old piano in the back. He'd suddenly appear out of the blue, give a concert and then disappear again. That's why we called him the phantom pianist.'

'How brave!' said Melinda.

'Bit foolhardy, if you ask me,' commented her father.

Merry felt Felix's eyes fixed on him but refused to return the gaze.

'I'll never forget one night,' Eric went on. 'We'd had a pretty hot day of it – and I don't just mean the weather. We ran into a detachment of Rommel's panzers unexpectedly and had to fight our way out. We'd taken a lot of casualties and were feeling pretty fed up. When darkness fell we leaguered the tanks in a wadi and were sitting around, eating our iron rations, when suddenly this truck comes bouncing into the middle of the camp. This chap here gets out, opens the back, gets a couple of squaddies to help him manoeuvre the piano on to the tailboard and starts to play. It was one of those amazing desert nights, absolutely still and blessedly cool after the heat of the day, and a full moon was just rising. And you played the Moonlight Sonata.' He had the total attention of the whole table now and Merry sat with his eyes downcast. 'I'm not normally much of a fan of the classics. More of a Glenn Miller man usually. But I do recognise that piece and the effect was magical. It was like . . .' He floundered for a moment. '. . . like a glimpse into another world, one that wasn't just a matter of killing or being killed.' He paused and swallowed. 'I'm not putting this very well. But I don't mind telling you that by the end the tears were running down my cheeks, and I wasn't the only one.'

There was a silence round the table. Merry kept his eyes on his plate. Eric said, 'I thought afterwards I'd like to have said thank you, but you'd gone by the morning. I never thought I'd run into you again. Anyway, better late than never. Thanks.'

Slowly Merry lifted his eyes, the lashes dewed with moisture he could not conceal. 'I'm glad you enjoyed it.'

'Thank you, Eric,' Lady Malpas said. 'You've illustrated my point perfectly.'

Felix said accusingly, 'I never heard about this.'

Merry looked at him. 'You weren't around at the time. I told you afterwards.'

'You never mentioned chasing around the desert in a soft-skinned truck,' Felix replied. 'What the hell were you trying to do? Get yourself killed?' Then he realised that the remark was too close to the truth for comfort and stopped abruptly.

After this the conversation became general for a while, until Merry heard, to his horror, Felix's great-aunt saying, 'Tell us about South Africa.'

'Oh yes!' the other aunt chipped in from his other side. 'We've never heard anything about your experiences there.'

There was an expectant silence round the table. Merry stole a glance at Lady Malpas, who appeared to have been turned to stone. He tried desperately to think of a way of intervening in the conversation but his organs of speech seemed to be paralysed. Felix smiled and with a sinking feeling in his stomach Merry recognised an expression of subversive mischief which he knew of old.

'I'm sorry, Aunt,' Felix said. 'I can't help you there. I've never been to South Africa.'

'Oh?' The old lady looked vaguely confused. 'Have I got it wrong? I felt sure your mother said that was where you were. Was it Kenya, then?'

'No, you were quite right the first time,' Felix answered. 'That was where I was supposed to be. That is to say, that was where the family decided to say I was in order to protect my shameful secret.'

'Secret?' queried his great-aunt. 'What secret?'

There was a rustle around the table, a stirring of people unsure whether to be alarmed or amused. Merry sneaked another glance at Felix's mother. She was sitting bolt upright, her face drained of colour.

Felix went on cheerfully, 'You see, all the time I was supposed to be seeking my fortune in Africa what I was actually doing was scraping a living on the stage.'

There were indrawn breaths of surprise. Merry thought for a moment that Lady Malpas was going to faint, and his own head spun as if he had been holding his breath for a long time.

Melinda exclaimed. 'The stage? How exciting! Do you mean as an actor?'

'No,' Felix said, still smiling, 'not as an actor.'

'What, then?' Eric joined in. 'A singer?'

'Heavens, no! Merry will vouch for the fact that I have a voice like a corncrake.'

'What, then?' Melinda demanded.

Merry was watching him, relieved and amused, and now for

the first time Felix returned his gaze. 'Merry knows. We used to work together. Do you want to tell them, Merry?'

Given his cue, Merry knew how to respond. 'Ladies and gentlemen,' he said, with a flourish, 'let me introduce you to Mr Felix Lamont, alias Mr Mysterioso, magician and *illusioniste extraordinaire.*'

Everyone stared at Felix. 'You mean,' said his uncle, 'that before the war you were earning a living as a conjuror?'

'Oh, much more than a conjuror!' Merry assured him. 'A magician, and a very good one.'

Lady Malpas rose to her feet. 'I think it's time we left you gentlemen to yourselves. Edward, there are cigars on the sideboard and port in the decanter. And perhaps later on Captain Merryweather will play for us. Shall we, ladies?'

Later, when they joined the others in the drawing room, Lady Malpas renewed her request for Merry to play. As he moved to the piano he found Melinda at his side.

'Can I turn over for you? I can read music.'

'Thank you,' he replied gravely, 'but I don't need music for what I'm going to play tonight.'

Even so, he had a nasty feeling she was going to stand by the piano and gaze at him with those disconcertingly admiring eyes. He was greatly relieved when Felix, seeing his danger, called, 'There's room over here, Mel. Come and sit by me.'

There was only one choice of music for that occasion. He played the Moonlight Sonata, and for once it was listened to throughout in silence – at least if you ignored the gentle snores of Colonel Weatherby.

Up in their room, after the guests had finally said their goodnights and gone to bed, Merry looked accusingly at Felix.

'What on earth were you up to at dinner? I suppose you realise that you nearly gave your mother a heart attack.'

'A small revenge for last time I was here,' Felix said.

'And what about me? I almost passed out on the spot, too.'

Felix paused, half undressed, and retorted, 'You're a fine one to talk! Careering around the desert in a soft-skinned vehicle, just asking to get blown up! What on earth were you thinking about?'

'You know what I was thinking about,' Merry replied quietly.

Felix came close to him. 'You bloody idiot! What would I have done if I'd got back and found you'd been blown to smithereens by a shell?'

'I wasn't expecting you to come back,' Merry pointed out.

Felix sighed and linked his hands behind Merry's neck. 'Poor old Eeyore! Cheer up. I'm here now.'

11

Richard moved silently to the edge of the trees and strained his eyes into the darkness. In the valley below him not a crack of light showed from the villages clinging to the hillsides. The only sounds were the rustle of leaves in the night breeze and the song of a nightingale far away on the other side of the ravine. *Where are they?* he asked himself. *Why don't they attack?*

Days had passed since the massacre at Stazzema and Richard had dragged himself painfully out of the swamp of despair that had threatened to engulf him. The thought that galvanised him was the prospect of revenge. Something had died within him, that day; his old self, which had been capable of feeling compassion, even for an enemy, had been snuffed out. He no longer recognised the man he had become. Together with Armando and Leandro, he had selected their position on the edge of the forest, at a point where the narrow mountain road made a hairpin bend on its way to Alpe di Sant Antonio. Now they were well dug in, three hundred of them, able to command the only route into the village. The enemy would have to attack uphill, across open ground. In daylight, the sentries would have a clear view of anyone heading in their direction and, night or day, they would hear any motorised vehicles approaching. All afternoon they had all heard the sound of heavy traffic on the road below. Richard guessed that the Germans in Fornovalesco had been waiting for reinforcements and now they were moving into position for an assault. But would they come by day or at night? Even now, Richard was well aware, men could be creeping towards them through the straggling vines that clothed the lower slopes.

He moved on, checking that all the sentries were alert, then turned back to the shepherd's hut where they had made their headquarters. Inside the hut the air was thick with the smoke of cigarettes and the stale-fish odour of the Primus stove. Armando had rolled himself in his blanket and appeared to be asleep. Leandro was playing cards with his second-in-command and on the far side of a rough table Antonia was methodically laying out bandages and instruments. She had returned to the hospital after Leandro's visit but Richard had been horrified that morning to discover her car parked behind the hut and roughly camouflaged with branches. He had first begged and then attempted to order her to go back to Castelnuovo but she had set her jaw defiantly.

'There is going to be a battle, no?'

'There is going to be a battle, *yes!*' he had responded. 'And that is why you should not be here.'

'In a battle men get wounded. You will need me.'

'Does Armando know you are here?'

She shrugged. 'He has seen me.' By which Richard deduced that her brother had had no more success in persuading her than he had.

Now, coming into the hut and seeing her calmly preparing, he felt a sudden rush of tenderness and pride.

Leandro looked up from his game. 'All quiet?'

'Yes, nothing stirring. And all the sentries are awake and on watch.'

'You should get some sleep. I'll go out and check again in an hour.'

Richard knew that he was right, but for him the attempt would be pointless. He found his eyes straying to Antonia. She looked up and met his gaze and on an impulse he made a slight movement of his head towards the door. To his surprise, she put down the tray of hypodermic syringes she was holding and came over to him. If anyone noticed them slipping out into the darkness, no one made any comment.

Outside, he took her hand and led her deeper into the trees. The moon was full, patterning the fallen leaves with lozenges of silver. The August night was balmy but Antonia shivered and Richard put his arm round her and drew her close to his side. She was wearing trousers and an old sweater that he suspected belonged to Armando but beneath the shapeless clothing he could feel the slender, fragile outline of her body. He felt a sudden urgent desire to protect her, in which the concept of protection was inextricably involved with the wish to hold her very close and cover her with his own body. He ducked his head and laid his cheek against her hair. It smelt of smoke and the night air. She lifted her face so that he felt the smooth skin of her cheek and then her lips were on his. They parted under his delicate pressure and her tongue eagerly sought his own. He could feel her body straining against him. At length he freed his mouth and murmured against her ear, '*Carissima*, we shouldn't. Think of your parents. Think of Armando.'

Her reply came in a breathy whisper. 'It doesn't matter. Gianni and I – we did not wait. I know the church says we were wrong, but I am glad that we had that, at least, before he died. Now, who knows what may happen tomorrow?' She drew back from him and looked into his face. 'We have always been drawn to each other, Ricardo, and now we are both free. Don't be afraid that I shall expect anything more from you. Just one night of comfort – that's all I ask.'

His body ached with desire. It was more than a year since he had said goodbye to Priscilla and there had been no one since, but it was not just long abstinence that sharpened his need. After all the months of tension, and the horror of Gianni's death and what had happened at Stazzema, he desperately needed simple human warmth and love. He held her close, murmuring endearments, and then took her hand and drew her along the path until they came to the base of a huge pine, whose shed needles, undisturbed for many years, formed a thick, springy carpet. There they lay down and abandoned themselves to a fierce, silent coupling. It was only when they lay, temporarily exhausted, in each other's arms that Richard realised how urgent his need had been. He kissed Antonia softly and whispered, '*Grazie, bellissima!* You have given me a wonderful gift.'

'I have not tired you?' she answered. 'Perhaps I was selfish to ask this tonight, when you have so much ahead of you.'

'No,' he answered. 'I shall fight with more energy and in better heart than before.'

'And you will win!' she murmured fiercely. 'You *will* win!'

They were brushing the telltale pine needles off each other's clothing when the first shout of warning echoed through the trees, immediately followed by the rattle of gunfire. Richard ran towards the hut, pulling Antonia with him.

'Go inside and stay there! We're under attack.'

The others were stumbling out, clutching their rifles, and around them in the forest the rest of the men were on their feet, groggy with sleep. Richard yelled at them to get to their positions and grabbed his Sten gun from where he had left it inside the door.

'Put out the lamp,' he ordered Antonia, 'and push the table against the door. Don't open to anyone except me or Armando.'

He left without waiting to see if she did as she had been told and ran to the edge of the forest. As he reached it there was a loud concussion from somewhere below him and a mortar exploded fifty yards short of the trees. He threw himself into a foxhole and levelled the Sten, aiming for the flash. Whether he hit his target or not he could not tell, because in the following seconds other mortars began firing all along a front that extended a hundred metres on either side.

'Bloody hell!' he muttered to himself. 'They're determined to get us this time.'

He glanced at his watch. It was 2.30 in the morning. From then on, time was measured only in the number of belts of ammunition he fed into the Sten and the frequency of the detonations of mortar shells before and behind his position. Three times the Germans attempted to rush their lines, and each time they were driven back by a hail of bullets. He no longer thought of the dark shapes he aimed at as human beings. Even the desire for revenge had faded. All that mattered was the instinct for survival.

It seemed to Richard that dawn came quite quickly. One minute he was firing blind, aiming for the flash of the guns, the next he could make out the grey shapes of men prone beside them or crawling forward between the rows of vines. Then the sun rose over the crest of the Apennines on the far side of the valley and the battleground was illuminated like a stage set. He could see bodies, and the scurrying shapes of stretcher-bearers with Red Cross armbands. He tried to count them, but gave up because the shifting curtain of gun smoke made it hard to be sure that he was not counting the same bodies twice. *How many men have we lost?* he wondered. There was no way of knowing. The Sten was red hot and he was afraid that it would seize at any moment, and his own throat was parched. In a momentary lull he reached for the water bottle hanging from his belt and took a swig. The water was warm and tasted of metal. Then the firing began again.

The sun rose higher. In his foxhole under the trees Richard was protected from the direct heat, but even so his body was running with sweat. He comforted himself with the thought that the enemy, lying out in the open, must be suffering worse. He could see them gathering themselves for another attack, and this time, when it came, he had the impression that the defensive fire was thinner and more sporadic. *We're running out of ammo*, he thought. *Or out of men to fire it!* It was enough, this time, to repel the advance, but he wondered how much longer they could hold out. It was contrary to everything he had learned about guerrilla fighting. The technique they had employed so successfully up to now had been to strike quickly and unexpectedly and then to melt away into the forest before the opposition could organise itself to retaliate. But this time, the partisans had made up their minds to stand and fight. He had tried to persuade them of the foolishness of the idea, but they were so incensed by what had happened at Stazzema that they refused to listen to reason.

In the lull as the enemy regrouped he drank the last of his water and looked at his watch again. It was midday. There was a rustle behind him and he swung round, prepared to resort to hand-to-hand fighting, but it was Armando who slid into the foxhole beside him.

'It's no good. We're losing too many men. Leandro's wounded. We can't hold out much longer.'

Richard scanned the battlefield. There was a brief respite in the assault while the opposing forces dealt with their casualties and reloaded their weapons. Then he heard a new sound, the grinding of engines. A moment later a tank appeared on the road below, its gun barrel already swinging round to bear on the partisan's positions. He turned back to Armando.

'Tell the men to abandon their positions and take to the mountains. There's nothing more we can do here. We'll regroup at Sassi after the Germans have withdrawn, but tell them to stay clear until the heat is off. Ask for a dozen volunteers to stay back and form a rearguard while we clear the casualties. Where's Leandro now?'

'In the hut. Antonia's doing what she can, but he's in a bad way.'

'See if he can be moved. I'll hold on here for the time being.'

Armando scrambled out of the foxhole and disappeared. Richard took aim and fired a short burst into the centre of the German line, where an officer appeared to be issuing orders. To his momentary satisfaction, he saw the man dive for the cover of a boulder, but it was clear that the enemy was regrouping for a new attack. There was movement behind him again and Silvano slid into the hole.

'Go back. I will take over here.'

Richard shook his head. 'No. I'll stay till the others have had a chance to escape.'

'No,' Silvano insisted. 'You must go. You are needed back there. Go!'

Richard hesitated a moment longer. Then he recollected that his job was to advise and facilitate and he was more valuable to the partisans alive than dead. He pressed Silvano's shoulder.

'Don't wait too long. When the next attack comes, the enemy should find nothing but empty holes.'

He scrambled out of the hole and, bending low, ran back to the stone hut. He could see men flitting through the trees, heading for the safety of the mountains. It was a defeat, but at least they would live to fight another day. At the door of the hut Armando was keeping guard. Inside, Leandro was lying on the table, with Antonia bending over him. She had opened his shirt and was pressing a pad to his abdomen, and already the pad was soaked with blood.

'How bad is he?' Richard asked.

She looked up and made a face that said 'Very bad'. Aloud she said, 'He needs to get to a hospital.'

'There's no chance,' Richard said. 'There will be roadblocks at every junction.'

'I know how it can be done,' Antonia said. 'Armando! In the boot of my car is my nurse's uniform. Bring it for me, please.'

'What are you thinking of?' Richard asked. 'You can't take a wounded man through the German checkpoints.'

'No,' she agreed calmly. 'But a woman in labour is a different story. And once we are there, the doctors are sympathetic to the cause.'

The door of the hut crashed open and a boy ran in, a bundle in his arms. 'Here,' he panted. 'They're my grandmother's. The biggest I could find.'

'Good! Give them to me.' Antonia took the bundle and shook out a voluminous black skirt, a shawl and a headscarf. She turned to Richard. 'Help me to raise him.'

Leandro groaned as Richard propped him into a half-sitting position, but he made no further protest. Antonia bound a fresh dressing tightly over the wound in his belly and then looked around her.

'We need something to pad him out, to make him look pregnant. There is a cushion in my car.'

Armando had come back with a bag. He dropped it on the floor and went out again, to return with the cushion. Antonia bound it over the wound with another length of bandage and then they slid the skirt over Leandro's head and fastened it round his waist. The shawl wrapped round his shoulders and the scarf tied over his head completed the disguise.

'He'll never pass as a woman,' Richard said. 'You can see he hasn't shaved.'

'That is something I can see to when we are clear of this place,' Antonia said. 'For now, take this.' She gave Leandro a large white handkerchief. 'Hold it over your face, as if you are trying to stifle your screams. But scream anyway!' She turned to the two men. 'Get him into the car.' Already, without false modesty, she was stripping off her trousers and sweater. Between them Richard and Armando carried the wounded man out and laid him on the back seat of the car, covering him with the rug Antonia always kept there. Huddled beneath it, with his face turned to the back of the seat and the scarf pulled low over his brow, he could pass as a woman at a brief glance. By the time he was settled, Antonia was there, neatly dressed in her uniform.

Richard lifted his head at a new outburst of firing. 'Go quickly! They'll be on us at any minute.'

Antonia got into the driving seat and started the engine. There was no time for goodbyes or counsels of caution. The car bumped over uneven ground and gained the forest track that led to the cottage. A moment later it had disappeared among the trees and they heard the sound of the engine changing gear as it descended the road towards the German lines.

'Will she get through?' Armando asked, wild eyed.

'Only God knows,' Richard replied. 'There's a good chance the Huns are too busy to pay much attention to a woman in labour. We can only hope.' The firing was getting closer. He put a hand on Armando's shoulder. 'Time we got out of here.'

As he spoke three men ran past them. 'Run!' One of them yelled. 'They're close behind us. *I mongoli!*'

'The guns!' Armando exclaimed. 'We can't leave them behind.'

He dived into the hut and Richard followed and grabbed the Sten gun. As they ran out again there was a burst of firing and a bullet ricocheted off the wall. Richard felt a searing pain as a fragment of stone sliced his cheek. For a moment he staggered, then recovered himself and began to run uphill. Already Armando was well ahead of him. He had not slept for more than twenty-four hours, had not eaten since the previous evening, and his breath rasped in his parched throat as he ran, but he forced himself onwards. *I mongoli*, the man had said. Richard knew what that meant. These were Russian troops from Kazakhstan, taken prisoner by the Germans and freed on condition they enlisted in their army. He had heard their reputation. In battle they were merciless, in victory they raped and pillaged. If he were caught, there would be no civilised handover to a German officer, just a brutal death.

The slope of the hill grew steeper and he could hear shouts behind him. He left the path and scrambled higher, cutting across the hairpin bends by which the path made an easier ascent. Fallen branches caught at his feet and brambles ripped his skin and twice he had to struggle across steep gullies worn by winter rains and now clogged with undergrowth. But at last the cries of pursuit were fading and in a small clearing where two paths met he paused, doubled over and gasping for breath. A movement above him brought him upright again, the Sten at the ready; but it was Armando who stepped out of the shadows.

'Thank God! I hoped it was you I could hear crashing around behind me. Are you hurt?'

Richard rubbed the back of his hand across his cheek. It came away dark with blood and soot. 'It's nothing serious.'

They moved together and embraced impulsively in the euphoria of finding themselves alive. Then Armando said, 'What now? Head for Sassi?'

'No, too risky,' Richard responded. 'The Huns knew where Leandro was hiding out. Someone may have betrayed our base, too. We need to stay clear until we're sure it's safe.'

'Keep to the high ground, then,' Armando concluded, and Richard nodded wearily.

Over the next two days, Richard learned what it was like to be a hunted creature. They slept in the open, with the trees for shelter, and drank from the streams. On the first evening a boy guarding his goats ran home and returned bringing bread and olives, all the sustenance his family could spare. Later, they came upon a rabbit warren and Richard set a snare, as he had been taught long ago at Arisaig. By morning, there was a rabbit in it. He had found it hard, during training, to kill helpless animals, but that day he wrung its neck without thinking twice. As he skinned and gutted it he caught Armando's eye.

'How hungry are you?'

'Not hungry enough to eat that raw, if that's what you're thinking.'

Richard looked down at the chunks of bloody flesh in his hands. 'No, nor am I – yet.'

At midday they found a small cave and decided they could risk lighting a fire. The rabbit was blackened on the outside and still red raw in the middle, but they ate it and felt better afterwards.

They worked their way steadily north and east along the crest of a ridge, until the following morning they were able to look down on the village of Sassi and the farm where they had made their headquarters.

'Looks quiet enough,' Armando said.

Richard nodded. 'Let's move closer.'

As they descended, keeping to the trees, a door opened and a man came out into the farmyard.

'It's Silvano!' Armando cried, and drew breath to shout.

Richard gripped his arm. 'Wait! It could be a trap.'

They watched tensely as Silvano was joined by three others, all their own men. They clustered around the well in the centre of the yard, and the sound of laughter carried up to where Richard and Armando crouched.

'It's all right,' Armando said. 'They wouldn't sound so happy if there was anything wrong.'

He jumped up and began to run down the hill. Richard followed. As Armando passed a rocky outcrop a figure appeared suddenly on top of it and, before Richard could shout a warning, dropped on to his back, bearing him to the ground. Richard threw himself down, levelling the Sten. The assailant was a big man and as he got to his feet Richard recognised him. *What fools we are!* he told himself. *We should have known our men would set a watch. God knows, I've dinned it into them often enough.*

He jumped up and yelled, 'Sasha! Don't be a fool. It's us – Armando and Ricardo.'

The big Russian turned to look at him, then stooped and dragged Armando to his feet. '*Padrone!* Forgive me! I didn't recognise you.'

'You bloody idiot!' Armando exclaimed. 'You might have broken my back!' Then, regaining control, he added with a rueful grin, 'No, it's all right. You were only doing your job.'

'The farm is safe, then?' Richard asked. 'No sign of the Germans?'

'Not a whiff,' Sasha assured him. 'Come! The others will be glad to see you. We have been worried.'

In the farmhouse kitchen they found a dozen of their men, some wounded but none seriously. Over the next two days others came in, in ones and twos, together with a few of Leandro's people who had decided to throw in their lot with Armando. Soon the farm was overcrowded and some of the men were dispersed, as before, to other abandoned buildings in the area. But there was no news of Antonia.

She reappeared on the fourth day, striding up the hill from the spot where she hid her car with the confident energy Richard had learned to expect. He saw her from a distance and ran down to greet her.

'*Carissima!* Thank God, you're safe!'

He was about to embrace her but stopped, embarrassed. Their lovemaking under the pine tree seemed to belong to another life and he was not sure how to approach her. She caught both his hands and kissed him on the cheeks. 'And you, *caro mio*. You are safe also. I was afraid that you had waited too long and *i mongoli* had caught you.'

'It was a close thing,' he admitted.

'And Armando?' she asked anxiously. 'He is safe too?'

'Yes, he's here. Come up to the house. He'll be so glad to see you.'

Armando was sitting at the kitchen table, cleaning a rifle. He jumped up as they came in and brother and sister embraced, weeping.

Richard gave them a moment and then said, 'Did Leandro make it?'

Antonia's expression grew sombre. 'I got him to the

hospital but the doctors could do nothing for him. He died yesterday.'

Armando crossed himself and murmured a prayer, and Antonia sat down opposite him and took his hand. 'He was a brave man, but we must not let his death dishearten us. We owe it to him to keep up the fight.'

'She's right,' Richard said. 'We should be grateful that there were not more casualties. But how did you get him to the hospital, Antonia? Weren't you stopped?'

'Twice,' she said. 'The first time, there was so much shooting going on I think the soldier did not want to stand in the road to argue. He waved me through. The second time, the man wanted to fetch his superior officer. I told him that if he delayed us he might have to help me with the delivery and as it was a breech birth, it would be a messy business. He let us go then.'

Armando gripped her hands. 'Tonia, you are magnificent! Don't you agree, Ricardo?'

'Yes,' Richard said, 'She is – magnificent!' But he turned away and occupied himself pouring wine for his companions. It seemed he had lost the capacity for enthusiasm. A year ago the end of the war had seemed so close. Now, the summer was passing and before long the Allies would be bogged down for another winter. He found himself hoping that he might be recalled before that happened. He must be due for some leave, surely. He looked across the room at Armando and saw how thin and fine-drawn he had become. It struck him that for his friend there was no hope of a recall to a relatively safe home country. For him, it was a matter of victory or death.

Richard forced himself to his feet. 'Come on. We've got work to do. What's our next objective?'

12

On the morning after the funeral at Malpas, when the guests had finally taken their leave, Felix said, 'Would you mind terribly if I went out for an hour's hack? I've been dying to get back on a horse ever since we got here.'

'Of course not,' Merry said, concealing his disappointment. He had hoped that, now that the formalities were over, they would have some time to themselves.

Felix disappeared and returned shortly afterwards in riding breeches and boots.

'Purloined from Anthony's room,' he confessed. 'Is that wickedly unfeeling of me?'

'I don't see why,' Merry said.

He accompanied him to the stables and watched at a safe distance while he helped Peter to saddle up the big bay hunter.

'It's a pity you don't ride, Merry,' he said, leading the horse out into the yard. 'I'll teach you one day.'

'No thanks,' Merry said, backing off a little farther. 'As far as I'm concerned horses are unreliable creatures with big teeth and bigger feet. Anyway, they make me sneeze.'

Felix swung himself up into the saddle as if he had been doing it every day for the last ten years. 'There, you see?' he said. 'You never forget. I'll see you in about an hour.'

'For God's sake take care!' Merry implored. 'Don't go

jumping any fences or anything.' But he knew he might as well have saved his breath.

He waited until Felix had disappeared down the lane and then turned back to the house. Suddenly he felt depressed and at a loose end. The sight of Felix mounting so confidently had somehow encapsulated feelings that had been building up over the last few days. This was no longer Felix Lamont, or even Ned Mountjoy, hero of the Battle of Britain. This was Edward, Fifth Baron Malpas, and he had slotted into his new role as if he had been preparing for it all his life. Merry had always known that for Felix the banishment from Malpas had felt like the expulsion from Eden, however insouciantly he had behaved in his exile. Now that the angel with the flaming sword had relented and allowed him to return, would he come to the conclusion that it was not worth risking another bite of the poisoned apple? Merry found himself wondering whether, in this allegory, he should cast himself as the serpent or as the temptress Eve.

Felix turned his horse's head across country, following remembered tracks and bridleways. The big hunter, well fed and under-exercised and feeling an unfamiliar hand on the reins, was inclined to be skittish, and for a while Felix's mind was occupied with calming him. After a good canter, however, the horse settled down, and Felix was able to look around him. Every field and hedgerow was familiar. Here, he had seen his first fox killed. There, he had had a bad fall. There was the bramble patch where he had picked blackberries with his mother. And over there, in that stream, he had bathed naked with the village boys and felt the first stirrings of an unfamiliar warmth.

Turning into a narrow lane that led homewards he loosened

the reins and let the horse amble at his own pace. This familiar landscape had brought to a head misgivings that had been stirring at the back of his mind during the last few days. For years he had assumed that he would never come here again. Now, he found himself not only readmitted to the land of his childhood but made its master and custodian. Was he qualified for the task? He remembered how his father had devoted himself to the land and the people who lived on it, determined to preserve a way of life that he already felt was slipping away. Now, after the disruption of the war, Felix realised that there was no question of maintaining the old ways. The task for him was to manage the inevitable changes so that they caused the minimum of disruption. But what did he know of farming methods or estate management? He could employ a farm manager, he supposed. But in that case, what role would be left for him? And was it, in any event, the kind of life he wanted?

Then there was his relationship with Merry to consider. What sort of life could they have together if he was settled here in Cheshire? Merry had a career to make, and there was no way he could do that from Malpas. Besides, public opinion would never tolerate it. Were they fated to go on as they had done so far, snatching secret meetings when they could manage to get away for a week or two? How long would their relationship survive under those circumstances? And would his mother ever be able to accept it?

His reverie was interrupted as they rounded a bend in the lane and the horse shied violently. An old woman straightened up from picking herbs along the ditch and backed away.

'It's all right!' Felix called, adding, to the horse, 'Stand still, you idiot! There's nothing to be frightened of.' He looked more closely at the woman. 'It's Mrs Harper, isn't it?'

She came closer, screwing up her eyes. 'Oh, it's you! I'm sorry, sir – your lordship. I didn't mean to frighten the horse.'

'It wasn't your fault,' Felix said, swinging down from the saddle.

'Fancy you remembering me!' She smiled at him, revealing a mouthful of broken teeth.

'Of course I remember you. I used to play with your son Georgie. You used to give us greengages from the tree in your garden. How are you?'

'Oh, not so bad. My feet give me a bit of trouble, but I'm used to that.'

Felix glanced down and saw that her feet were shod in ancient shoes that bulged around swollen and misshapen toes. He studied her face more closely. The skin was dark as leather and seamed with wrinkles. He would have guessed her age to be close to seventy, yet he knew that she must be only a few years older than his mother. 'You should see a chiropodist,' he said, unthinkingly.

She looked at him as if he had suggested that she might sprout wings and fly. 'A chiropodist? Me? Where would I find the money for that?'

Discomfited, he changed the subject. 'How's Georgie?'

She shook her head sadly. 'Georgie bought it on D-Day. Shot through the head, his CO said in the letter.'

'Oh, I'm so sorry. You must miss him terribly.'

'Aye, he was a good lad.'

'And Mr Harper? How is he?'

The same shake of the head. 'Harper passed away two year gone. He had a pain in his guts for three days and then he died. The doctors said it was 'pendicitis.'

'Appendicitis! Why didn't he see a doctor sooner?'

'I begged him to let me send for Doctor Weatherspoon. But

he said he wasn't running up no doctor's bills for a bit of indigestion. You get old Ma Rigley to make me up some of her herbal tea, he said. Well, she made it and he drank it but it didn't do him no good. He had a horror of getting into debt, you see, and he couldn't see how we were going to pay the doctor's bill.'

Felix felt a flush spreading up his neck, but whether it was from shame or anger or embarrassment he could not tell. 'You should have gone to my mother. She would have taken care of the bill.'

'Oh, no. We couldn't trouble her ladyship with that. She had enough on her plate. Besides, Harper would never take charity.'

'It wouldn't be charity!' Felix exclaimed. Then he added more quietly, 'Are you living on your own now?'

'Oh, bless you, no! I'm with our Ruth and her husband. They're very good to me.'

Felix came to a decision. 'Listen. When I get home I'm going to phone the chiropodist and ask him to come out and look at your feet. I'll tell him to send the bill to me. And I want you to see the dentist, too, and send his bill to me. If I'm not there my mother will deal with it.' The old woman opened her mouth to protest but he overrode her. 'It isn't charity. You're my tenant and it's my job to look after you. Besides, you were very kind to me when I was a kid, so I'm just returning the favour. And I want you to tell the other tenants that if they are ever in need of medical attention they are to apply to me. I don't want anyone else dying the way your husband died. Is that clear?'

Without realising it, he had reverted to the authoritative tone he employed when addressing his subordinates before a mission. The old woman goggled at him for a moment, then she nodded. He smiled at her. 'Now, you make sure you do what I say. I shall check with Ruth next time I'm home on leave and I shall be very annoyed if you haven't.'

To his intense embarrassment she suddenly lunged forward and seized his hand, kissing it. 'You're very good, sir. Thank you. But then,' she smiled up at him, 'you were always a good lad.'

Felix turned away and remounted. 'Give my regards to Ruth. And don't forget – I expect to see you walking like a dancer next time I'm home.'

He touched his heels to the horse's sides. 'Walk on!' At the bend in the lane he looked back. She was standing where he had left her, her hands pressed to her mouth.

As he rode across the next field the vague speculations that had occupied him earlier gave way to something more concrete, as an idea that had been germinating at the back of his mind for some time began to take shape. Perhaps there was a role for him, after all! He put Nutmeg into a canter. There was one more field between them and home and the horse was scenting his stable and the manger full of hay that awaited him. He strode out strongly. Between the two fields was a hedge, broken by a five-barred gate. Felix watched it coming closer. He had jumped it many times as a boy and he had no doubt that Nutmeg was capable of clearing it. But was he up to it himself? He felt a thrill of fear in his belly.

His usual response to that was to banish it by meeting the challenge head on but he suddenly heard Merry's plea. 'Don't go jumping any fences or anything.' Nutmeg was thundering towards the gate but, almost too late, Felix saw a compromise. Next to the gate the hedge was lower, its branches cut and laid to give a rounded top. With pressure of hand and leg he turned the horse's head towards that point and let him go.

As he flew towards the obstacle he found himself yelling the word with which he had so often led his squadron into battle. 'Tally-ho!'

Entering the house on his way back from the stables Merry was waylaid by Lady Malpas, standing in the doorway of her private sitting room.

'Captain Merryweather, I wonder if I could have a few words?'

With a heavy heart Merry followed her into the room and took the chair she indicated. This was what he had been expecting. He was about to be told, no doubt very politely, that his further presence would be de trop and that it would be better if his association with Edward were to be terminated.

Lady Malpas resumed her seat by her desk and seemed for a moment unsure how to begin. 'Captain Merryweather, you are obviously close to Edward – Felix, as you call him. I understand why now, after last night's revelations about his stage career.'

'I'm sorry,' Merry said, 'that was a slip. I try to remember to call him by his proper name when other people are around.'

'Oh, I have heard you use it between yourselves. I assumed it was a nickname of some sort. But that is not the point at issue. I am wondering if you are fully in his confidence.'

'I think I can safely say that we have no secrets from one another,' Merry responded cautiously, puzzled by the direction the conversation was taking.

'Can I take it that you are aware of the reason for his . . . sudden departure from home all those years ago?' his hostess asked.

Now we're getting round to it! Merry thought. Aloud he said, 'Yes, he has told me about that.'

Lady Malpas fidgeted with some papers on her desk. She seemed uncharacteristically diffident. She said, 'I want to say how very glad I am that he seems to have found such a good friend in you. Someone so level headed and sensible. He has always been . . . somewhat impetuous.'

Merry nodded, bemused.

'You came here once to plead his cause and I am afraid I was rather ungracious. I regret that now.' Lady Malpas went on, 'I have to say that I cannot approve of the lifestyle he has chosen. It seems to me both unnatural and ungodly.' She paused but Merry said nothing. 'However,' she resumed, 'I must admit that in all other ways Edward has turned out better than I expected. He does seem to be, in most respects, a quite admirable young man and I have been very favourably impressed with the way he has comported himself in the last few days.'

'He is,' said Merry loyally, 'a very remarkable person. I'm sure you will find that he will be a great credit to you.'

'I understand,' Lady Malpas continued, 'that he has formed a . . . a liaison with someone. I am not asking you to reveal the identity of this person, though I assume you know it. All I ask is that you should use your good offices to persuade him of the necessity for discretion. He has a position to maintain now and a great many people will be relying on him. I am sure I do not need to impress on you how vital it is to avoid any suggestion of scandal. He listens to you, I am sure. Will you be his counsellor? For all our sakes?'

Merry gazed at her. The ice-blue eyes met his openly, without any hint of duplicity. Was he being warned off? Was this a covert appeal to his better nature, asking him to break off his relationship with Felix? Or should it be taken at its face value? He decided that he must at any rate appear to accept it as the latter.

He said, 'Lady Malpas, I would like to assure you that I will always act in what I see as Felix . . . Edward's best interests. I would never willingly see any harm come to him – or to his family. I know how important Malpas is to him and I have seen how well he fits in here. I wouldn't want anything to happen to spoil that.'

Lady Malpas rose to her feet. 'Thank you. I felt sure that I could rely on you.'

Merry rose also and moved towards the door, but her voice stopped him.

'Captain Merryweather?'

'Lady Malpas?'

'I wonder, Captain Merryweather seems so formal. Would you mind if I called you Guy?'

Merry hesitated. The last person to call him Guy had been his father, dead now these five years. 'I'm usually called Merry,' he said.

She smiled. 'I know. But the use of a nickname implies, perhaps, too great a degree of intimacy. I should prefer Guy, if you have no objection.'

'Of course not,' Merry said, now completely at a loss. 'Guy will be fine.'

'Thank you,' she replied. 'Oh, and by the way, do feel free to use the piano at any time. I know pianists need to practise and you need not be afraid that the sound will disturb me.'

'That's very kind of you, Lady Malpas,' Merry said.

'I shall see you at lunch, then,' she said, and smiled at him again.

Feeling thoroughly dazed, Merry made his way to the drawing room and sat down at the piano. For the next hour he forced himself to concentrate on scales and arpeggios and at the end of that time it occurred to him that Felix should have been home. He walked down to the stables to find him, only to learn from Peter that 'his lordship' had returned a good twenty minutes earlier. Puzzled, he headed back to the house.

He found Felix in his bedroom, changing his clothes. He had a very odd expression on his face, a combination of incredulity and barely suppressed amusement.

'What's got into you?' Merry asked.

Felix sat on the edge of the bed and looked up, with a shoe in one hand. 'I've just had the most extraordinary conversation with my mother.'

Merry sat beside him. 'That makes two of us.'

'Really? What did she say to you?'

Merry frowned. 'That's the trouble. I know what she said, but I can't make up my mind whether it was actually what she meant or whether it was in some kind of code.'

'That sounds like my mother,' Felix agreed wryly. 'What did she actually say?'

'Well, she started off by being very nice to me and telling me how glad she was that you had me for a friend. Then she probed about a bit to find out how much I knew about why you left home and then we got to the really extraordinary bit. She said she knew you had formed what she termed "a liaison" with someone and I thought "oh-oh, this is it!" But instead of telling me to sling my hook she said she didn't want to know who it was. She just reminded me how important it was to avoid any breath of scandal and asked me to use my influence to make sure that you were "discreet".' He looked at Felix helplessly. 'Now, you tell me. Was that what she really meant, or was it a coded way of suggesting that if I really have your best interests at heart I should leave you alone?'

'Search me,' said Felix. 'Wait till you hear what she said to me.'

'Go on.'

'She started by saying that while she couldn't approve of my way of life she realised that there was nothing she could do to change it.'

'Oh yes, she said that to me, too. She also admitted that, contrary to her expectations, you had turned out rather well. Quite admirable was the phrase, I seem to remember.'

'Did she? Well I'm darned! Anyway, she repeated to me what she said to you, about this man I'm supposed to be having a relationship with. She doesn't want to know who it is and, while she can't approve, she is prepared to say no more about it *provided I never bring him into this house*!'

They gazed at each other in bafflement. Eventually Merry said, 'Is it actually possible that she hasn't realised who I am? It seems to me that she is either being extremely devious and cunning or incredibly naive.'

'Normally,' Felix remarked dryly, 'from what I know of my mother I would go for devious and cunning every time. But in this instance I really think it may be the other thing. You see, I suspect she has a very stereotypical picture of the sort of chap I'm likely to have taken up with.'

'Meaning?'

'Oh, I don't know. A pretty chorus boy? Or some outrageously camp old queen? Don't ask me how her mind works. The point is, she's obviously taken a liking to you and you don't fit the picture. Therefore you can't possibly be the man in question.'

'Alternatively,' Merry suggested, 'she knows perfectly well who I am but she doesn't want to admit it.'

'That would be in character,' Felix agreed. 'She can't bear to think of this person under the same roof so she's convinced herself, consciously or unconsciously, that you can't be the one. Anyway,' he finished putting on his shoes and smiled at Merry, 'it looks as though we've been given the green light, as long as we don't . . .'

'. . . do it in the street and frighten the horses, in Mrs Pat Campbell's famous phrase,' Merry supplied. 'I wonder.'

'What?'

'Are you sure it wasn't a covert invitation to me to fall on my sword?'

'Well, if it was she's backing a loser,' Felix said crisply. 'Come on, let's get some lunch. I'm starving!'

At dinner Lady Malpas remarked, 'I'm afraid you haven't had a very enjoyable leave. I do hope you don't feel that we have neglected you, Guy.'

Felix caught Merry's eye across the dinner table. '*Guy?!*' he mouthed silently.

In their bedroom, later that night, Felix paused in the act of removing his shirt and said, 'What was all that "Guy" business at dinner?'

'Your mother feels,' Merry responded sedately, 'that Captain Merryweather is too formal but Merry is too intimate.'

'Does she, by George!' Felix chuckled. 'How quaint! Particularly as everyone who knows you, even slightly, calls you Merry.' He moved closer and looked into Merry's face. 'Have you ever been called Guy?'

'Not since I was a child, except by my father, of course.'

Felix put his head on one side, quizzically. 'Should I be calling you Guy?'

'Only if you expect me to call you Edward from now on,' Merry responded heavily.

Felix's expression became serious. 'Something's wrong. What is it?'

'No, it's nothing. Forget it.' Merry would have turned away but Felix took him by the shoulders.

'There is something. You've got your Eeyore face on. What's up?'

'No, really,' Merry protested. 'It's just . . .'

'Just?'

'Oh, I don't know. I suppose I just feel I don't really fit in here.'

'That's rubbish!' Felix exclaimed. 'You've been a tower of strength over the last few days. And look how Mother's taken to you. You fit in perfectly.'

'Oh, temporarily, perhaps. But in the long term . . .'

'What about the long term?'

'Well, I can't see much chance of us being together a great deal in the future, can you?'

Felix frowned. 'I know it isn't ideal, geographically speaking. Me up here and you – wherever. But that was always on the cards, wasn't it? I mean, whatever I ended up doing after the war the chances are that we wouldn't have been in the same place for long. After all, you'll probably be touring, playing all over the place. We were never going to be able to settle down together permanently.'

'I know that,' Merry said unhappily. He knew at gut level what he wanted to say but could not find the words to express it. 'I'm not talking geographically. I just feel that your life here is going to be so different that there won't be much room for me.'

Felix's grip on his shoulders had tightened so much that it had become painful. 'Merry, are you saying that you're afraid I'm going to chuck you?' Merry, unable to meet his eyes, gazed at the floor between them. Felix shook him slightly. 'I thought we'd been over all this years ago and sorted it out. I told you, you must never doubt me, and you promised not to.' When Merry did not respond he went on, 'Listen the other night you said you'd rather spend a week in hell with me than eternity in paradise on your own. Don't you *know* that that goes for me too? If I thought this place was going to come between us I'd walk out tonight and never set foot in it again.'

'You couldn't,' Merry said bleakly. 'I've seen how you belong here. It's part of you and you're part of it. And you're needed here.'

'And so are you. I need you! Merry, I know we've each got our own lives to lead and our paths seem to go in different directions but I couldn't bear to lose you. Surely you know me well enough to understand that.'

'I don't know,' Merry mumbled unwillingly. 'I thought I did, but down there,' a movement of his head indicated the lower floors of the house, 'you seem different.'

'Down there I'm playing a role,' Felix insisted. 'Haven't you been around the theatre long enough to know when someone is acting?'

'Maybe,' Merry conceded doubtfully. 'But you've been acting a part ever since you left home and I'm not sure which one is real – Felix Lamont or Edward Mountjoy.'

The last words were stifled by the pressure of Felix's lips on his own.

'Come to bed,' Felix murmured, 'and I'll show you what's real and what's acting.'

Merry was woken the next morning by Felix singing 'Happy Birthday to You' in his ear. He was somewhat more surprised when Lady Malpas greeted him with the same phrase.

Over breakfast Felix said, 'I want to take Merry out for lunch, as it's his birthday. You won't mind, will you, Mother?'

'Of course not,' she replied. 'It's the least you can do, when he's given up his leave. Take the Daimler. I don't know how much petrol there is but there are some coupons in my desk.'

To begin with Felix refused to say where they were going but before long they were entering the City of Chester. Here Felix marched Merry into a jeweller's shop and insisted on buying him a very expensive pair of cufflinks. Later they lunched at a country pub overlooking a sleepy and largely overgrown canal, eating fresh bread and crumbly Cheshire cheese with tomatoes and pickled onions, washed down with pints of good bitter. In the afternoon they walked along a high sandstone ridge, grateful for the shade of forests of tall beech and oak. When they came to an escarpment looking out across the Cheshire plain towards the distant smudge of the Welsh mountains on the horizon, they sat down on the short grass. Felix lay back and gazed up into the sky.

'Peace, perfect peace – and not a contrail to be seen. You'd never think there was a war on.'

'No,' Merry agreed. 'It doesn't seem to have affected this part of the country.'

'It has, of course,' Felix said. 'It looks superficially unchanged but things will never be the same again – here or anywhere.'

'What do you mean?' Merry asked. 'Are you thinking about the new farming methods?'

'No, much more than that. I mean the people, basically. Think of all those men coming back from the services. They've been to places and seen things they would never have dreamed of before the war – and met all sorts of people, too. They're not going to just settle back into the old ways. Quite right, too. We need changes.'

'What sort of changes?'

'Changes in the way society is organised. The government has seen that. Look at this new Education Act. Everyone to stay at school until they're fifteen. Secondary education for everyone. That's going to make a huge difference.'

Merry looked down at him, mildly amused. 'I've never heard you talk politics before.'

'No?' Felix sat up and ran his hand through his hair, looking slightly embarrassed. 'I suppose it's coming back here that's brought it to a head, but actually I've been thinking about it quite a lot, on and off. I realise now I had a very privileged upbringing, but at the time I just took it for granted. People like us had a right to good schools and nice houses, horses to ride and cars to drive and a doctor on call if ever we were ill. It wasn't until I got thrown out that I realised what it was like for other people. I watched all you lot scraping by on the pittance Monty paid us, often with hardly enough to pay the rent each week. And even then I had Aunt Betty's little legacy to fall back on so I never went short. But it was the RAF that really made me think. Look at the way we treat our sergeant pilots, for example. They fly with us, share the same risks, and they're bloody good, too – better than some of the officers. We look out for each other in the air but when we get back on the ground they're not allowed to eat in the same mess or drink in the same bars and they sleep in tents or Nissen huts, while we're billeted in the best accommodation available. Because we're "gentlemen" and they're not! And what really gets my goat is the fact that most of the other chaps seem to think that it's perfectly natural and right.'

'Oh well, if it's snobbery you're talking about,' Merry said grimly, 'you should try the officers' mess in an old cavalry regiment. There it's nothing to do with your rank or how good you are at the job, it's who your parents are and which school you went to.'

'That's exactly what I'm talking about,' Felix said. 'And it's got to change. Mark my words, as soon as the war's over things are going to be very different.'

'Come the revolution!' Merry said with a laugh. 'You realise you'll be one of the first to be put up against a wall and shot?'

'Don't joke,' said Felix. 'If we don't learn, it could come to that.'

'I've never seen you take life so seriously,' Merry said.

'And on your birthday, too.' Felix smiled. 'Sorry. I didn't mean to lecture.'

Merry looked out across the fields. 'How long do you think it will be, until the war's over? Will we still be in uniform on my next birthday?'

'God, no!' Felix exclaimed. 'Hitler must realise that he's beaten soon. With us and the Americans pushing in from the west and the south and the Russians making inroads in the east, he'd be mad to fight through another winter. It must end soon.' He got up and stretched out a hand to pull Merry to his feet. 'We'll come back here on your birthday next year, in civvies, and talk about what we're doing with the peace.'

'Unless you're manning the barricades,' Merry said, with a grin.

They dined at home but afterwards Felix insisted on walking down to the local pub, where they were greeted with a respectful but rather tentative welcome, until Felix made it clear that he was not going to stand on ceremony. After that it turned out to be an extremely convivial evening. The newspaper cuttings retailing Felix's doings during and after the Battle of Britain were taken down and passed round and Felix bought drinks for everyone. Then Merry bought his round and after that Felix let slip that it was Merry's birthday, so they had drinks on the house. At some point Merry found himself seated at the old upright piano with Felix at his shoulder saying, 'Come on, let's have a sing-song.'

So they sang all the old favourites: 'Roll Out the Barrel', 'Tipperary', 'Pack Up Your Troubles in Your Old Kitbag', 'There's a Silver Lining', 'We'll Meet Again', 'There'll Always Be an England', until their voices were hoarse. At closing time they strolled back up the lane to the Hall, their arms round each other's shoulders, just drunk enough to have an excuse for hanging on to each other.

The next day, heavily hung over, they took the train back to London. When they reached Euston station, instead of directing the taxi to the friend's flat where they had stayed at the beginning of the week, Felix gave the driver a different address, and before long they were standing outside the entrance of a smart modern block on the fringes of Mayfair.

'It's still here, all in one piece, then,' Felix commented.

'What are we doing here?' Merry demanded. It had been a long day and his head ached.

'Come and see,' Felix said.

He led the way to the lift. Outside a door on the third floor he produced a set of keys and opened it with a flourish reminiscent of his days as a magician.

'Where are we?' Merry asked, following him inside.

'The family pied-à-terre. I'd forgotten it existed until Mother gave me the keys. Father kept it so he had somewhere to stay when he came to town on business. What do you think?'

The flat was beautifully furnished in art nouveau style. 'It's wonderful,' Merry said. 'Your own place in the centre of town!'

'Our own place,' Felix said. He produced a second set of keys and held them out. 'A quid pro quo for the use of your house in Seaford. I want you to come and go as you please, whenever you're based in London. There are two bedrooms, in case anyone jumps to conclusions. Understood?'

'Understood,' Merry said, taking the keys. 'Thank you.'

'Right!' Felix walked into the master bedroom and threw his case on the bed. 'We've got one night before I have to go back. What shall we do?'

It was then that Merry remembered George Black's offer. A phone call to the offices at Grosvenor Street produced an immediate result and a couple of hours later they were picking up two complimentary tickets for the best seats in the house at the Palladium. The theatre was packed, mainly with servicemen on leave, with their wives or girlfriends. Everyone was in the mood for an evening of hilarious escapism and they were not disappointed. They roared and stamped and whistled their approval and yelled back the chief comedian's popular, if ironic, catchphrase.

'*You lucky people!*'

13

Rose sauntered down the Champs Elysées with a lightness in her step that she had not felt for months. She had abandoned her ENSA uniform in favour of an expensively cut coat and skirt in hyacinth blue and a chic little matching hat. She had picked both up for a song in a shop on the Left Bank the previous day. They were second-hand, of course, but in pristine condition, and had obviously once formed part of the wardrobe of a very sophisticated lady. The shopkeeper, who spoke surprisingly fluent English, had explained that many wealthy Parisians had been forced to sell their couture clothes along with their jewellery and other valuables in order to buy food on the black market. Whatever the origin of her finery Rose felt that she 'looked a million dollars', an impression that was born out by the admiring looks and wolf whistles of passing British Tommies and American GIs.

The whistles were not only for her. Violet, walking on her left, was also arrayed in second-hand finery, in a dress of green silk that complemented her auburn hair. On her other side was Angela, the ingénue of the party, a petite blonde only just out of school, who could hardly contain her excitement at finding herself in Paris.

'Fancy me, walking down the Chumps Illisis!' she exclaimed.

'It's *Champs Elysées*,' Rose corrected and, unable to resist the temptation, added, 'It's very beautiful, but it's not a patch on the prom in Tripoli, with palms waving over your head and the blue Mediterranean just across the beach, is it, Vi?'

'You are so lucky, Rose!' Angela sighed. 'I don't suppose I'll ever get a chance to go somewhere really glamorous like that. Not now the war's nearly over.'

'It's not over yet, so don't count your chickens,' Violet said. 'Anyway, Paris is glamorous enough for me.'

'Me, too,' Rose agreed. 'Sorry, I didn't mean to shoot a line. It's fantastic being here.'

'Makes you think, though,' said Violet. 'All these beautiful buildings, and hardly any damage. When you think what poor old London's been through . . .'

'It doesn't seem fair, does it?' Rose looked around her. The October sun was bright but there was a softness to the light that seemed to smooth out the hard edges and lay a wash of misty gold over the scene. The leaves were turning, but autumn here was gently nostalgic, not soggily pessimistic, as it always seemed to her in England. 'Still, let's not think about London,' she went on. 'Let's make the most of being here.'

At the Arc de Triomphe they turned and crossed the river to the Left Bank.

'Tell you what,' Violet said. 'I'm parched. Shall we find one of those pavement cafés and have a drink?'

'Oh yes!' Angela chimed in. 'I'm dry, too.'

'OK,' Rose said, 'but it's bound to be expensive here, on the main boulevard. Let's try up this way.'

They turned into a side street and came, after a short walk, to a narrow alley where café tables were set out on the pavement.

'This do?' Violet asked.

'Anywhere'll do,' Angela said. 'My feet are killing me.'

Rose did not argue but she felt somehow uneasy about the place. The clientele was very different from that along the main boulevards and she was uncomfortably aware of suspicious and even hostile looks cast in their direction. They had hardly settled themselves at a table when her doubts were reinforced by a sudden commotion inside the café. Twisting in her chair, she was shocked to see the door flung open and a young woman ejected so violently that she fell full length on the pavement. Two other women, considerably older and wearing shawls crossed on their chests and tied behind, sleeves pushed up to reveal brawny arms, were close behind her, screaming at her. Behind them came a man in a raincoat, with a cigarette hanging from the corner of his mouth, and the proprietor of the café in his apron.

The girl started to pick herself up and Rose heard her two companions gasp in shock at her appearance. Her clothes had once been smart, but now they hung in ribbons. Her blouse had been ripped open, leaving one shoulder and part of her breast exposed, and her silk stockings were muddy and holed at the knees from her fall. But it was her face and head which shocked the three English girls. Her cheek showed a purple bruise, there was blood at the corner of her lip and her hair had been roughly shorn to within an inch of her head. The man in the raincoat stepped forward and grabbed the girl's arm, jerking her to her feet. He spoke to her for a moment, with a concentrated fury that was obvious to Rose although she could not understand a word of what was being said, and then gave her a violent shove. Sobbing, the girl stumbled between the tables towards the street.

Acting on instinct, Rose jumped up and caught her by the arm. 'What's wrong?' she asked. 'Do you need help? Can we do anything?'

The girl stared into her face for a moment in uncomprehending terror, then jerked her arm away and scuttled off down the alley. Rose turned to go back to her table and realised that the other two women were now standing close behind her, glaring suspiciously. One of them said something in a hoarse, hectoring tone, obviously asking a question.

Rose forced a smile and said, 'I'm sorry, I don't understand. We're English.'

The woman said something to her companion, who replied with a derisory snort of laughter. They both moved a little closer.

Violet and Angela were beside Rose now. Violet said, 'I don't like the look of this. Let's beat it.'

'Good idea,' agreed Rose.

She turned towards the street, only to discover that the other customers of the café had risen and formed themselves into a rough semicircle, cutting off their escape. Rose hesitated, then squared her shoulders and marched firmly towards a point where the group was thinnest. Without speaking, the men facing her drew together, closing the gap, their arms folded, lips smirking mockingly around their Gitanes. For an instant she considered trying to force her way through, but she could see that the result would be a humiliating defeat. She swung round again, looking for the café proprietor to demand his assistance, but found herself face to face with the man in the raincoat. He came closer and plucked at the sleeve of her jacket, demanding something in a menacing growl.

'Look,' Rose said, trying to stop her voice shaking, 'we haven't done anything. Don't you understand? We're English. *Anglais!* We're with ENSA. We're supposed to be your allies.'

Ever since the concert party had arrived in France they had grown to expect the warmest of welcomes. At every village they had been greeted with flowers and wine, handshakes and embraces. Of course, the most exuberant welcome had been reserved for the troops, but it had seemed that anyone English could rely on the same warmth of feeling. The hostility that now surrounded them was incomprehensible.

The man in the raincoat repeated his question even more aggressively and when Rose did not answer he reached up and made a sudden swipe at her hat, knocking it to the ground. Then, as Rose cried out in protest, he spat straight in her face. For a moment there was uproar. Violet was at Rose's side, grabbing the man's sleeve and screaming, 'Leave her alone, you bastard!' Alice was crying, the two French women were shouting and beneath all this there was a threatening undercurrent of voices from the crowd.

Then, over the chaos, came a single, authoritative voice. '*Taisez-vous! Taisez-vous, tout le monde!*'

In the sudden silence Rose turned to look at the speaker. A tall man dressed in an immaculate dove-grey, double-breasted suit was making his way through the crowd, which fell back respectfully to let him pass.

'*Qu'est-ce que se passe ici?*' he demanded, addressing his question to the man in the raincoat.

The man replied with a torrent of indignant French and the new arrival cut him short with a few contemptuous words. Then he turned to Rose and the other girls and removed his trilby hat.

'Mesdemoiselles, a thousand apologies. These are stupid, ignorant people and there is much fear and suspicion still in the city. They think anyone well dressed, who is not in uniform, must be either a spy or a collaborator. You are English, yes?'

'Yes,' Rose replied, breathlessly.

'And what are you doing here in Paris?'

'We're with ENSA. You know, the people who entertain the troops?'

'Of course. I am familiar with the work of ENSA. But why are you not in uniform?'

Rose looked at the other two, uncomfortably aware that they had broken regulations. 'It's our first visit to Paris,' she said after a pause. 'We didn't want to look dowdy compared with all the chic Parisian ladies.'

He smiled suddenly. The hair at his temples was flecked with grey and there were lines on his face that made it difficult to guess his age, but now she realised that he was younger than she had first thought – perhaps in his middle thirties.

'Mademoiselle,' he said, 'you certainly do not need to fear comparison. I doubt if there is a woman in Paris smarter than you. But it is not wise to go about out of uniform. As you see, it can cause misunderstandings.'

He turned and addressed the crowd in French and they began to move away, shrugging and muttering. The man in the raincoat dropped the butt of his cigarette on the pavement and ground it out under his shoe, with a look that suggested he wished it was Rose, and then turned and went back into the café, followed by the two women. Their rescuer watched him go, then turned back to Rose and her two companions.

'Forgive me, I have not introduced myself. Lucien de Vaucourt, at your service.'

Rose was shaking all over. With an effort, she pulled herself together and replied, 'I'm Rose Taylor. This is Violet Ferguson and Angela Brown. We're really very grateful to you, monsieur.'

He extended his hand and when Rose gave him hers he made a little bow and for a moment she thought he was going to kiss it, but he merely murmured, '*Enchanté, mademoiselle*,' and then turned to greet the other two girls in the same way.

While they were thanking him Rose started to look for her hat. It had been kicked under one of the tables and when he saw what she was doing he bent quickly and retrieved it for her.

'Such a chic little hat! What a shame. But I think with a good brush it will be all right.' He looked at her closely as she took it from him. 'But you are shaking still. You need something to calm your nerves. Allow me to buy you a drink – all of you.'

Rose began to demur but Violet, never one to turn down an invitation, cut in. 'Oh, that's very kind of you! I could really do with something after all that.'

'Of course,' de Vaucourt agreed. 'But not here. Let me take you somewhere a little more salubrious. Please, Mademoiselle Rose, take my arm. It is not far.'

Slipping her hand through his arm she felt a steady, reassuring warmth. He walked at an easy pace, making casual conversation to the other two girls, giving her a chance to calm herself. Within a few minutes they were entering a café whose pavement tables were sheltered from the street by glazed partitions and adorned with crisp white tablecloths and little vases containing red carnations. A waiter came hurrying forward as soon as they appeared and greeted de Vaucourt with a bow.

'*Champagne, Jean-Luc*,' their host ordered, as the man led them to a table.

'*Champagne, M. le Baron*,' the waiter repeated. '*Certainement! Tout de suite!*'

As they sat Violet caught Rose's eye across the table and mouthed '*M. le Baron!*' but Rose tried to pretend that she had not understood. She turned to de Vaucourt.

'What was going on there, at the café? There was a girl. They attacked her before they turned on us.'

De Vaucourt nodded. 'I saw her. Almost certainly she was a collaborator. There were girls who found it easier to survive by becoming the mistresses of German officers during the Occupation. These officers were able to give them smart clothes, silk stockings, and a good time. But, understandably, they were hated by those who refused to collaborate. Now the ordinary people are taking their revenge.'

'But why did they turn on us?' Rose asked.

'You were too smartly dressed,' he explained. 'Very few women can afford to dress like that now, and those that can are careful to keep the fact to themselves.'

'But I tried to tell them we were English,' Rose protested.

'I'm afraid either they didn't understand or they didn't believe you,' de Vaucourt said. 'I should explain that, for a long time, many weeks, after the Allies entered Paris there were still German agents hiding out in the city. You must have heard how they attempted to assassinate General de Gaulle, even in the cathedral of Notre Dame itself, during the thanksgiving service. People are still very suspicious. You might even say there is a certain amount of hysteria. That is why it is so important that you wear your uniform at all times.'

'Yes, I see that now,' Rose said meekly. 'I apologise for any trouble we've caused.'

'No, please,' he exclaimed. 'It is for me to apologise, on behalf of my countrymen.'

The champagne arrived and de Vaucourt raised his glass. 'To the *Entente Cordiale* – and the ultimate victory over *les Boches*!'

'We'll drink to that!' Violet said warmly.

They all drank and de Vaucourt said, 'So, you are with ENSA. What do you do?'

They told him and he said, 'Of course, I should have known. Three such lovely ladies would have to be dancers. And where are you performing? I should like to come and see you.'

Before either of the other two could answer Rose said, 'I don't think that would be possible. We're based outside Paris, at an army rest camp, but we probably won't be there for long. We're expecting to be sent up nearer to the front line very soon.'

She caught a look of puzzled irritation from Violet but ignored it.

'*Quel dommage!*' de Vaucourt murmured. 'I am a great lover of the theatre, in all its forms. I should have greatly enjoyed seeing your show. So, do you return to your base this evening?'

'No,' said Violet, before Rose could answer. 'We've got forty-eight hours' leave. We're staying in Paris.'

'Then you must let me show you round,' de Vaucourt insisted.

'Oh, we couldn't possibly trouble you,' Rose murmured.

'But I insist,' he returned, smiling at her. 'It will give me the greatest pleasure.'

To change the subject she said, 'Forgive me for asking, but the people at that café seemed to know you. They obviously have great respect for you. And yet it doesn't seem the sort of place you would normally go to. I'm puzzled.'

He nodded, holding her gaze. His eyes, like his hair except for the grey at the temples, were very dark. 'That is understandable. But, yes, these people know me. The man, Pierre, was active in the Resistance. I was his superior officer.'

'You were in the Resistance?' Angela breathed, overawed.

'*Bien sûr*, Mademoiselle Angela. After Dunkirk I escaped to England and joined General de Gaulle. Later I was parachuted back into France to help organise resistance to the occupiers. I have been here ever since.'

'How exciting!' Violet gushed. 'I do think you're terribly brave!'

'Do tell us about it,' Angela begged, eyes shining.

He shrugged. 'Alas, there is not much I can tell you. You understand, even now much of what we did has to remain secret. Perhaps, one day . . .'

'Of course,' Rose said quickly. 'We don't mean to pry into things that don't concern us. And anyway, we must be going. You've been very kind and we're all very grateful but we mustn't impose on you any further.'

'But you do not impose!' he exclaimed. 'It is my pleasure. Please, you will let me see you back to your hotel. I insist!'

In spite of Rose's protestations that they could perfectly well find their own way he insisted upon accompanying them. Taxis were almost non-existent but a short distance from the café one appeared, miraculously, as if it had been specially ordered, and he ushered them all into it. At the entrance to the hotel Rose turned and offered him her hand.

'Thank you again, M. de Vaucourt. You saved us from a very nasty situation and we're very grateful. And thank you for the champagne.'

He took her hand. There was a twinkle in his eye, as if he understood her embarrassment and her eagerness to be rid of him – which was more than she did herself.

'I am delighted to have been of assistance. I hope you have suffered no ill effects.'

'Oh, no. I'm sure we're all fine now. Goodbye.'

He bowed over her hand. '*Au revoir*, Mademoiselle Rose.'

As he said goodbye to the other two, she turned and hurried up the steps into the hotel foyer. At the desk she enquired whether there were any messages for her, but the reply was negative. She knew that Merry now had his HQ in Paris and had sent him a note suggesting that they might meet. She was disappointed that so far he had not responded. By the time she had collected her key the other two girls were behind her.

'Why did you give him the brush-off like that, Rose?' Violet demanded. 'He'd have shown us a good time if you'd let him.'

'Look, he was just being polite,' Rose said. 'You can't take advantage of people like that.'

'How do you know he was just being polite?' Angela said. 'I think he'd taken a real shine to you, Rose.'

'Oh, don't be silly!' Rose turned irritably towards the lift.

'I just don't understand you, Rose.' Violet pursued her. 'A really dishy gent offers to take you out and you turn him down flat.'

'It wasn't just me,' Rose pointed out.

'Is that the problem?' her friend asked. 'You're jealous because he asked all three of us out?'

'I am not jealous!' Rose said furiously. 'If you wanted to go with him you should have spoken up. Personally, I don't let strange men just pick me up on the street.'

They continued to protest until she reached her room, where she slammed the door before either of the other girls could follow her in. She threw the pretty little hat on to the bed, pulled off the jacket and sat down in front of the dressing table. Only then did she see that her hair was still in disarray from the struggle at the café and her mascara was smudged, and she blushed with furious embarrassment at the thought that she had sat drinking de Vaucourt's champagne in such a state. As she grabbed her hairbrush and began to pound her dark curls into submission she paused for the first time to wonder why she had reacted so violently. De Vaucourt had been charming and impeccably courteous. Why had she refused his offer to show them round? Was it simply that she did not want to impose on his good nature? She told herself that she had acted correctly but at a deeper level she was aware that this was not the real explanation. There was something about the look in his eyes when they first met her own which had disturbed an equilibrium it had taken her months to achieve.

After lunch she opted to stay in the hotel, giving the excuse that she was still shaken from the morning's events and wanted to rest. She was still hoping that Merry would get in touch. Suddenly she longed for his company. He was one of the very few people with whom she could have discussed the sudden tumult in her emotions. She was preparing to go down for dinner when the reception desk called to say that a gentleman was waiting for her. She completed her make-up in a hurry and almost ran to the lift, expecting to find the lanky figure of Merry in the foyer. Instead, she found herself face to face with Lucien de Vaucourt.

He was holding a bouquet of pink roses, which he offered to her with a little bow.

'Mademoiselle Rose, I hope you will forgive me for pursuing you but I could not let our encounter this morning end so inconclusively. I understand very well that you thought my offer this morning was simply a formality. I hope that this will convince you that it was more than that. I shall be most honoured if you will let me take you out to dinner.'

Rose was silent, struggling with contrary impulses. Her cautious nature insisted that she knew nothing of this man, other than what he had told her himself. On the other hand, his smile, the look in his eyes, the memory of the strong, supportive arm she had held called to something deeper than caution. She said, 'Do you mean just me? Or the other two girls as well?'

He made a slight, humorous grimace. 'If you feel that it would be improper for you to come with me alone, by all means invite the other two young ladies. But I should much prefer it if we could dine *à deux*.'

Rose met his gaze. For an instant longer she hesitated, then, like a swimmer nerving herself for a dive, she caught her breath and said, 'All right. Thank you. I should like that very much.'

He took her to a small restaurant near the Place de l'Opéra and apologised for the limited menu, which seemed to Rose to be full of unheard-of luxuries. Over the meal he drew her out about her experiences with ENSA and her life as a dancer before the war. He seemed genuinely knowledgeable about the theatre, and particularly about dance. He recalled performances by Diaghilev's Ballets Russes, which he had seen as a very young man, but also spoke warmly of the famous Bluebell Girls, the English dance troupe that had for many years been the toast of Paris. For his part, he told her about his early career as an officer in a crack cavalry regiment and about growing up on the family estate near Bourges. It made her uncomfortable to think of the difference in their backgrounds but, beyond asking where she had grown up and what family she had in England, he did not press her for details. He would not say much about his wartime experiences, but he had a fund of humorous anecdotes relating to the way his people had coped with the German occupation. He was a born raconteur and very soon her initial awkwardness had given way to laughter. By the end of the meal they were chatting as easily as old friends.

Afterwards he took her to Montmartre and they strolled arm

in arm through the narrow streets and ended up in a little bar, where they sat at enamel-topped tables around a clear space of bare boards that served as a dance floor and watched a couple perform a violent Apache dance.

He seemed to be on friendly terms with a wide range of people, and when Rose mentioned the fact he smiled and responded, 'The Resistance created some surprising bedfellows. I shall always be grateful for the opportunity to have worked with so many people from all sorts of backgrounds, all bound together by one common aim.'

On the way back to her hotel he said, 'I should very much like to come and see your show. Is it really impossible?'

'I don't know,' she replied. 'We're at the British army camp outside Fontainebleau at the moment but I've no idea how long we shall be there. I suppose you could come out there one evening, but I don't know if we're allowed to invite civilians.'

He smiled. 'Don't worry about it. Leave it all to me. I'm sure I can arrange an invitation.'

In the foyer of the hotel he took her hand. 'I have enjoyed myself so much this evening. Thank you.'

'No, I must thank you,' she answered. 'It's been a lovely evening. I'm sorry if I was rather ungracious earlier.'

'You were not ungracious,' he said. 'I do not think that would be possible for you. You were extremely correct and I found that very attractive. If you had been too ready to accept my invitation I think perhaps we should not have met again. When do you have to return to your base?'

'Tomorrow, I'm afraid,' she said regretfully.

'What a shame.' He sighed but added with a smile, 'Never mind, I shall just have to come out to Fontainebleau to find you. We can meet again, can't we?'

She returned his smile. 'Yes, I'd like that.'

'Good.' He bent his head and kissed her hand. '*Au revoir, ma chère* Rose.'

'Goodnight,' she answered. 'And thank you again for a lovely evening.'

On collecting her key from the desk she found that at last there was a note from Merry, hastily scrawled on a piece of hotel notepaper.

Dear Rose,

Just a very quick note to say I'm so sorry I missed you. I was out of town when your message arrived and have only just returned. I called this evening, hoping to catch you, but I understand you have gone out to dinner 'with a gentleman' – I wonder who the lucky man is! Unfortunately, I have just received orders to shift our HQ farther north to be nearer to the front line so we are off tomorrow. What a bind! I would love to have had a chance to catch up with you and hear all your news. Still, I've no doubt you and your company will be following us north very soon, so perhaps we shall meet then. Meanwhile, take care.

Love,
Merry

Rose looked at the letter in exasperation. If only he had come a little earlier! But then, she reflected, she would not have gone out with Lucien. It was a shame to have missed Merry but she could not pretend that she was sorry that things had worked out the way they had.

When she arrived back at the camp with the other girls the following afternoon she found Jack Holmes waiting for her in the converted mess hut where they gave their performances. Jack was still fat, even after seven months of army rations, and since they had come to France he had seen them through crisis after crisis with an unfailing energy and good temper that had forged a disparate and potentially volatile collection of artistes into a close unit. With Jack was a tall, slim man with fair hair and a deeply tanned face.

'Rose,' Jack greeted her, 'I want you to meet our newest recruit. This is Wilf Thompson. He's a dancer, so you'll be working closely together.'

'Pleased to meet you,' Wilf said, and Rose recognised the familiar accents of her south London childhood.

She shook hands and said hello, wondering as she did so what a man of his age, since by all appearances he was still in his early twenties, was doing in ENSA and not in one of the armed services. Jack obviously guessed her thoughts.

'Wilf was invalided out after the fighting at Monte Cassino,' he said.

'Bomb happy,' Wilf supplied with a grin. 'That's what we called it.'

Rose said quickly, 'I know what you mean. We played to men like you at the army rest camp near Amalfi.'

'You were in Italy?'

'Yes, for several months all through last winter.'

He looked intensely relieved. 'You'll have some idea what it was like, then.'

'Terrible,' Rose agreed. 'People over here have no idea.'

'No, they don't,' he said.

'Well,' Jack put in, heaving himself out of his chair, 'it's obvious you two are going to have a lot in common. I'll leave him to you, Rose. You can take him round and introduce him to the rest of the company. I've suggested he watches the show through tonight and then tomorrow we'll have a rehearsal with the band and if all goes well we can fit him into the bill tomorrow night. OK?'

In the course of the next hour Rose learned Wilf's story. It was not an uncommon one. The marvel was that more men had not finally broken as he had under the stress of what they had been through. It had begun with more than a year fighting his way across the deserts of North Africa, from the breakthrough at El Alamein to the final triumph in Tunis and the promise of a return to England and some desperately needed leave. Then had come the news that they were not, after all, to embark for England. Instead they were destined for the invasion of Italy. There had been the brief triumph of the landing at Salerno and then the reality of the long haul up the length of Italy, along roads mined and booby-trapped, under the incessant rain and the strafing of the Luftwaffe. Finally, after weeks living in a trench half full of water, under unremitting bombardment, Wilf's nerve had broken. He did not have to describe his condition to Rose. She had seen men like him, cringing and shivering, unable to sleep, diving for cover at the slightest noise.

Eventually he had been returned to England and declared unfit for further active service. Discharged into Civvy Street, he had hoped to return to his former career.

'I was in show business as a dancer before the war,' he told her, 'but when I looked for work back home there was nothing doing. Then someone offered me a job as a travelling salesman, selling kids' toys. I tried it for a week or two, but I couldn't stick it. It wasn't the job so much. It was the way people looked at me. I could see them thinking, 'What's he doing selling toys, instead of fighting for his country?' Some women actually came up to me and asked why I wasn't in uniform.'

'You should have told them,' Rose said. 'Tried to make them see what it was like.'

'I did, once or twice,' he replied. 'But you can't, you know. If they haven't been there, they've got no idea. They just think you must be a coward.' He stopped and lit a cigarette. Rose had noticed that he was constantly lighting up, inhaling a few breaths and then stubbing the cigarette out, only to light another a couple of minutes later. In between, his hands were never still, constantly reaching into his pockets or pulling at his clothes, while his eyes searched the NAAFI canteen where they sat as if he expected to see enemies in every corner.

'Anyway,' he went on, 'after a bit someone suggested I try ENSA. I didn't think they'd have me with my record but I went up to their HQ at Drury Lane and did an audition and they sent me out here.'

'Well, I'm very glad they did,' Rose said. 'But I'm afraid you may find you still have to answer the same questions.'

'I know that,' Wilf replied, 'but at least these chaps know what it's like. And at least I can feel I'm still doing my bit. Know what I mean?'

Rose agreed, but wondered silently whether he was going to find things more difficult than he anticipated. She introduced him to the rest of the company, who accepted him readily enough, and after the performance that evening he came to the hut they had been given as a combined dressing room and green room and warmly congratulated everyone. He was especially enthusiastic about the dancing.

'I'd heard terrible things about ENSA shows and I thought you might be . . . well, scraping the bottom of the barrel a bit, you know. But it's a real, slick professional show you've got here, Rose, and those girls of yours could go anywhere. As for your solo! Terrific stuff! You're a real star. You're wasted here.'

'I don't think so,' Rose said. 'I've been with the big, glossy ENSA shows that play the big theatres, but I'd much rather be with a small company like this that gets to perform right up where the fighting is. That's where we're really needed.'

'Good for you!' he said.

Next morning Rose went along to the mess hut to watch Wilf run through his act. She had learned that he was a tap dancer but she discovered now that there was more to his performance than that. To begin with it seemed to be a comedy turn, as he repeatedly muffed his steps and excused his mistakes with cheerful cockney humour. Then, quite suddenly, he seemed to get the hang of things and his gawky, uncoordinated movements resolved themselves into a slick, highly professional tap routine. Rose watched the transformation with delight. Not only had the bumbling comic disappeared, but the edgy, restless, shell-shocked man had been transformed into a sparkling, fleet-footed artiste, his face alight with the sheer pleasure of rhythmic movement.

When he came offstage she asked him, 'Why the comedy routine? You don't need that. Your tap dancing is brilliant.'

'Self-defence,' he said with a rueful grin. 'I found this out when I first joined up. I used to do the occasional turn in shows we put on in the regiment but I found out very quickly that if you just get up there and dance everyone thinks you must be a poofter. If you get 'em laughing first it seems to put them on your side, somehow.'

'Well, it's a great act, anyway,' Rose said. 'You even had the band laughing. That's always a good sign.'

That night, when she went to get dressed for the performance, she discovered that a bouquet of pink roses had been delivered for her. The note read, 'You see? I told you I would arrange an invitation.' Sure enough, when she went onstage, de Vaucourt was sitting in the front row, next to the commanding officer in charge of the camp. Afterwards, she was invited to the officers' mess, where she found him drinking brandy as if he were in the company of old friends.

'Rose!' he greeted her. 'You were magnificent! Such flair, such elegance! Don't you agree, Colonel?'

The colonel, who had up to that moment treated all the ENSA personnel as if they were a regrettable necessity, not susceptible to army discipline and therefore likely to be subversive, beamed at her and said, 'Oh, quite agree, old chap. Very – er – very pretty. Yes, good show!'

Shortly afterwards de Vaucourt declared that he must be on his way back to Paris and asked Rose to walk with him to his car. As they strolled he said, 'When can I take you out to dinner again?'

'I don't know,' she answered. 'I'm performing most evenings.'

'Lunch, then?'

'Perhaps. I'd have to clear it with Jack.'

He handed her his card. 'Telephone me at that number when you are able to get away. Any day will be fine. Will you do that?'

'Yes, all right. It might not be for a day or two.'

'Try to make it soon. I shall be waiting for your call.'

He kissed her hand, climbed into his car and drove off into the night. Rose headed for the hut she shared with the other girls, trying to rationalise an excitement she had not felt for a very long time.

After the show the next evening, Wilf sought her out.

'I've been thinking. We ought to get together, you and me,

and work out a routine. I reckon we could have a really good act going.'

Rose considered the idea and immediately saw its possibilities. She had been beginning to feel that her own solo items were getting a bit stale but she had lacked the incentive to develop anything new. The prospect of working with a partner was appealing.

'I think that's a great idea, Wilf,' she agreed. 'Let's get together tomorrow and see what we can come up with.' She paused, then added, 'But let's not say anything to the others yet. Not until we've got something to show them, eh?'

Wilf agreed, and that night Rose found herself lying awake, trying to decide on a suitable piece of music and thinking out possible moves and combinations of steps. The next day, they sneaked into the empty mess hut and prepared to rehearse. There was an old gramophone in one corner of the mess and a pile of dusty records, among which they found Cole Porter's 'Anything Goes'. Wilf wound up the machine and put it on. It was so scratched and filthy that the words were almost indistinguishable, but the beat was there and that was all they needed to get started.

Rose had felt instinctively that Wilf's style would match her own, and as soon as they started to dance she knew that she had found the perfect partner. A lot of the time they had no need to discuss what they were going to do. They each improvised and the other instinctively picked up the idea and carried it forward. At the end of an hour they had polished the movements almost to performance standard.

'Hey!' Wilf cried, at the end of the final run-through. 'How about that? Fred Astaire and Ginger Rogers have got nothing on us!'

The next day they asked Jack and the rest of the band to play for them and at the end of the number they all broke into spontaneous applause. That night, 'Anything Goes' was incorporated into the bill and brought the house down.

In her enthusiasm for the new venture Rose had pushed the thought of Lucien de Vaucourt to the back of her mind, but as soon as she woke the next morning the idea came to her that she would ask Jack for some time off and arrange to meet him for lunch. What was more, she decided, she would ask him to come and see the show again, so she could demonstrate the new number. The prospect was so enjoyable that she sang to herself as she went in search of the manager.

Jack was in the dressing-room hut, with a piece of paper in his hand. Rose said cheerily, 'Morning, Jack. Listen, I've come to ask a favour. Can you do without me for an hour or two? I've got a hot date in Paris.'

Jack looked at her for a moment. Then he said, 'Sorry, ducks. No can do. I'm afraid your date will have to cool down. We're on the move.'

14

'Ferrucio is here. He wants to talk to us.'

Armando put his head through the trapdoor leading into the loft where Nick Macdonald kept his radio. Richard looked up from encoding a message. 'I'll be back to finish this in time for your next scheduled transmission, Nick. It looks as if something may be brewing.'

Ferrucio Parri was the commissar of the Giustizia e Libertà brigade of the Partito d'Azione, who now controlled the whole of Emilia Romagna, the next province, just beyond the mountains to the east. As a representative of the CLN, the Committee of National Liberation, his authority was considerable. Richard knew that if he had made the dangerous journey across the mountains something important must be afoot. He climbed down the ladder from the loft, followed by Nick, and crossed the yard to the farmhouse, where Ferrucio was waiting. He wasted no time in coming to the point.

'We have a job for you,' he said with a grin that exposed a row of sharply pointed teeth, giving his face a curiously animal quality. 'With the Allies in control of Florence and attacking all along the Gothic Line, it can only be a matter of days before they reach this valley. Things are getting too hot for the Germans and our intelligence suggests that they are planning a withdrawal from Fornovolasco. We suggest that you mount an ambush here,' he stabbed at a map with a nicotine-stained finger, 'where the road passes through this ravine. Mortars placed on the cliffs on either side should cause enough confusion to give you the advantage.'

'We don't have mortars,' Armando objected.

'No,' said Ferrucio, 'but the Garibaldini up at Carregine do.'

'We're going to be working with the Garibaldini?' Armando exclaimed.

'We must all cooperate,' Ferrucio said. 'If we start to squabble among ourselves we are lost.'

Armando frowned. 'I don't like working with the communists. And why have they got mortars, when we haven't?' He darted a look at Richard, which all but accused him of holding back essential supplies.

Richard said quietly, 'I think we should concentrate on the plan. We can talk about this later.'

'There is a second element,' Ferrucio went on, 'and this is where you and your men come in. According to our intelligence, the commander of the German force in this area, General Hoffmann, has set up his HQ here,' the finger prodded the map again, 'in the Villa Bonaventura. It used to be the residence of a wealthy wine merchant until the Nazis requisitioned it. If we can eliminate, or better still capture, him, it would be a great coup and prevent, or at least postpone, any counter-attack if the initial ambush is successful. The High Command feels that your men, aided by the expertise of our British friend here, would be best suited to this enterprise. How do you feel about that?'

Armando's expression changed from sulky suspicion to enthusiasm. 'Of course. We shall be honoured! Ricardo, you agree?'

'If the conditions are right,' Richard said cautiously. 'We need to know a lot more about the location and the defences before we commit ourselves.'

For the next hour they studied maps and intelligence reports. Finally Richard said, 'OK. On the information we have it looks feasible. When is this due to happen?'

'Soon,' Ferrucio replied. 'It could be within a week.'

It was agreed that they should rendezvous with the rest of the brigade five days later. They spent the intervening time assembling their forces, many of whom were dispersed around the valley for greater security, checking weapons and packing stores. Most of the band were to take part in the ambush with the rest of the brigade. Only a select group, headed by Richard and Armando, were to go to the Villa Bonaventura. Richard spent most of his time with them, putting them through some intensive extra training. Nick Macdonald begged to be included, complaining that he always missed any excitement, but Richard was adamant.

'We can't afford to lose you, Nick. Radio contact is the most vital part of the whole operation.'

At noon on the appointed day, they moved to a clearing in the forest above the gorge where the ambush was to take place. Richard knew that the numbers of the partisans had grown enormously, but he could not suppress a thrill of excitement as he became aware of the size of the gathering. It was not easy to estimate at first sight, since those who had already arrived were encamped in the fringes of the forest, hidden from aerial reconnaissance. But once they were in among them it became clear that there were several hundred men, all of them well armed and organised.

They found Ferrucio in the tent that had been set up as command HQ, with George Oldham, another British officer who was working with the group from Carregine.

'Intelligence reports suggest that the German force is preparing to leave,' Ferrucio said. 'It seems probable that they will reach this spot early tomorrow morning.'

'Well,' Richard said, 'I must say I'm impressed. I'm beginning to think that this might actually work.'

'Don't worry about this end of the operation,' George said with a grin. 'You've got the sticky job. I wish you luck with it.'

Outside the tent, Antonia was brewing acorn coffee over a Primus stove. Richard exchanged looks with Armando, who raised his eyebrows and hands in a gesture of defeat.

'You shouldn't be here,' Richard said.

She met his eyes unsmilingly. 'You were glad to have me around last time.'

'I know. And I've no doubt we shall be glad of you again, when the fighting starts. But don't you understand that we worry about you – Armando and I?'

Her face softened. 'As I worry about you. Do you think it is easy for me to sit in Castelnuovo, knowing you are risking your lives out here?'

Richard sighed and shook his head. It was useless to argue.

The Villa Bonaventura was roughly three hours' march to the east and Richard and Armando planned to set out with their men at midnight, so as to reach it just before dawn. At the appointed hour the assault party set off, Armando at the head, Richard bringing up the rear. Each man was dressed in dark clothing, his face blackened with charcoal from the fire, and all were heavily armed. For some time they marched in silence, descending a winding track that led down to the valley. At the bottom of the slope they reached the main road and the signal was passed back to halt and lie low. Very soon Richard understood the reason, as the silhouettes of two German soldiers passed across his field of vision, outlined against the night sky. Once the patrol had disappeared into the darkness the men flitted across the road on silent feet and the march resumed.

By 3 a.m. they were crouching in a ditch beside a lane leading to the villa. Leaving the men in the charge of Silvano, Richard and Armando made their way through a vineyard to a point where they could look down on their target. It was a spacious building, completely surrounded by a high wall except for the point where an imposing wrought-iron gate led to the main entrance. Two sentries were on duty outside the gate, and as they watched two more, with dogs on leashes, passed across the front of the building.

Richard whispered, 'To stand any chance of getting inside we need to take out those two at the gate without alerting the rest.'

'Not easy,' Armando murmured. 'They look pretty wide awake from here.'

'There's one good thing,' Richard went on. 'The vines grow right up to the wall, except where the road cuts through. We can use them as cover. Let's see how often that dog patrol passes.'

After watching for a further twenty minutes they withdrew and spent some time huddled in the ditch, drawing up their plan of attack. Half an hour before dawn they led their men through the vineyard to take up their positions.

Richard crept forward until he reached the last row of vines in front of the villa. Flat on his stomach, he inched his way along the base of them until he lay only a few yards from one of the sentries. As Armando had said, the man seemed alert, but fortunately he was concentrating on the road. Beyond him, Richard could just make out the figure of the second sentry. He glanced at his watch. Four minutes to go. He had not allowed any too much time. He hoped Sasha, the powerfully built Russian ex-POW whom he had chosen as his opposite number, was in position. As the hands of his watch reached the agreed time he heard a sound from farther down the road – the sound of a drunken tenor voice singing 'O Sole Mio'. Both sentries jumped forward, unslinging their rifles, and one called out a challenge. Silently Richard launched himself across the intervening space. There was no time for thought. This was what his training at Arisaig had been all about, and in spite of the years that had passed he acted instinctively. He was aware of the impact with his opponent's body, the smell of unwashed clothes and stale sweat, the rasp of an unshaven chin under his hand as he forced the man's head back, his fingers clamped over his mouth. His other hand, carrying the knife, made a swift, horizontal stroke and he heard a faint, liquid gargle and something warm and sticky flowed over his wrist. Then the body in his grasp went limp and he laid it on the ground.

Looking across the road, he saw that Sasha had disposed of his victim with equal efficiency. Meanwhile, in a swift rush, two columns of men filled the verges on either side, while Armando, the drunken singer, joined Richard at the gate.

'I'm glad you were quick off the mark,' he whispered. 'I fancy that fellow was inclined to shoot first and ask questions afterwards.'

A postern gate proved to be unlocked and Richard led the

way through it. On the far side the drive was lined for a short distance with shrubs, giving cover until they were thirty yards from the house. Beyond that there was nothing but an open sweep of gravel. The front door, an imposingly solid affair, was closed and the windows were shuttered. Richard turned and gestured to the men behind him and two groups silently detached themselves and circled through the gardens towards the rear of the house. Richard waited until he thought they had had time to reach their positions and then he reached for something hanging from his belt.

'Let's see if we can stir up the ant's nest a bit, shall we?'

He had never been much good at games at school, but there was one event he had shown a talent for and that was throwing the cricket ball. The grenade whistled through the air and landed on the porch. While their ears were still ringing from the explosion Richard and Armando were racing towards the door, followed by the rest of their men. The grenade had blown the door inwards and already the hallway was filled with running figures and the clatter of boots on marble floors. Men in various states of undress, most of them armed, appeared on the staircase. Richard squeezed the trigger of his Sten gun and some of them fell, while others scrambled back to the safety of the upper storey. At his side, Armando dealt with the men in the hallway.

After that there was nothing but confusion. Richard could hear rending wood as the rest of his men forced an entry at the rear, but he did not wait for them to join him. As agreed beforehand, he led his men up the stairs while Armando and the rest cleared the ground floor. It seemed likely that the general would have been asleep in one of the bedrooms when the attack began. Men had been posted in the grounds of the villa to watch for anyone attempting to escape, but Richard was hoping to seize their quarry before the element of surprise wore off. In frenzied haste he flung open door after door along the corridor. The first two rooms were empty, their occupants having already either joined the fighting or decamped. Open windows and the sound of shots from the garden told their own story. In the next, two sleepy men in the act of pulling on their boots meekly raised their hands in surrender and were left under guard, to be dealt with later. As he opened the door of the fourth room a bullet sang over Richard's head, so close that he felt the wind of it, and ricocheted off the marble tiles on the opposite wall. He flung himself through the door in a rolling dive, while a shot from one of the men covering him from behind elicited a yell of pain. A German officer sagged on to the bed, clutching the arm from which a service revolver now dangled uselessly.

Richard levelled his gun at the man. 'Where is the general?'

The other man regarded him with malicious contempt. 'What general?'

'General Hoffmann. Don't waste my time.' He was speaking German, glad that he had picked up enough during his time in occupied France for this.

The answer was a brief, bitter laugh. 'Bad luck! The general left last night, for a meeting in Bologna.'

Richard stared at him for a moment, trying to determine whether he was telling the truth. Then he turned to the two men behind him. 'Francisco, take him downstairs and watch him. He's coming with us. Sasha, come with me.'

He completed his search, discovering the principal bedroom, the bed obviously undisturbed. It seemed the wounded officer had been telling the truth. Swearing under his breath, Richard turned back towards the stairs. As he rounded a corner he stopped abruptly at the sight of a German soldier who had apparently evaded their net. He was standing at the top of the stairs, his revolver in both hands, arms extended over the banister rail towards the hallway below – and from below came the sound of Armando's voice, issuing orders. It would be obvious to anyone who the leader of the attackers was; the one man to shoot if you had the chance.

Richard raised his Sten and pulled the trigger. Nothing happened. The mechanism had jammed. His revolver was in its holster and he could not afford the split second needed to reach for it. Without hesitation he launched himself bodily at the German. He felt the impact as he struck him in the middle of the back and heard the gun go off close to his head, immediately followed by a rending of wood as the banisters gave way under their combined weight. There was a brief, panic-stricken sensation of falling followed by a crushing impact and then a blank.

He came round to feel hands lifting him into a sitting position. Armando's voice penetrated the mist of semi-consciousness.

'Ricardo! Can you hear me? Where are you hurt?'

He didn't know, except that the left side of his body seemed to have gone numb and he could not remember for the moment where he was or what he was supposed to be doing.

'Ricardo, we have to leave. Can you walk?'

The urgency of the tone cut through the fog in his brain. 'Yes, yes,' he muttered, struggling to stand. He cried out as Armando grasped his left arm to help him up.

'What is it?'

'My arm! Can't move it. Think it's broken.'

Armando helped him to the stairs and sat him down. 'Did you find the general?'

'Not here,' Richard slurred. 'Left last night.'

It was Armando's turn to swear. Then he turned away and Richard heard him issuing rapid orders. Feet clattered as the men reassembled. The prisoners, except for the officers, were herded into one room and locked in. Then Armando returned.

'We must move. I caught one of them in the act of sending out an SOS. We'll have the Luftwaffe on us in a minute, unless we're very lucky. Can you walk?'

''Course,' Richard said. 'It's my arm that's broken, not my leg.'

Nevertheless, the stab of pain that shot up his arm and through his shoulder as he got to his feet caused him to stagger and grasp at Armando for support. Armando grabbed his good arm and drew it across his shoulders and half carried him out of the door and down the drive. Somehow, stumbling on the uneven ground and choking back cries of pain, he made it as far as the ditch where they had sheltered earlier. Here they paused, waiting for the last stragglers to come in, while Armando counted heads. Two of their number were missing and their comrades reported that they were quite definitely dead, so there was no sense in returning to look for them. Several others were wounded, fortunately none of them seriously. Field dressings were applied and one of the men, a shepherd who professed to have some experience of broken limbs, bound Richard's arm close to his side. Then they prepared to move out.

The next few hours were some of the most unpleasant Richard could remember, at any rate since Dunkirk. It was full daylight now and the way lay across open country until they reached the foothills. This late in the year the crops had all been harvested and the fields were bare, except where rows of vines gave some cover. Slinking along between them, or creeping close to hedges, they made use of what concealment they could find, their ears alert all the time for the sound of aircraft. The strapping on Richard's arm helped to lessen the jarring but every step sent a stab of pain through the left half of his body. Down here the sun was still fierce, even this late in the year, and before long his throat was parched and his shaken body cried out for water, but Armando clutched his good arm and urged him forward.

At one point they all flattened themselves against the earth as they heard aircraft approaching. Three Me 109s appeared, circling the position of the villa, and it seemed they must be spotted within minutes. Then suddenly all three broke off the search and sped away northwards and a cheer went up from the sheltering men as a formation of American Thunderbolts appeared out of a light morning haze and went in pursuit.

At last they reached the foothills and the fringes of the forest. As soon as they were under the shelter of the trees Armando called a halt, and Richard sank down on a fallen tree trunk. Armando squatted beside him and held out a canteen of water.

'I have to thank you. Sasha says the man you brought down was about to shoot me. You saved my life.'

'What happened to him – the German?' Richard asked.

'He fell, too, when the banisters gave way. But he fell head first. His neck was broken. Are you in much pain?'

Richard grimaced. 'I've felt better. And it was all a waste of time. The bloody general wasn't even there. So much for Intelligence!'

'Perhaps it wasn't entirely a waste of time,' Armando said. 'We have three prisoners for you to interrogate, when you are up to it. Also I made sure that all the radio equipment was completely destroyed, so their communications will be disrupted for a while. And then there are these.' He produced a sheaf of papers from inside his jacket. 'They were on the radio operator's desk. I don't know if they are useful at all.'

Richard rested the papers on his knee and flicked through them with his good hand. 'Signals traffic. Coded, of course, but that doesn't seem to be too much of a problem to the boffins back at HQ. They could give us some very useful information about enemy dispositions. Well done, *amico*. We'll send these through as soon as we can find a courier to take them.'

A shout ended the conversation. 'Listen!'

It was superfluous. They had all heard the rumble of heavy gunfire in the distance.

'The ambush!' Armando said. 'The battle has started.'

They marched on, up the winding track. It was much harder going than the outward journey for all of them, coming at the end of a long march and a night without sleep. For Richard it was pure hell. Every part of his body ached from the impact with the marble floor of the villa and his arm and shoulder seemed to be on fire. For most of the way the path was so narrow that they had to proceed in single file, which meant that Armando could no longer help him, and it seemed to be strewn with tree roots and tendrils of creeper, all lying in wait to trip him. Eventually he caught his foot and fell heavily, jarring his broken arm and momentarily losing consciousness for the second time.

When he came round he found he was being hoisted on to a muscular back and Sasha's voice said gruffly, 'Hold on, Major Ricardo. Don't worry. Sasha will not let you fall.'

Clutching round the Russian's neck with one arm and supported by strong hands from behind, he allowed himself to be borne along towards the sound of the gunfire. There was no doubt that there was a fierce battle going on in the valley, but it was impossible to determine from the noise which side had the upper hand. By the time they reached the leveller terrain above the ravine, however, the bombardment was diminishing. The heavy guns had fallen silent and only the occasional rattle of automatic weapons broke the silence.

'It's over,' Armando said. 'But who's won?'

Farther on they were halted by a shouted challenge. To their relief the words were in Italian and the password the one that had been agreed the day before. At once they were surrounded by an excited group of Garibaldini, and Richard was lifted bodily off Sasha's back and laid gently in the shade of a huge chestnut tree.

'What happened?' he demanded. 'How did the battle go?'

'It was magnificent!' the leader exclaimed. 'Exactly as we planned. We felled a tree across the road and when the convoy stopped the mortars opened fire. The road was too narrow for the trucks to turn round. We disabled one tank and set another on fire. After that, they were a sitting target. Some of them ran for it. We picked most of them off before they got far. Ferrucio sent us to round up the stragglers.'

'Any casualties on our side?' Armando asked.

The other man shrugged. 'Some, I suppose. I didn't see many.'

Somebody knelt beside Richard and offered him a leather bottle. It contained grappa, the fierce local spirit. He swallowed, choked, and took another mouthful. The spirit burned his throat but brought a welcome numbness to the rest of him. He was vaguely aware of the sound of axes at work and then a makeshift stretcher was laid beside him, contrived from the trunks of a pair of saplings with blankets stretched between them. With Armando's help he eased himself on to it and four muscular young men lifted the supporting poles on to their shoulders. He made the rest of the journey lulled into a half-doze by the grappa and the gently swaying motion of the litter.

This pleasant drowsiness was abruptly dispelled by the sound of a woman's scream. He opened his eyes and attempted to sit up. They were back at the tent where they had gathered the night before, and it was Antonia who had screamed. He heard Armando call, half-laughingly, 'It's all right, *cara*! It's all right! He's only wounded. A broken arm, nothing worse. Calm yourself.'

Richard was carried into the tent and laid on the ground and Antonia bent over him, her face stern though her eyes were full of tears.

'So, what is all this? A broken arm, is that all? And you have yourself carried back here, just to frighten me. How did you break it?'

'Fell downstairs,' Richard said apologetically. 'Careless of me.'

'Don't scold him, Antonia,' her brother said. 'He saved my life. He fell when he threw himself on a man who was about to shoot me.'

Antonia looked at him, then back at Richard. 'Then he is forgiven. Let me see this arm.'

There followed a painful interlude while the arm was unstrapped and the sleeve of his battledress jacket cut away. 'Do you mind?' he protested. 'That's army property. I'll have to . . . aah!' The sentence died as she ran her hands along his arm.

'It's broken all right,' she announced.

'Can you set it?' Armando asked.

'No. I don't have the skill. I shall take him to the hospital.'

'No!' Richard protested. 'It's too risky. It worked once. You can't expect to do it twice.'

Silvano stepped forward out of the shadows. 'There is a doctor in Vergemoli. He set my cousin's arm once, when we were kids. He is on our side. We could take him there.'

Ferrucio came into the tent and Richard raised himself on his elbow. 'Ferrucio, congratulations. I hear the ambush was a success.'

Ferrucio grinned his feral grin. 'A complete success. We captured three armoured cars and destroyed several tanks. Almost the entire force were either killed or captured. Very few escaped. You will tell your High Command that the partisans now govern in the Garfagnana, no?'

'I'll tell them,' Richard promised.

Antonia had been examining the contents of her medical case. 'I have one dose of morphine left. That will get you through until we reach the doctor. We must hope that he has some form of anaesthetic.'

As it turned out, he did not, and the ensuing moments were such that Richard did not care to recall later. But when the arm had been set and bound with a splint Antonia appeared at his bedside with a cup.

'Drink. It is a herbal mixture that has been used for generations in these villages to help women through the pains of childbirth. I don't know what goes into it, but I have seen it give great relief. Come, drink, *caro mio*.'

The concoction was so bitter that he had difficulty in swallowing it, but a few minutes later a pleasant numbness seeped through his limbs. He closed his eyes, but as his conscious mind relinquished control, images of the previous night took possession of his brain. He twisted his head restlessly, trying to dislodge them, and Antonia stroked his face and murmured, 'Sleep, *caro*. You're quite safe here.'

He looked up at her, but her face was blurred and he was not sure whether it was the drug or because there were tears in his eyes.

'I'm not a murderer, Tonia!'

'Of course not. No one is accusing you.'

'I killed a man in cold blood.'

'To save Armando's life.'

'No, before that. The poor bloody sentry. Just an ordinary soldier, doing his job. I cut his throat.'

'This is war, my love. He would have cut yours, if circumstances had been different. Think what they did to Gianni.'

He was losing his grasp on reality, and memories of his training at Arisaig became mixed with pictures from the previous night's battle.

'I'm not a killer!' he protested. 'They made me into one. All I ever wanted was to sing.'

'And so you will,' she assured him, 'soon, when this war is over. For now, you are a soldier fighting against a cruel and evil enemy. The Good Lord will forgive you for what you have done – and I bless you for the help you have given to my people.'

'You're not going to like this,' said Nick Macdonald.

Richard looked up from cleaning his revolver. 'What am I not going to like?' he demanded irritably. His broken arm was healing but it still ached when he tried to use it, especially in the damp November weather, and it made him short tempered. His radio operator laid a piece of paper on the table in front of him. Richard read it through twice and looked up.

'Are you sure you decoded this correctly?'

'Quite sure.'

Richard looked at the order from TAC HQ again. 'They're mad!' he said. 'If we pass on this order we're as good as signing the death warrant of all the people we've been working with.'

'I know,' Nick said simply. 'But High Command obviously doesn't understand the situation here.'

Richard thought for a moment. 'It could be a mistake. Don't mention this to anyone for the time being. We'll wait until we get definite confirmation.'

He went out into the yard and found Armando instructing a group of recruits in how to set an explosive charge.

'I need a word, when you've got a moment,' he said casually.

Armando looked at his face and turned to one of his lieutenants. 'Carry on for me, Francisco.'

Back in the farmhouse kitchen Richard showed him the signal. 'Of course,' he said, 'we could always say it had come over so garbled that we couldn't make head or tail of it.'

Armando studied the paper in silence for a moment. Then he looked at Richard, and his eyes were hard. 'You are here as a liaison officer only. I am not bound to obey your orders.'

'I'm not attempting to give you orders,' Richard replied. 'I can only pass on the instructions given me from above. You don't have to act on them.'

'Good!' said Armando, turning away. 'Because I have no intention of doing so.'

Richard felt a throb of pain greater than the ache in his arm. 'Armando, that order didn't come from me. If you decide to ignore it, I'm with you all the way. You know that.'

Armando shook his head. 'No, you will be ordered back. They will send a plane for you, and you will go back to England.'

'No, I won't!' Richard declared passionately. 'I don't care what orders I'm given. Even if they send a plane – which they won't – I shall refuse to get on it. They can court-martial me if they like, but I won't leave you and the others to fend for yourselves.' His common sense told him he was being foolhardy but for once he let his gut instinct rule him.

Slowly Armando turned back. His face softened and Richard saw tears come into his eyes. The next moment he was caught in a close embrace. 'Forgive me,' Armando said, releasing him. 'I should know you better by now. But how can your High Command do this to us? When we have fought so hard? We thought victory was just around the corner. Are the British and the Americans just going to sit on their hands through another winter, while we starve to death or are hunted down by the Nazis?'

'I suppose,' Richard said heavily, 'that they must have good strategic reasons for halting the advance. You know how impossible it is to fight through these mountains in the winter. I think perhaps that General Alexander honestly believes that the best way for the partisans to survive is to go home and try to pretend to be normal citizens.'

'And meanwhile our young men are taken off to Germany as forced labour, our bases are destroyed and our stores are taken over by the enemy. Has Alexander any conception of the numbers involved, that he thinks we can just disappear? Does he know what these *mongoli* are like? They are animals! If we move out, they will move in and rape and pillage unimpeded. I won't do it, Ricardo! I can't do that to my men!'

'Of course you can't,' Richard said quietly. 'I've told you,' he went on, 'I'm only passing on the message. You're in command and I'll fall in with whatever you decide. But say nothing to the others yet. Wait until we get confirmation, or otherwise.'

Confirmation was forthcoming all too soon. That evening

they gathered round the wireless set as usual to listen to Radio Italia Combatte, the voice of the Allied armies in Italy. General Alexander's message was broadcast in good Italian, without any attempt at code. The partisans were to desist from operations until further notice. No more supplies would be sent. They were advised to pack up and return to their homes.

'So now,' Armando said grimly, 'the Germans know that all they have to do is come and get us!'

15

The little convoy ground slowly along the deeply potholed road – a jeep, a bus, a truck and a motorcycle. Ahead of them the land was flat and colourless, marked only by the occasional stark outline of a building gutted by shellfire. Above, the sky was a uniform blanket of gunmetal-grey cloud, from which a steady, chill drizzle fell, adding to the water that already filled the bomb craters and turned the fields on either side of the road into a sea of mud. Rose slipped off her shoes and drew up her knees so that she could hold her icy feet in her gloved hands. They had been travelling all day and her bones ached from the constant jolting, and she felt cold to the very centre of her being.

'How much farther, do you think?' asked Maisie, who sat beside her.

Rose shook her head. 'God knows! I'm beginning to think the place doesn't exist. I think someone back in England put his finger on a pre-war map and said, "Send them there," without realising that it had been bombed out of existence years ago.'

'What's it called?' said Maisie. 'Nij-megen?'

'I don't think you pronounce the "j". More like "Nighmegen".'

'Far-megen, you mean,' said Maisie. 'I wish it was bloody nigh!'

They were jolted out of their lethargy by the bus coming to a sudden halt. Rose peered forward. There had never been much light and now the short winter day was almost over. The jeep that was leading the way had been halted by an army patrol and she could see the lieutenant who was escorting them speaking to one of the men. After a moment, he came back to the bus and climbed in.

'Sorry, everyone. Seems there's a bridge down over the canal up ahead. We're going to have to find another way round.'

'This is bloody ridiculous!' expostulated Leighton Dwyer, the company's male vocalist. 'We're all going to go down with double pneumonia at this rate. I vote we turn round and go back to Antwerp.'

'Hear, hear,' said his wife Ann, the other half of the duo.

'Listen!' Jack lumbered to his feet. 'There's lads up there who haven't had their boots off or seen a hot meal in days. They're looking forward to a bit of light relief – and by God we're going to give it to them. All agreed?'

'I'm with you, Jack,' came Wilf's voice from the back of the bus.

'And so are we,' Rose said. 'Aren't we, girls?'

The response, if not enthusiastic, was at least in agreement. The officer went back to his jeep and the whole convoy turned itself round with much grinding of gears and headed back the way it had come. Rose closed her eyes, lulled into an exhausted doze by the motion of the vehicle. She was not sure whether it was a dream or just a pleasant fantasy, but for a moment she thought she was back in Paris, having dinner with Lucien. Paris seemed a long time ago now. For nearly two months they had been grinding their way through Belgium and Holland, from one shattered village to another along the front line. They had had a brief break in Brussels, in the luxury of a proper hotel, which had been requisitioned as a rest centre for troops withdrawn from the battlefield. Now they were off again.

She woke again to the sound of voices. The bus was stationary.

'Are we there?' she mumbled to Maisie.

'Some hopes!' the other girl answered. 'I don't know what's gone wrong now.'

The lieutenant was talking to Jack at the front of the bus and Rose saw him hand over a map. She rubbed the condensation off her window and peered out. Ahead and to one side of her she could see the jeep, tilted at an angle while the driver hunched over one wheel, apparently struggling with something. The lieutenant had got out again and Rose leaned forward and said, 'What's going on, Jack?'

'The jeep's got a puncture and the nuts are seized on the wheel. Lieutenant Jamieson suggests we carry on without them. He thinks we're not more than a few miles from the place now.'

'Then for Christ's sake let's get on!' said Dwyer. 'Before we all perish from exposure.'

Jack started the engine again and they edged forward past the jeep and on, deeper into the forest. They had covered scarcely a mile, by Rose's reckoning, before the brakes were again applied, so sharply that they were all jolted forward against the seat in front. Peering out once more, Rose saw a figure in army uniform, holding up his hand and blocking the road. Jack leaned out of his window and called, 'What's up, Sarge?'

'You are!' came the reply. 'Up the wrong bloody creek!'

The sergeant moved forward and climbed into the front of the bus.

'Who the bleeding 'ell are you, anyway?' he demanded.

'We're ENSA,' replied Jack, with some dignity. 'We're on our way to Nijmegen.'

'No you effing well ain't!' was the retort. 'Not up this road, anyway. Jerry's dug in about two hundred yards down there. If I hadn't stopped you you'd have needed to tell your jokes in bloody German!'

With great difficulty the bus and the truck containing their props turned round and once again they headed back the way they had come. The lieutenant and his driver were still wrestling with the wheel on the jeep when they got back to them. When Jack explained what had happened they decided to abandon the vehicle and got into the bus with the rest.

The lieutenant said, 'I suggest we go back to that village we passed a dozen miles or so back. I know it has been heavily shelled but there must be at least one building with a roof on it. We'll shelter there for the night and try again tomorrow morning.'

No one had the energy to argue, so they set off once again. This village was no different from others they had passed through in the last month, the streets full of rubble, many of the houses reduced to crumbling ruins. Rose gazed out as the bus inched cautiously up the main street. In the darkness it was impossible to see what remained of the homes that had once housed ordinary, simple people. There were only gaunt silhouettes blurred by the unending rain.

The bus came to a standstill in what had once been the main square. Once the engine was switched off they could hear the distant gunfire that had become such a regular accompaniment to their daily life that now they only noticed it at moments like this. The village itself was silent and deserted.

Lieutenant Jamieson said, 'Wait here, all of you. I'll take my men and have a scout round. Don't leave the bus until I tell you. There could be unexploded shells lying around. We'll be as quick as we can.'

Rose watched him go, then dragged herself wearily out of her seat, unfolding arms and legs stiff from sitting and aching with cold, and looked at the five girls who were her special responsibility. Maisie was grim and silent, but in control. Alice was sniffing and shivering but Violet beside her had an arm around her and was whispering encouragement. In the seat behind, Angela was crouched double, her arms across her stomach and her face tense and pale.

Rose leaned over to her. 'What's wrong, Angie?'

The girl shook her head silently but her companion, Liz, whispered, 'It's her period. She's really bad and she's running out of STs.'

'Has she had any aspirin?' Rose asked.

'We ran out hours ago.'

'OK. I'll see what I can do.'

A request for aspirin elicited a reluctant response from Ann Dwyer. 'I was keeping these last two for an emergency. I get terrible migraine and I think I've got one coming on.'

'Thanks, you're an angel,' Rose replied, taking them.

Whispered enquiries among the girls, however, failed to produce the much-needed sanitary towels. Rose was still trying to think of a solution when the soldiers returned.

'One end of the church is still more or less intact,' Jamieson announced. 'It's the best we can do, I'm afraid. At least it's a roof over our heads. Follow me, and don't stray off the track.'

They climbed out of the bus and plodded single file after the faint glimmer of the lieutenant's torch. The church smelt of damp and of the smoke from a fire that had blackened the walls of one transept, but at least it was out of the wind. The tower had collapsed through the roof of the sanctuary, leaving it open to the sky, but, as Jamieson had said, the far end of the nave was almost undamaged. They filed into the pews and sat in huddled silence, as if they were waiting for a service to begin.

Jack clapped his hands together. 'Now then, we can't sit here all night without a bit of heat. Some of you lads give me a hand to break up some of these pews so we can get a fire going.'

'You can't do that!' said Dwyer, scandalised. 'It's a church.'

Jack looked at him for a moment, then he nodded towards the ruined sanctuary. 'After that lot, I don't think they're going to miss a bit of furniture, do you?'

Dwyer looked chastened. 'No, of course not. No, you're right,' he said, and got up.

Jack began wrenching at one end of a pew. Someone found a chunk of masonry and started smashing at the wood, reducing it to splinters. Someone else ripped the pages from a hymn book to serve as kindling.

Wilf came over to Rose and put an arm round her shoulders. 'You OK?'

'Just about. Nothing that a nice hot cuppa wouldn't cure. You don't happen to have a kettle and a packet of tea in your pocket, do you?'

''Fraid not,' Wilf said. 'But hang on a mo! There must be shops in a village this size. Perhaps we could find some.'

He called Jamieson over and suggested the idea to him. The officer looked dubious. 'In my experience places like this have usually been pretty thoroughly looted. You're unlikely to find anything worth having and it's a hazardous business looking. Most of these buildings are very unstable. They could collapse on you without warning.'

'I think it's worth a try,' Wilf said obstinately. 'These ladies need something hot inside them. I don't mind going, if someone else will come with me to lend a hand.'

'All right,' said Jamieson. 'Take White and Peters with you, but for God's sake be careful.'

The two corporals joined Wilf and they all moved towards the door. Rose went after them. 'I'm coming with you.'

'No, you stay here,' Wilf said. 'We can manage.'

'No, I'm coming,' she insisted. 'There's things we need and you men wouldn't know where to look for them.'

They picked their way across the square and found what had clearly been a row of small shops. The sign above the first declared it to have been a bakery but the interior had been gutted by fire. The second sold grain and agricultural equipment. The third appeared to have been a grocer's but, as Jamieson had predicted, everything easily consumable had been removed from the shelves.

'What about an ordinary house?' Rose suggested. 'There might be stuff in someone's kitchen.'

They moved on down the street. The rain had ceased at last and a full moon was making fleeting appearances through rags of cloud. They stopped in front of what must once have been a substantial residence. The whole of the front wall had collapsed, leaving the rooms open to view, their furnishings more or less intact. Like a child's doll's house, Rose thought.

'Right,' Wilf said. 'Let's try here. Kitchen will be at the back, presumably.'

They had to climb over a mound of rubble to get into the front hall, and then their way was blocked by a fallen door. The stairs leading to the first floor were still standing, however. While the men struggled with the door Rose said, 'I'm going to try up here.'

'Don't do that, miss,' one of the soldiers called. 'That staircase could come down if you put any weight on it.'

'Don't worry,' Rose answered. 'I'm not very heavy.'

Step by step, keeping close to the wall, she felt her way up the stairs. Just below the top one of the treads gave under her foot with an ominous creak but she stepped over it and gained the landing. She guessed that the master of the house and his wife would have occupied one of the front bedrooms. She prayed there had been a wife, and that she was a woman who had not yet reached the menopause. The passageway leading to the front had acquired a disconcerting slope, but seemed firm enough under her feet. As she crept forward she could hear the three men banging cupboard doors open in the kitchen.

As she stepped into the first bedroom the moon came out fully from behind the clouds. It was a strange feeling to walk into the brightly lit, fully furnished room, with its missing fourth wall – like being on a stage set. Rose pause and looked around. A double bed – that was hopeful. And on the far side of the room was a chest of drawers. She opened the top one. It was full of socks and underpants, quite obviously male. The next one down was more hopeful, containing flannelette knickers and woollen vests, sensible rather than glamorous but definitely a woman's. Rose slid her hand under the clothes and felt about. Her fingers encountered a paper wrapping. Triumphantly she drew the packet out. She did not need the moonlight to tell her it was what she was looking for. She stuffed it into the front of her coat and turned back towards the door.

From below Wilf's voice called, 'Come on, Rose. We've got what we came for. What are you doing up there? Trying on a new wardrobe?'

'Coming,' Rose called. She moved into the passageway and then froze. She had heard a sound, so faint that she thought it might have been her imagination. Then it came again, low and weak, but quite unmistakable to anyone who had heard it before. The sound of a baby crying.

'Rose!' called Wilf again, impatiently.

'Wait! Shut up a minute!' she called back. 'I heard something.'

'Heard what? Rose, be careful!'

The sound was coming from one of the rooms at the back of the house. Rose opened the door and retched at the smell of urine and blood and excrement. There was less light here and for a moment she could see nothing. Then she made out the shape of a bed and a huddled shape upon it. The child's cries were coming from somewhere on the bed.

Rose turned and called down the stairs. 'Wilf, come up here. Bring a torch. There's a baby here and someone . . . I think, I can't tell. Hurry!' She heard his feet on the stairs and remembered to call, 'Watch that next-to-last step!' A moment later he was beside her, a torch in his hand.

'Bloody hell!'

Together they crept over to the bed. From a tangle of bedclothes a white face looked up at them, eyes wide with terror, and a faint hoarse whisper issued from the cracked lips.

'What does she say?' Wilf asked.

'I don't know,' Rose replied. 'I think she thinks we're Germans.'

She leaned over the bed and said softly, as reassuringly as she knew how, 'It's all right. We're English. *Anglais*. We're going to help you. Let me look.'

Rose had never had any desire to be a nurse, nor had she ever been present at a birth. Her knowledge of what was required was limited to old wives' gossip and the scene of the birth of Melanie's child in *Gone with the Wind*. The birth itself was over, however, and the tiny child lay, bloodstained but undamaged, against its mother's side. All that was needed was to cut the umbilical cord, for which she commandeered Wilf's shoelaces and his penknife. Then between them they lifted mother and baby out of the soiled and fetid bed and wrapped them in clean sheets and blankets taken from the next room. By this time, the two corporals had come upstairs and stood helplessly at the bedroom door. Wilf delivered the mother into the arms of the stronger of the two and Rose, following with the baby, felt a lump rise in her throat as the big man cradled her, tenderly, reverently, and began the slow, cautious descent of the stairs.

Back at the church a good fire was blazing and some of the company had brought a couple of the costume hampers from the truck. The members of the company were incongruously decked out in velvet cloaks and feather boas. Someone had rigged up a tripod over the fire and suspended from it a big metal fire bucket full of water. The sight of the stalwart Corporal White and his burden produced screams of horror, which changed to cries of amazement and distress when Rose showed them the child. A pile of hassocks became an improvised couch and the woman was laid upon it, close to the fire, while Valerie, the only one among them who had ever had a child, took charge.

'What on earth was she doing there?' Maisie asked.

'Left behind in the rush to get out, I imagine,' Jamieson replied.

'You mean to say her own people ran away and left her to give birth all on her own?'

'Looks like it,' the officer said laconically.

Wilf and the other two had not found tea but they had acquired a bag of coffee and a couple of large pans and even, amazingly, several cans of condensed milk. Normally Rose loathed drinks made with the sickly-sweet stuff, but that night it tasted like nectar. She cradled the new mother in her lap and fed her spoonfuls of milk diluted with warm water, and after a while a little colour came back into her face. Meanwhile Valerie bathed the baby in water from the fire bucket and wrapped it up in strips torn from one of the sheets. Jamieson tried to question the girl in English and French but succeeded only in ascertaining that her name was Marie.

'She obviously only speaks Dutch,' he said. 'But at least I think she's understood that we mean her no harm.'

Rose drew Angela to one side and gave her the packet she had been carrying inside her coat and the girl gratefully retired to a sheltered corner and came back looking very much happier. By that time, some bottles of wine had appeared and were being passed from hand to hand. It was some time before they realised that they were drinking the communion wine.

'I don't think He'd mind, under the circumstances, do you?' said Jack.

Eventually, they stretched themselves on the wooden pews or huddled together on the flagstones around the fire and slept intermittently, while the soldiers took turns to keep watch.

Towards dawn Rose fell into a deeper sleep, and when she woke it was light and the girl, Marie, was sitting up supported by Valerie and feeding her baby. When Rose knelt beside them the girl looked up and whispered, '*Danke* – Tank you.'

Rose touched her arm and smiled, then looked at Valerie. 'How is she?'

'Very weak,' was the answer. 'But that's not surprising. Poor kid. She can't be more than sixteen or seventeen. And there's no sign of a wedding ring, you notice.'

'What on earth are we going to do with the two of them now?' Rose asked.

It was a question that was repeated in different forms as the others woke up.

'We could take her with us to Nijmegen, I suppose,' Jack suggested.

'Into a battle zone? Are you mad?' Valerie returned. 'She needs to be in hospital.'

'If only the jeep wasn't u/s we could send her back in that,' Jamieson said.

'Strikes me we'd all better go back and take her with us,' Leighton Dwyer suggested hopefully.

Jamieson lifted his head sharply. 'Hang on! Listen!'

At that moment Peters, who had been on watch outside, appeared in the doorway. 'Sir, there's a convoy coming up.'

'Ours?'

'Yes, sir.'

Twenty minutes later Marie and her baby had been dispatched in an ambulance to the nearest field hospital and they were all back in the bus, jolting along in the middle of a long line of troop carriers and supply vehicles. At midday they finally arrived in Nijmegen.

'Christ Almighty! They expect us to put on a show here?' said Dwyer.

The same thought was in all their minds, though they said nothing. At first sight Nijmegen seemed as deserted as the village where they had spent the night. Then they began to see signs that life went on – a fugitive, underground life to be sure, but one that refused to be extinguished. A woman emerged from a cellar, a basket on her arm, and scurried along the street to disappear into another. Two filthy children poked their heads above a shattered wall and cheered the convoy as it passed. A man rode a bicycle down the street at a furious pace, swerving crazily to avoid the shell holes. In some areas little remained that stood higher than three or four feet, and the sound of gunfire was continuous. The windows of the coach buzzed and Rose could feel the vibration from the explosions deep in her own chest.

Incredibly, in the centre of the town, some kind of community hall still stood, and it was to this that they were directed. There was a gaping hole in the roof of the auditorium and a puddle had collected in the seats beneath it, but the stage area was more or less intact. There was even electricity for the lights.

'Mad, isn't it?' grinned the young sergeant who had been detailed to help them. 'You won't believe this, but the power supply comes from the other side of the river.'

'You mean, from behind the German lines?' Wilf said. 'Why don't they cut it off?'

'I guess the engineers are Dutch and haven't let on,' the boy said. 'Either that, or the Jerries are too thick to work out which switch to throw.'

'Well, long may it last,' said Jack. 'Come on, folks, let's get busy. We've got a show to do.'

'God knows who to,' said Dwyer.

But by seven o'clock a long line of men had formed outside the hall. Squinting through the gap in the curtains, Rose saw the seats filling up with soldiers. Their faces and uniforms were caked in mud and many were swathed in filthy bandages, but there was a buzz of excited talk. Very soon, the auditorium was wreathed in cigarette smoke and the smell of unwashed bodies. Hugging her greatcoat over a flimsy costume, Rose shivered and hoped she would not pull a muscle. She and the other girls had all been exercising but in this unheated atmosphere it was impossible to keep warm.

The show opened with a high-kicking number from the dancers, always guaranteed to get a warm reception from the sex-starved troops. Almost simultaneously, the Germans opened up a fresh barrage, directed straight at the town, and a Bofors gun started firing back from somewhere close by, making it almost impossible to hear the beat of the music. They managed to keep more or less together, however, and the applause at the end had little to do with artistic appreciation. Valerie, the comedienne, was on next, but most of her punchlines were lost in the noise. Then Jack played a trumpet solo and the Dwyers sang a duet.

The first half was due to close with a big ensemble number, involving the Dwyers, all the girls and Wilf. They were halfway through when there was a splintering crash and a large window on one side of the auditorium was blown in, scattering shards of glass over the audience and on to the stage. Rose was knocked off her feet by the blast and for a few seconds she thought she had lost both sight and hearing. Then sound came back and the dust cleared and she staggered to her feet. There was a sharp pain in her leg and she looked down to see a splinter of wood protruding from her thigh. She jerked it out and looked around for something to staunch the blood. Around her the other performers were picking themselves up. Maisie had blood running from a cut on her forehead and Ann was tying a handkerchief round her husband's forearm. Down in the orchestra pit the musicians were shaking dust and broken glass from their instruments, but as far as Rose could see no one was seriously hurt. In the auditorium, a few soldiers were being attended to by medics and others were clearing glass and pieces of wood from the seats, but there was no sign of panic.

A soldier with a Red Cross armband jumped up on to the stage and came over to Rose. 'Hold still, miss. Let's have a look at that, shall we?'

She winced as he swabbed the wound with disinfectant and stuck a plaster over it.

'There you are, good as new.'

She thanked him and he moved on to attend to Maisie. Jack hauled his bulk on to the stage and asked, 'OK everyone? Anyone badly hurt?'

They looked at each other and shook their heads. It seemed too good to be true, but no one had suffered worse than cuts and bruises, though they were all trembling from the shock. Then Rose realised for the first time that one person was unaccounted for.

'Where's Wilf?' she asked.

She found him at the back of the stage, huddled into a corner with his arms over his head. She crouched beside him and put her arms round him. 'It's all right, Wilf. The bombardment seems to have stopped. Everyone's OK.'

He raised his pale face to hers and muttered, 'I'm sorry! I'm sorry!'

'There's nothing to be sorry about,' she told him. 'You just took cover, that's all. Come on, let's go back to the others, shall we?'

The rest of the company was busy clearing debris off the stage. Rose looked out into the auditorium and got a shock. There, in the gloom, were rows of expectant faces.

'Jack!' she said urgently. 'Look!'

He looked. So did the others.

'They're expecting us to finish the show,' Rose whispered.

Jack took in a slow breath. 'So they are. Well, are we going to disappoint them? What do you say, folks?'

'No!' said Violet.

'No!' echoed the other girls, rather less firmly.

''Course not,' said Wilf, and gave a high-pitched, shaky laugh. 'You know what they say. The show must go on!'

'Right!' said Jack. He turned towards the audience. 'Sorry about the interruption, lads. If somebody will sweep the stage while the cast get changed for the next number, the show will resume in approximately five minutes.'

Rose was afraid that the clapping and stamping that followed would complete the destruction that the German shell had begun.

'Blimey!' Wilf remarked, his voice stronger now. 'I've heard of bringing the house down, but this is going a bit too far if you ask me.'

Brussels, in the winter of 1944, was a brilliant city. While the armies battled it out along the River Scheldt, Brussels became the headquarters of every organisation involved in the conflict and a rest centre for troops withdrawn from the line. It was the place where men and women came to relax, to forget the war for a few hours and to seek entertainment, and entertainment was provided in plenty. For Rose and the company of *Lighten Up!*, returning to Brussels was like being reprieved from the torments of the damned, and yet, after the grim reality of the battle front, there was something brittle and ephemeral about the gaiety. Not that that stopped them from making the most of proper beds and hot baths and a theatre to perform in without holes in the roof.

They had been in the city for only three days when Rose

entered the dressing room to find a bouquet of pink roses waiting for her. The card read, 'You see? You can't escape me so easily!'

Lucien was waiting for her after the show. He took her hands and kissed her on both cheeks, as if something had happened while they were apart to banish all formality between them. To Rose it seemed quite natural. It was only when she thought about it later that she realised that something had changed in their relationship. Lucien took her out to supper and afterwards they went dancing. She had thought that she was tired after the show, but somehow she acquired a new lease of life in his company. He wasn't a particularly good dancer – nothing like as good as Beau. Nothing like as good as . . . she stopped herself. She had to stop comparing people with Richard. That was all years ago, and anyway Richard was married – if he was still alive. Dancing with Lucien was a different experience. He held her close and they swayed dreamily to the music and she melted into the warmth and security of his embrace.

'How did you find me here?' she asked him at one point.

'Oh, I have my connections,' he replied, teasingly.

He came to collect her every evening after the performance. They danced until the small hours and then she went back to her hotel and slept until lunchtime.

'You're burning the candle at both ends, you are!' Wilf said grumpily.

Rose laughed. 'My candle burns at both ends/It will not last the night/But Oh my foes and Ah my friends/it gives a lovely light!'

He was not impressed. 'If you're not careful you'll be ill. You don't want to be laid up for Christmas.'

Two nights later Lucien said, 'Rose, *chérie*, will you have to work all over Christmas?'

'Why do you ask?' Rose said.

'I wondered if perhaps we might get away for a day or two. Back to Paris perhaps? I have a flat there and my servants are very discreet.'

Rose gazed at him. Her heart was beating very fast. 'I don't know, Lucien. I . . . I'm not sure if I can get away. Can I tell you tomorrow?'

He smiled at her. 'Of course. But, dear Rose, try to make the answer "yes".'

The next morning Jack called a meeting of the whole company.

'Great news, folks! We're all going home for Christmas! Two weeks' leave and passages booked on the ferry.'

While the others cheered Rose could only think that it might be possible to spend those two weeks with Lucien. A pageboy pushed his way through the group towards her.

'Telegram, mademoiselle.'

She ripped the envelope open and read, *Bet's baby born yesterday stop A little girl stop All well stop. Wish you could be here stop Love Mum.*

16

Merry scribbled his name at the bottom of the last chit, shuffled the papers together and pushed back his chair.

'What am I doing here, Kate?' he asked his secretary gloomily. 'I'm a musician, not a blasted desk-wallah.' He extended his hands dramatically. 'Look at these fingers! I shall be suffering from writer's cramp soon. How am I supposed to play the piano?'

'I'm sure you'll manage, Captain Merryweather,' thc secretary replied dryly. She looked at her watch. 'Shouldn't you be getting back to your hotel to get ready for tonight? I'm really looking forward to hearing the Warsaw Concerto.'

Merry softened his tone slightly. He and Kate were old adversaries. Though she now wore the uniform of a sergeant in the ATS he had recognised her at once as the formidable dragon who, before the war, had guarded the door of a successful booking agent whose favour he had often solicited, usually unsuccessfully. Now that the roles were reversed he had begun to recognise her virtues. 'It's nice of you to say so, but it doesn't alter the case. I don't want to give the occasional concert for brass hats. I want to be up at the front line, where I'm really needed.'

Kate raised a finger and cocked an ear towards the window.

In the silence they could both hear the distant thunder of the guns. 'Antwerp's near enough to the front line for me,' she said. 'The trouble is, you're too good at your job. If you weren't so efficient perhaps Colonel Black would let you go. Have you asked him?'

Merry sighed. 'Many times, Kate. Many times.'

He lapsed into silence, gazing out at the grey sky beyond the window. After a little he said, 'Is this war ever going to end? When I came over to France in August everyone was so optimistic. It seemed as if it must be all over within a month or so. Now here we are nearly at Christmas and we're bogged down roughly where we started in 1940.'

'The Germans can't hold out much longer, surely,' Kate commented.

'That's what everyone's being saying for months,' Merry said gloomily.

There was a tap on the door and a corporal put his head round it. 'Excuse me, sir. Colonel Black's here.'

'Here?' Merry exclaimed, starting up.

Before the corporal could speak Black was in the room.

'Merry, good to see you. How are you?'

'I'm very well, sir,' Merry replied automatically. There was something about Black's arrival, so perfectly on cue, that almost made him feel the gods had been listening to his complaints. 'We weren't expecting you. Why didn't you let me know you were coming over?'

'Sudden impulse,' said Black, smiling his genial smile. 'Got the offer of a ride on a plane that was heading this way. Thought I'd like to come to your concert.'

'I'm very flattered,' Merry said. 'Kate, can you rustle up some tea for Colonel Black, please?'

When the secretary had left Black's normally cheery expression darkened. 'Have you heard the news?' he asked, seating himself in front of Merry's desk.

'News?' Merry queried, returning to his own chair.

'About Glenn Miller?'

Merry sat up abruptly. Battlefield reverses were commonplace, but Glenn Miller was an icon to any musician. 'What about him?'

'Missing. Took off from an airfield in England yesterday, heading for Paris, and never arrived.'

'Shot down?'

Black shrugged. 'Presumably. No one knows. His plane disappeared off the radar and no one's seen hide nor hair of it since. The Germans haven't claimed any planes shot down, but there's no report of it landing somewhere else. So I guess we have to assume he's dead.'

'Dear God!' Merry said softly. 'Of all the lives to be lost in this bloody war . . . I wonder, if they'd known who was in that plane, do you think they'd have left it alone?'

'Who knows?' Black replied. 'I imagine they might think it would be a pretty effective blow to morale – particularly to the Americans.'

'And they'd be right,' Merry said. He felt as if this was the final straw to be added to the mounting depression that he had been experiencing for some days. 'What was he coming over here for?'

'Planning a series of concerts.'

'The Yanks'll be heartbroken. His band must be pretty cut up. They worshipped him.'

'Along with a lot of other people,' Black agreed. He straightened in his chair. 'However, we mustn't let it interfere with our plans. Everything ready for tonight?'

'I suppose so,' Merry said listlessly.

Black leaned towards him. 'What's up, old man? You look a bit down in the mouth. It's not just this news about Miller, is it?'

Merry made an effort to shake off his gloom. 'No, no. That's tragic, of course, but . . . well, I suppose I'm just a bit browned off with the war.'

'Felix OK?'

Merry caught his superior's eye and was grateful, not for the first time, for the unspoken understanding. 'Yes, so far as I know. He's stationed at Eindhoven. We manage to get together occasionally. He's flying a lot of ops over Germany, strafing railway lines and depots. As far as I can make out the weather is more of a problem than enemy aircraft but he doesn't like what he's doing. Says it goes against his sporting instincts to shoot a sitting target.'

'This war stopped being a sporting fight a long time ago,' Black said grimly. 'If it ever was one. So, if Felix is all right, there must be something else. What's the problem?'

'You know what it is,' Merry said. 'I hate being stuck in an office. I want to be out there with the men.'

Black sighed. 'Merry, I don't know what to do with you, I really don't! You're not a youngster any more. You did your bit in the desert. Why can't you settle for a quiet life?'

'I'm only thirty-two,' Merry protested. 'I'm hardly in my dotage.'

'I know that. But there're kids of twenty-two or three who can go out there and entertain the men in the trenches.'

'And there are ENSA performers in their fifties out there, too,' Merry said. 'I know. I've seen them.'

Black shook his head. 'I don't want to lose you, Merry. That's the truth. You've got too much to offer this sad old world and we're going to need you when the war's over. But if you're really pining to get back out there . . .'

'You'll let me go?' Merry said eagerly.

'I'll see what I can do. I have to find someone to take your place, for one thing. Now, shouldn't you be getting ready for this show tonight?'

As soon as he entered the concert hall Merry's depression left him. This was his world, the only one he really felt at home in. The sound of the orchestra tuning up, the hum of an expectant audience, sent a surge of adrenalin running through his veins. While he was playing he forgot everything – the war, his frustration at spending so much time on paperwork, even the regrettable fact that Felix had been unable to get leave to come and listen.

The Warsaw Concerto, written for the film *Dangerous Moonlight*, had been an instant hit and it was enthusiastically received at the end of that night's concert. Merry had just returned to the platform for the third time, in response to the applause, when he became aware of sudden movement in the front row of the dress circle. All the high-ranking officers who were the guests of honour were leaving their seats and heading rapidly towards the exit. Backstage rumour was rife, but there was no concrete information until George Black pushed his way through the pass door from the auditorium.

'Brilliant performance, old chap,' he said. 'But I'm afraid the reception's going to have to be cancelled. There's a hell of a flap on. Jerry has just launched a massive counter-attack through the Ardennes.'

Rose reached Wimborne in the afternoon of 17 December. This time she telephoned from the station and Jack Willis came and picked her up in the van he used to deliver his vegetables.

Her mother opened the cottage door to her and, when Rose embraced her, exclaimed, 'Careful! Careful! My hands are all over flour!'

'Never mind that,' Rose said. 'It's lovely to see you. How is everyone?'

'Oh, we're fine, fine.' Mrs Taylor's face glowed. 'The baby's gorgeous and as for Bet – well, you wouldn't know she'd just had a kid! Out there feeding the chickens, she was, when I went up there this morning.'

'No, really?' Rose laughed. 'A proper little farmer's wife!'

'Oh, she's that, all right,' her mother agreed. She looked at Rose. 'No regrets?'

'No,' Rose said firmly. 'No regrets. When can I see them?'

'We'll go up there shortly. Bet's dying to see you. But come and have a cup of tea first. I bet you're worn out, aren't you?'

'It's been a long journey,' Rose agreed, 'and the ferry crossing was horrible, really rough. But at least there are no submarines to worry about these days.'

Mrs Taylor put the kettle on and went back to stirring a concoction of some sort in a large mixing bowl.

'What's that going to be?' Rose asked.

Her mother sniffed. 'Christmas cake, supposed to be. One of them recipes they give out on the wireless of a morning. Mostly dried egg and grated carrot. Can't see it being much good, myself. Still, you've got to try, haven't you?'

Rose sighed nostalgically. 'Remember those Christmases before the war? Christmas cake covered in icing, and real almond paste; mince pies, Christmas puds, tangerines . . .'

'Oh, give over!' her mother exclaimed. 'I don't know when I

last saw a tangerine. I queued up for forty minutes the other day because someone said Simpson's had got oranges in, but by the time I got to the front of the queue they'd all gone.'

'Poor Mum,' Rose said. 'It's no fun keeping the home fires burning, is it.' She noticed as she spoke how her mother's once ample figure had shrunk, so that her clothes hung loosely about her.

'Oh, we manage,' her mother said. 'There's a lot of folk worse off than us. Jack Willis is always very good and, of course, Matthew's able to keep a little bit extra back in the way of milk and eggs. He's very fair, mind you. Everyone gets what's coming to them on the ration. But he wouldn't be human if he didn't hang on to anything going spare for his own family.' She looked Rose over. 'Anyway, what about you? You're nothing but skin and bone. Don't they feed you in them army camps?'

'Of course they do,' Rose said. 'And I can tell you, there's more in the shops and restaurants in France and Belgium than there is over here. I've just been working hard, that's all.'

'Restaurants, is it?' her mother said. 'And who's been taking you out to restaurants?'

'Really, Mother,' Rose said, refusing to be drawn, 'a girl can go into a restaurant without a man taking her, you know.'

'Oh yes?' her mother replied sceptically.

Rose changed the subject. 'Tell me about the baby. What's her name?'

'Victoria.' The glow returned to her mother's face. 'I thought it was a bit old fashioned but Bet and Matthew were set on it. Mind you, when they chose it they thought she'd be born just about in time for the victory celebrations. But Bet says, never mind. She may be a few months early but who cares about that? You wait till you see her. She's a little beauty!'

'How have the boys taken to her?'

'Oh, they think she's marvellous. Of course, Billy tries to pretend he's not really interested. He's at that sort of age. But Sam just adores her. Then, he's always been one for young creatures of all sorts. Puppies, kittens, babies – it's all the same to him.'

Rose had thought that meeting Matthew and Bet again would be easy this time. After all, they had said everything that needed saying when she was last at home, back in March. On the journey back her mind had been full of her parting with Lucien, so she had not given a great deal of thought to what she would say or do when she arrived.

He had called for her as usual after the show and had refrained, with his usual impeccable manners, from asking for her answer to his invitation all through supper. In the end she had had to bring it up herself.

'Lucien, about what you asked me yesterday . . .'

He gave her a rueful smile. 'The answer is going to be no, isn't it?'

She reached out impulsively and laid her hand on his sleeve. 'It is, but not for the reason you are thinking.' She explained about the opportunity for leave and the telegram from her mother, and when she had finished he lifted her hand to his lips.

'Then of course you must go home and see your family. I would not try to keep you from that. But this gives me hope, *chérie*. Hope that, when you come back, your answer will be different.' He paused. 'You will come back, won't you?'

She looked into his dark eyes and sighed unhappily. 'I don't know. There's no guarantee. We could be sent anywhere – the Faroe Islands, or even the Far East. Our boys are fighting in Burma and Malaya, as well as here.'

He gripped her fingers more tightly. 'I can't bear the thought that this might be the last time I shall see you. Promise me that, if you are sent to one of those places, somewhere too far for me to follow you, when the war is over you will come back. Please, dear Rose, promise me that.'

She swallowed. 'I don't know, Lucien. One thing this war's taught me is that you don't know what's round the corner. But I will try. I promise you that.'

'And you will write to me?'

'Yes, as long as you write back.'

She had given him her address in Wimborne and he gave her his card with his Paris address and scribbled the name of the hotel where he was staying in Brussels. He wanted to come and see her off at the station the next day, but she had asked him not to. Already the rest of the company was agog with curiosity about their relationship. She didn't want any embarrassing scenes on the platform.

Now, walking up the lane to the farm, that conversation in the restaurant in Brussels seemed to belong to a different life – or perhaps it had happened to a different person altogether. That was a cosmopolitan Rose, who had been entertained by Free French officers and Italian aristocrats from Cairo to Naples and had eaten in the best restaurants of Paris and Brussels. This now was Rose Taylor, the chorus girl from Lambeth. The girl who might have been Mrs Matthew Armitage.

Bet enfolded her in a long hug and Matthew kissed her chastely on the cheek, and Billy and Sam were shy for two minutes until she produced the Belgian chocolate she had brought back for them. It was when Bet placed the baby in her arms that she found it hard to restrain her tears. As a child she had never been particularly interested in dolls and, though she was very fond of Billy and Sam, she had been away from home forging her career as a dancer most of the time when they were small. And even when she was home she had done her best to avoid the messy business of feeding and changing nappies. Sometimes it seemed to her that she lacked the maternal instinct. But when she felt the tiny, warm, living creature in her arms something rose up within her, something primitive and visceral that filled her eyes with tears. She remembered Marie cradling her infant in the dawn light of the ruined church, the huge eyes in the waif-like face glowing with gratitude and love, and she suddenly wanted to break down and sob.

'Did Mum tell you what we're calling her?' Bet asked.

Rose nodded and cleared her throat. 'Victoria. I think that's smashing. She'll be a real victory baby.'

'She didn't tell you the rest, then?' Bet said with a smile.

'The rest?'

'Yes, her middle name.'

Matthew was looking at her. 'It's Rose,' he said. 'She's Victoria Rose.'

Bet had prepared high tea for the six of them and before long they were all chatting easily. Rose told them about finding Marie in the ruined village, but not about the night when the hall in Nijmegen had nearly been hit by a shell. She told them about Wilf and their new dance number, but for some reason she could not explain to herself, she avoided all mention of Lucien. She described Paris and Brussels, but not the roads of Normandy where horses, still widely used by the Germans to transport stores, lay dead and rotting by the roadside, or the flattened towns and villages along the River Scheldt in Holland. She talked about the welcome they had received from ordinary French and Belgian families, but not about the day she had nearly been mistaken for a collaborator.

When the meal was over, Matthew went out to lock up the animals for the night and Rose and her mother washed up, while Bet fed the baby. Standing at the sink, Rose was pierced by a sudden shaft of nostalgia. Once she had stood here every evening, washing the dishes while Matthew dried, and talking over the day's work on the farm – which cow was yielding less milk than she should, whether Pippin the old carthorse needed shoeing, how many eggs she had collected that morning. She glanced round at Bet, feeding her baby by the fire. But for the twist of fate that had brought Richard to Wimborne that New Year's Eve, that would have been her, not Bet. She calculated briefly. Nearly four years had passed. Probably she would have had a couple of kids by now. She had told her mother she had no regrets. Was it true? She remembered the souks of Cairo and the elegant promenades of Tunis and Tangiers and the Bay of Naples in the last of the autumn sunlight. She had sweated in the desert and shivered in the mountains of Italy and wept secretly under the bedclothes in hotel rooms and Nissen huts in a dozen different places, and often she had been very, very frightened. Would she have swapped it for the chance to be sitting by the fire like Bet, with a baby at her breast? She glanced round again and caught her sister's eye and smiled. Finishing the last of the dishes, she began to hum.

'What's that tune?' her mother asked. 'I don't think I've heard that one before.'

Rose smiled. 'Oh, it's a little number I heard in Paris. Edith Piaf sings it.'

At nine o'clock all conversation stopped as they gathered

round the wireless set to listen to the news. As she listened, it seemed to Rose that the contented warmth of the kitchen had been swept away by an icy wind. The German panzer divisions had made a totally unforeseen attack in the snowbound forests of the Ardennes and forced their way through the American lines. They had penetrated deep into Allied territory and the Americans were now making a stand in the vital crossroads town of Bastogne.

Bet said, her voice breaking with a distress that sounded like anger, 'I thought the Germans were beaten. Everyone's been saying they're on their last legs.'

'Don't tell me we're going to have another Dunkirk,' her mother begged.

'Of course not!' Rose said firmly. 'Our lads aren't going to let the Germans push them around this time. The Yanks were caught on the hop, that's all. They'll soon push the Huns back to where they started. Wait and see.'

Back at the cottage Rose found a small pile of Christmas cards waiting for her. There were cards from Merry and Felix and one from Monty and Dolly Prince and others from girls she had worked with over the years. Among them was one that gave her particular pleasure. Under a picture of a bulldog with Winston Churchill's face and a sprig of holly in his collar were the words: *Bet you thought you'd never hear from me again! Sorry it's been so long. Things were bad for a while but now I seem to have turned the corner. Got a new job, as a barmaid in a posh hotel in Cheam – live in, very cushy! Hope you have a marvellous Christmas. Love, Sally.*

Rose smiled as she read it. In spare moments over the last nine months she had wondered what had become of her old friend, but now she recalled what she had thought as she watched her walk away from their last meeting. 'Sally will be all right!' And it was true. Sally, whatever her faults, was a born survivor.

It was a low-key Christmas. There was little in the shops to buy for presents and less in the way of luxuries to eat. The Willises joined them at the farm for dinner but it was clear that they were missing Barbara, who had married her Canadian and been persuaded by him to join his parents in the safety of Vancouver. Jack had fattened a capon, as usual, and Matthew had managed to shoot a brace of pheasants, so they were better off than many families, and the kitchen was decorated with holly and paper chains, but they all found it hard to be festive.

In the morning they joined the rest of the village in the little church and after dinner they clustered round the radio to listen to the king, but their main focus of attention was on the news and the war report broadcast every evening after the nine o'clock bulletin from one of the war correspondents in the field. From this they learned that the fog, which had prevented Allied planes from taking off, had cleared and that they were now in action against the German forces, and that an all-out attack on Bastogne had been repelled. In the days that followed they heard how the various units of German troops were being cut off and captured, or forced back towards the Rhine. What had been nicknamed the Battle of the Bulge was almost over.

For Rose, the high spot of the holiday came when they all went in Jack Willis's van to the local cinema to see Laurence Olivier in *Henry V*. She recalled how, as a schoolgirl, she had been taken to see him in *Romeo and Juliet* at the Old Vic. She had not understood much of the play, but she had conceived a romantic passion for the actor, and the memory of that schoolgirl crush was now somehow involved with another recollection – of an afternoon in the cinema in Fairbourne watching Olivier as Heathcliff and feeling Richard's arm steal round her shoulders. She guessed that much of the language of *Henry V* was lost on the audience in the village cinema, but there was no mistaking the patriotic fire of the story, and Olivier's ringing battle cry of 'God for Harry, England and St George' was greeted with cheers that drowned out the soundtrack.

On 1 January she reported, with the rest of the company, at the ENSA headquarters in the Drury Lane Theatre. There was a chill of apprehension in her stomach as she greeted her companions. There was no guarantee that they would be working together in the future. They could be split up and sent off to fill gaps in other companies, anywhere in the world. Rose had worked with a variety of other groups over the years but seven months together, under Jack's good-natured command, had drawn them all close, and she suddenly felt that she lacked the energy or the courage to make a whole new set of relationships.

Wilf came over and hugged her. 'Cheer up, girl! We're into the finishing straight now.'

'Do you think so?' she asked.

'Got to be,' he answered. 'But listen, if the company's not staying together, what say we tell them that we've got our own act? That way at least we might both be sent to the same place.'

Rose hesitated. 'I've got the girls to think about, Wilf. We're a troupe, too. I wouldn't want to leave them in the lurch.'

'OK, tell them we all belong together,' Wilf said. 'A job lot – take us or leave us. OK?'

She smiled at him with sudden affection. 'OK. We can try.'

In the event, they need not have worried. The company was

to stay together and, to Rose's secret delight, they were to return to Brussels and carry on where they had left off. She sent a telegram to Lucien, and when they got out of the train in the Belgian capital the thought uppermost in her mind was that he might be waiting for her.

She saw him before he saw her, a distinguished dark head protruding above the hurrying crowd by the barrier. Her heart began to hammer and she quickened her step, so that when he turned and saw her she was already almost running. He came towards her and, without pausing for thought, she ran straight into his arms. He held her for a moment in a close embrace and she felt the same warm strength, the same sense of security, that she had felt the first time he offered her his arm. Then he held her off and kissed her tenderly on the cheek.

'My dear Rose, I'm so happy to have you back! I have been so lonely for you. But you look so well! The rest has done you good. How are your family?'

'They're all fine,' she told him, smiling into his eyes. 'I've missed you, too.'

Then she looked behind her. The girls were clustered together, trying not to giggle, wide eyed with curiosity. Jack was looking uncomfortable, as if he felt he should move in and break up this ecstatic reunion. Then she saw Wilf's face. He looked, she thought in that first instant, like an abandoned child. Then she remembered his past history and decided that probably it was the prospect of returning to the sound of the guns which had made him look so pale.

Lucien wanted her to have dinner with him but she persuaded him that she was too tired and really just needed an early night. He insisted, nevertheless, on driving her to her hotel.

'You won't disappear somewhere tomorrow, before we have a chance to be together, will you?' he asked.

She shook her head. 'They're bound to give us a day or two to get ourselves organised.'

'Then I'll pick you up at seven tomorrow evening,' he said.

Later that evening Jack led her to a quiet corner of the bar. 'Look, Rose,' he said, 'I know it's none of my business, but are you sure you know what you're doing with this French character?'

'This French character, as you put it,' Rose replied loftily, 'is the Baron Lucien de Vaucourt.'

'Are you sure?' Jack asked.

'Of course I'm sure. It's on his cards.'

'Anyone can have a card printed.'

'Well, why shouldn't he be?'

'I'm not saying he isn't. It just makes me wonder a bit, the way he seems to hang around Brussels waiting for you. Doesn't he have a job?'

'He's independently wealthy,' Rose said. 'His family own vineyards in Burgundy.'

'So he says.'

'Well, it's obvious, isn't it? I mean, he's obviously got money.'

'But how did he get it?'

'I've told you how! Look, he's a very well-respected man. Everywhere he goes people recognise him. He was a leader of the Resistance.'

'Do you know that for a fact?' Jack leaned across the table towards her. 'Rose, I'm not trying to be a killjoy. I'm just concerned for you. From what I've heard, there are a lot of people going around today telling everyone they were in the

Resistance when they actually spent the war doing something quite different.'

Rose had been restraining her growing anger up to this point but now her patience snapped. 'Look, Jack, I know you mean well but it really is none of your business. You don't know Lucien and I do. Let's leave it at that, shall we?'

'OK, OK.' He sat back and lifted his hands in a gesture of surrender. 'You're a grown-up person, and it's your life. Just don't take everything on trust. Get me?'

Rose went up to her room feeling shaken. She was fond of Jack and it distressed her to have argued with him. But his words had provoked a much deeper disquiet, which she tried hard to ignore. Before she could sleep, however, the problem had to be confronted. The fact was that she really knew nothing about Lucien except what he had told her himself. She had not met any of his family, or any friends other than casual acquaintances encountered in bars and restaurants. But, she told herself obstinately, she had the evidence of her own experience. Lucien was kind, courteous, generous. There was something about him which instilled complete confidence. Did it really matter if he had estates in Burgundy, or if he had been in the Resistance? He was still the same person.

By the following morning she had dismissed the suspicions aroused by Jack and concentrated her mind on the preparations for the next tour. There had been changes to the company. The Dwyers had dropped out on unspecified 'medical grounds' and had been replaced by an amply built Yorkshire woman who obviously fancied herself as the next Gracie Fields and an elderly man who did a speciality act with an accordion. They also had a new comic, which was a relief because, although they all liked Valerie, they were all thoroughly tired of her repertoire of jokes. So there was to be a ten-day settling-in period, trying out the show in locations around the city, before they set off for the front line again.

By evening, when Lucien picked her up, she had more or less forgotten her doubts, and by the time they had eaten dinner and moved on to a nightclub to dance she was convinced that Jack was just being 'an old woman'. Swaying gently in his arms she found herself wanting more than ever to be close to him and, as if he sensed her feelings, he held her tighter than usual until her head was resting on his shoulder and she could feel his body moving against hers.

Finally, at midnight, he whispered in her ear, 'Perhaps we should make this the last dance.'

'Must we?' she asked, drawing back to look into his face.

He smiled and pulled her to him again. 'I wondered – perhaps you might come back to my hotel – for a nightcap?'

She knew what he was suggesting. The moment had come for a decision, but she found that her mind was already made up.

'Yes,' she murmured dreamily. 'Why not?'

In the taxi he kissed her properly for the first time and she was amazed that it had not happened before. The kiss seemed so natural and his touch so familiar that she felt none of the panic, the urge to control her own desire, that had always intervened when any other man tried to make love to her. He whisked her through the hotel lobby without giving her time to feel embarrassed and when they reached his room, he took her in his arms and kissed her again and she felt every nerve in her body respond. She felt his deft fingers undoing her blouse and then his hand on her breast and dimly, at the back of her mind, her conscience said, *You shouldn't let a man do this unless you are married to him*. But also at the back of her mind was the memory of a spotty youth and a few minutes of painful fumbling. She had crossed that barrier already and there was no point in turning back now.

Lucien's lovemaking was everything she had known it would be – tender, considerate, experienced. What she had not expected was the power of her own desire and the urgency of an orgasm balanced on the cusp between pleasure and pain, so that she sobbed and moaned without restraint. Afterwards he cradled her against his shoulder and stroked her face and hair until she fell asleep.

She woke to a perfect recall of the night's events and a sense of triumph. Finally she had escaped the bonds of her mother's warnings and her own inhibitions. Finally, she was a woman in her own right, and she felt that she inhabited her body in a totally different way. Her mind wandered to the boy on the riverbank, whose name she no longer remembered, and then further back to Beau. If only she had had the courage to offer him what she had given Lucien last night. If only he had had the sophistication to persuade her to give herself up to him. Then she might not carry with her the pain of knowing that he had died alone and unfulfilled. Escaping that thought, her mind delved farther back. Suppose she had given herself to Richard, back in those distant summer days in Fairbourne? Would he have married her? Or would she still be left with that empty space in her life, that unanswered question? Had he loved her, as he claimed? Or had his interest faded with the summer? She would never know, and now Priscilla had him.

She looked at Lucien on the pillow beside her, his face smoothed by sleep into a youthfulness that touched her heart. Why, she wondered, had it never occurred to her that she might marry him? The thought had never crossed her mind. Would he propose to her now?

He opened his eyes and drew her to him. 'My sweet Rose,' he murmured, 'thank you. Thank you so much. You have made me a very, very happy man.'

That evening he met her with a bouquet of red roses and that night, and for the next nine nights, she slept in his arms. Neither of them spoke of the future.

17

Merry swung himself up into the front seat of the truck and turned the collar of his greatcoat up around his ears. For a brief moment he wondered what had possessed him to exchange his nice, warm office for this nomadic life in a snow-filled landscape. Then he heard Chubby Hawkes chuckling over something in the back of the truck and smiled quietly. He had got his wish, finally. George Black had sent a replacement to take over his job and Merry had been provided with a truck and a young Belgian corporal as a driver. Best of all, he had a band that consisted of four members of the original Merrymakers, who had apparently been conspiring to return to his command ever since they were separated in North Africa. For the last month they had traced the roads along the German's much-vaunted Siegfried Line, from Nijmegen to the mountains of the Ardennes, and yesterday they had heard the news that the Americans had broken through the defences and were heading towards the Rhine. With the Russian armies across the Oder and only forty miles from Berlin, they all knew that the end of the war was, at last, at hand.

The truck drove out of the temporary encampment where they had played the previous evening and began to follow a road that descended in a series of hairpin bends towards the valley below, the young driver going cautiously because the surface consisted of hard-packed ice and on either side snowdrifts four feet deep were ready to swallow them up. As they dropped lower, Merry could make out the outlines of a village in the valley, and his cheerful mood evaporated again. They had passed through so many places like this. He could make out dark shapes against the snow around the village. The larger ones, he knew from experience, would be cattle, killed by shellfire. The smaller ones, only just distinguishable from here, were the bodies of men – Germans, Americans, English, Belgians, soldiers and local people, all caught up in the vicious fighting that had swayed to and fro across the region for the last couple of months.

This village was no different from any of the others, few of the houses standing above ground-floor level, the inhabitants eking out existence in the cellars, from the steps of which they regarded the truck with total indifference. Here they were not welcomed as liberators. There had been too many armies, too many soldiers in different uniforms, and in the end the result was much the same. Then, a few hundred yards farther on, they rounded a bend and came upon a sight so different and so unexpected that Merry laid a hand on the driver's arm.

'Stop here a minute, Jean-Jacques.'

The truck came to a standstill and Chubby stuck his head through from the back. 'What's up?'

'Look,' Merry said.

Just ahead of them was a steep hillside covered in virgin snow, brilliant in the sunshine, and plodding up it was a little group of dark figures, five lads pulling home-made sledges.

'God, that takes me back!' Merry murmured.

Jean-Jacques smiled. 'Me, also. I had a sledge when I was a kid.'

The leading pair had reached the top of the hill and now

careered downwards, their whoops and yells of excitement clear in the frosty air. Merry smiled but said nothing. He had not been thinking of childhood games but of a New Year's Day at Wimborne when he and Felix had taken Bet Taylor's two boys sledging, to get them out of everyone's hair for an hour or two. They had gone reluctantly but in the end they had enjoyed it as much as Billy and Sam.

The rest of the band had climbed out of the back of the truck to see what was going on and Merry and Jean-Jacques joined them.

'Cor!' exclaimed Dave Shadwell, who played the saxophone. 'Doesn't it make you wish you were still a kid?'

'Makes me wish I had a sledge,' said Hank Walsh, the drummer.

The two leading boys had reached the bottom of the slope and were turning to start back up it. On an impulse Merry turned to Jean-Jacques. 'Go and ask them if they'll lend us their sledge for a bit. Tell them there's a couple of bars of chocolate in it for them.'

The driver looked at him for a moment as if he suspected that this was an example of the strange British sense of humour, then he turned and jogged across to the two boys. Merry watched him in animated conversation for a few minutes, then he came back with the two lads in tow.

'They want to see the chocolate.'

Merry dived into the cab and retrieved two bars of NAAFI chocolate. The boys looked at each other, nodded and held out their hands. Merry gave the older of the two one of the bars. 'This one now, and the other when we've finished,' he said. The boy grabbed the chocolate and his younger brother handed over the rope attached to the sledge.

'Right!' said Merry. 'Who's first?'

Once the deal had been reported to the other boys they readily handed over the second sledge and the five of them huddled in the truck, under the genial supervision of Chubby, who was constitutionally averse to any form of physical exercise. For the next hour Merry and the others took it in turns to toil up to the top of the hill and come skimming down, yelling as loudly as any of the kids. By the end of that time their trousers were soaked to the knee, their greatcoats plastered with snow and their hands inside their wet leather gloves aching from the cold, but they were breathless with laughter and tingling with exhilaration.

Having handed over considerably more chocolate than in the original agreement, they said goodbye to the boys and clambered back into the truck. At first, Merry was glowing from his exertions, but after a while he became uncomfortably aware of the sweat cooling on his body and the water in his clothes turning to ice in the unheated cabin. Before long he began to shiver and an ominous tightness gripped his chest.

Jean-Jacques noticed and asked, 'Are you all right, *patron*?'

'Just a bit chilly,' he responded. 'I'll be fine as soon as we get somewhere where I can take these wet clothes off.'

Their objective that night was a forward casualty clearing station, which they knew to be somewhere just behind the front line, though its exact location was uncertain. The sound of gunfire led them in the right direction and late in the day they entered a ruined village much like the one they had passed through earlier. It was here that the casualty station had been set up. Casualties were being treated in a series of damp cellars, where medics carried out their necessary operations by the light of oil lamps and candles. Forward of them, an infantry regiment was conducting an assault on a line of German strongpoints and the wounded were being brought in in such numbers that no one had the time or inclination to attend to Merry and his musicians. They huddled in a corner, feeling dispirited and useless. Shells were regularly falling in the streets so it was obviously impossible to offload the piano and set up to perform in their usual manner, but after a while Chubby and Dave risked going back to the truck and returned with their instruments. Carrying these, they began to make the rounds of the cellars where men lay waiting for attention, or for the ambulances that would take them back to hospitals in the rear.

Merry could hear them asking, 'Any requests, lads?'

And then the strains of 'If You Were the Only Girl in the World' or 'We'll Meet Again' echoed softly through the rabbit warren of interconnected cellars. They played that infuriating nonsense song that seemed to be on the wireless every time you turned it on – 'Maisie Dotes and Dosie Dotes'. And they played 'Abide with Me' and 'Bread of Heaven' and 'What a Friend We Have in Jesus' – except that the words Merry heard being sung were not the ones he had learned in Sunday school.

Meanwhile, Merry sat huddled in a blanket, as close as he could get to a paraffin stove, unable to stop shivering. Someone gave him a cup of hot, sweet tea, which he gulped gratefully, but he could not stomach the cold bully beef, which seemed to be the only food on offer. There was clearly going to be no chance of drying his clothes and every stretcher and camp bed was in use, so in the end he rolled himself in his blanket in a corner of the cellar and succeeded in falling into an uneasy doze, woken every so often by voices crying out in pain or calling for water.

When he woke it was morning and his chest was so painful that it was several minutes before he could get enough air into his lungs to be able to stand up. When he did, his head swam so that he had to put a hand on the wall to support himself. One of the medics gave him a couple of aspirins and a hot drink, which enabled him to get himself up the cellar steps and into the truck. The others greeted him with concern, but he assured them that he would be fine. It was just a chill.

All day in the truck, as they skidded and swayed along the icy roads towards their next destination, he alternately sweated and shivered, drifting in and out of consciousness. That evening, they arrived at a supply base farther behind the lines, where there were at least tents and a cookhouse and a mess hut established in a farmer's barn. Another medic gave him some more aspirin and he was, at last, able to change some of his clothes, and by evening he had succeeded in convincing himself that the worst was over. They put on a concert in the mess, which seemed to go down very well, although the piano keys swam before Merry's eyes and he had no idea how many wrong notes he had played. He managed to keep going until the performance was over. Then he stood up in response to the applause and the barn, with its oil lamps and its appreciative faces, whirled around him and disappeared into blackness.

Felix had just finished giving a bollocking to a new young pilot who had failed to keep his logbook up to date when the phone in his makeshift office rang. An unfamiliar female voice said, 'Squadron Leader Mountjoy?'

'Speaking.'

'My name is Sister Mary Lovell.' The voice had a gentle Irish brogue. 'I'm stationed at the military hospital outside Liège. I'm sorry to bother you, but do you happen to know a Captain Guy Merryweather?'

Felix felt a jolt in the pit of his stomach. 'Yes. He's a . . . a close friend. Is something wrong?'

'I'm very glad I've managed to contact you, Squadron Leader. The fact is, he's very poorly and he's been asking for you. We weren't sure to begin with who it was he meant because he's got a very high fever and he's delirious a lot of the time. He kept asking for someone called Felix and to start with we thought he was looking for his pet cat or something. Then he had one of his more lucid patches and he managed to say your name. It's taken me a while to track you down.'

'What's the matter with him?' Felix asked tensely.

'Double pneumonia. He was brought in two days ago. I gather he'd been up at the front line and got thoroughly soaked and chilled. We're treating him with a new drug, which is supposed to have excellent results in this sort of case, but . . . well, the thing is this. If you want to be sure of seeing him, I think you should try to get here as soon as possible.'

'You mean . . .' Felix had to stop and swallow before he could get the words out. '. . . you're telling me that he's going to die?'

'No, not in so many words. We may pull him through. I hope we shall. But he won't rest until he's seen you and that isn't helping. Is there any chance you could get here? I know I shouldn't really ask that, but . . .'

'I don't know,' Felix said. He was unable to order his thoughts. 'It won't be easy. But I'll try. Look, tell him you've spoken to me and I'll do my best to get there. Tell him to hang on. Will you do that?'

When he had put the phone down Felix went to the map pinned on the wall. From Eindhoven to Liège must be getting on for a hundred miles by road. A hundred miles over roads deep in frozen mud and clogged with army traffic. It could take him all night. He looked out of the window. There was about half an hour of daylight left. There would be no further operations today. For a while he paced the floor, wrestling with the contrary demands of duty and love. Then he picked up the phone and spoke to his WAAF secretary.

'Call my fitter and tell him to get my Spit ready for immediate take-off. And then ask Flight Lieutenant Hervey to come and see me, at once.'

When Hervey arrived Felix said, 'Listen, Pete, I've been called away on a special mission. It's all very hush-hush so I can't talk about it, but with any luck I'll be back before anything happens tomorrow morning. You're the senior flight lieut. I want you to hold the fort till I get back. OK?'

Hervey looked understandably puzzled but he was too well trained to ask questions. 'OK, Skip. I hope you're not getting into something dicey.'

Felix was pulling on his flying jacket. 'I don't think so. Should be a piece of cake. Just don't mention it to anyone if you can help it. The fewer people who know about it the better.'

Ten minutes later he was in the air. It was dark by the time he reached the airfield at Liège and they had to light the flarepath for him. It was some time since he had needed to do a night landing and he was glad to get the Spitfire down safely. Then came the business of explaining his sudden arrival to the authorities. He had a certain reputation in the force, however, and his story of a secret mission was not questioned. He was even loaned a jeep to take him into town. It took him some time to locate the hospital but at last, with a terrible sinking in his stomach, he reached the ward and asked for Sister Lovell.

'I'm Edward Mountjoy. You phoned me about Captain Merryweather.'

'Oh, Squadron Leader, you made it! I'm so glad. I hope I did right to call you.'

'Yes, of course. I'm very grateful to you.' And then the question he could hardly bring himself to ask. 'How is he?'

The nurse looked grave. 'I'll not try to hide it from you. He's very poorly indeed. But this new penicillin drug is supposed to be a wonderful thing. The doctor reckons if we can get him through tonight he stands a chance. Come along, I'll show you where he is.'

Felix followed her down the long ward with its rows of militarily tidy, white-sheeted beds. At the far end screens were drawn around one bed, and when the sister led Felix through them a young nurse who had been sitting by it rose quickly to her feet. Merry was propped up on pillows, his face white, except for two bright spots of red on skin that seemed to be stretched unnaturally tight across his cheekbones. Felix could hear his breathing, rapid and cffortful, and although his eyes were closed his lips moved incessantly, framing a low, urgent but incoherent plea. The nurse had been bathing his face with cold water but, at the sister's instruction, she put down the sponge and slipped away through the gap in the screens.

Sister Lovell laid a professional hand on Merry's wrist and shook her head.

'He's very weak. Try to get him to rest, if you can. That's what he needs more than anything. I'll leave you with him for a little while. If you want anything just call. The nurse will be near by.'

She went out through the screens and Felix moved closer to the bed. He reached out and laid a hand over Merry's, which was plucking restlessly at the sheet. It was burning to his touch.

'Merry, it's me, Felix,' he said, feeling oddly foolish and

inhibited. Merry made no response. Felix looked behind him. Through the gap in the screens he could see the bed on the far side of the ward, but the occupant appeared to be sleeping. He perched on the edge of the bed and leaned over Merry, smoothing his hand over his forehead, pushing back the lock of hair that persisted in defying army regulations. 'It's Felix, Merry. I'm here. It's all right. Everything's going to be all right.'

The muttering stopped and for a moment there was silence. Then Merry's eyes suddenly opened and his hand grasped at Felix's sleeve.

'Hold on to me, Felix,' he whispered hoarsely. 'Don't let me go!'

Felix cast one more glance behind him, then he leaned down and scooped Merry into his arms, laying his cool cheek against the burning face. 'I've got you,' he murmured. 'It's all right. You're safe now. I won't let you go.'

Merry reached up and for a few seconds he clung with a preternatural strength around Felix's shoulders. Then Felix felt his grip loosen, until he became a dead weight in his arms. He almost cried out for help until he realised that, though the stertorous breathing had quietened, it had not ceased and that Merry's eyelids had closed and his hands were still. He seemed to be sleeping. He went on holding him until his arms and shoulders ached with the strain and then, very carefully, he laid him back against the pillows. Merry murmured briefly, unintelligibly, and then was quiet again.

Keeping hold of his hand with one of his own, Felix reached out for the sponge that the nurse had left and began carefully to bathe Merry's face and neck. Feeling the need to keep a line of communication open, he said the first things that came into his head.

'What have you been up to, to get yourself in this state? I don't know, I turn my back on you for five minutes and look at you! Why couldn't you stay in Antwerp, where you were safe? Trouble with you is, you don't know when you're well off.'

The two crescents of dark lashes, more striking than ever against the pale skin, flickered slightly and the ghost of a smile hovered on the dry lips. Felix felt his throat constrict with the sudden upsurge of love. He glanced round. The dark space between the screens was empty. He leaned down and kissed Merry on the forehead, then laid his face against his friend's and whispered in his ear, 'I love you. You know that, don't you? I can't manage without you. You've got to hold on, for my sake. The war's nearly over. We've made it through this far. You can't let me down now.'

There was no answer, but he felt Merry turn his head a fraction so that his cheek pressed his own. He straightened up and went on with his sponging. After some time the sister came back and he looked up at her, but did not let go of the hand he held. She put her fingers on Merry's other wrist and regarded him for a few seconds with her head cocked to one side, then nodded and said, 'That's better. His pulse rate has come down a bit. Are you all right there, or shall I send the nurse back to do that?'

'No, I'll carry on,' Felix replied. 'I'm sure she's got other things to do.'

'Oh, no shortage of those!' Sister Lovell said, with grim humour. 'Right, then. Keep up the good work.'

Time passed. Someone brought Felix a cup of tea and a sandwich, which he ate automatically. Merry seemed to be either asleep or unconscious but Felix thought his hand felt a little cooler. Eventually a doctor came, and Felix was asked to wait outside the screens. Through the gap he watched the doctor as he took Merry's pulse and listened to his chest. Then he took from an attendant nurse a syringe, the size of which made Felix wince in sympathy, and injected the contents into Merry's thigh.

Felix heard him say, 'Well, maybe this stuff is the miracle cure they make it out to be. I thought we were going to lose this one earlier, but now I think we may just pull him through.'

'Well now,' said Sister Lovell, following him out into the ward, 'isn't that a mercy? Sure, it's wonderful what medicine can do . . .' She caught Felix's eye and he was almost sure that she winked. '. . . with a little help from our friends.'

Felix went back to the bedside and Merry opened his eyes and murmured, 'Thirsty. Need some water.'

Felix poured water from a jug on the locker by the bed and lifted his head so he could drink. Merry sighed and relaxed again. The ward was dark now, except for a distant glow from the nurse's desk, and the only sounds were heavy breathing and the occasional snore, punctuated at times by the groan of a man in pain. Felix was suddenly aware that he was very tired. He had been up at dawn and had flown two sorties that day, aside from his last-minute dash to Liège. He shifted from the bed to the chair, rested his forearms on the edge of the bed and his head on his arms and fell into a doze, which deepened by degrees into sleep.

He woke abruptly, stiff and chilled, aware that something had changed. He could no longer hear Merry's short, painful breaths. He sat up quickly and reached for his hand. It was still dark and it was a moment before he realised that Merry's eyes were open and fixed on him. His voice thick with sleep, he murmured, 'Hello, old chap. How are you feeling?'

It was a moment before there was any response. Then

Merry whispered huskily, 'You're real. I thought I was hallucinating.'

Felix stifled a yawn and shook the sleep out of his head. 'Yes, I'm real enough. Don't worry about that.' He touched Merry's forehead. It was cool and slightly clammy. 'Feeling any better?' he asked.

'I think so,' Merry answered. Then, 'Have you been here long?'

'Since this evening. I suppose I mean yesterday evening, You don't remember?'

'Did you pull me out of the well?'

Felix frowned. 'You haven't been in a well. You're here, in hospital, quite safe.'

Merry shook his head. 'I was falling down a deep, dark well, down and down. And I called out to you and asked you to hold on to me. And you reached out and grabbed my hand and pulled me up.'

Felix leaned closer and murmured, 'I was here then. You asked me to hold you, and I did. But there was no well.'

The hazel eyes gazed up into his own. 'You saved me,' Merry said. 'I was going. If you hadn't held on to me I should have gone right down. You saved my life.'

Felix swallowed hard and gripped his shoulder. 'It's a good job I was here, then.'

Somewhere at the far end of the ward a trolley rattled and then the lights came on. Felix sat up and looked at his watch. It was almost 6 a.m. He calculated rapidly. It would not be light enough to take off for another hour, but he had to get back to the airfield and go through the usual formalities. He looked at Merry. He had closed his eyes again, but his face had lost the drawn, taut look of the previous night.

Felix said, 'Merry, I'm going to have to go soon. I've got to get back to my squadron before anyone misses me, or there'll be hell to pay. Will you be all right now?'

Merry opened his eyes and there was a glint of amusement in them. 'You mean to say you're AWOL?'

Felix grinned back. 'I suppose you could say that.'

'Better get back then,' Merry said.

Felix found his hand and pressed it. 'I'm sorry I can't stay. I'd like to say I'll visit, but it's such a bloody long way. I can't keep on borrowing a Spit.'

'You borrowed a plane – to come here?'

'It was the only way to get here in time.'

'Christ!'

Felix said, 'I'll phone this evening to see how you are. You are on the mend, I can see that.'

Merry nodded weakly. 'I'll be OK. Don't worry. You get off. Don't want you facing a firing squad.'

'I don't think it'll come to that,' Felix said, smiling. He glanced round, then stooped quickly and kissed him once more. 'As soon as you're well enough, we'll get together somewhere. That's a promise. Take care!'

'And you. You're the one in the aeroplane.'

'Don't worry about me. I'll be fine.' Felix stood up and then hesitated. It was painfully hard to leave but, on the other hand, the consequences of lingering could be disastrous. He picked up his cap and raised a hand in farewell. ''Bye, old chap. See you soon.' Then he turned and walked away down the ward. He paused to speak to the sister on duty, who was not Sister Lovell, and asked her to promise to contact him if there was any change. Then he headed for the airfield.

As he brought the Spitfire into land at Eindhoven he was relieved to see that the airfield was quiet and the other planes were drawn up in their blast pens. Obviously, there had been no call to scramble, which meant he should not have been missed. So he was somewhat surprised to be greeted by his senior flight lieutenant as he climbed out of the cockpit. The young man looked worried.

'What's up, Pete?' Felix asked. 'Problem?'

'I'm not sure, Skip,' Hervey replied. 'The wingco's here and he doesn't seem to know anything about a special mission.'

'Well, of course he doesn't!' Felix said, trying to sound mildly testy. 'It's secret, isn't it? It was arranged at a higher level.' He patted the young man's arm. 'Don't worry. I'll sort it out. Where is he?'

'In your office. He's in a bit of a bate, I'm afraid.'

Wing Commander 'Chips' Chatterley was an old comrade of Felix's from the Battle of Britain. In fact, they both recognised that if Felix had not been missing for over a year he would probably have been equal, if not senior, in rank. Felix strolled into his office as casually as he could manage, skimmed his flying helmet on to a peg on the wall, and said insouciantly, 'Hello, Chips. How's tricks?'

Chatterley glowered at him from behind his desk. 'Where the hell have you been? And it's *sir*, if you don't mind.'

Felix dropped into a chair. He felt deathly tired but he knew that to win this battle he had to keep cool. 'I've been visiting a friend in hospital.' He had worked out on the way over that it was pointless to stick to the story of the secret mission. Chatterley could check up all too easily and if his deception was discovered it would only make things worse.

'You did what?' Chatterley exclaimed. 'You're telling me that you took a Spitfire in order to visit a friend in hospital?'

'He's in Liège. It's too far to go by road,' Felix said reasonably.

'So you just took off, without a by your leave or a word to anyone?'

Felix dropped his flippant manner. 'Look, Chips, he's a very old and dear friend and the sister phoned me from the hospital to say he was in a bad way and if I wanted to see him I had to get there quickly. It was the end of the day, I knew there wouldn't be any more ops and I could be back here before anyone had really noticed I'd gone. Which I should have been, if you hadn't happened to come by.'

'So you took one of His Majesty's aircraft for your mercy dash.'

'Only borrowed, old man. I've brought her back unharmed.'

'And suppose you'd met up with a couple of Me 109s? That could have been the end of an invaluable Spitfire – to say nothing of a bloody good pilot.'

'I haven't seen an Me 109 in weeks,' Felix pointed out. 'I think the Luftwaffe's saving them up for something.'

'That doesn't alter my case!' Chatterley snapped. 'All sorts of things might have happened – friendly ack-ack fire, engine failure, anything. Then you would have pranged a perfectly good plane on an unauthorised mission.'

'But I didn't,' Felix said. 'It's out there, safe and sound, and no one need be any the wiser.'

Chatterley glowered at him in silence for a moment and Felix could see him struggling to balance duty against friendship and regulations against expediency.

'By rights,' the wing commander said, 'I should take this to a higher authority. Have you considered the penalties for being absent without leave?'

'Yes, I know,' Felix agreed. 'The powers that be would feel they had to court-martial me. But just think of what would happen then. Imagine the effect of that on morale. Imagine the headlines in the papers.' He sketched a block in the air between them. 'BATTLE OF BRITAIN ACE COURT-MARTIALLED AFTER MERCY DASH TO BEDSIDE OF FRIEND. It wouldn't look good.'

Chatterley glared. 'Are you trying to blackmail me?'

'Of course not. I'm in no position to, am I? I'm just trying to point out the consequences, for both of us. I don't think our lords and masters would particularly want this landed in their laps, at this juncture, do you?'

Chatterley sat back and looked at him. Then he grinned. 'You're a cunning bastard, Ned Mountjoy!'

'Who, me? Surely not!' Felix replied meekly.

There was a pause. Then Chatterley said, 'By the way, this friend – all right, is he?'

'Yes, thank God! At least, he seemed to be on the mend when I left. They're filling him full of some new miracle drug – penny-something.'

'Penicillin? Yes, I heard about it.' Chatterley seemed to recall himself to the business in hand. 'Don't get the impression that I approve of what you did. It was thoroughly irresponsible. I mean, if it had been a family member, a brother say . . .' He remembered something and blushed. 'Sorry, bad example, but you know what I mean.'

'Merry means more to me than any brother,' Felix said quietly.

Chatterley gave him a searching look, which Felix met unflinchingly until the other man looked away. 'Right! As long as you understand that I'm not condoning your behaviour. Less said the better. We'll stick to the story of a secret mission for public consumption, if you don't mind.'

Felix gave him his most dazzling smile. 'Thanks, Chips. I really appreciate it. I owe you a drink.'

'Forget it,' said Chatterley, looking uncomfortable.

Fortunately, it was a quiet day. The weather closed in about mid-morning, putting an end to all flying for the day, so Felix was able to spend the afternoon lying on his bed. He tried to rest, but his sleep was troubled by images of Merry sinking out of reach in a deep well, and every time he managed to reach his hand it was cold and as slippery as a fish and he could not keep hold of it. At six o'clock he managed, after some difficulty, to get a call put through to the hospital and waited with a thumping heart for Sister Lovell to come to the phone. The Irish lilt was more pronounced than ever.

'Squadron Leader? I'm glad you called. Yes, he's doing fine. We're not out of the woods yet, mind, but he's making very good progress.'

'Thank God!' Felix said. 'Has he mentioned me? Does he remember that I was there last night?'

'To be sure he does! He's spoken of you several times.'

'Will you tell him I telephoned, please?'

'I will that. And I'll tell him you sent your love, will I?'

'Yes, do that, please.'

Felix called every evening after that, until at the end of a week there was a longer wait than usual and then Merry's voice came down the line.

'Hello, Felix?'

'Merry! How are you?'

'On the mend, thanks. Sister says they're going to throw me out of here soon.'

'Where to?'

'A convalescent home somewhere. Not sure where yet.'

'Let me know as soon as they tell you. I'm due for some leave soon. I'll try to get to wherever it is they send you.'

'Brilliant! I'll let you know. I'm . . . I'm really looking forward to seeing you again.'

'Me, too.'

Merry was sent to convalesce at a hotel in a spa town in the Auvergne. He wrote to say that it was a place much favoured by the French military establishment, who apparently had great faith in the healing power of the waters and had sent sick soldiers to recuperate there for generations. Following their lead, the British army had commandeered two hotels for their own wounded. Felix pulled every string available to him, but in spite of his efforts he was unable to arrange for more than seventy-two hours' leave. It took him most of the first day to get to Chatelguyon, where he was disappointed to find Merry still pale and lethargic, and even more so to discover that the hotel was overcrowded and Merry was sharing a room with two other convalescents. It was a frustrating interval. Merry was too weak to walk far, although there was at last a hint of spring in the air, and in the crowded rooms there was no opportunity for intimacy. Felix's only consolation was that, by the end of his brief stay, there was a little more colour in his lover's cheeks.

On the last evening they shared a bottle of wine. Raising his glass, Felix said, 'Now, you look after yourself. The war's nearly over and soon we'll be able to spend some proper time together. Next time we meet, we'll be drinking to victory.'

18

'Someone's coming!'

It was a low, urgent call from the man on guard outside the shepherd's hut. Richard looked across the table at Armando and they both got up and went outside. Below them, on the narrow path that zigzagged up the scree slope, two small figures were plodding upwards. Richard lifted his field glasses and studied them.

'It's Ferrucio,' he said.

'And Antonia,' said Armando, lowering his own glasses and glancing sideways at him. Richard nodded and went on watching the approaching figures. He had never been quite sure whether Armando knew about his relationship with his sister or not. They had made love three or four times since that first occasion, always hastily and secretively, snatching a few minutes when the opportunity presented itself. In the circumstances of that winter, that had not been very often.

'If Ferrucio's made the journey out here it must mean something is about to happen,' Armando said. 'And not before time!'

'I quite agree,' Richard responded. He looked around him. The valley was deep in snow but on the opposite slope, where the sun caught it, bare rock was beginning to appear, glistening darkly against the blinding whiteness of the surroundings. The mountain peaks stood out now against a sky of an improbable delphinium blue. Down below, hundreds of feet down and out of sight, on the meadows that bordered the river, it was already spring. Richard drew a deep breath and flexed his shoulders. Thank God, the running was over and the time for action was near.

It had been a bitter winter, in every sense of the word. Bitter in its unrelenting sub-zero temperatures and in the stratagems they had had to employ to stay alive. Deprived of the support of the Allies and the regular drops of supplies and ammunition, the partisans had been unable to hold on to the gains they had made the previous summer. The Germans, no longer needing to concentrate their forces on repelling the Allied advance, had turned their attention to the guerrillas who had proved such a thorn in their flesh. They had launched *rastrellamento* after *rastrellamento* with ever larger units, leaving terror and destruction in their wake. Unable to resist, and yet aware that to take the advice of General Alexander and return to their homes would amount to an act of collective suicide, the partisans had done what they had learned to do in the early days when there were only a few of them. They had broken their battalions down into small units, each headed by a trusted lieutenant, and melted away into the countryside. For four months Richard and Armando, together with Nick Macdonald, the radio operator, and half a dozen others, had moved from mountain hut to abandoned farmhouse, living on their dwindling supplies of food and what they could beg or buy from peasants, who had little enough for themselves. As the German columns moved into one valley, they had moved round the shoulder of a hill into the next. When they found themselves encircled they had split up into twos or threes and filtered through the Nazi lines, to meet up again at a rendezvous behind them. Once, they had been forced to ford a freezing river to escape and had been saved from death from hypothermia only by the kindness of a farmer's wife, who had taken them in and dried their clothes in front of the kitchen range, and fed them bowls of hot turnip soup. They were all aware of the price she and her family would have paid if the Germans had come upon them, but no one referred to it.

Their two visitors reached the level ground in front of the hut at last. Ferrucio was panting for breath, but Antonia, though her cheeks were flushed with the effort, looked as if she could have gone on for several hundred feet more. Richard shook hands with Ferrucio and kissed Antonia on both cheeks, in the same manner as her brother.

Inside the hut Ferrucio produced a flask of grappa and they settled round the rough wooden table. Nick, at Richard's invitation, left his precious wireless and joined them.

'Well,' Armando said eagerly, 'what news?'

Ferrucio looked at Richard. 'What instructions have you had from your headquarters?'

'To hold ourselves in readiness until we receive the word to move.'

Ferrucio gave a sharp, contemptuous snort. 'And this is what you propose to do?'

'Do you have a better idea?'

The small man leaned forward, his expression intense. 'The Allied offensive will be resumed very soon, we all know that. We must be ready. Soon they will be at the gates of cities like Bologna on the east and La Spezia and Genoa to the west. When the Germans start to withdraw there will be a power vacuum before the Allies move in. That is our opportunity. We must be ready to take over the administration of the cities. We do not want them to fall into the hands of fascist sympathisers or the old, corrupt regime that existed before the war.'

Armando glanced at Richard. 'How will your people react to that?'

'The usual form seems to be to establish Allied Military Government until such time as proper elections can be held,' Richard said. 'But I think they will work with whoever happens to be in charge at the time.'

'So, what are you proposing?' Armando asked Ferrucio. 'My men have no experience of running a city administration.'

'There is no need for that,' Ferrucio said. 'There are enough members of the CLN in Bologna with the right experience. Over the winter we have been making our plans. Every man knows what his job will be when the moment arrives. But we need your men to prevent the Germans from wreaking havoc before they leave. We must take over the key points by force and hold them until the Allies arrive.'

Armando looked again at Richard. 'For that we shall need ammunition, supplies. We need your backing. But the orders you have go against what Ferrucio suggests.'

'Not necessarily,' Richard said. He grinned. 'There was another directive too, which seems to contradict the latest one. We are required to perform what they call "anti-scorch" operations. Ferrucio is right. The Germans will try to do as much damage as they can before they leave. Railways, bridges, aqueducts, electricity substations, water pumping stations – they are all possible targets, to make life as difficult as possible for the people coming after them. My instructions are to prevent that wherever possible. I think we can assume that covers the sort of operation Ferrucio has in mind.'

The other three round the table grinned back at him and Armando slapped him on the arm. 'Good! So, Ferrucio, when do you want us to move?'

'Not too soon,' Ferrucio cautioned. 'We may be able to seize the key points if we take the Huns by surprise but we should never be able to hold them against a determined counter-attack. We must wait until the Allies are on the point of entering the city and then move in in force. How long do you need to collect your men together?'

'A week, perhaps,' Armando said.

'And your equipment, what have you done with all your guns and ammunition?'

'Buried them under four feet of snow,' said Armando with a grin. 'Unless the Germans knew where to dig there was no chance of them coming across them.'

'So, assemble your people, collect your weapons. Already the Germans are pulling their troops back, ready to defend their lines. You shouldn't have any trouble. I will contact you again in a few days to let you know where to rendezvous with the other companies.'

'Just a minute,' Richard put in, 'if Armando and his men are only going to take over at the last minute, who is going to stop the Huns blowing up key installations before they arrive?'

Ferrucio smiled his sharp-toothed smile. 'That is where you come in, my friend.'

That evening Nick called Richard over to the corner where he was crouched with his wireless set.

'Have a look at this, sir. You'll like the look of this!'

Richard leaned over him and read the message that he had just finished decoding. Then he slapped him on the shoulder. 'At last! The brass hats have seen sense and realised what a valuable asset we can be, given the opportunity.'

The message was an instruction from TAC HQ to mount all-out guerrilla attacks on the German lines of communication, in preparation for the Allied advance. Supply drops would be resumed forthwith.

Some days later Richard stood outside the farmhouse that had been their headquarters the previous summer. Once again, he had discarded his uniform and was dressed as a simple working man. His army dog-tags and other identification were safely stitched into the lining of his boots, though he suspected that if things went wrong he would have little chance to produce them. He turned to Armando and held out his hand.

'Until we meet again. Don't forget our rendezvous.'

'The City Hall, as early as possible on the day the Allies take over,' Armando said. 'I shall not forget. Make sure you are there.'

'You, too,' Richard said.

Armando gripped his hand. They both knew that there was a good chance that one or other of them would not arrive at the meeting place. 'Good luck, *caro mio*,' he said.

'Good luck to you, too,' Richard said, and suddenly there flitted across his memory a heart-shaped face and a pair of violet eyes and Rose's voice saying, 'In the theatre you never wish people luck! You have to say break a leg. Silly, isn't it?' He cleared his throat and forced his mind back to the present. He held Armando's gaze for a moment, then pulled him closer and embraced him.

Turning to Nick Macdonald he said, 'See you in Bologna, Nick.'

The young Scotsman frowned at him. He had still not forgiven Richard for ordering him to stay with Armando, though they both understood that the Italian needed to maintain a line of communication with TAC HQ. Then his expression changed.

'You watch your back, sir. I don't like the idea of you being down there on your own.'

'I shan't be on my own,' Richard said. He offered his hand. 'Take care of yourself.'

'You too.' Nick shook hands and, after a moment's hesitation, Richard embraced him, too. Despite the discrepancy in rank they had forged a close bond over the months they had spent together.

Richard saluted the rest of the small group who had escorted them down the mountain and shouldered his rucksack. He had left his Sten gun with Armando but, as in France, he wore his pistol strapped to his thigh where it could be easily reached via a false pocket. With a final wave he turned away and followed Ferrucio down the track leading to the road.

He had expected a long walk, but when they reached the road a small car was waiting for them – a car that Richard recognised, as he did the young woman standing beside it.

'Antonia! What are you doing here?'

'Driving you to Bologna. Is that the best you can manage in the way of a greeting?' She offered her cheek to be kissed. '*Ciao, caro*.'

He kissed her but said, 'You shouldn't be here. Why have you let her come, Ferrucio?'

'She has as much right to be here as you have,' Ferrucio pointed out. 'Let's get in, shall we?'

'What about your parents?' Richard persisted as they got into the car. 'What about your job at the hospital?'

'I have given up my job in Castelnuovo. Now I work for the City Hospital in Bologna, as a midwife.'

'Where are you living?'

'With you, *caro*. As your wife!'

'Ferrucio?' Richard twisted in his seat to look at the little man in the back of the car.

Ferrucio leaned forward and handed Richard a packet. 'See, here are your papers. You are Fabrizio Tebaldi, employed by the city council as a general odd-job man. And this,' indicating Antonia, 'is your wife Isabella Tebaldi.'

'But why?' Richard demanded. 'Why a wife?'

'Do you not think it will be useful to you, *caro*, to have a wife who has a car and a permit to be out after curfew?' Antonia enquired.

'Of course!' Richard said, beginning to understand. 'But I don't like to see you taking such a risk.'

'Pah!' interrupted Ferrucio. 'Do you think you are the only one who takes risks? This girl has been at risk every day of her life for the past year. What difference does it make whether she is back in Castelnuovo or with you in Bologna?'

There was no easy answer to that so Richard fell silent and Antonia started the car and began the long drive to Bologna.

When they reached the city they dropped Ferrucio at a street corner and Antonia drove on to the apartment they were to share. It was simple, clean, sparsely furnished, in a working-class suburb.

In the kitchen Antonia turned and looked at him. 'Ricardo?'

'Fabrizio,' he corrected.

'You are angry with me?'

'Angry? No, of course not.'

'But you do not want me here.'

He put his arms round her. 'Tonia – no, Isabella – I'm thrilled to have you here. It just worries me that you are sacrificing so much, risking so much.'

'Ferrucio was right. The risk is not greater here than at home.'

'But what about . . .' He had been about to say 'your reputation', but it sounded so trivial and old fashioned that he stopped. Instead he said, 'What would your parents think if they knew we were living as man and wife?'

'They need never find out,' she replied, with a little shrug.

'All the same,' he said, 'you should think of your future.'

She wound her arms round his neck and gazed provocatively into his eyes. 'You are afraid that after this I shall expect you to marry me. Forget it! When all this is over, you will go home to England and I shall marry a nice Catholic Italian boy.'

'Who won't mind that you're not . . .'

'A virgin? *Caro,* I do not think that, when this war is over, men and women are going to worry about that sort of thing so much. The men will have to make the best of it, because there won't be enough virgins to go round!' She laughed. 'Anyway, it's too late to worry about that now.'

This was unavoidably true, so Richard banished his scruples and kissed her and later they went to bed and made love unhurriedly and, for the first time, without keeping one ear cocked for approaching footsteps.

From the following morning Richard's life assumed a new routine. Each day he set off, carrying the worn bag of tools that he had found waiting for him in the apartment, for a council depot where he met up with Marco, an older man who had been a member of the CLN from the very early days. Richard remembered him from his first visit to Bologna, back in the summer of 1943. He was a master carpenter who could turn his hand to any job and had for years been foreman of a gang of workers who carried out repairs to city council property. In his company, Richard got to know most of the key installations in the city. He found himself on one day painting some railings that overlooked the railway marshalling yards, on another sweeping up leaves in a public garden next to a water pumping station or mending a broken window in the telephone exchange. In Marco's office they studied a map and Marco pointed out places where a charge of dynamite would do most damage, and as they criss-crossed the city on buses and trams Richard began to learn the layout. He made mental notes of the numbers of guards and which units they were drawn from, and watched to see how alert they were and when they were relieved.

In the evenings, hidden under a rug in the back of Antonia's car, he travelled to empty warehouses or small garages and workshops in different quarters of the city. Quite often the car was stopped and Antonia was asked to produce her papers. He lay still, breathless with admiration for her courage and steadiness of nerve, as she explained that she was hurrying to the bedside of Signora X or Y, who was experiencing a difficult confinement. If the soldier who had stopped her seemed inclined to be officious she was quite ready to supply some gruesome details, which invariably caused him to wave her on her way without further ado.

At his destination Richard would find six or seven tense, eager men, and for the next hour or two he would demonstrate the use and handling of explosive charges – not, this time, how to set them but how to make them safe. Finally, at midnight, Antonia would drive him home and they would fall into bed, too tired very often to make love.

On some evenings, instead of the lectures on explosives, he met with the members of the Committee of National Liberation at one of the safe houses they used in different parts of the city. Here again, there were many who remembered him from his first visit and he was received on the whole with warmth.

He detected certain reservations however, among the communist component, who suspected that the Allies intended to hand the running of the city over to the royalist government that had been set up in the wake of Mussolini's downfall. It took a good deal of tact to keep everyone's mind focused on the immediate need to protect the city from the spite of the retreating Nazis, and not let them indulge in factional wrangling.

It was to this committee that intelligence reports came in from sympathisers all over the area. Bit by bit, they built up a picture of the Germans' intentions. Charges had been set in a railway tunnel here, under a viaduct there, in electricity distribution stations around the city. It was from here, too, that orders went out. There were more ways than one to prevent the enemy from carrying out the planned destruction and of disrupting the withdrawal that was already in progress. Strikes and go-slows hampered movement of goods and passengers. Key parts of certain machines unaccountably disappeared. In many cases, demolition charges could only be set with the complicity of local personnel, and a propaganda campaign made it clear to such people that, whatever the perceived threat from the occupiers, they would soon be gone, whereas the CLN would remain. Those aiding and abetting the common enemy could not expect mercy. On the other hand, it was not difficult to leave a loose wire or fail to connect a vital component, and the departing Germans would be none the wiser.

Over a period of three weeks the plans were drawn up until every man knew his job and all that remained was to wait for the signal that the American forces that were advancing on the city were about to launch their final attack. That signal would come via a coded message broadcast by the BBC's Italian service. Abruptly, after the frenzied activity of recent days, Richard found himself with time on his hands. He decided to employ it, in line with his original training, to familiarise himself in more detail with the layout of the city streets. Carrying his bag of tools and having memorised several legitimate-sounding destinations, he set off on foot, taking careful note of strategic positions, such as buildings from which snipers might control important intersections and back-streets by which infiltrating guerrillas might bypass roadblocks or security checks.

In the course of his wanderings he found himself suddenly in front of the Opera House. He came to a standstill, gripped by a kaleidoscope of memories and half-forgotten dreams. Central to these was the image of a rubicund little man in the uniform of an officer in the Italian army. Massimo Parigi! Once *répétiteur* at this very Opera House, later attached to the German/Italian Armistice Commission in Marseilles and most recently encountered as a prisoner of war in North Africa. Richard recalled vividly how he had sung for Parigi in Marseilles, in exchange for a pass that would enable him to cross the demarcation line into occupied France, and how he had wished at the time that he was auditioning for a place in the opera company instead. He moved closer to the main entrance and saw, to his surprise, that there were bills advertising current productions. Tonight they were giving *La Bohème*, tomorrow *La Traviata*, the next day *Carmen*. Reading the titles, Richard experienced an almost physical ache of desire to attend one of those performances. It gave him a strange sensation of unreality to think that such things were still going on in a city about to be attacked, but he reminded himself that theatres had continued to function throughout the London Blitz. Moreover, had not Gigli sung in a gala performance of

Un Ballo in Maschera in the presence of General Kurt Mailtzer on the night before Rome fell to the Allies?

It occurred to him that there might be a rehearsal in progress at this very moment for one of the operas, and as soon as the thought crossed his mind the temptation to find out became irresistible. His training told him that it would be taking an unnecessary risk, but he rationalised his impulse by deciding that if he was challenged he could always say he had been sent to check up on some faulty electric wiring. The fact that no fault had been reported could be put down to the sort of administrative cock-up that was a regular feature of life in most Italian cities. Without pausing to think further he tried the door leading into the foyer.

Slightly to his surprise, it gave to his touch. The foyer was deserted so, emboldened, he made his way up the stairs leading to the circle. As he approached he could hear that there was, indeed, a rehearsal in progress. The familiar music of Act II of *Carmen* filtered out to him through the swing doors. Cautiously he pushed them open and slipped into the back row of seats. It was a principals-only rehearsal, the accompaniment being provided by a single piano rather than the full orchestra, and onstage Carmen was taunting her lover Don José. Richard settled back in happy anticipation. Soon his favourite character would appear – Escamillo the toreador, the baritone role that he had studied as part of his training in Milan. But to his great disappointment the rehearsal was stopped just at the point where Escamillo should have made his entrance, and the singers were told to take a break.

Regretfully, Richard made his way back down the stairs. As he crossed the foyer, swing doors on the far side opened explosively and Richard turned quickly to face the newcomer, then froze in stunned recognition. From twenty feet away,

Massimo Parigi stared back in equal amazement. Then he hurried forward.

'Ricardo?'

Years of indoctrination in subterfuge came to Richard's aid. 'Fabrizio, signor,' he corrected with what he hoped was an ingenuous smile. 'Ricardo was the other one. You remember?'

He stared into Parigi's eyes, praying that the little man would keep his wits about him. Internally, he was cursing his own stupidity, which had brought him face to face with the one man in the city who knew him not only as Ricardo Benedetti, singer and one-time cabaret entertainer, but also as Major Richard Stevens of the British army. His mind was racing. In the prison camp Parigi had offered himself as a double agent and Richard had sent him to London for training. Had he been accepted? Was he now here in that capacity? If so, there was no danger. Meanwhile, his peripheral vision was registering that the foyer was still deserted. If the worst came to the worst, he could dispose of Parigi and be away before anyone was any the wiser.

'Of course!' Parigi smiled broadly. 'How stupid of me. Fabrizio, of course. But tell me, my friend, what are you doing here?'

Richard raised the bag of tools. 'Come to repair some damaged wiring, signor. The Clerk of the Works sent me.'

'Damaged wiring? Ah yes, to be sure. You have finished?'

'Yes, I was just on my way out.'

'Then perhaps you have time for a drink with an old friend. Yes?'

Richard hesitated. On balance it seemed best to accept, to make sure that Parigi understood the importance of keeping quiet. It was always possible, of course, that the invitation was a trap, but from everything he knew of him it seemed unlikely. Their previous encounters had convinced Richard that this was a man after his own heart, to whom music was far more important than politics. Parigi might be a patriotic Italian, but he was no fascist.

'*Sì, signor. Grazie*,' he responded.

'Excellent! Come, I know just the place. Somewhere quiet, where we can talk.'

As they walked Richard said, 'I was not expecting to see you here, signor. Last time we met the situation was rather different.'

'Yes, indeed!' Parigi agreed. There was a twinkle in his eye, and Richard had the impression that he was greatly enjoying the little drama they were enacting. 'But then we Italians came to our senses and realised that we had been fighting on the wrong side. After that, there was nothing to stop me returning to my post here with the opera company.' He gave Richard a meaningful look. 'And it is convenient. You know? I am well placed to be of use.'

They came to a small bar in a side street and Richard noticed appreciatively that his companion had chosen a slightly run-down little place, not the sort likely to be frequented by members of the opera company. There were few customers and Parigi led him to a table in a corner where they could talk without being overheard. Richard was careful to choose a seat that gave him a clear view of the door.

Parigi ordered coffee and brandy, remarking, 'The coffee is terrible, of course, but if you pour the brandy into it it becomes almost drinkable.'

Richard met his gaze. 'So, we are both working for the same organisation?'

Parigi leaned forward and lowered his voice, his expression now totally serious. 'You set me free from that hellhole in Africa and gave me the chance to strike a blow for my country – for the true spirit of Italy. I have to thank you. I planned, when this damned war is finally over, to seek you out. But now, see, God has brought you to me!' He sat back and looked at Richard, the small dark eyes as sharp as a bird's. 'Were you listening to the rehearsal?'

'Yes. I was up in the circle.'

'What did you think?'

'The Carmen is charming,' Richard said. 'It is a beautiful voice. Perhaps a little strained on the top notes? Your Don José is a little long in the tooth, but I can understand the reason for that. But what happened to Escamillo? I was looking forward to hearing him.'

Parigi raised his shoulders and spread his hands. 'My friend, I believe you have been sent here by the good Lord. You are the answer to my prayers.'

'I'm sorry,' Richard said, shaking his head. 'I don't know what you mean.'

'Escamillo is terrible. Once he had a good voice but he is old and he drinks too much. Today he did not even turn up for rehearsal. But what is one to do? All the younger men have been called up or have gone into hiding to escape being sent to Germany.'

'But what has that got to do with me?' Richard asked. Somewhere, deep in his guts, he could feel a flutter of excitement, a foolish, incredulous hope.

'You have studied the role, no? Didn't you tell me that you had sung it with that Belgian opera company, before the war?'

Richard contemplated explaining that the opera company had been a fiction, dreamed up as part of his cover, but thought better of it. 'I learned it when I was a student. But that was years ago.'

'But one does not forget such things.'

'Perhaps not, but what are you suggesting? I haven't sung seriously for months.'

'But you are fit. I can see from looking at you that you are in good condition. If the muscles here are strong . . .' Parigi patted his ample diaphragm, '. . . then all the rest follows. You know this.'

'Well, maybe. But I am still terribly out of practice. You are not seriously suggesting that I should take over the role?'

'It is for one performance only. After that – well, who knows what will be happening here? And there are two days left for rehearsal.'

'You want me – Fabrizio Tebaldi – to sing in your Opera House?' Everything in his training, not to speak of common sense, was telling Richard that the whole idea was madness. And yet, to sing in an Italian opera house . . . It was the realisation of a dream. And who was to know what it might lead to? The war was almost over. He had to think of the future. All the carefully laid plans he had made with Priscilla had fallen apart. How could he turn down an opportunity like this?

'Perhaps you might sing under another name? I could introduce you as someone I met while I was a prisoner of war, perhaps?'

'As Ricardo Benedetti, you mean?' Richard said. His brain was racing. No one in the audience would connect Ricardo Benedetti with Fabrizio Tebaldi. Under the make-up he would be unrecognisable. True, some of his colleagues in the CLN had known him under that alias when he first visited the city, but even if one of them happened to be in the audience, what harm could it do? He still had his papers as Ricardo Benedetti, if he was challenged by anyone in authority, and who would ever imagine that a British agent would dare to appear in opera in front of an Italian audience?

'No, tell them you met me in Marseilles,' he said. 'We'll stick to the story you know. But surely it's impossible. Why should your director allow me to sing?'

'Listen,' said Parigi, leaning towards him. 'Come back with me now. I will ask Signor Valente to hear you and I will suggest that perhaps you might understudy the part. I am quite sure that the old man will not turn up on the night. He knows he is past it and he is terrified of what the audience will do to him. I will tell him, in confidence, that we have found an understudy. I will flatter him a little, tell him that this young man can never equal him in his prime, of course, and suggest that it will be better for his reputation to let people remember him as he was then, rather than facing the possibility of a debacle. He will be delighted to bow out, I can promise you.'

'But suppose I can't do it?' Richard was suddenly gripped by panic. 'I've told you, I haven't sung seriously for months – years, even.'

'You know the famous aria?'

'Oh yes, of course. I couldn't forget that.'

'Then come and sing it for Signor Valente. After that, I will coach you with the rest. After all, it is not a large part. Will you do it?'

For a moment Richard hung, like a diver on the edge of a high board, but like a diver he had gone too far to regain his balance. Now he must take the plunge and make his dive as perfect as possible.

'I'll try it,' he said. 'But you may wish you had never run into me!'

Fifteen minutes later he was standing on the stage in front of a bemused Signor Valente, who could not quite grasp where this strange young man had sprung from. His knees were shaking so hard that he felt sure the tremor must be visible to the director, and it crossed his mind that he had faced enemy gunfire and possible capture by the Gestapo with greater equanimity. The thought put his current situation into perspective and the first notes of the introduction, played by Parigi, stilled the trembling. He had sung the toreador's aria for Laszlo Brodic, who had coached him while he was at Beaulieu, and it had been a popular part of his repertoire when he was in the Follies. For an instant he had the illusion that it was Merry smiling up at him from the orchestra pit, not Parigi. He drew a deep breath and sang. He was aware that some of the higher notes were not as true as he would have wished and that his phrasing was not perfect, but the acoustics in the auditorium were excellent. He lifted his head and felt his voice filling the theatre. This was what he was made for! Everything else – skirmishing with the partisans, sabotaging trains, skulking on street corners – was just play-acting.

When the aria came to an end the director came over to him, his hands clasped in front of his face. 'But where have you been, my young friend? Why have I never heard you sing before?'

Richard raised his shoulders slightly. 'The war, maestro.'

'Ah, the war, the war! But soon it will be over. And the day after tomorrow you will sing Escamillo for us. Yes?'

Richard felt a smile well up from somewhere deep in his chest. 'Yes, maestro.'

It was late afternoon before he set off back to the apartment. He felt giddy with excitement and the music coursed through his veins like wine. He had not felt like this since his first night with the Follies. As he walked, however, more sobering considerations came into his head. The immediate question was, should he tell Antonia what had happened? His training suggested that the fewer people who knew about it the better. On the other hand, he was in such a state of excitement that he doubted he could behave normally in front of her. It was not that he did not trust her implicitly, simply that he was unsure how she would react. Over the past months he had come to admire her courage and her fiercely independent spirit more than ever, but it was exactly that spirit which made living with her a somewhat exhausting experience. She was too volatile, too easily moved to fury over what seemed to him relatively trivial incidents, for his comfort. He told himself that it was the Latin temperament, that her outbursts meant nothing and passed over as quickly as storms in April, but all the same he had caught himself thinking once or twice that it was a good thing they were not really married. He would not wish to live like this permanently. The more he thought about it, the more he came to realise that their original relationship had been the right one. As comrades in arms and mildly flirtatious friends they had got on very well. As lovers, they were doomed to failure.

Nevertheless, he determined to share his news with her. He guessed that she would be anxious about its possible repercussions. He hoped that he could persuade her to rejoice with him at the wonderful opportunity. In the event, she was furious.

'You fool!' she railed at him. 'What do you think you are doing? How can you put everything at risk to satisfy your own ambition?'

'I'm not putting anything at risk,' he returned. 'There is no reason why anyone should connect Ricardo Benedetti with Fabrizio Tebaldi.'

'And if someone recognises you?'

'They won't. I shall be in full make-up.'

'Going into the theatre, and coming out?'

'The only people likely to recognise me are our friends. Why should that cause trouble?'

'And what about the cause? What about everything we have worked for over the past weeks?'

'That is all in hand. You know as well as I do that nothing more can be done until the Americans arrive.'

'And suppose they arrive while you are onstage?'

'Then I presume the performance will come to a sudden end. Anyway, we both know they are not likely to be here for at least another three days. If the invasion was imminent the BBC would have broadcast the warning.'

'And what if one of the company is an informer? The Gestapo are still active, you know. What if you are arrested?'

'Then the others will be able to carry out all that needs to be done without me.'

'And if they torture you to make you disclose your accomplices?'

'Why should they? I am simply Ricardo Benedetti, a singer. I have my papers and Parigi and I have concocted a story about how I came to the city looking for work and applied to him as an old acquaintance. He is willing to say that I am staying at his apartment, if they ask for an address.'

'And suppose they torture him? He knows who you really are.'

'But no more than that.'

'It is enough. The fact that you are an English officer will not protect you. They will treat you as a spy. Can you hold out against what they will do to you?'

Richard was silent for a moment. The scenario she had

outlined was unlikely, but not impossible. He remembered that, hidden in the removable heel of his shoe, was a pair of gold cufflinks, given to him by Maurice Buckmaster before he left for his first mission in France. He had carried them with him ever since. One of the links was hollow and contained a small yellow pill. When he went to perform the day after tomorrow, he would make sure that he was wearing them.

He said, 'If the worst should happen, I shall make sure that they can get nothing from me.'

She stared at him for a moment and then flung her arms around his neck. 'Don't you understand, I am afraid for you!'

He held her tightly, rubbing his face in her hair. 'I know, *carissima*. But it will be all right. It's the chance of a lifetime. I have to take it.'

They went to bed then and made love, but even so he was not quite sure that she had forgiven him.

19

On returning to his squadron at Eindhoven, Felix found that, with the improvement in the weather, operations were becoming more frequent. It was clear that the Allied armies were preparing for an all-out assault on the Rhine crossings, and one of the jobs allotted to the RAF fighter squadrons was to tempt the Luftwaffe into the air in order to reduce their numbers before the main attack. They flew a sortie over a Luftwaffe base at Rheine, losing several planes to heavy flak, but the Luftwaffe pilots remained obstinately on the ground. Later they learned that the ME 109s had been withdrawn deeper into German-held territory. The squadron flew a number of sweeps east of the Rhine, which they nicknamed 'rodeos', but without persuading the Germans to engage. Returning from such operations, Felix could see the Allied armies massing on the west bank of the Rhine.

Then, on 23rd March, came their orders for 'Operation Varsity'. Felix's squadron, along with several others, was to provide a protective umbrella over the northern end of the dropping zone as airborne troops went in to establish a bridgehead on the eastern bank of the river. As they flew over the target area Felix looked below him. The night before, the whole area had been carpet-bombed and it was pitted with still-smoking craters. He shook his head, disbelievingly. This was Germany, for God's sake! Had Hitler no more pity for his own people than he had for those of any other country he had overrun? Then, turning back for base, he saw the vast array of tanks and men pushing forward across the Rhine and said aloud, 'Please God, it can't go on much longer now!'

At the beginning of April he received a letter from Merry. They had kept in touch with some difficulty in the intervening weeks. Sometimes Felix was able to get through to the hotel on the telephone but very often it proved impossible and letters took many days to arrive. He had been encouraged, however, by the increasingly positive tone of Merry's communications and the fact that he was obviously gaining strength and was able to do a little more each day. Now he wrote to say that he had been passed fit for active service and would be returning to Brussels to put together a new and much more ambitious show.

> *George came to see me* (he wrote), *which struck me as very decent of him. We had a long talk about the new show. He reckons that the fighting will be over in a matter of weeks and that we are then going to be faced with large numbers of men, including ex-POWs, all waiting impatiently to be shipped home. Of course, it's going to take time, so we're going to need some pretty good entertainment to keep them occupied while they wait. He's right, of course. I think we all have the idea at the back of our minds that as soon as peace is signed we shall just be able to pack up and go home and carry on where we left off. But of course it ain't going to be like that.*

Felix was worried by the idea of Merry taking on the responsibility of a big show at that juncture, but he comforted himself with the idea that he was always happiest when he was working and that it had, perhaps, been the enforced idleness of the convalescent home that had so depressed him.

On 23rd April he received orders to move the squadron to Celles, some ten miles east of Hanover. This airfield had been one of the Luftwaffe's principal training bases and he expected some improvement on the temporary accommodation they had endured at Eindhoven, but the reality was such that for the first hour or two he and the rest of the squadron wandered round, speechless with wonder and bitter envy. For months they had lived in rickety huts, with no proper washing facilities and no laundry. In the winter they had clustered round paraffin heaters for warmth. Then, after that first hint at the beginning of March, spring had come with a rush, bringing weeks of unseasonably warm weather and temperatures in the eighties. The men had slept in their clothes and their uniforms were caked in grease and dirt and the smell of unwashed humanity had become almost overpowering. Here in Celles there were luxurious bedrooms, pristine sanitary blocks and spacious communal areas. There were even carpets in the lavatories, and a chandelier hung from the ceiling of the officers' mess.

Their pleasure in their new surroundings was soon sullied, however, by rumours that started to circulate about a concentration camp near by, which had recently been liberated by Allied forces. These rumours were so horrific that everyone concluded that they must be grossly exaggerated. Celles was being used not only as a fighter base but as a transit centre through which certain privileged ex-POWs were being repatriated and high-ranking German officers were being sent for interrogation by judicial units. Busy with regular sorties to escort the bombers, which were still engaged in reducing Hitler's Germany to rubble, or to shoot up anything that moved behind the enemy lines, Felix had little time to talk to these transitory visitors and pushed the rumours to the back of his mind.

One evening, just as he was preparing to pack up for the night and head for the mess for a well-earned drink, the corporal at the gate rang through.

'There's a Captain Harry Forsyth asking for you, sir.'

'Harry Forsyth? Never heard of him,' Felix returned brusquely. 'What does he want?'

'It's not a he, sir. It's a lady,' the corporal corrected, in some embarrassment. In the background Felix heard a low chuckle.

'Harriet!' he yelped. 'Good God, man! Send her over immediately.'

He just had time to run a comb through his hair before Harriet arrived. She was immaculate in her ATS captain's uniform but Felix was struck at once by the change in her. Her face was pale and drawn and she had aged ten years since he last saw her at his brother's memorial service. He caught hold of her hands and kissed her on both cheeks.

'Harry! It's wonderful to see you! But what have you been up to? You look exhausted.'

Harriet took off her cap and ran her hand through her auburn hair. 'Yes, to be quite honest, I am. I've had some pretty nasty experiences just lately. How about you?'

'Oh, muddling along, you know. Listen, I was just about to head for the mess. You look as though you could do with a drink.'

She seemed to hesitate for a moment. Then she said, 'Actually, would you mind if we just sat here for a bit? I'd like to talk quietly, just the two of us.'

'Of course,' Felix said. 'Have a seat. How about some tea?'

'Tea would be wonderful,' Harriet said, dropping into the chair he indicated.

He sent the WAAF in the outer office for tea and then drew a chair close to Harriet's.

'Now, tell me what's been happening.'

She looked at him for a moment, as if unsure where to begin. Then she said, 'Have you heard about the concentration camp just up the road from here at Belsen?'

'There have been some pretty wild rumours,' Felix replied.

'Take the worst, wildest rumour you've heard and multiply it by a hundred,' Harriet said wearily. 'It's worse, far worse, than you could possibly imagine. Worse than anyone in their right mind could imagine.'

'You've been there?' he asked.

She nodded and put her hand over her eyes for a moment. 'I was with Eleventh Armoured, covering their advance towards Luneberg, hoping to be one of the first to get pictures of the final capitulation. We were camped in the forest about ten miles north of here – it must be nearly three weeks ago now. I saw some German officers being brought into camp, blindfolded. They were taken to Brigadier Fitzgeorge-Balfour's caravan. Did you ever meet Victor? I came across him several times at parties and such before the war. He's the chief of staff for Eight Corp now. Several hours later, the Germans left and he went with them and didn't come back until nearly midnight. After that, rumours started going round about an outbreak of typhus somewhere up ahead of us, and a prison camp of some kind. For a day or two no one seemed to know what was going on, except that a detachment of tanks and men had been sent on ahead. Then Victor sent for me. He said that he was going to ask the other press photographers attached to the division to go and take pictures of what they'd found in the camp, but he didn't want me to go with them. He said,' Harriet paused and smiled bitterly, 'that it was no place for a nice, well-brought-up girl like me. Of course, I insisted on having the same opportunities as the rest of the press corps and he said, "Very well, but don't say I didn't warn you."'

The WAAF arrived with the tea and Felix opened a drawer of his desk, produced a bottle of whisky and poured a generous slug into each cup.

'I think you need this,' he said. 'I think we both do.'

Harriet swallowed a gulp of tea and murmured, 'Oh, that's good.' Felix offered her a cigarette, took one himself and lit both, then said, 'Go on.'

'We were taken in a convoy of jeeps and a short way along the road we passed a big sign, in English and German, saying "DANGER. TYPHUS". Then we drove through a gate in a high fence into a compound. At first it all looked quite normal and reasonable. There were huts, a garage, what looked like a hospital – all quite neat and tidy. Apparently that was where the SS guards lived. The only thing wrong was the smell.' She stopped and took a long drag on the cigarette. 'When you came through Normandy last summer, did you smell the cattle rotting in the fields? Cattle that had been caught in the cross-fire and that no one had time to dispose of?'

'Yes,' Felix said. 'It's one of my most vivid memories of that time.'

'That's what I thought I was smelling,' Harriet said. 'Then we were taken through another gate, into the part of the camp where the prisoners were kept. My God, Felix!' Her voice broke. 'I don't know how to talk about it. There were people everywhere. Some of them came surging round us, some just stood and looked, some sat or lay on the ground. But they were all like living skeletons. I tell you, there was one man sitting, leaning against a hut wall, and I thought it was a corpse, just skin stretched across a skull and a set of bones. And then he moved! I never knew life could go on existing in a body like that. And the stench! Excrement and decay and filth of every kind. And then we saw why. Everywhere we looked there were dead bodies. Some of them were just lying where they had fallen but others . . .' She gulped and choked back tears. 'There were heaps of dead bodies, Felix, just flung one on top of the other. Hundreds of them, thousands, all nothing but skin and bones.'

'Who were all these people?' Felix asked, stunned.

'No one knows for certain. It will take months, years, to identify them all. The brigadier was told by the camp commandant that they were common criminals, but they aren't. There are people there who had been caught helping POWs to escape, or who had worked for the Resistance in France, and many, many of them are Jews. Anyone Hitler and his cronies took a dislike to or thought might oppose them, they rounded up and thrust into that place to starve to death or die of typhus or dysentery or TB.' She raised a tear-streaked face to Felix. 'The medical corps has set up a hospital. They are doing everything that's humanly possible, but five hundred people are dying every day! Five hundred, Felix! And there's nothing we can do to prevent it.'

Felix reached out and took her hand. It was shaking as if she herself had a fever.

'And you've been in there, among all that? Are you all right?'

She nodded. 'Oh, don't worry. I haven't brought any infection out with me. We've all been thoroughly deloused, four or five times a day, and regularly checked. Physically I'm fine, except that I can't sleep.'

'I'm not surprised,' Felix said softly. 'And you've been taking photographs of all that horror?'

'Yes!' she said passionately. 'Because people have got to know! They have to be shown. You said yourself you thought the rumours must be exaggerated. That's what everyone is going to think because it's inconceivable that human beings can inflict that kind of suffering on each other. So we have to have proof. Incontrovertible proof.'

'Yes, I can see your point,' Felix said, looking at her.

She met his eyes. 'I know what you're thinking. You're thinking, this is the girl who ran out of a hospital room because she couldn't bear the sight of the disfigured face of the man she loved. Well, I've learned a lot since then, Felix. Sometimes I think that I've been forced to face up to all sorts of horrors – not as a punishment, but to compensate for the way I behaved that day.'

'My dear girl!' he exclaimed, and leaned closer to put an arm around her shoulders. 'No one blames you for that day. It was a terrible shock. It would have been to anyone. And we've all had to learn to look horror in the face since then. You mustn't see anything that's happened since as a consequence of that.'

'No,' she said, 'you're right. It's the height of egoism to relate what I've just witnessed to my own petty concerns. What matters is that I may have been able to do a little bit towards bringing it home to people who haven't seen it, so it can never happen again.'

'Do you think the ordinary Germans knew what was going on?' Felix asked.

'God knows! Apparently the locals pretended that they had no inkling. But they know now. Victor had them all rounded up and forced to tour the camp, to see for themselves. But the ordinary German soldiers, the Wehrmacht, didn't know. The camp was run by the SS. The Wehrmacht officers who took our people in there were just as horrified as we were.'

They were silent for a moment. Felix squeezed her shoulders gently. 'What can I say? Is there anything I can say or do to help?'

She sighed and gave him a rueful half-smile. 'If we were anywhere else I'd say take me out somewhere there's music and dancing and good food and let's get totally plastered.'

'I'm afraid the best I can offer you on that score is dinner in the mess. You can get as drunk as you like but I'm afraid I have to fly in the morning.'

She said, 'I'll settle for dinner. Anything's better than sitting around on my own, thinking.'

'Where are you staying?' he asked. 'Are you still with Eleventh Armoured?'

'No, they've moved on. I stayed to document the situation at Belsen, but now I'm on my way home. I've had enough, Felix. It . . . it isn't just what I've seen in the last few weeks. I'm flying out from here tomorrow.'

'How did you know I was here?'

'Oh, a chance remark from one of the reporters staying in the same hotel. I'm so glad you are here, Felix. More than anything in the world just now I need a friendly shoulder to cry on.'

'It's at your service,' he said. 'Feel free, any time.'

Over dinner he kept the conversation away from the horrors Harriet had described. If circumstances had been different, it would have amused him to see the reaction of his junior officers to her appearance. He had kept up the fiction that he had a long-standing relationship with an aristocratic young lady but no one in his present unit had ever met her and he suspected that they had begun to regard her as a mythical creature. They greeted her arrival as if a unicorn had suddenly appeared among them.

After the meal Felix offered to drive Harriet back to her hotel. In the jeep she said suddenly, 'I haven't told you the whole story.'

'No?' he said, wondering what further horrors she had to relate.

'It's nothing to do with the camp. It's a personal thing.'

'Go on.'

'I'm afraid you'll think I've behaved very stupidly, very unpatriotically even.'

'How so?'

'I've . . . I've been having an affair – with a German officer.'

Felix drew the jeep to the side of the road and stopped the engine. 'How on earth have you managed that?'

She looked at him in the light from the instruments on the dashboard. 'You're not horrified?'

'No, I don't think so. If you fell for him I imagine he must be . . . OK. But how on earth did it happen?'

'Have you got a cigarette?'

'Of course.'

When they had both lit up she went on, 'It was last December. I was travelling with an American woman reporter, a girl called Martha Thompson. We were planning a piece together about "how our boys are celebrating Christmas". At least, that was the idea. We had a driver, a Corporal Phillip Hanks, and a jeep. We were driving through the Ardennes, looking for an American unit we had been told was just up ahead of us. Well, you remember what happened last Christmas.'

'The German offensive, the start of the Battle of the Bulge.'

'That's right. All of a sudden we found ourselves in the middle of it, with no idea whether we were heading towards our own lines or the enemy's. The main roads seemed too dangerous, so we took off into the hills. You remember what the weather was like?'

'Foul. We were grounded until December twenty-third.'

'Exactly. There was thick snow on the ground and freezing fog. Suddenly, we rounded a bend in this narrow lane – more of a forestry track, really – and there was a German tank right in front of us. It must have hit a mine or something, because it was burned out and there were several bodies in the snow around it. It was a shock, as you can imagine. Phil tried to brake and swerve to avoid it and lost control of the jeep and hit a tree. Martha and I were OK, more or less, but he got a nasty crack on the head, and the jeep broke an axle. So there we were, stranded in the middle of nowhere. I can promise you, I thought we'd had it.'

'Not surprised,' Felix agreed sympathetically.

'Then we saw footprints that couldn't have been more than an hour or two old leading along the track ahead. There were drops of blood, too, so we thought we'd better follow. A couple of hundred yards farther on we found a house. Not a woodsman's cottage but quite a grand place. It must be some wealthy family's summer retreat, I should think. Probably when the roads are clear of snow it doesn't seem quite so remote, but that day it was like the Sleeping Beauty's castle, buried deep in the forest, practically invisible.' She drew on her cigarette. 'The footprints went right up to the front door, so we knocked but no one came. Then we saw that a window had been broken on the ground floor, so we climbed in. It was a scary business, knowing someone was in the house but not knowing who or where. We found him eventually. A German colonel, sprawled out on one of the beds, unconscious. It wasn't hard to guess that he had come from the tank. He had a nasty gash on his head and was obviously suffering from delayed concussion, and his hands were quite badly burnt.'

'What did you do?'

'Well, we disarmed him, for a start. Then Martha, who is a practical sort of girl, found some linen in a cupboard and bandaged his head and hands and Phil and I reconnoitred the house. Whoever owns it must have stocked up in case they were ever stuck out there. There was a larder full of tinned stuff and a whole pile of logs just outside the back door. So we lit a fire and made ourselves at home. After a bit, Axel – that was his name, Axel von Duisdorf – came round. Phil wanted to keep him tied to his bed but somehow that just seemed inhuman. He spoke very good English and he offered to give us his parole, so we accepted.'

'What was he doing there, in the middle of nowhere?' Felix asked.

'We couldn't think how he found the house, to begin with,' she said, 'but he told us that it was marked on the map and he and his men had been heading for it when they hit the mine. They thought there might be an American field headquarters there.' She laughed, but there were tears behind her laughter. 'He was so charming. Really good company. And Phil found the wine cellar, so we all got a bit drunk on Christmas Day. And from then on, we really had quite a jolly time! We found a gramophone and a stack of records and we pulled back the carpet and danced and played silly parlour games.'

'How long were you there for?' Felix asked.

'Ten days altogether. We knew the battle was still going on all round us, because we could hear the gunfire and tanks grinding by in the distance, but we didn't know which side was winning. Anyway, the weather was still pretty awful and we had no transport, so we just had to sit tight. In the end, a detachment of American tanks came along the forest road and we flagged them down and they took us with them back to their HQ.'

'And you had an affair with this Axel von Duisdorf.'

She stubbed out her cigarette. 'It wasn't the way it sounds, Felix. It wasn't just casual sex because we were all stuck in the same house with nothing to do.'

'No, I'm sure it wasn't,' he said gently.

Harriet turned her face towards him and in the faint light he saw that her cheeks were wet. 'I loved him, Felix! I'd never understood what falling in love was like until then. Earlier on today I said something about running out on the man I loved – and I did love you, Felix. I still do! And if I hadn't found out otherwise, I should have always thought that that was what being in love was like. But it's not! Being *in love* is quite different from just loving someone.'

'I know,' he said quietly.

She nodded. 'Yes, of course you do.' She reached for the packet of cigarettes he had left on the dashboard and lit another one. 'I can't explain how it happened, except that to begin with we talked and talked. For the last five years we've all been told that the Germans are inhuman monsters – and after what I've seen lately I can believe that some of them are. But not all! We forget that most of them are just like us. The more Axel and I talked, the more we discovered that we had in common. We both grew up with the same sort of background – I suppose what people call "landed gentry". You know what I mean. You're the same. Horses, dogs, the countryside, the seasons. But he belonged to one of those old Prussian military families, so it was always assumed that he would go into the army. He didn't want to at all. He would much rather have been a farmer, he said. But his father insisted on it. And he'd fought all through the war believing that he was doing his patriotic duty, just like the rest of us. But by the time we met, he was completely disillusioned. He hated Hitler and everything he stood for and he could see that they were going to be defeated and he couldn't forgive Hitler for not surrendering sooner and saving all those thousands of lives.'

She stopped and Felix said, 'He sounds a nice sort of chap.'

'Yes,' she said, 'he was.'

'Was?' Felix queried.

'When the Americans came, I couldn't bear the thought of Axel being made a POW. I persuaded the others not to say anything about him and we left him there in the house. For the next two months, more, I went back there every few days to be with him. I've always worked as a freelance, so there was no editor laying down where I should be or what I should be photographing. I managed to get hold of a jeep and persuaded the powers that be that I didn't need a driver, so I was able to come and go whenever I liked. I bought food on the black market and took it up there and for those few weeks we were blissfully happy. I mean blissfully, Felix. I've never felt like that before – and I don't believe I ever shall again.'

'What happened?' Felix asked.

'One day I arrived and there was no sign of Axel, but there were fresh tyre tracks in front of the house and American army mess tins in the kitchen. Obviously a patrol had come by and found him, so I had to assume he was a prisoner. I waited all day, in case he was hiding out in the woods somewhere, but he didn't come back. I'd given him a contact address in case of emergencies and a week or two later I got a letter. He was being held in a prison camp behind the lines. I thought . . . I thought, soon the war will be over and he will be set free and then . . . I don't know what I thought would happen then.'

Felix put his arm round her shoulders. 'Harry, you must look to the future. If you really feel like this, and he feels the same, what's to stop you being together after the war?'

She gave him a strange look, full of bitter, ironic amusement. 'Quite a lot, actually. We always knew it couldn't work out, when we stopped to think about it. For a start, Axel was married, with two little children, and as a devout Catholic he wouldn't contemplate divorce. But even if he had been prepared to abandon his family, where could we have lived? An Englishwoman married to a German? We'd have been ostracised in both countries. The only way we could have been together was to go to somewhere untouched by the war – South America, Brazil perhaps. Neither of us liked the idea of spending the rest of our lives in exile. Anyway,' she stubbed out the second cigarette, 'it's all irrelevant now. He's dead.'

'Dead!' Felix felt as if he had just walked into a brick wall. 'How?'

'Apparently some reporter took pictures of the conditions in Belsen back to the camp and the commandant made all the prisoners look at them, to see what had been done in their name. Axel was found hanged by his belt the next morning. He'd left a note with a friend, asking him to contact me. He couldn't bear it, you see. He couldn't bear the shame.'

She was weeping openly now and Felix took her in his arms and held her. 'Poor darling! Oh, my poor, poor Harry. What a ghastly thing to happen. I'm so sorry, my dear.'

Eventually she regained control and sat back. 'I'm sorry. I shouldn't burden you with all this. But I needed to talk to someone.'

'My dear girl, who else would you talk to? We've always

been the best of friends, haven't we? Maybe we should never have been lovers, but I've always been very, very fond of you. You know that.'

She nodded and took the handkerchief he offered her to mop her eyes. 'I'm so glad you were here, Felix. I couldn't have told anyone else. You will keep this to yourself, won't you? I don't want my family or anyone finding out.'

'Strictly *entre nous*,' he promised. 'You can rely on me.'

After a few minutes he restarted the jeep and drove on into the town.

She said, 'How's Merry?'

He told her about Merry's illness, though not about his mercy dash to Liège or the frustrations of his visit to Chatelguyon. 'But he seems fine again, now,' he concluded. 'Back to work on a new show. That will keep him happily occupied.'

When he drew up outside the hotel she said, 'Will you come up with me? I don't want to be alone.'

He looked at her, assessing the implications, then he said, 'Yes, of course.'

In her room she put her arms round his neck and leaned her head on his shoulder. 'Stay with me, Felix. I don't want to sleep by myself tonight.'

He said, 'Do you want me just to be here, share a bed, hold you? Is that all?'

She looked at him and it crossed his mind that, after all these years, he could not have said what colour her eyes were. Green, blue, hazel? A mixture of all three? She said, 'You can still do it, can't you? With a woman?'

'With you,' he said. 'I don't know about anyone else.' She kissed him and he felt his body's response. He murmured, 'Are you sure you want this?'

'Once more,' she whispered. 'For old times' sake. Please, Felix?'

'For old times' sake,' he repeated.

A week later his tour of duty came to an end and he was posted back to his old job at the Air Ministry in London.

20

For two days after his meeting with Parigi, Richard spent all his waking hours in the Opera House, either rehearsing on the stage with the rest of the cast or practising alone. As the *répétiteur* had predicted, his predecessor in the role failed to put in an appearance, on the grounds of ill health. At first Richard was afraid that his voice would give way under the unaccustomed burden but he was physically very fit and Parigi proved to be a sensitive and expert coach. By the evening of 20th April he still felt unsure of his moves but musically he was on firm ground.

Antonia refused to come to the theatre to listen to him, saying that one person at risk was more than enough, but she kissed him tenderly as he left and wished him luck. All through the opening scenes, sweating in his costume and make-up, he endured agonies of nerves. He had attended many a performance at La Scala in Milan during his student days and he knew how cruel an Italian audience could be. He tried to breathe deeply and concentrate on the music. Then his cue came and he walked out into the glare of the lights. The familiar smell of packed humanity, well spiced with garlic, mingled with the scent of stage make-up and size from the scenery, filled his nostrils and suddenly he was at home. This was the little theatre at the end of the pier in Fairbourne, or the Opera House in Naples with Merry smiling up from the pit.

He glanced at Parigi, in his little box in the centre of the stage, only his head visible above stage level, then at the conductor. He began to sing.

It was only when he heard the cheers and the shouts of 'Bravo, bravo!' at the end of his big aria that he knew that he had actually succeeded in impressing one of the most critical audiences in the world. From then on, until the final curtain, he forgot the war and gave himself up entirely to the world of the opera.

He walked into his dressing room, still high on adrenalin and applause, and found Antonia, taut as a wound spring with anxiety and excitement.

'Thank God! You're finished at last. It's happening. The Americans are already in the outskirts of the city. The Germans are pulling out.'

'Already? Are you sure? Have we had the confirmation from the BBC?'

'Half an hour ago. Hurry!'

He was already scrubbing the make-up off his face with removing cream. The call-boy stuck his head round the door.

'Signor, your curtain call! The audience is shouting for you.'

'Too bad,' Richard responded. 'Please give my apologies to Signor Valente and tell him that I have been unavoidably called away.' To Antonia he said, 'Why haven't we been given more notice? How do they expect us to get our people in position when we aren't told until the last minute?'

She shrugged. 'Ask your BBC, not me.'

He pulled on his street clothes and retrieved his revolver from where he had hidden it during the performance. He checked that it was fully loaded and shoved it into his pocket.

'Go back to the flat, Antonia. Wait for me there.'

'No,' she exclaimed, 'I am coming with you.'

He gripped her shoulders. 'You can't. You have to be at the apartment, to act as liaison. That was what was agreed, remember? Messages may come for me and I will either telephone or send a runner to collect them.'

She nodded unwillingly at that and he led the way quickly out of the stage door to where she had left her car. As soon as they reached the street they could hear the roar of engines, and as they rounded a corner a column of German tanks ground past them. Farther on Antonia had to brake sharply as three staff cars with their escort tore down one of the main boulevards. Richard could hear small-arms fire in the distance.

'Our men are in action already,' he said. 'They must have moved up right to the edge of the city, waiting for the signal.' He jerked his head after the retreating cars. 'Obviously the top brass aren't staying to fight it out.'

She stopped the car at an intersection and he took her in his arms. 'Go straight back, *cara*. Promise me! We must all be at our allotted posts.'

'I know,' she answered. 'Take care, my darling! I'll see you soon.'

'Yes, very soon,' he promised. He got out and watched for a moment as the little car disappeared into the night, then turned and began to walk swiftly in the opposite direction.

His first objective was the main telephone exchange, since it was through this that orders to set off the charges placed around the city would be transmitted. In the shelter of a doorway he found a group of eight men waiting for him, as arranged. He wished at that moment that they were some of Armando's men, whom he had trained over the past months, but they were still with Armando on the outskirts of the city. These were men he had hand picked from those he had worked with since his arrival, and he had taught them all they needed to know. What remained to discover was how cool they could remain under fire.

After a few brief words he gave the order to move out, and two shadowy files slipped along beneath the arcades that shaded the ancient street, to converge on the entrance to their target. The sentry at the gate was distracted, clearly wondering what all the unusual activity was about. As they approached he turned to shout a question to someone in the building behind him. Richard, materialising out of the darkness, swung him round, doubled him over with a kick to the groin and then felled him with a double-handed chop to the back of the neck. Jumping over his prostrate body, he led his men into the building.

Most of the operators were civilians and were only too eager to surrender. One or two of the German NCOs, whose job it was to supervise them, put up a token resistance but none of them were front-line troops. Once two of their number had been wounded they gave up, and Richard ordered his men to herd them into a convenient cellar and lock the door. Leaving four of them to keep an eye on the activities of the civilian operators and monitor all calls, he mustered the others and headed for the City Hall.

As they ran through the streets it became obvious that the whole organisation had swung smoothly into action. Outside every public building dark-clad figures wearing the armband of the CLN stood guard, but the Germans had not given up completely and here and there localised firefights were in progress. In one square a sniper had taken up a position at the top of an ancient bell tower, and it was only Richard's forethought in marking the place down as a likely site for such activity which saved his men from being mown down. When they reached the City Hall, however, all was quiet. The main foyer was occupied by CLN fighters, and when Richard made his way upstairs he found the principal members of the committee in session in the Council Chamber. One of them, a tall, saturnine man who went under the nickname of Il Moro, came over and shook Richard by the hand.

'Congratulations, my friend! The city is under our control and from the reports we are receiving there seems to have been no damage to any essential services.'

'I'm delighted to hear it,' Richard returned. After the weeks of preparation he felt a sense of anticlimax. It had all been too easy. He could not even be sure that his teams had been responsible for the success of the anti-scorch policy. Maybe they had dismantled the charges, or perhaps the men who were supposed to set them off had simply deserted their posts. It was even possible that the orders had never been issued. Anyway, that was not important now. 'And the Germans?' he asked. 'Havc they pulled out completely?'

'There was no one here but a few clerks and NCOs,' Il Moro replied. 'All the senior officers have gone and I understand most of the garrison has moved out. There are reports of some fighting still going on in the vicinity of the main railway station. It seems the enemy are trying to load some of their heavy equipment on to trains and are defending the area with some determination.'

Richard thought rapidly. 'Do you have any need of me here?'

'No, my friend. Everything is under control, I can assure you.'

It crossed Richard's mind that, as the only British officer in the city, he should perhaps be taking charge, but he dismissed the thought. These men had planned their own action and carried it out without a hitch. The city was theirs. If the military authorities who would move in at dawn wanted to change that, it was up to them. Officially, he reminded himself, he was not even here.

'I'm going to the station,' he said. 'I may be able to make myself useful there.'

Running downstairs he came face to face with Armando. They embraced breathlessly and Richard exclaimed, 'You're here already! I didn't expect you so soon.'

Armando laughed exultantly. 'There was no opposition. We came straight here. Almost, anyway. We managed to capture one of the Nazis' arms dumps on the way! The men are disappointed. Not enough fighting!'

'Do you fancy a bit more?' Richard asked. He explained rapidly about the action at the railway station and Armando immediately called his men together. They had commandeered several jeeps and a truck on their way through the city and they now set off at high speed, the men who had not found seats clinging precariously to the running boards and hanging on to the back of the truck.

As they approached the station they could hear that heavy fighting was in progress around the main entrance. Richard directed them up a side street, to a point where a high embankment overlooked the marshalling yard. Lying flat, he and Armando examined the situation through night glasses. Below them a long line of tanks was being loaded on to a specially adapted train. A little farther off, infantry were boarding a troop train. In the direction of the main concourse they could hear that the attacking partisans were being held at bay by a spirited defence.

Richard turned to Armando. 'There's no point in trying to stop the troop train. We should just have several hundred more of the enemy to hold down until the Yanks arrive. But if we could stop the tanks from leaving . . . Have you brought any plastique with you?'

Armando called softly to two of his men, who came forward and displayed the contents of their rucksacks. One carried plastic explosive, the other the necessary detonators. Richard said, 'Can you cover us while we set the charges?'

'Of course,' Armando replied.

They conferred briefly and Armando issued orders. Then someone made short work of the fence with a pair of wire-cutters. To partisans who had lived for the past year and more in the mountains the steep embankment was no impediment, and within minutes they were all at the base of the slope. While Armando and his men faded away into the night to take up their positions, Richard led the two with the explosives towards the track. The engine had steam up and the driver was occupied with his dials and levers. Bent double, below his line of sight, Richard and his two assistants crept up alongside the hissing, wheezing machine. Richard was remembering his time at Arisaig, where he had been taught exactly where to lay a charge to do the maximum damage. He found himself smiling at the recollection of a night when he and two others had been detailed to set a dummy charge on the harmless passenger train that plied along the branch line from Fort William to Mallaig.

He turned to the young man who carried the plastic explosive and nodded approvingly as he produced it from somewhere in the region of his armpit. If overheated, plastique became volatile and extremely dangerous, but when cold it was difficult to manipulate into the correct shape. Working fast, with the never-to-be-forgotten almond smell of the stuff in his nostrils, Richard applied it to two crucial positions and then reached for the detonators. Here he hesitated for a moment. They were of the type known as time pencils and could be set for any length of delay. He tried to work out the optimum period. If he allowed too much time there was always the possibility that the Germans might conduct an inspection and find the charges. They were, after all, aware of the possibility of sabotage. Or, if the train started off, the detonators could be shaken loose. On the other hand, if the explosion occurred before the troop train left, the station would be flooded with men searching for the perpetrators. As he wrestled with the problem, whistles blew on the opposite platform and the other engine gave a series of violent snorts. Then came the rattle of couplings and the quickening rhythm of the wheels. The troop train was pulling out. Richard set the time pencils for one minute and gestured to his two companions to get clear.

At the back of the train there was an area of brightly lit, clear space, occupied by a number of Germans engaged in loading the tanks. Richard looked around him. To one side was a signal box, which appeared to be empty. The soldiers' attention was on the job in hand, not on the space behind them. He touched one of the men with him on the arm and nodded towards the signal box, then waved them off with a sharp gesture. When both had safely reached the shadow of the building he followed. Crouched there, he looked at his watch. Ten seconds to go. He peered round the corner. In front of him was another clear area, as brilliantly illuminated as the stage he had so recently trodden. On the far side of that was a warehouse, whose open door he had noted from the top of the embankment. That was where Armando had stationed himself. Thirty yards without cover. In the confusion it should be possible.

He looked at his watch again. Five seconds – three, two, one.

Richard swore softly. Those time pencils were notoriously unreliable! Then came the roar of the explosion and he saw the engine judder in a violent hissing of steam.

While the echoes were still reverberating he shouted to his men, 'Over there! Now! Go!'

They sprinted away and he followed. As he ran he was aware of shouts of confusion, then of the rattle of automatic fire as Armando and his followers opened up and the crack of return fire from the troops around the tanks. He saw the first man gain the shelter of the door, then the second. He was ten feet away when he heard a shout behind him. He half turned, glimpsed a muzzle flash and felt a violent impact somewhere in his lower back. After that, there was nothing but blackness.

21

Rose was humming 'The Man Who Broke the Bank at Monte Carlo' and trying on a new hat. Behind her in the mirror she could see Lucien watching her with an indulgent smile. Catching her eye, he came over and laid his hands on her shoulders.

'Rose, my sweet, you look delightful. But aren't you going to get changed so we can go out to dinner? I'm starving.'

She laughed and tilted her head to kiss him. 'Oh dear, we can't have that, can we? I don't want you fading away. I shan't be a minute.'

The company had been given a week's leave and this time Rose had chosen to spend it with Lucien in Paris. She felt slightly guilty, knowing that her mother would be disappointed, but justified the decision on the grounds that the war must soon be over and then she would be home for a long holiday, whereas there was no knowing when she might get the chance to go to Paris again.

She continued humming happily as she changed her clothes. Whatever was in store in the future, she was having a wonderful week, and she had made up her mind to enjoy every minute of it. They were staying in Lucien's apartment close to the Place de l'Opéra. She loved its high-ceilinged rooms with their long windows giving on to little balconies, though the furnishings, while indisputably luxurious, struck her as being rather heavy and old fashioned. It was staffed by a housekeeper and a manservant and Rose, unused to being waited upon, had felt rather shy with them to begin with, but they had accepted her with such perfect tact and courtesy that their presence had quickly come to seem perfectly natural.

Lucien himself had set out to spoil her in every possible way. Paris in the first week of May was picking up the threads of its pre-war existence and, though there were still shortages, it had an elegance and a *joie de vivre* that Rose had felt was missing from poor, battered old London on her last visit. During the day they had strolled along the Champs Elysées and the banks of the Seine or explored Montmartre, and he had taken her to the Louvre and introduced her to his favourite pictures. And he had taken her shopping and insisted on buying her the sort of clothes she had only ever seen in the pages of *Vogue* magazine. They had eaten out every evening and afterwards either gone dancing or to a show. Best of all, in Rose's estimation, he had taken her to see the Sadler's Wells Ballet, which was performing for a short season in the city, and she had seen and been totally captivated by their new young star, Margot Fonteyn.

Tonight, he took her to a different restaurant, a small, intimate place where they ate in a booth with faded plush-covered seats, attended by elderly waiters in long white aprons. At the end of the meal he ordered champagne and, when the waiter had poured it and retired, he raised his glass to her.

'So, *ma petite*, you like this Parisian life, do you?'

'I'm having a wonderful time,' she said, smiling at him. 'You've made it wonderful.'

'And do you think you would like to live like this permanently?'

She laughed. 'Oh, I don't know if I could keep it up indefinitely. All this wonderful food, for one thing. I should get terribly fat.' Then she saw from his face that it had not been an idle question. 'What are you asking me?'

'I am asking if you would consider staying with me permanently.'

'Do you mean . . .' She stopped, suddenly short of breath. 'Are you asking me to marry you?'

He lifted a hand and let it drop again. 'If only I could, *ma chère* Rose! But I think you must already have guessed the truth. I am already married. I have a wife and three children in Burgundy. But surely you understood this, no?'

Rose gazed at him in silence. She was not sure what she felt, except that she was not surprised. At length she said, 'So, what are you suggesting?'

He smiled and leaned towards her. 'My wife never comes to Paris. She hates the city as much as I loathe the country. If you agree, the apartment would be yours, as your home. For eight, ten months of every year I shall be here with you. Sometimes I am obliged to return to my estate, to make sure everything is being run correctly, but most of the time I am here in Paris. We would continue to live as we have done this week. Oh, perhaps not at quite the same pace! As you say, one cannot keep this up for ever. But there will be parties, balls, the theatre, the opera, the ballet. And financially you would want for nothing. I will make you a generous allowance.'

Rose sat in silence. She was being offered the chance to become the mistress of a French nobleman, like Marguerite in *The Lady of the Camellias*. The image of her mother's face swam before her mind's eye. 'You, Rose! A kept woman! The shame of it!' And yet, why was it shameful? Were not most wives kept women, also? She tried to imagine life as Lucien's mistress. A small devil of mischief envisaged her inviting Bet and Matthew to stay with her. Or Sally Castle! *Why don't you come over and spend a weekend at my apartment in Paris? I'll ask Louise to prepare a room for you.* But what about the rest of the time? She looked at Lucien.

'What about my career?'

'Your career?'

'As a dancer.'

'But surely you do not intend to keep that up indefinitely.'

'I don't know. I should miss it. Perhaps I could get work here. Maybe I could audition for the Bluebell Girls.'

He shook his head. 'Oh no, my dear. I do not think that would be quite appropriate. After all – forgive me, I don't mean to be rude – a dancer's career is not a long one, surely. You are now what, twenty-five?'

'Twenty-six.'

'And you could go on until what – thirty, perhaps.'

'Pavlova went on until she was a lot older than that. Not that I'm trying to pretend I'm in the same class, of course. Anyway, I'm a choreographer as well. I've made a bit of a reputation there. I'd like to keep it up.'

He was looking hurt and puzzled. 'So you would rather pursue your career? Even if that means that in the end you are alone?'

The spectre of a lonely, old-maidish end raised itself once again in Rose's mind but a flicker of anger had been roused too.

'It might not come to that,' she said sharply.

'There is someone else perhaps?'

'No, not at the moment. That doesn't mean there never will be.'

'Of course not. You are a beautiful woman. But think,

chérie. Compare what I am offering you with marriage to a *petit bourgeois* back in England. Are you not worth more than that?'

'I don't know about being worth it,' Rose replied. 'It would be marriage, at least. I should be able to hold up my head in decent society.'

He tried to take her hand. 'My dear, you must understand. For us, here in France, this is not a matter of shame. For generations it has been recognised that men and women marry for convenience but for romance they take a lover or a mistress. I have never loved my wife. Our marriage was arranged for us by our families. It has always been understood between us that each will go his own way. I do not pretend to you that there has been no one before you. But not like this, Rose! I have never wanted to share the rest of my life with someone before. Don't you love me enough to want the same?'

His eyes beseeched her and she longed to kiss the sadness from them. She sighed deeply. 'I just don't know, Lucien. I do love you. Of course I do. But I don't know if I could live like this. I should feel so . . . so insecure.'

'I will make a legal settlement on you. I am a rich man, Rose. I can afford to be generous.'

'And suppose there were children?'

'I would adopt them and give them my name. They would want for nothing.'

She hesitated. 'I can't make a decision now, Lucien. You must give me time to think about it.'

'Of course,' he said at once. 'But, please, don't be too long. I am afraid that once you go back to England you will forget me.'

She shook her head. 'I'll never do that, Lucien. But I'll give you an answer before I'm posted back home. I promise you that.'

He called the waiter and paid the bill. As they left the restaurant he seemed to have regained his cheerful mood of earlier in the evening, almost as if her decision was a foregone conclusion.

Outside, they discovered that the street was crowded and the people were all heading in the same direction, towards the Arc de Triomphe. There was an excited babble of voices.

'What's going on?' Rose asked.

'I don't know,' he replied. 'Some kind of parade perhaps. Let's go and see.'

The crowds thickened as they reached the Champs Elysées and suddenly they heard singing, hundreds of voices raised in the 'Marseillaise'. Rose stopped dead and turned to Lucien.

'Do you think . . .? It can't be, can it?'

He put his arm round her and hugged her tightly. 'I believe it is, *ma chère*. At last!'

She clung to him, burying her face in his shoulder. 'Oh, thank God! Thank God!'

At a camp outside Hamburg, Merry was about to conduct the overture to his latest show. In the audience were troops who had been detached from the fighting to help organise the massive job of dealing with the inmates of the camps and the vast numbers of refugees who were now wandering the countryside. There were also many ex-POWs who were waiting to be repatriated, with a sprinkling of nurses to care for them. He had watched them coming in, seeing their gaunt figures, their faces worn by starvation and forced marches, but their eyes alight with triumph and anticipation. They had survived. They had come through and they were going home! Mentally, he promised them a show to remember.

When the hall was full he made his way to the podium and

was about to raise his baton when a young corporal threaded his way hurriedly through the musicians and handed him a folded piece of paper. Merry opened it and read. For a long minute he stood still, blinded by tears, fighting the constriction in his throat that prevented him from speaking. Then he turned to face his audience.

'I have just been handed a message. I should like to read it out to you. It reads as follows: "This afternoon, in the city of Rheims, Field Marshal Jodl, on behalf of the German government, signed the instrument of surrender to the Allies under General Eisenhower." Ladies and gentlemen, the war is over!'

His last words were drowned in a storm of cheering and whistling and drumming of feet. Under cover of the noise he turned to the band and mouthed, 'The king!' At the first drum roll silence fell in the hall, except for the scrape of chairs as the audience rose. Then, from behind the curtain, came the rich bass voice of Bart Bradshaw, the company's chief vocalist.

'God save our gracious king, long live our noble king . . .'

And from behind Merry the massed voices of the audience joined in. 'God save the King . . .'

As the national anthem came to a close the curtain rose and Merry caught Bradshaw's eye and called, 'There'll Always be an England,' and the band launched into the opening bars.

After that they played 'Land of Hope and Glory' and then someone from the audience shouted out 'Let's have "Jerusalem".' So they played that too.

By this time the entire company was onstage, singing and embracing each other and blowing kisses to the audience. Merry knew that tears were running down his cheeks but, looking around at his fellow musicians, he saw that many of them were in the same condition. As the last notes died away he turned to look at the audience and saw that many of them were weeping too.

The officer commanding the camp stepped forward and said a few words, congratulating the men and promising them a swift return to their homes and families. Then he turned to Merry.

'What now?'

'Now?' Merry said. 'Now we start the performance proper. You know what they say. The show must go on!'

It was not, perhaps, the most polished performance they had ever given, and they knew that the laughter and cheers from the audience were not entirely prompted by appreciation of their efforts. But it was certainly the happiest show Merry could remember.

When it was over it was clear that the audience were still in a ferment of excitement. The CO made a little speech thanking the performers and then murmured to Merry, 'Can you keep them busy a bit longer? If we let them out in this mood, God knows what will happen.'

'How about a sing-song?' Merry suggested.

So they sang 'Doing the Lambeth Walk' and 'Knees Up Mother Brown' and 'Roll Out the Barrel' and then, as the mood quietened a little, 'We'll Meet Again' and Ivor Novello's new song, 'We'll Gather Lilacs'. Finally, the chaplain stepped forward and said a prayer and then suggested that they finish with 'Oh God Our Help in Ages Past', which was sung with as much gusto as any of the previous numbers. The evening ended with the members of the cast coming down off the stage and joining the audience in an impromptu party that went on into the small hours.

Alone in his room at last, Merry took the photograph of Felix that he had carried with him all through the war out of his suitcase and gazed at the handsome, scarred face with its faint, dreamy smile. Suddenly he was gripped by a longing to be with him so intense that it felt like a physical pain. It was more than two months since they had seen each other – nine since they had slept together.

Feeling the tears start again he whispered, 'We've made it, my dear! It's over and we're both still here. Thank God!'

Felix received the news in his office at the Air Ministry and, when the first delirious celebrations were over, he picked up the phone and asked for a London number.

'Harriet? Wonderful! I'm so glad you're in town. What are you doing?'

They met for dinner, then went on to a nightclub and finished up back at Felix's flat in Belgravia. Next day, they joined the crowds in the Mall to celebrate VE Day. They cheered Winston Churchill as he drove to lunch with the king and queen at the palace and then listened to his speech to the nation, which was carried over loudspeakers to the crowd.

'Advance, Brittania! Long live the cause of Freedom! Long live the King!'

Later they found themselves dancing the hokey-cokey and the conga round the statue of Queen Victoria, in a long line of men in uniform and girls in summer dresses, rank and class divisions forgotten in the general hysteria. They stood and shouted, 'We want the king!' until the royal family appeared time after time on the balcony of the palace, then moved down Whitehall to cheer Winnie again on the balcony of the Ministry of Health. They sang 'For He's a Jolly Good Fellow' and then responded enthusiastically as he conducted them in 'Land of Hope and Glory'. After that, the whole of the West

End was given over to a huge street party and, since the licensing laws had been suspended for the night, it was dawn before the two of them staggered back to the flat, too exhausted to do anything more than fall into bed.

Next day Harriet took the train north to be with her family.

Rose returned to Eindhoven two days after VE Day. Everyone in the company was under the impression that they would now be free to return to England and take up their interrupted lives where they had left off. It was a shock when they received instructions from their HQ that they were to remain where they were for the time being. Eindhoven was to be an important transit point for troops returning to England and they needed to be kept entertained. Many of her colleagues were deeply disappointed, but to Rose the news came as a relief because it meant that she had a little more time to make up her mind about Lucien's proposal.

A few days later Wilf asked her to join him for a drink in the bar of the hotel where they were quartered. It was mid-morning and the bar was almost empty. He bought her a gin and lime and led her to a quiet corner table.

'Got any plans for when they finally let us go home?' he asked.

'Not really,' Rose said, feeling guiltily deceitful. 'See the family, have a bit of a holiday. Then look for some work, I suppose. How about you?'

'Well, that's just it,' he said. 'I've been thinking. We make a good pair, don't we? Maybe we should stick together.'

'As a double act, you mean?' Rose said. She was beginning to wish she had made an excuse to avoid this conversation.

'Yes, partly. I mean, it's a good act. Everyone says so. But I was thinking of a bit more than that. You're a brilliant choreographer, Rose. And I've seen how good you are with the other girls. And I reckon I could do anything Jack does. How about you and me starting our own company?'

'Our own company?' Rose stared at him. 'I wouldn't have any idea how to begin.'

'Well, it can't be that difficult,' he said. 'First of all you need some really good acts. Well, we've met enough people in this job to be able to pick out some top-rank performers. People who are going to be top rank soon, anyway. Then you have to find a theatre and persuade a manager to book you for the season. There are bound to be plenty of places looking for a summer show, now the war's over. After that, Bob's your uncle!'

Rose took a sip of her drink and choked slightly. Suddenly a whole new prospect was opening up before her, adding to her existing confusion.

'You'd need capital,' she objected, taking refuge in practical considerations. 'For costumes, scenery, props – and salaries until the audiences got big enough.'

'I know that,' he said. 'But there's my gratuity – you know, the handout all ex-servicemen are getting from the government. And then there's my parents' house in Streatham – well, my house now.'

'What happened to your parents?' Rose asked, realising that she had never heard him mention his family before.

'They were killed by a bomb in '41. Bit of rotten luck really. They'd gone to stay with friends in Bristol. Thought it would be safer than Streatham. The place where they were staying got a direct hit and the house in Streatham never had so much as a window broken. Sod's law, I suppose.'

'I'm terribly sorry,' Rose murmured. 'I never thought to ask before.'

'Well, there's no point in going on about it, is there?' he said. 'After all, they weren't the only ones, not by a long chalk. Anyway, the point is, the house is mine. I'm an only child, you see. But I can't see much point in hanging on to it if I'm going to spend most of my life touring. So I thought I'd sell it and use the capital to start the new company.'

'It would be a terrible risk,' Rose said. 'I'm not sure you should do that.'

'Well, you know what they say. Nothing ventured, nothing gained. I reckon it's worth a try. And if it went wrong, well, we'd still have our own act.'

Rose looked at her glass. She remembered the old times with the Follies, the happy days on the beach, the fun and excitement of the show each evening. It had been precarious, of course, but Monty and Dolores had done all right. When she and Wilf were too old to dance they would still be able to work in thc theatre if they ran their own company. The idea was certainly attractive.

She said slowly, 'I wouldn't be able to contribute anything like that sort of money.'

'I wouldn't expect you to,' he returned. 'All I want you to bring is yourself.' He stopped and she saw him flush. 'I'd better put this to you straight. I'm very fond of you, Rose. I think you know that. What I'd like to do is ask you to marry me. There's just one snag . . .'

'You're married already,' Rose guessed.

'No!' He sounded quite shocked. 'No, it's nothing like that. I wouldn't try to pull that trick on you. There's never been anyone else, cross my heart. No, it's just that . . .' He stopped and blushed more deeply. 'Ever since Monte Cassino I've had this . . . this problem. The doc says it'll probably put itself right in time. He says there's nothing physically wrong and probably when the war's over and I've had a chance to, well, get back to normal it'll be OK. But just at the moment I can't . . . can't . . .'

'Can't get it up?' Rose finished for him, and then blushed in her turn at the realisation that a few years ago she would never have dreamt of using that term in conversation with a man.

'Yes,' he said gratefully. 'But like I say, it may put itself right – or it may not. That's why it isn't really fair to ask you. On the other hand, if we were going to work together permanently it might make it easier if we were married. You know the way people talk. But of course, if there was someone else . . . I mean, I know there's this Lucien bloke, but I can't see you settling down permanently with him. I mean, if there was someone else in our line that you wanted to marry, I'd understand that.' He stopped. 'I'm not putting this over very well, am I?'

'I think I understand what you're saying, Wilf,' Rose said gently. 'And I'm very flattered, and very grateful. But there's a lot to think about.'

'Oh, of course, I know that,' he said. 'I'm not expecting you to give me an answer straight away. I just want you to have all the facts at your disposal, as they say. And there's one more thing. Kids. If you wanted kids and we couldn't – I couldn't – we could always adopt.'

Rose murmured vaguely, 'Yes, I suppose we could.' She emptied her glass. 'Give me time to think about it, Wilf. I really don't know what to say right now.'

'That's fine with me,' he said. 'Just as long as you haven't turned the idea down flat. You take as long as you like.' He paused. 'About this Lucien chappy . . . It wouldn't bother me that there's been someone else, so you don't need to worry about that. I know I can't show you the sort of good time he's been giving you but, like I said, that's all very well for now, but it's not going to last. What I'm offering you is for life. You've got to think about the future, Rose.'

'Yes,' she agreed soberly. 'You're absolutely right, Wilf. I've got to think about that very seriously.'

22

Richard spent VE Day on a hospital ship, pitching around in the Bay of Biscay. His memories of what had happened in the marshalling yard at Bologna were confused. It was all perfectly clear up to the moment of the explosion. After that, it was a muddle of pain and darkness, from which faces and voices sometimes emerged. He recalled being half lifted, half dragged and thinking that he couldn't feel his legs. Then nothing until Antonia was bending over him, being efficient and businesslike in spite of the fact that her face was wet with tears. Then the pain had come and he had lost consciousness again. After that there seemed to be a long period of time during which he was sometimes lifted and moved on some kind of stretcher, sometimes left to lie still, hearing, dimly in the background, the voices of Antonia and Armando. Finally, there had been a moment of clarity. A strange face bending over him and an American voice saying, 'What's your name, buddy?'

He had not answered at once. What was his name? Was he Ricardo Benedetti or Fabrizio Tebaldi? Was it all right to break his cover? Was this a trap? At Beaulieu they had tried to confuse you like this, waking you in the middle of the night and firing questions at you. If you broke your cover then you were out on your ear. He mumbled something.

'What's that?' the American demanded.

Armando's face swam into his field of vision. 'It's all right.

You're safe now. This is an American military hospital. You must tell them who you really are.'

The American said sharply, 'Can't he speak English? Why are you talking to him in Italian?' and Armando replied, '*Che? Non capisco.*'

Richard made a great effort and said, in English, 'My name is Richard Stevens – major. My identification tags are in my boot.'

'In your boot!'

They must have found them in the end because they stopped asking him questions and the next time he came round he was in bed and a nurse was saying reassuringly, 'It's all right. You've had an operation but you're going to be fine.'

Later he asked them, with desperate urgency, where Armando and Antonia were. No one had any idea who he was talking about. Bologna was in American hands, but what had happened to the partisans who had enabled them to enter unopposed no one seemed to know. A few days later he was transferred to a ship and began the voyage home.

When the ship docked at Southampton he was transferred to a hospital onshore and the next day he opened his eyes from an afternoon doze to find Victor, his one-time Conducting Officer, sitting by his bed.

'Ah!' he said. 'I hope I did not wake you.'

Richard struggled into a sitting position, wincing as he did so. 'Victor! Good to see you. How are you?'

'Me? I'm fine. It is I who should ask you. You are in much pain?'

'No, not really. It just catches me when I move. But at least I can move. That's the great thing.'

'So I understand,' Victor said gravely. 'I spoke to the doctor in charge of your case. He tells me that if it had not been for some very skilled surgery you might have been paralysed from the waist down. The bullet had lodged very close to the spine.'

'So they told me,' Richard agreed.

'How did it happen?'

Richard hesitated and Victor laughed. 'Come, the war is over. You may not be able to talk to other people, but at least you can tell me.'

Richard recounted what he could remember of the actions of that night, omitting any reference to how he had spent the earlier part of the evening, and said finally, 'Do you have any information about how things are out there now? No one has been able to tell me anything and I never had a chance to say goodbye.'

'I know very little more than I read in the newspapers,' Victor said, 'but before I came down here I did have a word with your Head of Section. I gather he is extremely pleased with what you and your men did that night. Bologna was handed over to the Americans without a fight and I'm told the Allied Military Government is working hand in hand with the existing authorities.'

'Meaning the CLN?'

'I imagine so.'

'Not *my* men,' Richard added as an afterthought. 'I was only there in an advisory capacity.'

'Advisers do not end up with a bullet in their backs,' Victor commented dryly.

Richard said, 'I feel bad about not saying goodbye, though. We were friends as well as comrades. Now I shall never know what has happened to them.'

'I suppose you know them only by their *noms de guerre*,' Victor said.

Richard looked up suddenly. 'No, as a matter of fact! I do know their real names – the people I'm most concerned about. Of course, what an idiot I am. I know where they live, if I can just remember the address. The father is a prominent lawyer in Viareggio. I'm sure a letter would find him, even if I haven't got it quite right.'

'So, that is one problem solved,' Victor said, with a small smile. 'And soon you will be well enough to go home, so the doctor says.'

'Yes,' Richard agreed. He looked at Victor. There was something about his expression that made him feel nervous. 'There's something else, isn't there? What's wrong, Victor?'

Victor spread his hands in a small gesture of helplessness that betrayed his central European origins. 'I wish I was not the one to bring bad tidings, my friend. But you must be told. It concerns your wife – your ex-wife.'

'Priscilla?'

'Yes. She was killed in one of the last air raids on London.'

'Killed?' Richard gazed at him blankly. He felt unable to summon any kind of reaction to the news.

'I'm afraid so.'

'What was it – a V2?'

'Not cxactly. The air-raid warning had sounded, but as you know – or perhaps you don't – the V2s came over so fast that by the time the warning sounded they had usually already hit their target. That was exactly what happened. Priscilla was running across the street to an air-raid shelter when she was run over by a fire engine on its way to the scene.'

'Oh no!' Richard murmured. 'So in the end it was just an ordinary street accident?' He shook his head and felt the first hint of distress. 'Poor Priss! She would have wanted a more romantic end than that.' He was silent for a moment, until a new thought struck him. 'Hang on, I thought she'd gone to live in France.'

'Not yet,' Victor said. 'I believe her new lover had to return to Paris with de Gaulle but he did not want her to join him until the decree absolute came through. That was what she told people, at least, but I wonder if in fact he was glad to get away.'

'You mean, he wasn't in love with her after all?'

'I am not in a position to judge. But I saw them together a few times and it always struck me that she was more infatuated than he was.'

Richard sighed and said again, 'Poor Priss!'

'It is tragic, of course,' Victor agreed. 'But at least for you it is not such a personal tragedy. The marriage was over, after all.'

Richard nodded. 'Sir Lionel and Lady Vance must be distraught.'

'Yes, indeed. I went to call on them, to give them my condolences. They adored Priscilla.'

'Everyone adored Priscilla,' Richard said.

'Apart from you,' Victor suggested.

'Including me, for a while,' Richard said. 'She was a lovely girl, Victor. She just couldn't accept that I had a job to do that didn't fit in with her plans.'

'She should have understood, she of all people,' Victor protested. 'After all, she was in a position to know what kind of work you were engaged on.'

'She should have done,' Richard said. 'She saw enough of us off on the first leg of it. But she always felt that there were more important things in life. And maybe she was right, after all. Perhaps I would have been better employed bringing a bit of culture to the masses. At least I wouldn't have killed anyone that way.'

'My dear boy,' Victor said gently, 'you must not begin to think like that. All of us have been responsible for deaths, directly or indirectly. That is what happens in war. You must concentrate on the lives you have saved. You have seen how brutal the Nazis could be. Imagine what it would have been like if they had been allowed to go unchecked.'

Richard looked at him bleakly. 'I suppose you're right. All I can see at the moment is that it's all been such a stupid, senseless waste of time and human lives – on both sides.'

Victor laid a hand on his arm. 'You have been very ill, my friend, and before that you have lived a life of great danger. It is no wonder you are exhausted. When you have had a chance to rest you will see things differently.'

'Will I?' Richard said. Then he added, 'I must write to Sir Lionel and Lady Vance.'

Victor left shortly afterwards and Richard lay trying to decide what he felt about Priscilla's death. The answer, which frightened him, was nothing. He could express an abstract regret. It was a tragic waste of a young life. But so many other young lives had been lost and he felt no more for Priscilla than he might have done for a casual acquaintance. He rationalised his lack of feeling by reminding himself that he had not actually seen her for two years. In reality she had been his wife for a few months only. It had been one of those passing things that happen in wartime, like his temporary infatuation with Ginny or his affair with Antonia. Even his passionate love for Chantal now seemed dreamlike and insubstantial. It was all finished now. He had a clean slate and must start again, but how and in what direction he had no idea.

At length he asked a nurse for some writing paper and wrote a brief, formal note of condolence to Priscilla's guardians and expressed the hope that he might be allowed to call on them when he was fit again. Then he wrote a letter to Armando, apologising for the fact that he had not said goodbye and hoping that he and Antonia were now back home, safe and well, and that they might all meet again one day. He sent his love to Antonia, but felt it better not to write to her directly. He racked his brain for the address and thought he had remembered it correctly, but in the confusion of post-war Italy he had little faith that it would reach its destination.

The letters written, he turned over and shut his eyes. A phrase from the Bible came unbidden into his mind. 'Sufficient unto the day is the evil thereof . . .' He wasn't sure what it meant, but he felt he had had more than enough evil for one day – more than enough for a lifetime.

Richard was discharged from hospital two weeks after VE Day and sent home to convalesce. His father met him at the station and slapped him on the shoulder.

'Hey up, lad! Good to see you. How's tha feeling?'

His face was unusually red and it took Richard a few seconds to realise that it was with the effort of suppressing his emotion. 'I'm fine,' he answered, automatically, though the truth was that he still felt weak and the journey had exhausted him.

'I've got a car waiting outside,' his father went on. 'You'll be glad to get home and put your feet up, I expect.'

'A car? You shouldn't have gone to that expense, Dad. I can manage perfectly OK on the tram,' Richard protested. Before the war they had owned a car, but he knew his father had sold it when petrol rationing came in.

'Nonsense,' his father responded. 'Can't have our returning hero coming home on the tram!'

The words echoed hollowly in Richard's mind all through

the journey. He knew that that was how his parents wanted to see him, but he knew equally well that he could tell them nothing to justify the picture they wanted to paint.

They were still living with his aunt, who came running down the steps from the front door to greet him. 'Oh, welcome home, Richard! We're that glad to see you! Thank God you're safe!' She kissed him on both cheeks and then drew back. 'Oh, look at you! You're so thin! Haven't they been feeding you in that hospital? Look at him, Ada! He's nowt but skin and bone.'

He climbed the steps to where his mother stood waiting at the door. 'Welcome home, son. It's good to have you back.' Her voice was quiet, her expression perfectly unruffled. Only common people gave way to public exhibitions of emotion. But when he put his arms round her to kiss her he could feel that she was trembling.

His aunt ushered them into the sitting room, calling to the maid to bring tea, fussing round him to take his suitcase and his cap, asking questions. He decided his mother's restraint was preferable. They had exchanged letters while he was in hospital and he had been relieved to discover that they already knew about Priscilla's death. Victor had taken it upon himself to write to them with the news.

His father patted him on the shoulder. 'Mother and I were right sad when we got your letter about the divorce. And then the lass goes and gets herself killed! I feel right sorry for her guardians but, to be honest, lad, I never thought she was the girl for you. So happen it's for the best, in the long run.'

Over tea his mother said, as if she was vexed with him for some act of carelessness, 'I can't think how you came to get yourself wounded in the first place. I thought you were supposed to be doing a safe desk job.'

Richard felt as if someone had placed a great weight on his

chest. 'I didn't spend all my time behind a desk,' he said carefully. 'When the Allies took Bologna I was sent in as part of the AMG – the Allied Military Government. You see, all the public institutions – police, law courts, city administration – had been in the hands of the pro-Mussolini Fascists. Once they were ousted someone had to take over until new men could be appointed. And there was a danger that Fascist supporters who had stayed behind in the city might try to sabotage essential services. I was sent with a detachment to guard the main railway station. Unfortunately there was a sniper hiding out in an empty warehouse near by and he got his shot in before we had time to clear him out.'

'You did see some action, then,' his aunt said.

Richard forced a smile. 'Just a bit, from time to time.'

'Let the lad be,' his father advised. 'The war's over. He wants to forget all about it now.'

The war, however, was far from being forgotten. Over the course of the next two weeks there was a constant procession of visitors to his aunt's house, ostensibly to welcome him home. Some of them were members of his parents' generation, bringing stories of sons and daughters awaiting demob in various parts of the world or still fighting out in the East. Others were grieving for children lost in the past years. Then there were some of his own age, men he had grown up with. Two had been released from prisoner-of-war camps by the advancing armies. One had been wounded in the D-Day landings, another torpedoed while escorting a convoy in the North Atlantic, a third had lost a foot when the bomber in which he was serving as navigator crashed on its return from a mission. All had stories to tell, either in person or through the mouths of their parents. One had won the Military Medal, another the DFM, a third had been mentioned in dispatches. Richard listened and congratulated or commiserated and answered their enquiries with a self-deprecating shrug and the murmured comment that he had had 'a very boring war, really'.

It was the sight of his mother grimly accepting the felicitations of her friends on his survival and trying to imply by subtle hints that her Richard, with his intelligence and his command of Italian, had been too valuable to the war effort to be risked on the battlefield as a common soldier which hurt him most. She made great play of the fact that he had risen to the rank of major, while few of the other boys had been commissioned, but Richard was simply embarrassed when his one-time playmates made a pantomime of saluting him.

He was also deeply disturbed by some of his more extreme reactions. One afternoon he was strolling through the park with a couple of old friends when one of them grabbed him playfully round the neck. A second later he was flat on his back, with Richard's hands around his throat. It was only the sudden sharp stab of pain from his barely healed wound that stopped him from doing further damage.

'Bloody 'ell, Dick!' the friend exclaimed when he had recovered his breath. 'There was no need for that.'

'Sorry,' Richard muttered, extending a hand to help him up. 'You caught me by surprise.'

'Where the 'eck did you learn to do that, anyway?' the other man persisted.

'Oh, basic training, you know,' Richard said vaguely.

'Basic training be blowed,' was the other's response. 'They never taught me that at Catterick.'

From then on he was aware that his friends looked at him with slightly different eyes, but he was more disturbed by how instant and unreflecting his reaction had been. It was years since he had been through the training at Arisaig, yet it was still so deeply ingrained that an unexpected encounter could trigger it. He knew that he was capable of breaking a man's neck before he had a chance to cry out, and wondered whether he was fit to rejoin normal society. He was glad when the two weeks' leave came to an end and he was able to return to London.

On reporting to the Baker Street offices of SOE he was instructed to check into a small hotel in Ebury Street and await instructions. There were several other men, in the uniforms of various services, in the hotel already, and Richard suspected that they, like him, were waiting on orders from Baker Street, but, true to their training, none of them ever 'talked shop' and conversation was confined to the barest generalities. Richard, idling the days away in acute boredom, remembered with irony the way agents waiting to be sent into the field had been cosseted and entertained by girls from the FANY – girls like Priscilla. Now that the war was over no one was bothered about the mental state of the men who had risked their lives behind enemy lines.

For several days Richard tried to pick up the threads of old acquaintanceships. By the very nature of things he had lost touch with the men he had trained with at Arisaig and Beaulieu. He rang Baker Street and tried to locate Victor, only to be told that he was abroad somewhere. There was no direct line to Beaulieu, for security reasons, so he called the number that was supposed to pass on messages, but that service had apparently been deactivated. There were, of course, people he had met through Priscilla when he was last in London, but he regarded them as more her friends than his and felt reluctant to contact them.

There was one bright spot in those weary days. Trawling through the few old friends who might still be in London, he made his way to Room 900 at the War Office, the tiny cubbyhole that housed the HQ of MI9. There, to his delight, he discovered Airey Neave and, more surprisingly, Ian Garrow, whom he had last seen in a small flat above a dress shop in Toulouse.

'Richard!' the Scotsman exclaimed. 'Where have you sprung from? I've been wondering ever since we parted at the end of '42 what had happened to you.'

For the next hour they exchanged reminiscences and Neave described his frantic efforts the previous summer to extricate British servicemen still trapped behind enemy lines when the Allied invasion started.

'One piece of excellent news,' he added. 'O'Leary survived.'

'Pat? That's wonderful! Last time we met you told me he'd been arrested by the Gestapo. What happened?'

'For about a year we had no idea,' Neave answered. 'Then a woman arrived at Jimmy Langley's club with a strange message. Apparently her son was a POW and he had made contact at some point with prisoners being held in Buchenwald. His letter home contained the address of the club and the message "tell Jimmy that Pat is alive and in Germany". Of course, we knew no more than that until the camp was liberated and, miraculously, Pat had survived.'

'That is excellent news!' Richard said. 'Where is he now?'

'Back in his native Belgium,' Neave replied.

'Belgium? So that's where he came from. I knew he couldn't really be Irish.'

'I suppose there's no harm in telling you the truth now,' Neave said with a smile. 'His real name is Albert-Marie Guérisse. He's a qualified doctor, who served in the Belgian army. He escaped when the Belgians capitulated in '40 and joined SOE and was commissioned as a lieutenant commander in the navy. That was when he adopted the Irish name. He was operating in "Q" ships off the South of France when he got left on shore by mistake and arrested. It was Ian here who got him out of the prison in Fort St-Hippolyte.'

'So that was it!' Richard said.

'Pat took over when I was picked up in my turn,' Ian added. 'And then he returned the compliment by getting me out of Fort Meauzeac, with your help.'

'He's a remarkable man,' Richard said. 'One of the bravest I've ever known. I'm so glad he's survived. What about the others? Dr Rodocanachi?'

'I'm afraid he didn't make it,' Neave said. 'He was in Buchenwald with Pat, but he wasn't strong enough to survive those conditions.'

They talked for a while longer, until Neave tactfully pointed out that he and Garrow had work to do and suggested that they meet again at some future date for dinner. Richard left his phone number and found himself once again out in the street with nowhere particular to go.

At length, a message came telling him to report to a Major Wilkins at Baker Street. He went with mixed feelings. Surely, he reasoned, they could not be planning to send him into the field again. Admittedly, the war was still being fought in the East, against the Japanese, but he spoke no Eastern languages and had no knowledge of the area. That, however, as he well knew, was not necessarily regarded as an impediment by his masters at SOE.

In the event, it transpired that the purpose of the interview was to prepare him for life in the civilian world. Major Wilkins was a small man in his forties, with round spectacles perched on a remarkably long nose. A typical bureaucrat, Richard decided, taking an instant dislike to the man.

'Well, now,' Wilkins said, when the initial social niceties had been performed, 'have you got any ideas about what you might do when you get back to Civvy Street?'

'I intend to go back to what I was doing before the war,' Richard informed him.

'Which was?'

'I'm a singer.'

'A singer!' The look of cheerful encouragement faded from the little man's face. 'What sort of singer?'

Richard explained about his opera training in Italy and his subsequent, brief career with the Follies. Wilkins looked glum. 'The fact is, old chap, there are dozens of men coming out of the services who have made a reputation for themselves in the entertainment world. Did you by any chance sing with any of the regimental concert parties or anything like that?'

Richard considered telling him that he had made a living as a cabaret artiste in France during the Occupation and that he had recently performed with a prestigious Italian opera company, to considerable acclaim. He could not do so, however, without revealing the nature of his wartime service and he was not sure to what extent this man was privy to the doings of SOE. So he said, 'No, I'm afraid not.'

'Pity, pity,' murmured Wilkins. 'You see, there are all those chaps who were with outfits like Stars in Battledress looking for jobs and then there are all the entertainers who worked with ENSA. Some of them are household names now, through programmes like *Forces' Favourites* on the wireless. People like – oh, what're their names – that couple that sing duets? Isabel St Claire and Franklyn Bell, that's it. The point I'm trying to make is that with people like that already established you're going to find it very hard to break in.'

'Isabel and Frank?' Richard said. 'I used to work with them, in the Follies.'

'You did?' The spectacles flashed with renewed optimism. 'Well, could you get in touch with them again? Perhaps they could give you some useful introductions.'

'Possibly,' Richard said, without enthusiasm. The prospect of begging Frank Bell for assistance stuck in his throat.

'Do you have any other contacts?' Wilkins asked. 'Anyone at the BBC, for example?'

'I . . . used to,' Richard responded hesitantly. They had all been contacts he had made through Priscilla and he was not sure how he would be received after the divorce.

'Well, the best I can suggest is that you try to pick them up again and see what they can do for you. But I'm afraid it's going to be hard work. Anything to do with the stage is always very insecure.'

'I know that,' Richard replied.

Wilkins leaned forwards with his elbows on the desk and steepled his fingers. 'May I make a suggestion?'

'Of course,' Richard agreed, repressing the impulse to add, 'I thought that was what you were here for.'

'Why don't you consider the idea of finding a proper job – one that will bring in a regular salary, pay the mortgage and the school fees, etc. – and keep your singing as a hobby? There must be hundreds of amateur operatic societies that would be delighted to have someone with your background as a member.'

'A *proper* job?' Richard repeated.

The note of irony in his voice was lost on Wilkins. 'Yes, exactly! Now, let's see. Do you have any qualifications?'

'Only as a singer.'

'Pity, pity. Still, you've been an officer in the army. You obviously have management skills and you're a personable young chap, well spoken, smart. You shouldn't have too much difficulty. How about looking at the house agency business? There's going to be a tremendous boom in house sales as people get resettled. I know that a lot of reputable companies are looking for young men like yourself to take charge of offices up and down the country. Or what about banking? You could make a very good career in banking. You might end up as a bank manager. Nice house, secure salary, pension, all that. Then you could sing in your spare time and maybe take on a few private pupils. What do you think?'

Wilkins sat back with an expansive smile, as if he had solved all Richard's future problems at a stroke. Richard looked at him for a long minute in silence. For the first time in his life he actually wanted to pounce on another human being and exercise some of the techniques he had been taught at Arisaig. He rose to his feet. 'Thank you. I'll think about it.'

'Do that!' exclaimed the little man. 'And if I can be of any further help, don't hesitate to come and see me again.'

Somehow Richard got himself out of the room and out of the building. Automatically he started walking back towards Ebury Street, then changed his mind and headed for Green Park. He walked fast, as if he had an appointment to keep or was trying to get away from someone. For some time he could only think in disjointed phrases. *The house agency business . . . a bank clerk . . . amateur operatic societies . . . private pupils.* Was this really the prospect he faced in the future? After everything that had happened, everything he had been through? A job sitting behind a desk, a 'nice house' with a mortgage, a wife presumably, school fees for the children. He knew it was a lifestyle that many men would have embraced with enthusiasm – but not him. Not him!

He found himself sitting on a bench in the park. Panic and despair gave way to grim determination. He would remake his career without help from the likes of Wilkins – even if it meant going cap in hand to Frank Bell. He took out a diary and began to make a list of every person he could think of who might be able to offer him a job or introduce him to someone who could. It was not a very long list. He went back to the hotel and spent the afternoon on the telephone.

His first call was to Sir Lionel Vance. He had had no reply to his letter asking permission to call on him and his wife but he told himself that there could be a number of reasons for that. The butler took his name and returned after a pause to say that Sir Lionel was out of town and Lady Vance was not available. Richard left his number and a request that Sir Lionel be told that he was very anxious to get in touch with him.

Then he tried to telephone the man who had been his agent before the war. The number was unobtainable and an enquiry to the exchange produced the suggestion that the building concerned had probably been destroyed in the bombing. Recourse to the telephone directory resulted in a blank. The agency had apparently ceased to exist. After that he tried various other possibilities. Harrison from the BBC, who had once offered him a job, was 'in the studio at present'. Richard left his name and number and a reminder that they had met through Priscilla Vance. Other similar contacts were either unavailable or, if he actually managed to speak to them, murmured platitudes about everything being up in the air at the moment, nothing actually to offer him right now, but they would bear him in mind for the future. Determined not to give in, he followed up every call with a letter and posted them that same evening.

Next day he sought out a photographer who specialised in theatrical work and had some new portrait photographs taken, and then went to a small recording studio in Wardour Street and arranged to make a demonstration disc. As soon as both that and the photographs were ready he intended to begin the thankless task of trudging from agent to agent in the hope that someone would take him on. Finally, he bought a copy of *Variety* and spent the rest of the day combing through the advertisements. There was depressingly little that he could apply for.

After dinner, unable to bear the thought of another evening spent reading the papers and chatting idly to men he scarcely knew, he set off for a walk. It had been a hot day and the atmosphere in the streets was still muggy and oppressive. London was crowded with servicemen waiting to be demobbed and every few yards he encountered groups of them, with girls in tow, heading for clubs and pubs, intent on celebrating their survival. It seemed that he was the only man in town not part of the universal euphoria. In a side street off Piccadilly a woman approached him, asking if he was looking for company. She was not unattractive underneath the garish make-up and for a moment he was tempted, but he shook his head and turned away.

Eventually he found himself on Westminster Bridge. Street lighting was still subject to restrictions that reduced it to dim pools of light at intervals across the span of the bridge, but although it was after eleven the summer sky was not completely dark. The tide was full and below him the river surged, sleek and muscled as a stallion, half seen, half felt as a moving presence. Richard leaned on the parapet and hung his head. For years he had lived a life of tension and deceit, perpetually watchful, never able to relax. Then had come the wound and the long weeks in hospital, with their consequent debility. Now, it seemed, he was to be cast out into the world with nothing but his gratuity and a cheap civilian suit. He was not even sure if he was fit to live in normal society. He remembered his violent reaction to the friend who had playfully wrestled him and the desire he had felt to attack the unfortunate Wilkins.

He shifted his position and the lamplight caught a faint reflected gleam at his wrist. Slowly, he unfastened the gold cufflink and held it in his palm. It had been with him ever since he left on his first mission, Maurice Buckmaster's parting gift. Sometimes it had been hidden, in the heel of a shoe or the shoulder pad of a suit, but he had never been parted from it. Now he pressed the hidden catch and the face of the cufflink clicked open. He contemplated the small yellow pill hidden inside – the L pill, given to all departing agents as a last recourse in the face of torture. He had never needed it – never even contemplated using it. But now . . . perhaps he was no longer fit to live in peacetime society. Certainly, it seemed to have no place for him. If he swallowed it, there would be just time to throw himself off the parapet before it took effect. Bodies in the river were not all that unusual. No one would query the actual cause of death.

He stood gazing at the dark water, against which his imagination conjured up the faces of people he had worked with over the past years. Antonia and Armando, Ginny, Dr Rodocanachi, Pat O'Leary. Abruptly he raised his head. O'Leary had survived Buchenwald. God alone knew what tortures he had suffered. And he, Richard, had never even been captured. He had led, it seemed, a charmed life. Was he to throw it away now, out of pure self-pity? He turned the cufflink over in his hand and watched the tiny pill drop out of sight. Then he straightened up and headed back towards his hotel.

23

The war had been over for nearly a month before Merry was recalled to London. From Dover he telephoned Felix at his office in the Air Ministry.

'Merry? Where are you?'

'Dover. I'm on my way to London. George wants me back for some reason.'

'Terrific!'

'The thing is, I was wondering . . . will it be OK for me to stay at the flat with you?'

'Good God, Merry! Don't be a clot! Of course it's OK. Where else would you stay? When do you expect to get here?'

'God knows! It's chaos here. Hundreds of men milling about and all the trains chock full. Some time this evening, I hope.'

'OK. I'll get us something to eat and expect you when I see you. You remember the address?'

'Oh yes. I've got it written in my diary. I'll see you soon, then.'

'Make it as soon as you can.'

It was after eight o'clock when Merry reached the flat. He was about to ring the bell when he remembered and felt in his pocket for the key that Felix had given him the previous summer. At the sound of the door closing behind him Felix appeared from the living room. Merry put down his case and hung his cap on the hallstand. His heart was beating so hard that it seemed to shake his whole body. For a long moment they stood looking at each other in silence. Then Felix crossed the space between them, put his arms round Merry's neck and kissed him on the mouth.

The kiss prolonged itself and Merry felt that time and the outside world had ceased to exist. His senses were filled to overflowing with Felix – the taste of him, the smell of him, the feel of the lean, agile body in his arms.

At length Felix drew back and looked into his eyes. 'Welcome home, my dear. Come on in. I've got the champagne on ice.'

He led Merry into the sitting room and then released him to open the bottle. Merry looked around at the room he had known only for that one brief evening the previous August. He said, 'Do you realise, the last time we were really on our own was here, last summer?'

'I don't need to be reminded of that!' Felix replied. 'It's been far too long.'

Merry said, 'I'm afraid I wasn't much good to you last time we met, back in the winter.'

The cork came out of the bottle with a soft *pffft* and Felix filled two glasses and carried them over to where Merry stood. 'That wasn't your fault. You'd been very ill. Anyway, here we are at last. I told you next time we met we'd be drinking to victory.'

'It's a bit late for that perhaps,' Merry suggested. 'How about to peace?'

'To peace, then. And to us. We've made it, Merry. Against all the odds we've come through and we're both still here. There were times I never thought we would.'

'There were times when I thought you hadn't,' Merry reminded him.

'I know,' Felix said tenderly. 'But here we both are. To peace – and the future, together.'

'Peace and the future,' Merry answered, from a constricted throat.

They drank and Felix said, 'Hungry?'

'Yes,' Merry answered apologetically. 'I'm afraid I am, rather.'

'Then let's eat!' Felix said with a laugh. 'We've waited the best part of a year for the rest. I expect we can wait a little bit longer.'

There was cold chicken on the table in the dining room.

'Good heavens!' Merry said. 'Are you still in the magic business after all? Where did that come from?'

'Nothing up my sleeve!' Felix returned. 'Just a chum at the ministry whose dad keeps chickens.'

As they ate Felix said, 'By the way, I've been down to Seaford a couple of times. The house is fine and I'm getting the garden into some sort of order.'

'That's very good of you. Perhaps we could both go down at the weekend?'

'Good idea. I've got the old Lagonda out of mothballs. We can drive down.'

'Excellent!'

'Have you heard anything from Rose lately?'

'I had a letter a few days ago. She's still stuck in Eindhoven, poor girl, helping to amuse the troops on their way home. But from what I can gather, she's having quite a good time. She seems to have taken up with a French aristocrat.'

'Serious?'

'I don't know. Rose always plays her cards pretty close to her chest in these matters.'

'They must bring her back soon, surely. Isn't ENSA being wound up?'

'Not my pigeon any more, thank God. But I should think so. I'll see if George knows anything.'

A little later Merry asked, 'What was it like here on VE Day? From the reports on the wireless it sounded extraordinary.'

'Oh, it was! I've never seen such crowds. It was just one huge party from Buckingham Palace to Piccadilly Circus. I wish you could have been here.'

'So do I. Were you all on your own?'

'No, actually. I ran into Harry so we joined forces for the evening.'

'Harriet? She's in London, then.'

'Not any longer. She went north to be with her people.'

They finished eating. Felix said, 'Want anything else?'

Merry shook his head. 'Not in the way of food and drink.'

Felix rose and held out his hand. 'Right. Let's leave all this and go to bed.'

After the euphoria of victory and reunion they both found it hard to settle to the routine work of helping to dismantle the organisations that had been the centre of their lives for so long. Felix complained bitterly that he was just 'twiddling his thumbs' at the Air Ministry and waiting to be demobbed. Merry was busier, interviewing men and woman who had worked with SIB about their plans for the future, but he was not prepared for the surprise that awaited him a few days later, when he was summoned to George Black's office.

His CO settled back in his chair and smiled at him genially. 'So, how's it going?'

Merry sighed. 'It's a sad business, breaking up what we spent so long putting together.'

'Has to be done, old boy,' Black commented. 'All these lads have got to be found jobs in Civvy Street, somehow or other.'

'I know,' Merry said, 'but that's easier said than done. Of course, some of them have already got well-established careers to go back to. Then there are some who have got themselves pretty well known through the work they've done with us and have already got offers, and others who have jobs or careers outside show business that they want to go back to. But that still leaves the rest. Some of them have got real talent and just need a bit of help to get started. But then there are those who have thoroughly enjoyed being onstage and want to make a career out of it but just haven't quite got what it takes. They're the ones that worry me.'

'You'll sort them out, Merry,' Black said easily. 'I have every confidence in you. That's not what I want to talk about now. The question is, what about you?'

'Me?'

'What are your plans for the future?'

Merry frowned. Over the last weeks he had given some passing thought to that problem but there always seemed to be something more pressing to think about. Or perhaps it was just that he didn't want to confront it.

'I don't know,' he said. 'Go back to what I was doing before the war, I suppose. I imagine there will still be summer shows, when things get back to normal.'

'Conducting third-rate concert parties at the end of the pier?' Black said scathingly. 'Is that the summit of your ambition?'

'They're not all third rate,' Merry protested mildly.

'Listen to me.' Black leaned forward and rested his arms on

the desk. 'For the last two years you've been putting on shows in big theatres with large casts and some of the biggest names in show business. And you've done it superlatively well. There isn't a single one of those big stars who hasn't come back to me and told me what a splendid MD you are.'

Merry blinked. 'That's frightfully kind of them.'

'*Frightfully kind!*' Black echoed his words satirically. 'Merry, these people are not in the business of being frightfully kind. If they don't think the MD knows his job they say so. But they've all been singing your praises. You're far too good at the job to waste yourself on piddling little concert parties.'

Merry looked at him warily. A small gleam of something that might be called ambition flickered in his mind.

'What do you suggest, then?' he enquired.

Black leaned back again. 'Think about what things are going to be like once we all get over the euphoria of winning the war. People think life is going to go back to being just like it was before – but it ain't! This country's taken a beating and it's going to take a long time to recover. There's going to be rationing and shortages for a long while yet and too many houses have been destroyed by the bombs. People are going to have a job to find anywhere to live. So what are they going to need, to take them out of themselves and give them a bit of a lift?'

'Entertainment?' Merry offered.

'Exactly! They're going to want glamour and fun and music. You mark my words, Merry, there's going to be the biggest explosion of all sorts of theatre since Shakespeare's day – musicals, straight plays, variety, specially variety. Now, my old dad, who's been in the business longer than almost anyone else, has seen this coming and he's taken the leases of several London theatres and between us we're going to fill them with the best variety shows in the country.' Black paused and regarded Merry with a gleam in his eye. 'How do you fancy being MD at the London Palladium or the Victoria Palace?'

'Me?' was all Merry could manage.

'Yes, you! You're just the man for the job. 'Course, if you've had a better offer . . .'

'No!' Merry gasped. 'Of course I haven't. There couldn't be a better offer. I can't imagine anything I'd like more.'

'That's OK, then,' Black said, beaming. 'I'll get the contracts drawn up. Let's go and have a drink on it, shall we?'

Merry waited to impart his news until Felix was settled with a pre-prandial gin.

His lover looked at him quizzically. 'You look like the cat that got the cream. What's happened?'

Merry gave him the gist of his conversation with Black and Felix jumped up, almost spilling his drink, and hugged him.

'Merry, that's terrific! And it's no more than you deserve. Haven't I always said you're the best MD in the business?'

'You're biased,' Merry said, smiling.

'Anyway,' Felix said, returning to his seat, 'it fits in perfectly with something I've been planning. You're going to be based in town, instead of trekking off to some seaside resort every summer, or touring the provinces. And I shall be here, too, a lot of the time, if things work out.'

Merry dropped on to the settee beside him. 'What things? I thought you were set on the life of a country gent.'

'Yes, well, I've thought a lot about that over this last year. You're right. I should be bored to death after a month or two.'

'You're not back on the idea of becoming a test pilot, are you?' Merry asked with alarm.

Felix chuckled. 'No, it's all right, you can relax.' He became serious again. 'Do you remember that conversation we had on your birthday last year, about the changes that need to happen in society after the war? You said you'd never heard me talk politics before.'

'Yes, I remember.'

'Well, I've realised that that is what really interests me now. I want to make a career in politics.'

Merry looked at him, sharply aware that the frivolous, devil-may-care Felix of the old days had matured into something very different. 'You can't stand for Parliament,' he pointed out. 'Peers of the realm are excluded, aren't they?'

'Along with criminals and lunatics,' Felix agreed with a grin. 'But don't you see? I don't need to. All I have to do is take my seat in the Lords. But I'm not going to be one of those red-faced old geezers who are wheeled out every time the Tories want to win a vote. I want to really get involved. After all, there have been cabinet ministers who were members of the Upper House.'

'On which side of the House will you sit?' Merry asked curiously.

'Neither, to begin with. I'll sit as a cross-bencher until I feel I know enough to make a decision. But there are various possibilities. I've already been putting out feelers, though nobody is making any sort of promises until after the general election, of course.'

'Well, at least you haven't got to worry about getting elected,' Merry murmured. On top of George Black's offer this new idea was almost too much to grasp, but an unforeseen and delightful prospect seemed to be unrolling before him.

'Do you think I'm crazy?' Felix asked.

'Not at all. I think it's a wonderful idea. It's exactly the sort of thing you should be doing.' He raised his glass. 'Here's to a brilliant career!'

'Thanks!'

They drank and looked at each other. Merry said, 'So you really will be spending a lot of your time in London.'

'Oh yes. That's definite.'

Merry smiled at him. 'Do you realise this is the first time we've actually lived together without the feeling that in a week, or two weeks, we've got to part, with no idea when we might see each other again?'

Felix reached out and put an arm round his neck. 'Of course I realise. I have to pinch myself every morning to make sure I'm not dreaming. Long may it last!'

But then he looked away and changed the subject and something in his manner left Merry feeling vaguely uneasy.

Two days later he came home from the office in Grosvenor Street to find Felix already busy in the kitchen, which was unusual since Felix's contribution to their domestic organisation usually consisted of pouring the drinks and laying the table. When the meal was ready he insisted on opening a bottle of wine from the pre-war stock laid in by his father. The late Lord Malpas had had a good palate – or perhaps just a good wine merchant – and the contents of the cellar at the Hall had hardly been depleted during the war years. He had also laid down a reasonable stock at the flat, but they had already started to make inroads into that.

'I thought we agreed to lay off the wine except for special occasions,' Merry said. 'God alone knows when decent French wine will be available again.'

'I can always bring some down from Cheshire,' Felix pointed out. 'I feel like a glass or two tonight.'

All through the meal Merry had the impression that Felix had something on his mind but could not bring himself to broach the subject. So when they had finished eating he said, 'Come on, get it off your chest.'

'What?' Felix asked defensively.

'Whatever it is that you've been brooding over all evening.'

Felix gave him a brief smile. 'You read me like a book, don't you.'

'Always have,' Merry agreed, and added fondly, 'It's one of my favourite stories.'

'OK.' Felix paused, fiddling with the stem of his wineglass. Then he looked up and met Merry's eyes. 'First, though, I want to get a few things straight – lay down some ground rules, if you like.'

'Good Lord!' Merry said, beginning to be disturbed but trying to maintain a light tone. 'This sounds serious.'

'It is serious,' Felix agreed. 'But the most important thing for you to bear in mind is that what I'm going to suggest is only an idea. If you don't feel you can live with it, it will be forgotten and never mentioned again. Understood?'

'Not really. I haven't got the vaguest notion what you're talking about.'

Felix reached across the table and laid a hand on Merry's wrist. 'Merry, you do know, don't you, that the most important thing in the world to me is what we have together? I would never, *never* do anything that might hurt you or spoil our relationship. So this is not the moment for noble self-sacrifice. The last thing you must do is agree to something you hate the thought of, just because you think it's what I want.'

'For God's sake, Felix,' Merry broke in, 'get to the point! You're frightening me to death!'

'That's just what I'm trying not to do,' Felix said earnestly.

'I just want to be sure that you understand that you only have to say "no" to kill the whole thing stone dead.'

'*What thing?*' Merry implored him.

Felix sat back and took a mouthful of wine. 'What would you say if I told you I was thinking of getting married?'

Merry stared at him and said the first thing that came into his head. 'You can't.'

'Well,' Felix responded judicially, 'from a legal point of view there's nothing to stop me, of course. And I can – you know – I can perform the functions of a husband, when required.'

Merry felt physically dizzy, as if he had suddenly found himself on the edge of a precipice. 'But why?' he said, helplessly. 'I don't understand.'

Felix reached out again and gripped his hand. 'I know. Just let me try to explain. OK?' In response to Merry's dazed nod he went on, 'There are several reasons, all bound up with inheriting the title. As you know, it's not something I ever imagined happening until last summer, but now that it has it does bring various other considerations along with it.'

'Of course. You want an heir.' Merry felt he was beginning to see some glimmerings of reason.

'That's certainly an important part of it. I'd like to be able to leave the place to someone who'll care for it. If I die without issue it all goes to Cousin Eric, and, while I've nothing against him, I don't think he's the right man for the job. He doesn't care about Malpas as I do. He wasn't born and brought up there as I was and, quite frankly, I don't think he'd be interested. So, yes, I'd like to continue the direct line, if I can. But there are other considerations. If I'm going to take up residence in Cheshire, at any rate for part of the time, I shall be expected to fulfil various social obligations – entertaining and so forth. And that really needs a hostess. Obviously, my mother can continue to fill that function for the time being, but it's not really fair to expect her to go on indefinitely. Besides which, I'm fed up with the "eligible bachelor" routine. It was bad enough when every squadron I served with was trying to pair me up with a suitable girlfriend. Can you imagine what it would be like when the whole county got at it?'

'On the basis that "it is a truth universally acknowledged that a single man in possession of a good fortune must be in need of a wife",' Merry murmured.

'Exactly,' Felix agreed. 'I don't know who said that, but he got it spot on. So, I want protection from the society marriage market. And I want a wife who will take on the burden of running the house and entertaining people and opening bazaars and village fêtes, and also look after the place when I'm away. Am I beginning to make sense?'

'Sort of.'

'There's more to it yet. The next point to consider is my political ambitions. That sounds pompous, but if I'm actually going to try to make a career in politics it rather seems that a wife is a *sine qua non* for success. And that brings me to the final point, which could be the most important. Protective camouflage. You know how people gossip. If we both remain single and continue to share this flat you know what people are going to say. Now that may not matter too much in your job. People in the profession are fairly broad minded as a general rule. But it could put paid to my chances of getting anywhere in politics. And if anybody decided to go in for a bit of blackmail or to get really vindictive it could, in the worst event, put us both in jail.' He sat back and looked at Merry. 'Does all this sound horribly cynical?'

'Yes, it does rather,' Merry said. 'Are you talking about a marriage of convenience?'

'I suppose so. But one that is convenient to all parties concerned.'

'But you can't!' Merry reiterated. 'It wouldn't be fair to any woman to ask her to marry you on that basis.'

'It would if the woman in question knew exactly what she was getting into.'

'You mean you'd tell her?' Then the truth came to Merry in a flash of revelation. 'Harry! You're thinking of asking Harriet to marry you!'

'There's nobody else I could even contemplate marrying,' Felix said.

'But what makes you think she'd agree? I mean, I know she's been carrying a torch for you all these years but surely she's not going to be prepared to marry you under those conditions. Unless . . .' A cold fist gripped his stomach. 'Felix, the only possible reason would be that she thinks she can break us up. Once she's married to you she thinks you'll break off our relationship rather than risk a scandal.'

'No!' Felix responded vehemently. 'Harry's not like that. I know you've never forgiven her for running out on me when I was in hospital after the crash but that was just shock. She's changed a lot since then. You must realise that from the photographs of hers that you've seen.'

'Then why should she be prepared to accept the sort of deal you're offering?' Merry asked obdurately. 'It's a non-starter, Felix.'

'No, it isn't,' Felix replied with quiet certainty.

Merry caught his breath. 'You've spoken to her? You've already asked her?'

'There didn't seem to be any point in worrying you with it until I was sure it was a genuine possibility.'

'But why? What's in it for her?'

'Security. A recognised position in society. Children, hopefully.'

'I take the point about the children. But security? Social position? She's the daughter of an earl, for crying out loud!'

'Yes, but the title and the land are entailed, just like Malpas. And Harriet's one of two sisters. There is no heir. When her father dies the land goes to a second cousin she hardly knows. She says she doesn't want to end up as the spinster aunt depending on his charity. Of course, she could earn a living as a photographer. She's made her reputation there. But she says she's had enough of that. She wants marriage and a family. After all, she's my age – thirty. It's getting late for her.'

'But all the same, doesn't she want love, romance, all the rest of it?'

Felix paused, frowning slightly. 'She's had that. Look, what I'm going to tell you is in the strictest confidence. Poor old Harry's been through the mill. It's no wonder she's looking for a bit of peace.'

Briefly, he outlined the story Harriet had told him in the jeep on the way to Celles. When he had finished Merry sat back and ran a hand through his hair.

'OK, it begins to make a sort of sense. I can see the advantages of the arrangement for both of you. But what are you suggesting? Some sort of *ménage à trois*?'

'Perish the thought!' Felix exclaimed. 'What do you take me for? No, the way it would work is like this. Harriet would be installed at Malpas and I should divide my time, as I always intended, between there and here.'

'And would she be happy with that?'

'Perfectly. She's ideally suited to it, Merry. I mean, we grew up together. She knows the people and she understands what they will expect. She enjoys the country life and she's an excellent organiser. She'll look after things when I'm away – and when I'm there we shall be company for each other. We've always been good friends. The only question is, can you be happy with it?'

'I don't know,' Merry said. He still felt as if solid ground had given way under his feet. 'It seemed as if life was finally sorting itself out and everything was going to be fine – and now this. I don't know.'

Felix got up and came round the table. 'Come in the other room and sit down,' he said. 'I can't talk properly with the table between us.'

He took Merry by the hand and led him into the sitting room, where he sat down beside him on the sofa and put his arm round him.

'Just remember what I said at the start of this conversation. This is the most important thing to me – us, together. If I thought for one moment that what I'm suggesting would come between us I'd never have contemplated it. If you aren't happy with it all you have to do is say no and that's the end of it.'

'How can I say no, when it's obviously the best thing for you?' Merry asked.

'Because it won't be the best thing for me if it makes you unhappy.'

Merry gazed into space, trying to imagine a future on the terms Felix had outlined.

'Suppose Harriet wants to come down to London with you, when you come?'

'She won't – except for the occasional shopping trip perhaps.'

'And on those occasions, what happens? I move out?'

'No. She sleeps in the spare room.'

'Felix, we couldn't do that!'

'Why not? She knows what the situation is. I've made it perfectly clear to her where my priorities lie.'

Merry shook his head. 'It won't work.'

'OK,' Felix said. 'End of story. Come to bed.'

24

Merry woke in the summer dawn. There was hardly any traffic about yet and somewhere near by a blackbird was singing. He turned his head and looked at Felix. He was sleeping as he usually did on his right side, the scarred left side of his face hidden in the pillow, and Merry felt a lurch of desire in the pit of his stomach. He allowed his mind to drift back over the past weeks since his return to London. For the first day or two they had been unable to keep their hands off each other, falling into bed as soon as they both arrived home and getting up only to forage for something to eat. That first weekend in Seaford they had hardly bothered to get dressed. Since then, they had settled into a more routine domesticity. Merry would prepare a meal and then, unless they were going out, they both settled down to read or listen to the wireless. Even so, it was never long before one or other would look at his watch and suggest an early night. Nevertheless, lying there as the outlines of the room slowly sharpened in the growing light, Merry found himself considering the prospect that before long they would begin to take each other for granted. He had sometimes marvelled at the fact that their love had remained so intense, so all consuming over a period of more than four years. Now he realised that it had been the repeated meeting and parting, the constant threat of danger and loss, which had kept it sharp, like an appetite never quite satisfied. If they settled now into a comfortable routine he saw that there was a danger that they might lose that sharp edge of desire. There had been no question of that last night. Felix had set out to prove otherwise and Merry had responded with equal passion. But it was impossible to live at that pitch of emotion indefinitely. The foundations for their future must be broader based than that.

Felix stirred and opened his eyes. Seeing Merry watching him, he murmured drowsily, 'Penny for them?'

'I think you'd better invite Harriet round to dinner,' Merry replied.

The dinner was arranged for the following Saturday. Felix suggested that they should go to a restaurant but Merry pointed out that it would be impossible to conduct the kind of conversation they needed to have in a public place. That meant that he had to cook and he spent some time wondering what he could contrive with the unpromising ingredients available on the ration. In the end he called in a favour from a trumpet player whom he knew to be moonlighting at the Savoy Grill. The trumpet player spoke to one of the chefs and, as a result, Merry returned in triumph from Grosvenor Street bearing a parcel containing a delicate rack of Welsh lamb. He found Felix already in the kitchen, unpacking a sturdy box to reveal three shiny, fresh brown trout.

'Where on earth . . . ?' Merry asked.

'Chap at the Air Ministry has a place down in Hampshire with its own trout stream. I had a word yesterday, before he went home for the weekend. He went out with a rod this morning and caught these three little beauties, put them on the next train to town and I collected them from Paddington half an hour ago.'

'Brilliant!' said Merry. 'It'll be a meal to remind you of the days before rationing.'

Harriet arrived a perfectly judged five minutes after the appointed hour. She was wearing a simple dark green dress, her only adornment a single row of pearls. Her auburn hair was drawn back in a chignon and her face was only lightly made up. Greeting her, Merry understood that, consciously or unconsciously, she was signalling that he need not regard her as a dangerous rival. She kissed Felix lightly on the cheek and handed him a small package.

'I knew you'd have wine, so I thought these might be welcome instead.'

Then she came to Merry and extended both hands. 'Thank you so much for asking me to come tonight, Merry. I can't tell you how much I appreciate it. May I?' She leaned towards him and he lowered his head for her kiss, saying, 'I'm glad you felt able to accept.'

Looking at her more closely, he saw that her face was thinner than he remembered it and her eyes deeply shadowed. She looked a good deal more than one year older since their last meeting at Anthony's memorial service. It was obviously true, as Felix had said, that she had been 'through the mill'.

Behind her Felix exclaimed, 'American cigarettes! You're a genius! I've been smoking filthy Turkish tobacco for the past week.'

Over cocktails he filled his cigarette case and offered it to Harriet. 'Poor old Merry's had to give up because of his asthma,' he explained as he lit her cigarette, then took one himself. 'But he's allowed one drag.' He lit the cigarette, then took it out of his mouth and handed it to Merry. It was a familiar gesture, one they had used often over the past years as a coded message of intimacy, and glancing at Harriet as he drew in the smoke, Merry saw that the significance had not escaped her. He handed the cigarette back to Felix and excused himself on the grounds that something in the kitchen needed his attention.

When the meal was served Felix proposed that they should leave discussion of the business in hand until after they had eaten. Merry could see the sense of this but felt rather at a loss for a subject of conversation, since both future plans and the immediate past seemed strewn with pitfalls. Felix and Harriet, however, fell easily into reminiscences of growing up in Cheshire and of the changes that had taken place since the outbreak of war, and Merry realised, listening to them, how much they had in common. They were, in almost every sense, natural partners.

Later the conversation turned to the present state of the country, now that the war was over.

'Not long now till the general election,' Harriet remarked. 'Will Winnie get in, do you think?'

'No,' Felix said. 'We shall have a Labour government by the end of July.'

'Do you think so?' Merry asked. 'Will people really turn their backs on Churchill, after he got us through the war?'

'Believe me, I've got the greatest respect for the old man,' Felix said. 'And it does seem ungrateful to kick him in the teeth, after all he's done. But people don't want to go back to the way things were before the war, and quite right, too. Things have to change, and Clem Attlee and Co. are the men to change them.'

'Will you vote for him?' Merry asked.

Felix grinned. 'I'm spared that choice, thank God. Peers of the realm can't vote, remember?'

The meal over, Felix poured them all a brandy and then

took himself off to the kitchen to make coffee. Normally Merry would have gone too, to clear up, but he recognised that Felix was deliberately giving him a chance to talk privately to Harriet. It was she who took the initiative.

'I'm so grateful to you for even being prepared to consider what Felix is suggesting.'

'I couldn't do otherwise,' Merry responded. 'Felix's happiness is more important to me than anything.'

'I know,' she said softly. 'And I hope you'll believe that it's more important to me, too. I want you to understand one thing. I would never attempt to come between you. For one thing, I know it would be useless, and if I ever tried to it would finish me with Felix for ever. And for another, I know he could never be happy if you two split up.'

Merry looked into her earnest, green-flecked eyes. 'I believe that,' he said. 'What concerns me more is the effect on you. Why should you want to embark on something like this?'

'Because it's what I want. What I've always wanted, in a way.'

'Are you in love with Felix?'

'No, not in the usual sense of the word. I was, for a long time. When we were both in our teens I thought if he didn't ask me to marry him I'd die of misery! Then I began to realise it wasn't going to happen. I thought for a while that it was because we knew each other too well. We were more like brother and sister. Then, of course, that horrible business at Cambridge happened and I understood.'

'But you and he had an affair after that.'

'Oh yes. He swore that he'd finished with . . . with all that. And he did try, but that was just the point. He had to try. He wanted to fall in love with me, but he couldn't. I knew that all along, but I kept hoping we could make a go of it somehow. I ruined it all, of course, when I ran out on him that day in the hospital. I've never forgiven myself for that, but perhaps it was for the best in the long run. It gave us all a chance to see what the real situation was. You were able to give him what he needed and I couldn't.' She smiled briefly. 'I guess the best man won.'

'But now,' Merry said, 'are you really happy to settle for . . . well, for second best?'

She looked down at her glass. 'I've got my reasons. I won't go into details. Just let's say all I want now is someone I can trust and feel safe with.' She raised her eyes again. 'I can be the sort of wife Felix needs, Merry. All I ask is the chance to show that.'

'And you're prepared to share him?'

Harriet made a small, wry grimace. 'Half a loaf . . . no, not even that. Crumbs from the rich man's table?'

Merry felt a sudden wave of pity for her. 'Harry, are you sure? You're worth more than that.'

'That's what I keep telling her,' Felix said, coming in from the kitchen with the coffee.

She looked up at him. 'It's all I want, Felix. All I need. If you and Merry are willing to go along with it.'

Felix put the tray down. 'You know my answer. It all depends on Merry.'

Merry looked from one of them to the other and something wrenched at his heart. 'In that case,' he said very quietly, 'all I can say is "Bless you, my children".'

He heard Harriet make a small noise of relief. Felix held his eyes for a moment and then he said softly, 'Thank you, my dear.' He reached for his brandy glass. 'A toast, then. To the three of us! May we all live happily ever after!'

Merry drank the toast with a strange feeling of unreality.

Was he really consenting to this bizarre arrangement? On the other hand, what was the alternative? And then, was it after all quite so bizarre as it seemed?

To cover his confusion he said, 'So, when's the wedding to be, then?'

Harriet and Felix looked at each other. She said, 'We've never even talked about that. It's all seemed such a pipe dream, until now. What do you think, Felix?'

'I don't know,' he replied. 'I suppose there's no point in hanging about. After all, we've known each other long enough. Unless,' a look of dismay came into his face, 'unless you want a big society do. That will take some time to arrange, I suppose.'

'Oh, God forbid!' Harriet exclaimed. 'I couldn't face all that. My mother would want to invite half the county. Let's have a quick, quiet wedding here in London, with only immediate family and our own friends.'

'Suits me,' agreed Felix. 'Mind you, people will talk.'

Harriet laughed suddenly. 'Let them! They'll never guess the true story.' Then she paused. 'There is one thing. It'll have to be a church wedding. My mother would never forgive me if I got married in a registry office.'

'Nor would mine,' Felix admitted.

Merry cleared his throat. 'Look, this is between the two of you. I'll go and wash the dishes, if you'll excuse me.'

Harriet swallowed the last of her coffee and got up. 'No, this can all wait until another day. I'm going to leave you two to yourselves now.' She turned to Merry. 'Dear Merry, thank you again – and for the lovely dinner, too. One thing's for sure. I'll never be able to bear comparison with you as a cook!'

She kissed him again, on the cheek, and went out into the hall. Felix accompanied her and Merry heard him promise to telephone her the next day. There was no time for more than a peck on the cheek before the front door closed and Felix came back into the sitting room. Merry had begun to gather up the dishes but Felix came over, took them firmly out of his hands and replaced them on the table. Then he put his arms round him and kissed him with an ardour that took his breath away.

'You are quite sure about this, aren't you?' he asked, drawing back slightly. 'It's not too late to change your mind.'

Merry shook his head. 'I wish I could say I'm sure it's going to work, but I'm not. But on balance it seems to be the best plan, for all of us. I'm so lucky to have you, and Harriet seems to ask for so little. It would be churlish to refuse.'

'I'm the lucky one,' Felix said. 'You won't regret this, Merry. I swear you won't.' He kissed him again. 'Come to bed.'

'What about the washing up?' Merry protested half-heartedly.

'Sod the washing up!' said Felix.

Felix lunched with Harriet a couple of times during the following week and after the second occasion he came back and announced that everything was settled. The wedding would take place on 18 July at St Peter's, Eaton Square, which was close to where Harriet had a flat. The banns would be called for the first time in just over a week.

'I wonder if they have a resident organist at present,' Merry murmured speculatively. 'I'd like to do the music, if that's OK with you.'

Felix grinned and curled a hand round the back of his neck. 'It's a nice idea, but you're going to be too busy to play the organ that day.'

'Too busy?'

Felix's intensely blue eyes gazed into his. 'I'd like you to be my best man, if you can bring yourself to do it.'

For a moment Merry hesitated, then he said, 'Yes, of course. That seems fitting. I'll be glad to.'

The next weekend Felix and Harriet went north to announce their engagement to their respective parents. Felix urged Merry to accompany him but Merry resolutely refused, maintaining that this was a time for him to remain in the background.

When Felix arrived back on the Sunday night Merry asked, 'Well, how did your mother take the news?'

Felix gave him a strange grin. 'You'll never guess what her first words were.'

'Thank God?' Merry offered.

'Try again.'

'Congratulations?'

'Wrong both times,' Felix said. 'Her first words were "But, Edward, what about Guy?"'

They stared at each other for a moment. Then Merry began to laugh. 'So she did know, all the time.'

'Of course she did,' Felix said. 'No fool, my mother! She just didn't want to admit she knew.'

'What did you say to her?'

'I told her you were going to be my best man and that seemed to satisfy her. Anyway, I think she realised by that time that she had rather given herself away, so she dropped the subject.'

'Fancy her thinking of me, at a moment like that,' Merry mused. 'But apart from that, she's pleased?'

'Oh, delighted. Everyone was. It was always assumed that Harry and I would marry, so they all feel smugly self-satisfied that their predictions were correct. Mother would have preferred a big county wedding, of course, but I think she understands why we don't want that.'

'And Harriet's family?'

'Equally delighted. I think they'd begun to be afraid they'd got an old maid on their hands. So, everything's in order. The announcement will appear in the papers the day after tomorrow.'

25

On the morning after his dark moments on Westminster Bridge Richard woke with one name ringing in his ears, as if someone had shouted it.

'MERRY!'

Merry! Of course! Why had he not thought of him before? Of all the people in the world Merry was the one who might be able to put him in touch with someone who would give him a job. If only he knew where he was! At breakfast, he was scanning the paper, more to avoid conversation with the other residents than out of any real interest, when a headline struck him as if somehow it had insinuated itself into his dreams.

BATTLE OF BRITAIN HERO TO WED

Lord Malpas, who will be better known to most people as Squadron Leader the Hon. Edward Mountjoy, DFC, is to wed Lady Harriet Forsyth, the elder daughter of the Earl of Pembury. The wedding will take place at St Peter's Church, Eaton Square, on July 18th. Lord Malpas, who succeeded to the title after the death of both his father and his elder brother due to enemy action, was awarded the DFC after shooting down eight enemy aircraft during the Battle of Britain. He was subsequently shot down himself and suffered serious burns to his face and hands. Lady Harriet also has a distinguished war record, having established herself as a brilliant and intrepid photographer whose pictures of battle scenes have appeared frequently in this paper.

Richard finished his breakfast without tasting it. A single thought dominated his mind. He ought to contact Merry somehow and make sure he was all right. He racked his brains to recall every detail of their previous conversations. What was the name of the outfit Merry had said he was working for? Central Entertainment Bureau, that was it! He rang one of the secretaries at Baker Street, who had always had a soft spot for him, and asked her to find out the telephone number. Half an hour later she called back to say that the organisation he wanted was the Central Pool of Artistes, which had headquarters in Grosvenor Street.

Richard dialled the number without a great deal of hope. Merry might well still be abroad, perhaps in France or Germany or even out East, or perhaps he had been demobbed already. When a switchboard operator answered he said, 'I don't know if you can help me. I'm trying to contact a Captain Guy Merryweather . . .'

'Hold the line, please,' came the crisp reply. There was a pause, a couple of clicks and then Merry's voice. 'Merryweather.'

Richard was so taken aback that for a moment he could not think what to say. Merry said, 'Merryweather here. Can I help you?'

'Merry, it's me – Richard.'

'Richard? Richard Stevens?'

'Yes. I didn't know if I'd be able to get hold of you. I wasn't expecting to be put straight through. How are you?'

'I'm fine. Fit as a flea! How about you?'

'I'm OK. Well, I was wounded, but I'm OK now.'

'Wounded? Not seriously, I hope.'

'Well, it could have been, but I was lucky. Merry, I've just read the item in the paper.'

'Item? Ah, the announcement of the wedding.'

'Yes. I was . . . well, it took me by surprise. Are you sure everything's OK?'

A brief pause. Then, 'Don't worry, everything's fine. Look, we ought to meet. Where are you?'

'In London. Just round the corner, more or less – Ebury Street.'

'No, really? That's marvellous! Can we have lunch?'

'Yes, of course. I'd like that very much. When?'

'Are you free today?'

'Yes, as it happens.'

'Excellent. There's a little Italian place called the Amalfi in Wardour Street. Do you know it?'

'Yes, I know where you mean.'

'I'll meet you there at twelve thirty. OK?'

'OK, fine! I'll look forward to it.'

When Richard reached the restaurant Merry was already there, sitting up at the bar in the reception area sipping a pink gin. Richard paused in the doorway for a moment to take him in. He had filled out over the six years and in the immaculately tailored uniform he looked lean and fit, rather than the slightly gangling figure Richard remembered from Fairbourne. His face was tanned, and in defiance of army protocol the rebellious lock of hair still fell forward over his brow. He looked round, saw Richard and came towards him. For a moment they faced each other awkwardly. A handshake seemed inadequate but it was all that convention permitted.

'Richard, it's good to see you!' Merry's hand-clasp was warm, the light green-grey eyes sparkling with pleasure. He did look, Richard assured himself, as if everything was, indeed, OK. 'I was absolutely stunned when you said your name. I've been trying to locate you for weeks.'

'Locate me? Really?'

'Yes, you *damned elusive Pimpernel*! What are you drinking?'

'I'll have a dry martini, if they've got such a thing.'

The barman was desolated. They had gin, yes, but the genuine Martini vermouth was totally unobtainable at present. Would the *signore* settle for the French Noilly Prat instead? Richard settled.

Merry said, 'I'm sorry to hear you were wounded. Where did that happen?'

While they sipped their drinks Richard told the story of the sniper in the warehouse, glossing over the exact circumstances and the immediate consequences. Then he said, with some hesitation, 'Have you seen Felix lately?'

Merry's eyes glinted. 'Oh yes. I see him every day. We share a flat.'

'You do?' Richard waited but Merry remained teasingly silent. 'He's in London, then.'

'Attached to the Air Ministry, in theory. In practice, waiting to be demobbed.'

'How is he?'

'Very well.'

Richard saw that if he was going to get the answer to his question he would have to approach it more directly. 'Merry, this wedding – I don't understand.'

Merry's look became serious but still reassuringly sanguine. 'I know,' he said quietly. 'It must seem strange to you, and I can't go into details. Just take it from me that we all know what we're doing. It suits everyone concerned. OK?'

Richard met his eyes. 'Of course, if you say so. I was just afraid that you might . . . well, you know.'

'I know.' Merry touched his sleeve briefly. 'I appreciate your concern.'

The waiter approached to tell them that their table was ready. The menu was very limited but, when he discovered that they both spoke fluent Italian, a number of other, more attractive, items suddenly became available. When they had ordered Merry said, 'So! How's Priscilla?'

Richard felt a sudden jolt in the pit of his stomach. He had put Priscilla's death to the back of his mind and it came as a shock to realise that his friends did not know what had happened.

'Priscilla was killed by one of the last V2s,' he said. 'At least, that isn't quite true. She was knocked down by a fire engine while running for shelter during one of the last raids.'

He heard Merry's quick intake of breath. 'My dear chap, I had no idea! I'm most terribly sorry. What a tragedy!'

'Yes, it was,' Richard agreed. 'At least, it was for her and for her family. Not so much for me. You see, we were divorced several months earlier.'

'Divorced?' Merry studied his face for a moment. 'Well, I'm sorry but not entirely surprised.'

'No,' Richard accepted. 'It was a mistake from the start. I mean, I thought it would work. We had so much in common, and I did love her – or so I thought.'

'I can certainly see that you had interests in common,' Merry commented. 'And I can see that the marriage would have had great advantages for you, personally – in career terms, I mean. But I never thought Priscilla was the right person for you. What happened?'

'Oh, partly just the war. She didn't like me being away for

such long periods. She didn't like being alone – not that she was, if you see what I mean. And also, she had ideas, ambitions for me that I just couldn't go along with. Not while the war was still going on.'

'What sort of ambitions?'

'She arranged for me to be seconded to CEMA. She thought culture for the masses was more important than fighting Hitler. I didn't agree.'

'Ah,' Merry said dryly. 'I know the dilemma well.'

Richard looked up quickly from his spaghetti Milanese. 'You did your bit. For God's sake don't think I'm criticising. You didn't get that DSO playing sonatas in village halls in rural England. It's just that I was . . . well, I thought I could be more useful elsewhere.'

'Such as blowing up bridges behind enemy lines,' Merry murmured, adding in response to Richard's look of alarm, 'It's all right. I'll keep my voice down and I'm not going to ask awkward questions. But I did have a vivid account from Felix of your last meeting.'

'Of course.' Richard smiled. It was a great relief to talk to someone who at least had some inkling of what he had been doing. 'I'd forgotten that for a moment.'

'So, what are your plans now?' Merry asked. 'Once you've been demobbed.'

Richard felt his face tighten. 'A job in a bank. Or what do you think of going into the house agency business?'

Merry stared at him, open mouthed. 'You are joking, of course!'

'That's what the chap who's supposed to advise us on new careers after demob suggested.'

Merry laughed. 'How bloody ridiculous! He obviously has no idea how good you are.'

'It seems that doesn't matter. What matters is whether you've got a name that people will recognise from hearing you on the radio – like Frank and Isabel.'

'Those two!' Merry exclaimed. 'Frank Bell was the biggest pain I had to cope with in all my dealings with ENSA.'

'Just the same, he's got his career made,' Richard said.

Merry looked at him seriously. 'Are you telling me that you've got nothing lined up? No offers at all?'

'None at all. I've spent the last few days trying to contact agents and producers. No one wants to talk to me.'

'Well, we'll soon change that!' Merry said emphatically. He went on to outline the proposal that George Black had made to him. 'It's not really what you should be doing,' he ended. 'You ought to be using that voice to sing serious music. But if nothing better comes up I'm sure I can find you a couple of spots on a variety bill and at least that will give you a chance to get heard. And there are a few people I can put you in touch with who might be able to offer you something better. How about musical comedy? I hear there's going to be a revival of *Show Boat*. I might be able to get you an audition.'

'Merry, could you?' Richard felt suddenly like weeping. 'I'd be eternally grateful. I don't mind telling you, I've been feeling pretty depressed recently.'

'My dear chap, why on earth didn't you contact me before?' Merry asked.

'I didn't know where to find you. It was that item in the paper that set me racking my brains to think how I could get in touch. Did you say you'd been trying to contact me?'

'Yes, but I didn't know where to start looking either.'

'Why did you want me?'

'To invite you to the wedding, of course. Felix is very keen that you should be there. He was tickled pink when I phoned him after your call to tell him you'd surfaced. He'd have been here now except he has a lunch date with some of Harriet's cousins. That girl has more relations than anyone I know and they all want to meet the bridegroom. Anyway, how about dinner tomorrow? Are you free?'

'Yes, I've got nothing on. In fact, I'm at a bit of a loose end.'

'We'll soon put a stop to that!' Merry was writing on a paper napkin. 'Here's the address. About seven o'clock?'

'Great! I'll be there.'

'You'd better be!' Merry said. 'I don't want you doing another of your disappearing acts.'

The next evening Richard presented himself at the Mayfair flat. Felix opened the door in his shirtsleeves and broke into a broad grin of welcome.

'Richard! Wonderful to see you again! Come in!'

He extended his hand and at the same moment Richard offered the bottle he was carrying. He saw his mistake and swapped hands but by then Felix had stepped back to usher him inside. He reached for the bottle as Richard attempted to shake hands. The awkward little dance ended in laughter and Felix exclaimed, 'To hell with this! We've both lived in Italy,' and embraced him.

Stepping back, Richard said, 'How are you, Felix?'

'Never better!' Felix said cheerfully. 'Merry tells me you stopped a bullet in Bologna. Are you completely recovered?'

'Yes, pretty well. I was lucky. They got me to a brilliant surgeon in an American field hospital. Otherwise I might be in a wheelchair now.' He studied Felix's face. It was the first time he had seen him in daylight since their meeting in the Willises' kitchen before he underwent plastic surgery, and he had a vivid memory of the hideous disfigurement wrought by the flames in the cockpit of his burning Spitfire. 'I must say, you're looking well. That surgeon chappy certainly knew what he was doing.'

Felix tilted his chin. 'Not bad, is it?'

'Bloody brilliant, I should say.'

Merry came out of the kitchen with a tea towel hung over his shoulder. Felix said, 'Richard is inspecting Archie McIndoe's handiwork.'

'Be careful what you say, Richard,' Merry advised. 'In this household the Holy Trinity consists of the Father, the Son and Archibald McIndoe.'

Felix chuckled. 'And not necessarily in that order.'

'I can see why,' Richard agreed. 'Hello, Merry.'

Merry came over to him and, ignoring his outstretched hand, took him by the shoulders. 'I couldn't do this in the restaurant,' he said, and kissed him firmly on both cheeks.

Richard drew back, laughing. 'Well, the last man to do that to me was a Frenchman.'

'French?' queried Felix. 'Not Italian?'

'Come to think of it, it probably was an Italian. Anyway, the chap I was thinking of wasn't French after all. He was Belgian, masquerading as an Irishman.'

'What the hell is he talking about?' Felix asked, looking at Merry.

'No idea,' said Merry. 'Why are we standing in the hall? Take the man through and give him a drink, for God's sake.'

Felix led the way into a large sitting room that reminded Richard of Maurice Buckmaster's flat. A shiver went down his spine as he recalled the hours spent there prior to being dispatched on a mission.

Felix was saying, 'What will you have, Richard? We've

managed to find some gin, but I'm afraid there's no vermouth to be had for love nor money.'

Richard held up a paper carrier he had been clutching all the while. Felix took it and extracted a bottle. 'You're a genius! Did you bring this back with you?'

'A parting gift from one of the nurses,' Richard said with a smile. 'I thought tonight might be a good moment to open it.' While Felix mixed the drinks he added, 'Felix, I'm sorry, I don't know whether congratulations or condolences are in order. I was sorry to read about your father and brother.'

Felix turned and held out a glass. 'Life's been a bit of a mixed bag for the last year or so,' he agreed. 'But then that goes for all of us. You probably realise that I didn't actually see a great deal of my family. There werc areas of my life on which we didn't exactly see eye to eye. I was sorry to hear about Priscilla, too.'

'Thanks,' Richard said. 'But like you I can't pretend it was a personal tragedy. How does it feel to be a peer of the realm?'

'You do realise,' Merry interjected, 'that you should have bowed three times and addressed him as "my lord"?'

'Oh, should I?'

'Only if you want a punch on the nose,' said Felix. He raised his glass. 'Well, here's to absent friends.'

'On which cheerful note I shall adjourn to the kitchen,' Merry commented dryly. 'Unless you have a taste for burnt offerings.'

'Merry's cooking,' Felix said, his face relaxing into a smile. 'Don't worry. He's brilliant. He can make something delicious out of the most unpromising ingredients.'

'Don't speak too soon!' Merry warned him. 'It's supposed to be lasagne, in Richard's honour, but I'm not at all sure that Spam is the ideal meat for the job.'

'Can I help?' Felix asked.

'No, you stay here and entertain Richard.'

'We'll both come,' Richard said. 'Felix can help and I'll watch.'

So he leaned in the kitchen doorway and watched with growing amusement as Felix meekly fetched and carried under Merry's instructions and the two of them bickered amicably about who had mislaid the corkscrew or failed to wash up a pan. Eventually Felix looked over and caught him smiling.

'What are you grinning at, young Stevens?' he demanded.

'You two,' Richard said. 'You're like an old married couple.'

As soon as the words were out of his mouth he felt himself flush scarlet with embarrassment. Felix and Merry consulted each other with raised eyebrows. Then Felix grinned.

'We are an old married couple,' he said. 'Fortunately, the law doesn't regard what I'm about to do as bigamy.' Seeing Richard's confusion, he patted him lightly on the arm. 'Don't worry. I know it seems bizarre, but we're all quite comfortable with it and, after all, that is what matters, don't you think?'

'Yes, of course,' Richard murmured. 'Please don't think I'm being judgemental. I just want you all to be happy.'

'Bless your heart,' Felix smiled. 'Well, we are. Aren't we, Merry?'

'Happy as Larry,' said Merry. 'Dinner's ready.'

Over the meal the talk naturally turned to what they had all been doing over the past years. Richard heard, for the first time, the story of Merry's exploits in North Africa and Felix's experiences in the defence of Malta, and the tale of how he had 'stolen' a plane in order to visit Merry in hospital.

Towards the end of the meal Felix fixed him with a look and said, 'Now then, young Stevens, you're sitting there very quiet, letting us do all the talking, but I suspect you've had a more interesting war than any of us. Come on, give!'

Richard returned his gaze for a few seconds in silence. The urge to pour out his experiences to sympathetic ears was almost overpowering. In the end he said, 'I'm sorry. I can't tell you.'

Felix frowned. 'I appreciate you've been involved in something clandestine, something not for public consumption, but after all, we already know part of it. You weren't there in Italy by accident, as I was. And the fact that you were able to summon up a plane to get me home suggests you were in a pretty influential position. What's the point in pretending it's a secret?'

Richard smiled faintly. 'I'm afraid you've got a mistaken impression of my "influence", as you call it. The plane was coming anyway. My masters back at base wanted a face-to-face briefing. I'd probably have got the boot if they'd discovered I'd squeezed you in as well.'

'Is that why you dropped me on the far side of the airfield and smuggled me into that lorry headed for Naples?' Felix asked. 'I thought it was all for my benefit.'

'Well, it suited us both.'

Merry said, 'I've never had a chance to thank you, Richard, for bringing him back. You know how much it meant to me.' He reached over to refill Richard's glass. 'Look, neither of us wants to press you to reveal anything you feel should be kept secret, but as Felix says, we already know part of the story and you can be absolutely sure that anything else you say will ever go beyond these four walls.'

'And the war is over,' Felix added. 'I can't see how it can do any harm.'

Richard hesitated for a moment longer. Then he said, 'OK.

I can't give you details or names or anything about the organisation itself. But I will tell you a bit about what I've been doing personally.'

'What I should like to know, more than anything,' Merry said, 'is how you came to be mixed up in that sort of cloak-and-dagger business in the first place. I can see that your fluency in Italian makes you very useful to Intelligence, but that's a far cry from blowing up bridges behind enemy lines.'

Richard shrugged wryly. 'That's simple. I volunteered.'

'Volunteered? Forgive me, but that seems completely out of character. As I recall you originally refused even to go for a commission.'

'It was, as I very soon discovered. But by then it was too late.'

'Why?' asked Felix. 'I mean, why volunteer?'

'Two reasons. One was that I'd had so much help from some wonderfully brave people when I was escaping from France. I wanted to go back and help them in return. The other . . . well, after that ghastly New Year's Eve when I turned up at Wimborne I couldn't settle down to army routine again. I had to do something. The irony was that, after it was too late, I discovered I'd volunteered for the wrong outfit.'

'How so?'

'Nobody knew what was going on at the time. Talk about right hands and left hands! A completely separate organisation was tasked with helping escapers and evaders out of occupied France. The outfit I'd joined was intended to stir up resistance and make things generally uncomfortable for the Huns.'

'So you ended up with the partisans in Italy instead.'

'Well, not immediately. I did actually spend some time in France helping an escape line. I was there for two spells, actually.' He paused, toying with his wineglass, and then looked across at Merry. 'Look, there is one story I want to tell you. Somebody ought to know and you were her friends – or the nearest thing to friends she had.'

'She?' Merry queried.

'Chantal,' Richard said.

'You came across Chantal? What happened?'

'I did rather more than "come across" her,' Richard replied. Briefly he outlined how the escape line had led him to Chantal and how they had made their way through France in the guise of a pair of cabaret entertainers. Felix and Merry exploded into guffaws.

'You're telling us you earned your living singing in night-clubs, to Germans?' Felix exclaimed.

'Mostly to Germans,' Richard agreed.

'This I must hear!' Felix cried. 'Come on, give us an example.'

'Wait,' Merry said, his eyes on Richard's face. 'There's more to this.'

Richard drew a breath. 'Yes, I'm afraid there is. Chantal got me out of France that first time and then, when I was sent back, I was told to contact her and take up my old cover. For a while everything went well. I started setting up my own team, and we found a beach in Brittany where a submarine could sneak in to take men off. Then, in the November of '41, the escape line was betrayed to the Nazis.' His voice had tightened and he paused to sip his wine.

'Betrayed?' Felix prompted.

'By an Englishman! A bastard calling himself Paul Cole. By chance I was out of town when the balloon went up. But Chantal was arrested. I managed to organise her escape, with the help of a priest and a warder at the prison. The trouble was . . .' His throat closed up completely and he had to stop and clear it. 'The trouble was the bloody Nazi bastards had tortured her. They'd beaten her on the soles of the feet until they were raw.' He stopped again and took a gulp of wine. 'I tried to get her to Brittany because I knew that a sub was due a couple of nights later. But it all went wrong. All the bridges were guarded and we had to abandon the car. We realised we'd have to swim the river. It was midwinter and bitterly cold but there was no other way. We ended up hiding in a barn waiting for dawn.' Suddenly his throat was aching with unshed tears. He realised his hands were shaking and tried to still them by clenching them on his table napkin. 'I shouldn't have fallen asleep. I didn't mean to. I intended just to lie there beside her and keep watch but I must have dropped off. When I woke up she was gone. I searched the barn, then outside. I thought perhaps she'd gone to the river to get water to drink. I found her . . .' There were tears on his cheeks now and he rubbed the back of one hand angrily across his eyes. 'I found her in the end, some way downstream. She was dead . . . quite dead. She'd drowned herself rather than be a burden on me, because she thought we'd never make it to the beach in time to catch the submarine.' He was sobbing now, in the grip of an anguish too deep to be controlled, which had suddenly ambushed him after years of denial. 'I carried her up to the farmhouse and laid her on the doorstep, with a note saying that she was a heroine of France and asking them to give her a proper burial. I hope they did. I couldn't do it for her, but I hope they did. I hope they did.'

For a long moment the only sound in the room was his choking sobs. Then a chair scraped as Merry rapidly repositioned it in order to put his arm round Richard's shoulders. Eventually Richard fell silent and drew back, sniffing and gulping. Merry silently proffered a clean handkerchief and he wiped his face and blew his nose, muttering, 'I'm sorry! I'm so sorry. I don't know what came over me.'

'Don't apologise,' said Felix, close to his other side. 'It sounds to me as if you needed to get that lot out of your system. Here.'

He put a glass of brandy into Richard's shaking hand and guided it to his lips. Richard sipped and choked, then drank some more. He said shakily, 'I didn't mean that to happen. I had no idea it still upset me so much. I thought I'd got over it.'

'Is that the first time you've told anyone?' Merry asked.

'Yes. Well, I had to report the bare facts to my senior officer when I was debriefed. But I didn't mention how it had affected me. Not supposed to get emotionally involved with fellow agents, you know.'

'I take it you and Chantal were lovers,' Merry murmured. 'I mean, we all thought at Fairbourne there was something . . .'

Richard nodded. 'Oh yes.' He felt tired but curiously relaxed. 'At Fairbourne it was just a bit of a fling, you know. A couple of nights, no more. But when we started working together in France we got very close. I actually,' he caught his breath, 'I actually asked her to marry me, that last night before we fell asleep. She said,' the tears were falling again, 'she said no because I had to come back to . . . to . . .' He struggled for a moment and suppressed the memory. 'We'd always agreed that it wasn't going to be permanent.'

Merry's arm tightened around him. 'Was there no one you could talk to?'

He shook his head. 'It's not exactly something I could discuss with Priscilla, is it?'

Felix said, 'Are you sure what she did was deliberate? Perhaps she did go down to the river to drink and fell in. It could have been an accident.'

'No,' Richard said. 'There was a note, inside her boot. She was wearing a man's wellington boots. They were the only ones she could get on over her poor bandaged feet. She left them on the riverbank. It was deliberate.'

'You made it to the rendezvous with the sub, I take it?' Felix asked.

'Yes. I crossed the river before it got light and then I got a lift with a local doctor. Chantal was probably right. I shouldn't have made it with her to carry. I owe her my life.'

Merry said, 'I'm glad you felt able to tell us. If there's anything we can do . . .'

Richard sniffed again and straightened up. 'I think, when things have quietened down a bit over there, I'd like to go back. See if I can find the farm and ask what happened to her. There might be a grave.'

'Let us know when you're ready, and we'll come with you,' Merry said.

'Yes,' Felix agreed. 'I'd like to pay my respects, too.'

'Thanks,' Richard murmured. 'I'd like that. I think she would have liked it too. We often used to talk about the old days in Fairbourne and wonder how you two were getting along.' He rose unsteadily to his feet. 'I could do with freshening up a bit, if I may.'

'Of course. I'll show you.'

Felix led him to the bathroom and handed him a towel. When he came back, his face scrubbed and his hands and breathing more or less steady, Merry was on his own in the sitting room and there was a smell of coffee from the kitchen.

Merry looked at him with a smile. 'OK?'

'Yes. Look, Merry, thanks for being so . . . understanding. I'm really grateful.'

'Oh, my dear chap . . .' Merry murmured dismissively. He

offered a cigarette from a box on the table, then flicked a lighter into flame. Richard inhaled deeply and sank into the easy chair that Merry indicated. Merry seated himself on the sofa.

'Did Priscilla know what you were doing while you were overseas?'

'She must have had an inkling. She was with the FANY, you know. Part of her job was helping to look after agents waiting to go into the field. But we never discussed it. That was taboo.'

'So all this time you've had to pretend you were doing something quite different?'

'Yes. My parents think I spent the war behind a desk. That's why it's such a relief to talk to you two.'

Felix came in with the tray of coffee. 'Surely you'll be able to tell them now,' he said, setting it down.

'I doubt it,' Richard replied.

'But there must be some form of recognition for what you've done, you and people like you,' Felix objected.

'I don't see how there can be,' Richard said. 'It would mean the government acknowledging that all sorts of dirty tricks had been going on, with their connivance.'

'So what?' Felix returned. 'All's fair in love and war, et cetera.'

Richard shook his head. 'I doubt if the powers that be will see it that way.'

'Well, if you ask me, that stinks!' Felix persisted. 'I mean, look at us. Here am I with a DFC and old Merry here with a DSO and you probably deserve a medal ten times more than either of us.'

'I quite agree,' Merry put in.

'Nonsense,' Richard said. 'You both thoroughly deserve

what you got. I knew when I signed up for this that there would be no recognition.'

'All the same, it must be hard,' Merry suggested.

'Yes,' Richard admitted, 'it is, sometimes.'

Felix poured coffee and passed it round. 'Changing the subject for a moment – I want to ask you a favour, Richard.'

'Ask away.'

Felix dropped into a seat beside Merry. 'Will you sing at my wedding, while we're signing the register? I'd much rather it was you than the choir.'

Richard felt a sudden flood of warmth. 'Of course I will. I'll be honoured.' Then he added, 'Provided, that is, I can have my favourite accompanist.'

'Sorry, old boy,' Merry said. 'Otherwise engaged.'

''Fraid so,' Felix nodded. 'Can't really have the best man dashing off to the organ loft when he's supposed to be witnessing my signature.'

'Best man!' Richard said. 'Of course, I should have thought. Oh well, I suppose I'll have to make do with whoever's playing the organ. What do you want me to sing?'

'I'll leave that up to you,' Felix said. 'I'm sure you can think of something suitable.'

'We'll put our heads together over lunch one day, eh, Richard?' Merry suggested.

'Good idea,' Richard agreed. 'I'd like that.'

Shortly afterwards he rose to take his leave. In the hall he turned to his hosts.

'Thanks for a wonderful meal, Merry. Felix, I'm afraid I ruined your dinner party. I do apologise.'

'Forget it!' Felix said. 'We regard it as a great compliment that you chose to confide in us, don't we, Merry?'

'We'll get together again soon,' Merry said. 'I'll ring you.'

When they were washing up after Richard's departure Merry remarked, 'He never mentioned Rose.'

'True,' Felix agreed. 'Do you think he's got over her?'

'Probably. After all, it was a long time ago and he never answered her letters. He's been married and divorced in the interval. It sounds as if his closest involvement was with Chantal.'

'What about Rose? Does she still carry a torch for him?'

'I doubt it. You know what she always says if his name comes up. "Water under the bridge." Anyway, she's got her Frenchman now.'

Felix paused in the act of drying a plate. 'Do you think we ought to warn them both that they might meet at the wedding?'

'Is Rose definitely coming?'

'Not definitely. She said she'd pull all the strings she could, but you know what the transport situation is like over there, with returning servicemen and refugees all milling about. I hope she does make it but we can't be sure.'

'In that case,' Merry said, 'perhaps it's better not to mention it for the time being. We don't want either of them pulling out because they're afraid of a repetition of that ghastly New Year's Eve business.'

'On the other hand,' Felix added, 'we might get exactly that if they suddenly come face to face without any warning.'

'I suppose you're right.' Merry washed the last dish and dried his hands. 'OK. Suppose we wait until we're sure Rose is going to be there, and tell them both when it's too late for them to change their plans? They ought to meet again, if only to clear the air.'

'Right,' Felix said. 'That's agreed. Unless Richard asks, of course. We'd have to tell him then.'

26

As the weeks passed the ENSA company in Eindhoven grew restive. They had seen trainload after trainload of soldiers heading for home but still there seemed to be no prospect of an early return for them. Only Rose was grateful for the delay, since it gave her more time to decide between Lucien and Wilf. At the same time, the longer she had, the more the strain of her indecision told on her. At night she lay awake, imagining different scenarios, first life with Lucien and then with Wilf. During the day her mind was more on the choice facing her than on her work. Others in the company noticed her loss of appetite, her absent-mindedness and the dark shadows under her eyes, but when questioned she simply insisted that she was tired, fed up with the constant pressure of performances and longing to be at home.

Lucien, mercifully, had written to say that business affairs kept him in Paris, though she wondered whether it was a deliberate move to give her time to make up her mind without pressure. Wilf, of course, was constantly with her but he, too, was behaving with great tact and never mentioned the decision he had left her to make. Nevertheless, the necessity of giving them both an answer in the course of the next week or two pounded at her brain day and night. Sometimes she lay in bed remembering Lucien's loving arms around her and felt that that was all she could ever want. She pictured herself permanently installed in the flat in Paris, beautifully dressed, going to the theatre or a party, or perhaps entertaining friends to dinner. It was at this point that doubts usually began to creep in. She had met few of Lucien's friends. Those to whom he had introduced her were mainly ex-comrades from the Resistance and seemed to inhabit a shadowy world where the precise nature of their origins or business interests were never revealed. Still struggling with the French language and unfamiliar with the nuances of French social life, she nevertheless felt that she was not meeting the sort of people who would be natural associates of M. le Baron de Vaucourt. This in turn raised the suspicion that, in spite of what he said, he did not regard her as belonging to the same sphere as his wife. Not that he was exactly ashamed of her, but he intended to keep her apart from friends of his own class. From here her thoughts naturally turned to the reactions of her own family and friends. There was no doubt in her mind that her mother would be deeply ashamed to admit that her daughter was 'living in sin' with a French aristocrat. Would she refuse to have anything more to do with her? Almost certainly she would refuse to visit her in Paris or to meet Lucien. If she herself went back to England, how would she account for herself when people asked her what she was doing now?

Wilf had assumed that her relationship with Lucien was only temporary. She had wanted to tell him he was wrong, that Lucien was in love with her and she with him. But she was not even certain in her own mind about that. Certainly she enjoyed his company and he was wonderful in bed, but was that love? Was it enough to base a whole future life upon? And could she be sure that his feelings for her would last more than a few months or years? She was clear headed enough to recognise the fact that part of her attraction for him was the idea of arriving at the theatre or a party with a beautiful woman on his arm. He enjoyed buying her clothes and supervising her make-up and coiffure, but would that continue when she was older, beginning perhaps to lose her looks or her figure? Would it persist if she were pregnant?

The question of children was another point to agonise over. He had said that he would adopt them, treat them as his own legitimate offspring, but could that ever be a satisfactory solution? How did you explain to your children that, though they bore their father's name, their mother was not his wife? Also, she imagined that once the children were born she would be expected to entrust them into the care of nursemaids and nannies, so that she could resume her role as a decorative partner. She could not imagine herself, somehow, bringing them up as she would wish to in that apartment in the middle of Paris.

And then, of course, there was the question of her own career. She had made a reputation for herself over the last few years and she was justly proud of the fact. She was loath to throw that away, quite apart from the fact that she still loved to dance and wanted to go on as long as she was physically able. From that point of view the alternative option of life with Wilf recommended itself. She had some doubts about the advisability of starting their own company but on balance the risk seemed to be worth taking and the challenge excited her. There was no doubt about the fact that she would be exchanging a life of ease and luxury for one of hard work and insecurity, but at least there would be no shame to it. She could hold up her head among her mother's friends and she was reasonably confident that once Wilf had committed himself to her she need never fear his continued loyalty. But that assumed marriage. Marriage to a man whom she had never even kissed and who, by his own admission, was unable to consummate the union. How important was that? Her brief time with Lucien had opened the hitherto carefully guarded doors of her senses and revealed a passionate nature she had only guessed at, but on the other hand she had lived without sex until then and presumably she could do so again. So she told herself in the small hours of the morning when accepting Wilf's offer seemed the only sensible solution, but the thought left her with a chill emptiness at the centre of her being that would not be consoled by common sense.

That left the possibility of accepting Wilf's suggestion that they form a professional partnership but declining his offer of marriage. This seemed in many ways the best option, but even so it had its drawbacks. Rose was unhappily aware of the fact that the years were passing and that, for women of her age group, there were going to be a limited number of available men. She was sure of one thing. She wanted marriage and children, even if they had to be adopted children. If she turned Wilf down now he might well look elsewhere, and there was no guarantee that she would get another chance.

Tossing and turning in the sultry summer night, Rose shut her eyes and allowed herself to recall for a moment a half-forgotten face. She could no longer clearly picture him and she had no photograph to aid her memory. The pictures and newspaper cuttings from that summer of 1939 had been consigned to an album in a cupboard somewhere in the flat above the shoe shop – if the shop still stood after the onslaught of the V1s and V2s. Grinding her teeth, she admitted to herself that she was not in love with either Wilf or Lucien. She had only ever been in love with one man, and she had let him go because she had been too prim, and too unsure of herself, to seize her chance when it was presented to her. So now she had better make up her mind to take what fate offered as a consolation prize. If only she *could* make up her mind between the two of them!

Felix's letter, enclosing an embossed invitation card, came as a shock but also a welcome distraction. A letter from Merry, arriving in the same post, set her mind at rest to some extent, but she found it hard to believe that he had agreed to such a bizarre arrangement. She knew that he was capable of martyring himself on the altar of his devotion to Felix, and she could not be certain that he really was happy about the marriage until she could look him in the eye and hear him say so. In any case, she was determined to go to the wedding. She loved both men like brothers, and the thought of missing such a momentous event was insupportable. She sought out George and told him about the invitation.

'Felix is one of my oldest friends, and I really would be terribly unhappy if I couldn't get to the wedding. The girls will be fine without me for a few days and you could just cut my solo and my duet with Wilf. Please, George! It's months since any of us had any leave. Can't you swing it for me, just this once?'

The manager smiled at her. 'You know I'd do anything for you, Rose. As it happens, I heard yesterday that we're all going home in a few weeks' time. It'll be back to Civvy Street and the dole for most of us, I expect. I'm sure we could do without you for a day or two if the order doesn't come through in time. The problem is transport. Every train and plane out of here is crammed to bursting already. But if you can find a seat, then I won't stand in your way.'

Rose's next call was at the army's temporary HQ in a nearby hotel. After several enquiries and a frustrating wait she found herself in a busy office where a young sergeant looked up from behind a desk strewn with papers. Rose gave him her sweetest smile and explained her problem.

'If you knew how many sob stories I've listened to over the last week or two,' he replied, 'you'd understand how difficult my job is. I'm trying to shift half the army on railways that have been bombed to smithereens to ports that are ditto, where there are only half the number of ships we need. I've got top brass bending my ear for flights home, journalists thinking they can waft in and out like it was pre-war, and people like you who want to get home because the wife's had a baby or the old man's gone off with another woman, and so on and so on . . .' He sat back and caught her eye and suddenly smiled. 'Tell you what, leave me a phone number and if anything comes up I'll give you a call. No promises, mind, and it might be at very short notice. Best I can do, I'm afraid.'

Rose thanked him and turned away. The more she thought about it, the more urgently she wanted to be at the wedding, but she had learned the hard way that what you want and what you get are often two very different things. And meanwhile, there was the problem of Wilf and Lucien to resolve.

Returning to her lodgings, she was met by Jack. He had a newspaper in his hand and was looking uncomfortable. 'Rose, I think you ought to see this.'

Rose looked at the paper. It was in Dutch and the headline meant nothing to her but on the front page there was a photograph of Lucien between two policemen. She raised her eyes to Jack.

'I don't know what this is about.'

'I didn't either,' Jack said, his tone apologetic. 'But I recognised the picture so I got one of the chaps behind the desk to translate it for me.' He handed Rose a sheet of paper. 'This is what it says.'

The scribbled translation read: 'French con man arrested for profiteering. Lucien Vaucourt, who liked to masquerade as the Baron de Vaucourt and claimed to have been active in the Resistance, was arrested yesterday on charges of illegal dealings on the black market . . .'

Rose gazed around the hotel lobby. For a moment her only thought was that she must sit down. Jack took her by the arm and guided her to a chair.

'I'm sorry, love. I should have found a better way to break it to you. But I did try to warn you . . .'

Rose looked at the crumpled paper in her hand. 'I don't believe it! It's a mistake. The police have got the wrong man.' She staggered to her feet. 'I'm going to phone Lucien.'

'He won't be there . . .' Jack began, but she ignored him.

It took a long time to get a call put through to Paris and then the phone rang and rang without an answer. Eventually Rose put the receiver down. She was trembling but a small, cold voice of reason was beginning to make itself heard. Why had she never met any of Lucien's family, or any of his upper-class friends? How was it that he always seemed able to obtain luxuries that were unavailable to most people? Why had she always felt that there was something a bit shady about his friends? She recalled the occasion of their first meeting, when he had instantly commanded the obedience of the unpleasant crew who were victimising the woman collaborator.

Jack was at her elbow with a glass of brandy. 'I'm sorry, Rose,' he repeated. 'But I always thought he was a wrong'un. Here, drink this.'

She pushed the glass aside. 'I'm going out.'

'Where are you going?' He sounded alarmed.

'I'll be back,' she called over her shoulder.

At the Hotel Metropol she asked the desk clerk if Andrew Logan was available. Logan was a journalist with the *Daily Express*. He had been to the show a couple of times and had taken Rose for a drink afterwards. She guessed that he fancied her but she had been careful not to give him any encouragement. Her personal life was complicated enough as it was. Today, however, she was prepared to use whatever means came to hand.

By good luck, Logan was in the hotel bar, hammering away at a decrepit typewriter. He stood up as she approached with a welcoming grin.

'Rose! What a nice surprise!'

She came straight to the point. 'Andrew, I need your help.'

'And I thought it was my body you were after.' He gave a pout of simulated disappointment. 'Well, what can I do for you?'

'There's a man I've been involved with, a Frenchman. He told me he was an aristocrat, and high up in the Resistance. Now I've just seen this in the paper.' She held out the newspaper, together with the crumpled translation.

Logan scanned them both. 'What do you want me to do?'

'Find out if it's true. Is there any evidence, or have the police got the wrong man?'

He looked at her closely. 'This really matters to you, doesn't it.'

She nodded, swallowing hard. 'Yes. And I'll be eternally grateful.'

He smiled ruefully. 'I'd ask for a reward, but I guess the only thing I want would be off limits. OK. Leave it with me. I'll call you as soon as I have anything.'

Rose returned to the lodgings and shut herself in her room.

She wanted to cry, but something told her that it would only make her feel worse. One thing was becoming clear. If the story was true, and increasingly she felt in her bones that it was, her dilemma was solved. Wilf's offer was now the only one on the table.

Logan rang late that afternoon.

'I'm sorry, Rose. I've been on to my contacts in Paris and it seems that there's no mistake. The story is all over the French papers, too, and the evidence is pretty damning, by all accounts. I wish I could tell you otherwise, but there it is.'

27

Richard did not ask after Rose. Not because he had forgotten, but because he was afraid that the mention of her name might precipitate another emotional breakdown, like the one that had embarrassed him at the dinner table. That had left him with a sense of catharsis that he recognised was probably healthy, but he did not want to risk another similar episode. Besides which, he had other things on his mind. Coming down late to breakfast the morning after the dinner party, he was given a message by the receptionist telling him that he was required to report to Baker Street.

Striding along the crowded streets, he made up his mind that if the summons was to a repeat meeting with Wilkins he would tell him, politely but succinctly, what he could do with his house agent's job and walk out. On reaching his destination, however, he found that the interview was with none other than his old boss, Maurice Buckmaster. The news sent a sudden surge of alarm through his intestines. What could Buckmaster want with him at this juncture? In a few moments of panic he wondered if somehow word had already reached him of his indiscretions of the previous evening. The notion of hidden microphones presented itself to his whirling thoughts, and even the idea that either Felix or Merry, or both, was also an agent of SOE and had reported him. That kind of breakdown under stress and desire to confide in an apparently friendly companion was one of the things he had been repeatedly warned about.

Sitting in the outer office, waiting for Buckmaster to see him, he calmed down a little. It was impossible for Buckmaster to know about last night. Why, then, was he here? Had he said too much to someone at the hotel? He couldn't recall doing so. Was it possible that he was about to be sent on another mission? Surely not. He wondered briefly what would happen if he refused to go. Would he be court-martialled? No, more likely he would be sent to the 'cooler', the remote house in the north of Scotland to which agents who failed in the training course or were unable to withstand the rigours of work in the field were sent, until such time as they could present no danger to the rest of the operation. He clenched his teeth. It would be too cruel to be sent into isolation at this point. Then the buzzer on the secretary's desk sounded and he was instructed to go in.

He came to attention, saluted and removed his cap. Buckmaster came round his desk and extended his hand with a genial smile.

'Richard. Good to see you again. How are you?'

'I'm well, sir, thank you.'

'Good. I heard you had a bad time in Bologna. No ill effects?'

'No, sir. I was lucky to be treated by a brilliant surgeon.'

'I'm glad to hear it.' Buckmaster returned to his seat and waved Richard to a chair opposite him. 'By the way, I was sorry to hear about your wife. Tragic business. But I gather that hadn't worked out for you, anyway.'

How well informed you are, Richard thought, and wondered how much more of his private life was known to his superiors. Aloud he said, 'No, unfortunately not.'

'Rest of the family well?' Buckmaster asked. 'Your parents are still alive, aren't they?'

'Yes, sir. They're both well, thank you.'

'Good. Tell me, did your wife know what you were doing?'

So that was it! Buckmaster thought he'd said too much to Priscilla and that she might have passed it on.

'I think she had an idea. After all, I met her when she was given the job of entertaining me before I went into the field. But we never discussed it.'

'Can't have been easy.'

'No, but I think she understood the reason.'

'What about your parents? Did they have any idea?'

'No, none at all. They think I've spent the war pushing paper and interrogating prisoners.'

'Ah. That must have been difficult, too.'

'I think it was for them. Particularly when the only mail they got were those deliberately uninformative postcards we all wrote before we went away.'

'I was thinking of you, more than of them. Hard not to drop the odd hint.'

Richard stiffened in his seat. Was this what he was being accused of? 'I'm certain nothing I said would have given them any notion of where I was or what I was doing.'

Buckmaster took his pipe out of his mouth and allowed himself a smile. 'Well, you'll need to tell them some of it now.'

'Need, sir?' Richard frowned at him, thrown by the sudden change of expression.

'To explain the medal.'

'What medal?' Suddenly his heart was beginning to thump.

'I've recommended to His Majesty that you should receive the DSO and I'm glad to say he has agreed.'

'The DSO!' The words came out in a strangled whisper.

'It's no more than you deserve.'

'But what am I going to say?' Richard asked. 'What shall I tell them?'

'The citation will say *For courage and initiative beyond the call of duty, while working behind enemy lines*,' Buckmaster told him.

'You mean I can actually tell people what I've been doing?'

'Not in detail. No names, no pack drill. You must not reveal anything about the organisation or the people involved, or the location of any of the training establishments. Nor can you discuss operations in detail. But you can tell people that you were infiltrated behind enemy lines and in general terms the kind of operations you were involved in. Understood?'

'Understood!' Richard breathed. 'Thank you, sir. Thank you very much!'

'As I said, it's no more than you deserve.'

'I'm not the only one, sir. There are dozens of others.'

Buckmaster's smile broadened. 'Don't worry. They haven't been forgotten. We set up an awards committee several months ago and you'll find a number of your fellow agents have received medals too.'

His mind racing to keep up, Richard said, 'Would it be in order for me to take a couple of days off, sir, and go up to see my people? I'd like to tell them in person.'

'Of course,' Buckmaster said. 'After all, you're only hanging around waiting for your demob papers, aren't you? Get the office to make out a rail warrant for you.' He sat back and began to refill his pipe. 'Speaking of demob, got any plans for civilian life?'

'I'm hoping to pick up my singing career again.'

'Ah, the cabaret act?'

'No, something a little bit more . . . more ambitious,

perhaps. I'm not really a cabaret artiste. Musical comedy, perhaps.'

'Excellent! Well, you must let me know what show you're in and I'll come to your first night.'

Buckmaster rose and held out his hand and Richard shook it with a sudden sense of nostalgia. This might very well be the last time they would meet. Certainly, it was the end of a very crucial period in his life. He said, 'Goodbye, sir, and thank you. Not just for the decoration. For everything.'

'Not at all,' Buckmaster responded. 'I'm just glad that you came through all right. So many others didn't. Good luck!'

Richard put on his cap, saluted and marched out of the room. With a curious sense of unreality he collected his rail warrant, and it was not until hc was out of the building that the full realisation of what had happened came to him. Then he had an almost irresistible urge to shout aloud, jump up and down and punch the air in triumph. Forcing himself to maintain a suitably dignified pace, he headed back towards the hotel, intending to pack. Passing a shop window, he caught sight of his reflection and automatically checked the street behind him to see that he was not being followed. Suddenly he began to laugh aloud, oblivious of the stares of passers-by. It was over! He didn't need to watch out for someone on his tail. He didn't need to censor every move, every word, in case it gave him away, or to feel for his pistol at the sound of a step on the stairs. It was over and he had survived – and what was more, he could tell his story.

The thought came to him that he could not go tamely back to his hotel. He had to tell someone, at once. He turned and headed for Upper Grosvenor Street.

After the efficient formality of Baker Street the atmosphere at the offices of the Central Pool of Artistes was reassuringly chaotic. Men and women came and went, mostly in uniform, mostly with a casual disregard for army regulations that would have had the average drill sergeant on the verge of apoplexy. Buttons were left undone, shoes were of suede rather than regulation army boots, ties were loosened or in some cases abandoned in favour of a silk cravat. Everyone seemed to address everyone else by their Christian name, regardless of rank. The building throbbed with a cheerful, creative bustle. Eventually Richard found his way to Merry's office, where a pretty girl in ATS uniform told him that the captain was busy. Richard felt like whisking her out from behind her desk and waltzing her round the room but he restrained himself and said only, 'Just tell him Major Richard Stevens is here and would like a word when he has a minute.'

The girl duly passed the message over the intercom and a couple of minutes later a rather plump man, wearing a silk shirt under his battledress tunic and carrying what looked liked a trumpet in a case, came out, and Merry appeared at the door and beckoned him in. Once inside, Richard was suddenly overcome with diffidence. It seemed unacceptably vainglorious to blurt out his news without preamble.

Merry said, 'Richard? It's nice to see you but I wasn't expecting to so soon. Is there a problem?'

Richard, tongue-tied by shyness, could only stand and smile at him.

Merry perched on the edge of his desk and looked at him quizzically. 'Well, are you going to tell me what's happened? Or are you just going to stand there with a silly grin on your face?'

Richard's grin broadened further. 'You remember what we were saying last night, about recognition?'

'Yes.'

'Well, they're giving me a medal.'

Merry shot off the desk as if it had suddenly become red hot. 'A medal? What?'

'The DSO.'

Richard felt his shoulders gripped and Merry's eyes sparkled triumphantly into his own. 'Richard, that's wonderful! I'm so pleased! Nobody could deserve it more.'

'Thanks,' he responded sheepishly.

'When did you find out?'

'Just now. You're the first person I've told.'

'My dear chap! I'm flattered. What about your parents?'

'I'm going home to tell them face to face.'

'Yes, of course. When?'

'I don't know. I thought perhaps this afternoon. If there's a train.'

Merry looked at his watch. 'Damn! It's only just after eleven. I was going to say we must have a drink to celebrate but I really can't get away this morning. I've got a whole lot of appointments.' He looked at Richard affectionately. 'Tell you what. Can you bear to hang around until lunchtime? I could give Felix a ring and we could all meet up. What do you think?'

'Great!' Richard said. 'I'd really like that.'

'OK. The Amalfi at twelve thirty. That suit you?'

'Yes, that'll be fine. I'll see you there.' He turned to the door, then paused and looked back. 'Merry?'

'Yes?'

'Don't tell Felix. I mean, not about why we're meeting.'

Merry grinned. 'Of course not. I'll leave that to you.'

This time Richard was the first to arrive at the restaurant. Merry joined him a few minutes later and soon afterwards Felix breezed in, his face alight with curiosity.

'Well, come on!' he demanded, as Richard handed him a drink. 'What are we celebrating? Merry was very tight lipped on the phone.'

Richard was seized by the same diffidence he had felt in Merry's office. He caught Merry's eye and his raised eyebrow said, *Well, go on. You asked for this*. He mumbled, 'Oh, it's just that the powers that be have apparently decided that you're right about some form of recognition.'

'What sort of recognition?' Felix asked, beady eyed.

'They're giving me the DSO.'

He had tried to speak quietly and in an offhand manner. Felix's reaction, however, left no room for false modesty.

'The DSO!' he exclaimed at the top of his voice. 'Well, I should bloody well think so!'

The words carried easily to the ears of the half-dozen or so people who were sipping pre-prandial drinks in the little bar, and eyes turned in their direction. Felix, unabashed, swung round to address the company.

'This chap,' he announced, 'has just been awarded the DSO! And what's more, he bloody well deserves it!'

His voice had carried through the archway leading to the restaurant, where several tables were already occupied, and there was a ragged splutter of applause and glasses were raised in Richard's direction. Ignoring Richard's sotto voce pleas, Felix then proceeded to order champagne and, when it arrived, explained to the barman in his fluent if ungrammatical Italian that the medal being celebrated had been earned while fighting with the partisans. At this point the proprietor, an enormous Italian with shoulders like a prize-fighter and a huge, drooping moustache, arrived to find out what all the fuss was about. When the circumstances were related to him he insisted on embracing Richard and delivering two smacking kisses that left the moist, garlic-scented imprint of his moustache on both cheeks. After that, the champagne was on the house.

Over lunch Felix could not be dissuaded from ordering a second bottle, and Richard was just thinking that perhaps he should reciprocate by buying a third when it arrived, unbidden, with a message from a small party of Italian émigrés dining at a table on the other side of the room. When he went over to say thank you he was immediately invited to join them, and after that his recollections of the meal became somewhat vague. His intention of taking the train home that afternoon evaporated. Instead, he found himself being helped out of a taxi at the door of his hotel and half carried up to his room. He was dimly aware that Felix was divesting him of his tunic, while Merry pulled off his shoes, and then nothing until he woke in the dusk of the summer evening.

The next day, more or less recovered from a thundering hangover, he caught the train north. His father and mother, and his aunt, met him at the station. He could see from his mother's eyes and his aunt's bright chatter that they were puzzled and rather worried by his unscheduled return, but he managed to remain silent until they were all sitting round the tea table in his aunt's living room. Then his father gave him the opening he was looking for.

'Well, lad. We'd not expected to have you back so soon. We thought perhaps you'd had your demob papers but I see you're still in uniform.'

'Yes, but not for much longer,' Richard said. 'I came because I've got some news for you.'

'News?' his mother said sharply.

He looked at her and thought, *You think I'm going to*

announce that I'm getting married again. Well, you can relax. Aloud he said, 'They're giving me a medal.'

His aunt gasped. 'A medal! Oh, that's grand!'

His mother said, 'A medal? What sort of medal?'

'The DSO.'

'The Distinguished Service Order?' His mother's eyes were fixed on his face. Even now she was prepared to be disappointed. 'Is that because you got yourself wounded?'

Is that all? was unspoken, but Richard knew it was there, hanging in the air between them. 'No,' he said. 'That's part of it, but not the whole story. You see, I'm afraid I haven't been telling you the whole truth about what I've been doing these past few years. Not because I didn't want to, but because I wasn't allowed to.'

He was interrupted by a sudden cackle of triumph from his father. 'There you are, Mother! What did I tell you? I always said there was more going on than we were getting to hear about.'

Richard smiled at him. 'I'm sorry, Dad. I should have liked to be honest with you, but I couldn't.'

'So what have you been doing?' his mother demanded. 'What's this medal for?'

'The citation is going to say *For courage and initiative shown while working behind enemy lines*,' Richard told her.

'Behind enemy lines?' she repeated. 'You mean, like a spy?'

He could see her trying to reconcile the social cachet of having a son with an exciting story to tell with the rather unsavoury connotations of spying.

'No,' he said. 'I wasn't a spy. We left that to the boys from MI6. My outfit was more concerned with making life uncomfortable for the occupying power.'

'Uncomfortable? How?' his father wanted to know.

'Sabotage, mainly. Blowing up bridges, derailing trains, holding up supply convoys.' It crossed his mind even as he spoke that he had listed inanimate objects, as if his activities had had no connection with human beings; had resulted in no loss of life.

His aunt gasped and clasped her hands together. 'You've been blowing things up behind enemy lines? And all this time your poor mother's been thinking you were safe behind a desk somewhere.'

'I'm afraid so,' Richard agreed, wondering whether anyone was going to congratulate him.

There was a brief silence, broken by his father.

'Well, I'll go to the foot of our stairs!'

The phrase brought back so much of his childhood that Richard found himself laughing out loud. His father got to his feet.

'Where's that bottle of sherry we opened on VE Day, Mother?'

'But Arthur,' she objected, 'we've only just had our tea.'

'Tea be blowed!' her husband retorted. 'We can't drink the lad's health in tea. This deserves summat a bit stronger than tea.'

While his father ferreted in the sideboard his mother said, 'So is that how you got wounded, not the way you said at all?'

'No, that was pretty much as I told you,' Richard answered, 'except that it happened before the Allies entered Bologna, not afterwards. We were trying to stop the Germans getting away with a whole trainload of tanks. I managed to blow up the engine but in the fighting that followed I got shot.'

'But how did you go on for medical treatment?' his aunt asked. 'Who looked after you?'

'A wonderful girl called Antonia,' Richard told her with a

smile, 'who also happened to be a nurse. I probably owe her my life.'

His father returned triumphantly with the sherry, two bottles of beer and some glasses.

'Now then,' he said. 'I expect you'll prefer a beer, Richard. That sweet stuff's no sort of drink for a man.' He poured sherry for the two women, and passed a beer over to Richard. 'Here's to you, lad. We're right proud of you, aren't we, Mother?'

For the first time he saw tears in his mother's eyes and was quite disconcerted when she got up from her place and came round the table to kiss him.

'Yes, we are,' she said. 'Right proud!'

After that, he spent the next hour talking almost solidly, answering their questions and relating stories of his activities in France and later in Italy. He was careful, as he had been cautioned to be by Buckmaster, not to reveal any operational details, and he avoided all mention of Chantal or Ginny, or Antonia, beyond what he had already said. They were fascinated by the thought that he could pass himself off as an Italian, that he knew how to handle explosives. The news that he had jumped out of an aeroplane with a parachute was greeted with gasps and hands clasped over mouths in horror.

Later, sitting in the front room, he had the satisfaction of hearing his mother on the telephone, calling friends and relations on a variety of pretexts and just happening to remark that 'our Richard is home for a couple of days. Yes, we're having a bit of a celebration, as a matter of fact. He's won the DSO, you know . . . Oh, it's all been very hush-hush. I can't talk over the telephone. But of course, we always knew that the desk job was just a cover for something else.' The rest of the evening was spent in the local, repeating his story to his father's cronies and absorbing more beer than he had drunk in a very long time.

The next day, as a result of his mother's hints on the phone, there was a constant procession of visitors to his aunt's house, people who had 'just dropped in to say hello to Richard, since he's home'. By bedtime, all the aunts and uncles and cousins and boyhood friends whose stories he had had to listen to in silence a few weeks earlier had been regaled with variations on the theme of 'our son, the secret agent'. Richard tried hard to be modest and dismissive but beneath his carefully casual manner he relished every minute of it.

Two days later Richard returned to London and made his demonstration record. The result convinced him that he was seriously out of practice and must do something about it quickly. The thought brought back to his mind the memory of Laszlo Brodic, the professor at the Royal College of Music who had coached him during his training at Beaulieu. To his relief he found him still occupying the small flat in Kensington where he had gone for his lessons in those now seemingly distant days. Brodic remembered him at once and greeted him with a warmth that surprised him, bearing in mind the irascible manner he had affected during their previous sessions. He insisted that Richard sing for him there and then, and the affable manner was rapidly replaced by the familiar tetchiness as he pointed out the mistakes and bad habits he had developed over the intervening years. The sooner these were corrected the better, he declared, before some permanent damage was done, and Richard had better come to him for lessons three times a week for the time being. In between lessons he must practise, practise, *practise*!

This last injunction presented Richard with a problem. He

was embarrassed to be heard practising in his hotel room, and besides, he really needed a piano. He considered looking for a room he could rent by the hour but Brodic's fees were already stretching his resources to the limit. The difficulty was solved by his next visit to Felix's flat. He was aware that Felix and Merry were 'keeping an eye on him'. A day rarely passed without a phone call from one or the other and an invitation to join them for lunch or go to a theatre in the evening. Merry seemed to have unlimited access to complimentary tickets for all the best shows and Richard was happy to be a beneficiary of his good fortune.

One evening, soon after his first session with Brodic, he was invited to dine at the flat again, and the first object that struck his eye on entering the sitting room was a magnificent grand piano.

'I say!' he exclaimed, crossing to touch the keys. 'A Steinway! Where did this spring from?'

'It was a wedding present,' Felix informed him.

'Really? Who from?'

'Me,' said Felix, enigmatically. Then Richard caught Merry's eye and understood.

After the meal Merry suggested that Richard should sing for them.

'I daren't,' Richard said, and recounted his dressing-down by Brodic.

Merry insisted he should sing anyway and he managed to get through the toreador's aria from *Carmen* without any significant errors.

'Nothing serious wrong there,' Merry declared. 'You're out of practice, that's all.'

'The problem is,' Richard said, 'finding somewhere to practise. I don't suppose you know of any spare rehearsal spaces, do you, Merry?'

'All you need is a room and a piano, isn't it?' Felix put in. 'That's no problem.' He left the room and returned a moment later with a key. 'Spare key to the front door. Merry and I are out all day. Just let yourself in whenever you want to practise and make yourself at home.'

The summer days slid by. London continued to seethe with returning servicemen. Richard continued to pester agents and work on his voice. Then, out of the blue, Harrison, the BBC producer, returned his call. Would Richard care to audition for him? Richard was delighted to accept. A few days later he signed a contract to sing on three successive Sunday evenings with the Palm Court Orchestra.

The first broadcast seemed to be well received and there were hints of future engagements, and he knew that Merry had mentioned his name to several people and was keeping an ear to the ground for news of suitable auditions. It was frustrating that there still seemed to be nothing concrete, but at least the spectre of a job behind a desk was receding.

Then, one morning, there was a letter beside his place at breakfast. It had been sent on from Baker Street, but had previously been redirected so many times that it was almost impossible to tell where it had started from, except that it had come by airmail. Turning it over, he found the sender's name and address on the reverse and felt an electric thrill of surprise as he read the name *Parigi* and an address in Bologna. He slit the letter open and read,

Caro amico,

I do not know if this letter will ever reach you. I heard that you had been wounded and evacuated from Bologna. I

pray that the wound was not as serious as it seemed and that you are now completely recovered.

Now, let me come to the point. Since you sang for us on that one magical night all those who heard you have been asking after you. As you must guess, we are in the process of recreating our opera company, but so many of our young men have been lost in the war that it is hard to find enough who are sufficiently gifted to fill up all the places. No doubt, if you are recovered from your wound, you have already been offered a prestigious role in your Covent Garden Opera Company or elsewhere in Britain. But I recall what you told me about the ridiculous prejudice against English-born singers and so I have some hope that my suggestion may not come too late. If you would like it, there is a place for you in our opera company here in Bologna.

Richard read and reread that last sentence several times. If he would like it! Would a man dying of thirst like water? Would a lost soul like to go to heaven? He controlled his shaking hands and read on.

I cannot immediately promise you leading roles. There are those who have established their reputations here who cannot be displaced so easily. But you would sing the second-rank roles, many of which I am sure you have studied, and understudy the principals. It would be good experience and I am convinced it would not be long before your great talent would be recognised and you would have the chance to graduate to leading roles.

Of course, you may not wish to leave your own country and make your home among those who were, for so long and so misguidedly, your enemies. That would be understandable. But if you can bring yourself to return to the city that rewarded your triumphant performance so badly, I can promise you the warmest of welcomes. Please let me have your reply as soon as possible.

I remain, your loving friend,

Massimo Parigi

Feverishly Richard returned to the top of the letter. It was undated. The postmark was obscured by the frequent redirections. There was no way of telling how long ago it had been written. It made him want to howl with frustration at the thought that this wonderful opportunity might have slipped through his grasp simply because the letter had not reached him in time. He knew that there would be other men, native Italians, returning from POW camps or coming down from the hills, many of whom must be capable of filling the vacancy that he had been offered. But even if that had gone, there was still the chorus. Parigi might be surprised to hear it, but he would give anything on earth just to sing with the chorus of a prestigious opera company.

His next thought was how to get a reply through as quickly as possible. Postal services were disrupted all across Europe and he knew that a letter sent by conventional mail might take weeks to reach its destination. Then inspiration struck. Before he had been shipped out of the American Military Hospital in Bologna he had had one visitor. His fellow British Liaison Officer, Mike Newman, had come to see him and had told him in passing that he was going to remain in the city as part of the Allied Military Government. Richard left his breakfast almost untasted and set out for Baker Street. There he went straight to the Signals Office and found the friendly ATS sergeant who had helped him contact Merry.

'Carol, can you do me a favour? I need to get an urgent

signal through to Major Newman with the AMG in Bologna.'

She looked at him with a frown. 'I didn't think you were operational any more.'

'It's a bit of unfinished business,' he told her. 'I was with the partisans there, if you remember. I really need him to pass a message to one of my contacts there.'

Carol hesitated. 'You'll get me into trouble, you will.' Then she giggled. 'No such luck, eh? Oh, go on, then. What is it you want to say?'

He leaned over the desk and gave her a smacking kiss. 'Carol, you're a darling! OK, this is the message. Please contact Massimo Parigi at the Bologna Opera House and tell him that Major Stevens has received his letter and the answer is yes. And a letter follows. Got that? Mark it Most Urgent, will you? Bless you!'

He left the office and headed for Felix's flat, almost light headed with excitement. This time, his daily practice would be sheer pleasure.

28

The wedding was due to take place in two days and Rose had almost given up hope of getting back to England in time. She could not rouse the energy to pester any more overworked officials with her request. The revelation of Lucien's true character had left her numb with shock. He had deceived her, had tried to lure her into heaven only knew what kind of sordid existence, and yet she ached for the sensation of his arms around her. The memory of the happy days they had spent together was poisoned for ever, but still she missed him.

That morning, Wilf asked her to come for a walk with him. 'I was wondering,' he said, 'now that you've had a chance to think about it – have you made up your mind?'

She looked at him despairingly. 'Oh, Wilf, I'm sorry! I keep going over and over it but it's such a big decision to make. I really don't know.'

'It's just that I've had this letter,' he said, 'from an uncle of mine in Los Angeles.'

'Los Angeles? You mean America?'

'Where else? The thing is this. Uncle Fred used to be in the profession, as a comic, mainly, but he had a good singing voice too. For a while he had his own show. That's where I got my start as a youngster. A few years ago he decided to try his luck in the movies, so he took himself off to Hollywood. Never made it, unfortunately, but he ended up running a bar just off

Sunset Boulevard. He's done very well out of it, too. It's very popular with a lot of movie folk, apparently. When I first had the idea of forming my own company I wrote to him for advice. He's just written back saying he reckons there are going to be great opportunities out there for dancers soon. According to him, all the studios are looking for a couple to take over from Fred Astaire and Ginger Rogers. He thinks we ought to go and try our luck there. He'd put us up and he says he can introduce us to lots of producers and casting directors. It's a fantastic opportunity, Rose. What do you think?'

'America?' Rose swallowed hard and shut her eyes for a minute. The kaleidoscope that had been revolving in her head for the past weeks had been given another shake and had settled into yet another pattern. 'Oh, Wilf, that's asking a bit much!'

'Is it?' he said. 'It's a beautiful country, so my uncle says, and the climate's wonderful. He reckons there are opportunities there that just don't exist back here. Let's face it, Rose. England's been battered into the ground. It's going to take years to get back to where we were before the war. Rationing, shortages of decent places for people to live – what's this word they keep using in the papers? – austerity, that's it. That's not going to go away in a hurry. In America they haven't had all that. We could have a great life there, Rose. Think of it! A beautiful villa, our own swimming pool, a posh car . . .'

'You're really keen, aren't you?' Rose said, looking at him.

He straightened his shoulders and she suddenly realised that he no longer twitched and fidgeted as he had done when he first joined the company. His eyes were clear and bright and there was a new, determined set to his mouth.

'Yes,' he said, 'I am. I reckon it's too good a chance to miss. It's up to you, Rose. What do you say?'

'You're telling me,' she said slowly, 'that you've made up your mind to go, with me or without me. Is that it?'

He hesitated for a moment. Then he said, 'Yes, I reckon that is what I'm saying.'

She walked on a few yards in silence. Then she said, 'I'll tell you tomorrow. Is that OK?'

'Tomorrow will be fine,' he said.

That evening, Rose was just about to leave for the theatre when the desk clerk called her to the telephone again. She raced down the stairs, her heart pounding, hoping against hope to hear Lucien's voice. Instead it was one she did not recognise.

'Miss Taylor?'

'Yes?'

'It's Sergeant Browning from the Transport Department. I've managed to get you a seat on a plane going to Northolt. Only snag is, it leaves at two a.m. Can you make it?'

'Two a.m. Tonight – tomorrow, I mean?'

'Yes.'

'I'll be there. Tell me what I have to do.'

Rose landed at Northolt in the dawn of the next day. She had to wait for some time before she was able to cadge a lift into London, and it occurred to her that it would be daft to make the journey down to Wimborne, in inevitably packed trains, only to return the next day for the wedding. At the bottom of her handbag was the key to the flat above the shoe shop where she had grown up and which she had always used as a base when she was in town, so she got the driver of the truck to drop her at Charing Cross and took the Tube to Kennington.

The windows of the shop were boarded up but the building

was still intact, though every surface in the flat was coated with a film of soot and brick dust from other houses in the street that had been bombed. Rose dumped her bags and went down to the phone box at the corner. After some difficulty she managed to get a call through to the farm. Bet answered and Rose could hear the baby grizzling in the background.

'Rose! Where are you?'

'In London. Listen, Bet. There's no sense in me coming down to Wimborne now. I'll meet you all at the church about ten forty-five tomorrow, OK?'

'So you'll be able to make the wedding after all. That's great. Mum will be ever so relieved.'

'Why relieved?'

'Oh, you know what she's like. Felix insisted that we were all to come, even if you couldn't make it, but she's been going on about not knowing what to say to all his posh friends.'

'Oh, really!' Rose spoke more sharply than she intended, but she was tired and hot. 'When is she going to get it into her head that we're as good as anyone else?' She softened her tone. 'For goodness' sake, Bet, tell her not to worry. There will be lots of Felix's old friends from his Follies days. It'll be fine.'

'We'll see you tomorrow, then,' Bet said.

'Quarter to eleven at the church. Make sure you're there on time.'

'We'll do our best. 'Bye for now.'

Rose rang off and walked along to the corner shop with her ration book. She returned to the flat carrying some tea, half a pint of milk, a small loaf, two eggs and a tin of Spam. She dusted off the essential surfaces, made herself a sandwich and fell into bed.

It was evening when she woke, and a thought struck her the moment she opened her eyes. She had promised to give Wilf an answer to his proposal that morning, but in the rush to catch her plane she had left the theatre at the end of the performance without any explanation, without even saying goodbye. She was overcome with guilt, but at the same time there was a sense of relief. At least she could put off making a decision for a little longer. She went over in her mind their last conversation. The thought of chancing their luck in Hollywood terrified her. But perhaps Wilf could be persuaded to return to his original plan? Then she remembered the look of determination in his eyes. He had said he would go, whether she came with him or not. In that case, he couldn't really be in love with her, could he? He had changed in the last weeks, and she felt convinced that he could cope on his own. 'Wilf will be all right,' she told herself. It was the way she had felt about Sally Castle, and she had been right there. But what did that mean for her? Had she only ever contemplated the marriage out of pity for him? And had he only thought of it as a professional convenience? That had been his approach from the beginning, but was it any basis for a marriage? She dreaded ending up like Frank and Isabel, acting out love on the stage and fighting like cat and dog off it.

So, if not marriage to Wilf, what then? A few weeks ago she had had too many choices. There was her job, the possibility of becoming Lucien's mistress, or marriage to Wilf. Now ENSA was being disbanded, the company that had come to feel like her family would be broken up. Lucien had turned out to be a con man and Wilf was ready to strike out on his own. So now, suddenly, her own future was a blank sheet. She had no doubt that she could find work easily enough. There were plenty of people who had seen what she could do and would be happy to give her a job. But the life of a single career woman had lost its appeal. She was twenty-six and aware that, with so many young men lost in the war, husbands were going to be at a premium. But her time with Lucien had introduced her to a passionate side of her nature that she had long sought to suppress. She wanted to feel a man's arms around her. She wanted security – and she wanted children.

The sight of her blue silk coat and skirt hanging on the wardrobe door brought another thought. She had not let Felix know that she would be able to come to his wedding after all. She got up, washed in cold water, since there seemed no point in lighting the boiler, dressed and cooked herself a boiled egg. As soon as she had finished eating she went down to the phone box again and dialled Felix's number. It rang for some time and then Merry answered.

'Merry, it's me, Rose. I'm in London. I managed to catch a plane last night, so I'll be able to make the wedding after all.'

'Rose! That's excellent. Felix will be delighted. Where are you staying?'

'At the flat. I'm meeting the rest of the family at the church in the morning.'

'I'm so glad you're going to be there. Look, I don't mean to be rude but I can't chat now. We're just about to leave. Felix's stag night, you know? The taxi's waiting.'

'That's all right. We can have a good old chinwag tomorrow. You go and have a good time. Just don't let Felix drink too much.'

'I'll do my best.'

She was about to put the phone down when he said, 'Oh, Rose! Are you still there?'

'Yes.'

'One thing you ought to know. Richard will be there tomorrow. He's back in town and he's singing a solo while we sign the register. I just thought you should be prepared.'

She heard Felix calling in the background. 'Must go! See you in the morning. 'Bye!'

Rose replaced the receiver and left the phone box as if sleepwalking. Richard would be there tomorrow! They would meet again at last. She wondered if he had changed much. She knew she had. Would he still find her attractive? But, of course, he was married. Presumably Priscilla would be with him. She felt a loosening of her bowels. That would be hard! How would she manage to greet her, to behave politely as if nothing had happened? Did Priscilla know that Richard had once proposed to her? For a moment she considered faking illness and staying away, but then a grittier emotion took over. She would not let Priscilla, or Richard, prevent her from attending her friend's wedding. Shc would go and show them that she was not an embittered old spinster, was not consumed with regret for her lost opportunity. That she was her own woman and could stand on her own feet. She would put on thc blue silk outfit that suited her so well, and the beautiful hat that Lucien had bought her to go with it. She would shampoo her hair and make up her face and let them see that she had come through, that she had her own victory to celebrate.

29

Merry had been working on the preparations for Felix's stag night for several days, along with certain secret arrangements of his own connected with the wedding itself. His job at the Grosvenor Street HQ was coming to an end. Stars in Battledress would go on, of course. Indeed, several companies were still performing in the battlefields of the Far East and he felt the occasional twinge of guilt when reports reached him of the appalling conditions they had to endure, but, for him, the war was over. Most of the men who had passed through his office had been found employment of some sort, though not always in the area they hoped for. (He secretly had some sympathy for the embattled Major Wilkins at SOE.) His own future was secure. He had signed a contract with the Blacks, father and son, and waited only to learn which theatre he was to be assigned to. For now, in the hiatus between jobs, he could concentrate on Felix's wedding.

There was one distraction, in the form of the general election on 5 July. Although no result could be declared until the votes of men and women serving overseas had been counted, the newspapers were full of rumours of a Labour landslide. Merry had been brought up in a deeply conservative tradition but the war had radicalised him in a way that he now found faintly surprising. Whatever his inbred instincts might urge, it was clear to him that there was only one way he could vote. Change was not only desirable, it was inevitable. All the same, it distressed him to see how the decision of the populace was received as a slap in the face for the man they all held responsible for bringing them through to victory. Churchill had declared in a broadcast that the Labour Party would require an organisation comparable to the Gestapo to carry through their plans, but that misjudgement of the popular mood had only hardened the opposition against him. The result would not be declared until the 26th but already there was excitement in the air, a sense of new beginnings. New beginnings for the country, and for himself, he reflected, in more ways than one.

He had told Felix that a dinner had been arranged with some old friends for the night before the wedding, in case he started to make plans of his own, and Felix had docilely agreed to leave it all in Merry's hands. Then, just as they were about to enter the taxi taking them to the Savoy, Felix exclaimed, 'Damn! Left my cigarette case upstairs. I'll just pop up and get it.'

Merry was about to go in search of him when he returned, patting his pocket. 'It had got down the side of the sofa somehow. Couldn't find it to begin with. Right, shall we go?'

Merry had purloined Felix's address book and he and Richard had been busy phoning and writing letters, so the group awaiting their arrival in the bar was a good deal larger than Felix had anticipated. Merry watched with pleasure as he recognised one familiar face after another. The first man to be greeted was rather older than the rest, a solidly built man in civilian dress with horn-rimmed glasses and broad, capable hands.

'Boss! This is terrific! It's so good to see you again. How are you, sir?'

'I'm pretty well, thank you. Now, let's have a look at you.' There was little trace of the man's New Zealand origins in his voice. Many years of performing plastic surgery on the elite of British society had long ago smoothed that away. Archibald McIndoe turned Felix to the light and examined his face critically. 'Well, I reckon I did a pretty good job on you.'

'You did a wonderful job,' Felix said. 'What was more important, you gave me the chance to get back in the air.'

'And you've survived, thank God,' McIndoe remarked. 'And so have the rest of these fellows.'

He turned with a smile to a small group of men who stood together. Some were in air force uniform, others in civilian dress. All had one thing in common. They bore the marks of McIndoe's surgery. For several, his ministrations had been less successful than with Felix, largely because their injuries had been more severe. One was in a wheelchair, and Merry remembered that Felix had told him he had lost both feet to frostbite after ditching in the North Sea. Another had fingers formed by slitting between the bones of his hands, to replace those lost to the flames. Merry searched their faces, trying to recognise them from the visits he had paid to the ward at East Grinstead. It was no good. His memories were of grotesque figures growing new noses from flaps of skin cut from their foreheads or with features so blackened and distorted that only their eyes were recognisable. These men, though several bore far more obvious scars than Felix, at least had human faces. He knew that a powerful comradeship of suffering had been forged in that special ward at East Grinstead and that they had all kept in touch over the years, and felt a lump rise in his throat as he watched Felix greet each one in turn.

Then the other guests came crowding round. Most were still in uniform and air force blue predominated. There were men who had served with Felix during the Battle of Britain, others he had known in Malta or more recently in Europe. Some now wore the badges of very senior ranks. Two were still sergeant pilots. Tonight distinctions of rank were forgotten.

As they moved towards the dining room Merry noticed that Felix had drawn Richard to one side and was murmuring conspiratorially in his ear. *What's he up to now?* he wondered, but there was no time to speculate further as the party got into its swing.

It was a noisy and bibulous affair. Fortunately, the management had grown used to the excesses of young servicemen celebrating their survival and was prepared to make allowances. What surprised Merry was that Felix seemed to get drunk unusually quickly. Admittedly, they had started with cocktails in the bar and now the wine was flowing freely, but normally Felix could hold his drink better than most. Tonight, as the evening progressed, he became more and more uninhibited and hilarious. Merry put it down to the emotional impact of meeting so many old friends and the unavoidable tension associated with the wedding the next day. The important thing was, he seemed to be enjoying himself.

At length it became obvious that they were the only diners left and the waiters were hovering, wanting to clear the table. As they rose to leave, Felix lurched suddenly and grabbed Merry's arm for support.

'Oops!' he exclaimed, with an uncharacteristic giggle. 'I seem to be feeling a bit squiffy!'

As they made their way through the foyer the talk turned to the subject of where they should go next. A number of nightclubs were suggested and there was good-natured argument about the relative merits of each. When they reached the pavement, however, Felix raised his voice and declared,

.ry, chaps. I don't think I'm up to going on anywhere. Got keep a clear head for tomorrow, you know. Don't want to .ry in the middle of my big scene.'

There was a chorus of dissent. Of course he must come. He couldn't go home this early, on his last night of freedom. In the middle of it Felix clutched again at Merry's arm. 'Take me home, Merry,' he pleaded. 'I feel a bit woozy.'

At that instant, as if by magic, a taxi glided to a standstill beside them and Richard jumped out and took Felix, who was now singing 'Show me the way to go home', by the other arm. Before Merry had a chance to either agree or demur, he found himself in the taxi beside Felix and pulling away into the Strand. Felix twisted round in his seat and waved cheerily to the disappointed crowd outside the hotel. Then he sat back and said, in a perfectly normal voice, 'Well, that seems to have worked very satisfactorily.'

Merry stared at him. 'You're not drunk at all, are you?'

Felix grinned. 'No more than you are.'

'Then why . . .?'

Felix put his head on one side and looked at him. 'I didn't really want to spend my last night getting pissed with that lot, nice chaps though they are. Did you?'

Merry met his gaze and thought he understood.

'Don't get me wrong,' Felix added. 'It was a great night out and I really appreciate the trouble you went to to round up all those old friends. It was wonderful to see them again and have the chance of a good chinwag. But I'll see most of them again tomorrow, and tonight I have other priorities.'

When they reached the flat Merry went straight to the bedroom door but Felix headed instead for the kitchen.

'Fancy a nightcap?'

'No, not really. I think I've had enough for one night.'

'Oh, come on! I'm having something.'

Merry followed him into the kitchen, where he reached into the fridge and produced a bottle of champagne.

'Where did that spring from?' said Merry. 'It wasn't there just before we went out.'

Felix chuckled. 'Why do you think I had to go back for my cigarette case?' He moved to fetch glasses from a cupboard. 'There's a little snack in the fridge, too, if you wouldn't mind having a look.'

Merry looked. 'I don't believe it! Caviar? How on earth . . . ?'

'Chap I know at the Air Ministry is good pals with the Russian air attaché. He was very happy to swap that for a couple of bottles of the old man's good claret.'

Felix loaded the bottle and glasses on to a tray and added a packet of water biscuits. 'Let's go through and sit down. Bring that caviar, can you?'

In the sitting room Felix set the tray down on a low table but did not immediately open the champagne. Instead, he came and stood facing Merry, his expression suddenly serious.

'Before we drink, there's something I want to say.'

Merry put the jar of caviar down, mildly puzzled by the sudden change of mood. 'OK. Go ahead.'

'Tomorrow,' Felix said, 'I'm going to stand up in front of a whole church full of people – not to mention God, if He exists – and make a lot of promises. *For better, for worse . . . till death us do part . . . forsaking all others.*' He gave a faint, wry smile. 'I thought of asking the vicar if I could leave out the last bit. But I don't think he'd wear it, do you?'

Merry felt a lurch of alarm. At this late juncture, Felix was having second thoughts! For an instant his brain raced through the possible repercussions, if he was about to announce that he couldn't go through with it.

Felix went on. 'If I could, I'd be happy to stand up in front of the congregation, in front of the whole world, and make the same promises to you, you know that. But the law won't let me.'

Merry felt as if he had stepped into a lift that was going down very fast. This was not about the wedding. It was about himself and Felix. Felix, with his God-fearing upbringing and his natural honesty, had finally come to the conclusion that he could not make solemn promises that he had no intention of keeping. Now that it had come to the crunch and he had to choose between the safety of marriage and the dangerous, deceptive course that he and Merry had steered for the past five years, he had done what Merry had always feared and opted to return to what society regarded as normality. This champagne and the caviar were not a happy prelude to the wedding breakfast. They were a Last Supper. Numbly, unable to think of any words of protest or appeal, he waited for the axe to fall.

Felix was fumbling in his pocket. 'That being so, I thought we ought to have our own little private ceremony here.' He produced a small box and flicked it open to reveal a gold signet ring, set with jade. 'My grandfather brought this back from China and left it to me in his will. I've never worn it.' He looked up and met Merry's eyes. 'Will you wear it for me, Merry?'

Dizzy with conflicting emotions, feeling as if a hand was clamped around his throat, Merry had to struggle to speak. 'Yes, of course – if you want me to.'

Felix reached for his left hand. 'I'd like to put it on the fourth finger, but that might result in you having to answer embarrassing questions. Anyway, it's really made for the little finger.' He slid the ring into place, then looked up again. 'For better, for worse, my dear, till death us do part.'

For a moment Merry thought his knees were going to give way. The blood hammered in his ears and he seemed to have stopped breathing altogether. The violent plunge into the abyss had left him unable to take in the reality of what was happening.

Felix's gaze became sharper. 'My God, you're shaking like a leaf. What's the matter? For Christ's sake, Merry, what did you think I was going to say?' Then, as Merry struggled to formulate words, he went on, 'You thought I was giving you the brush-off, didn't you. That's it, isn't it?'

'I'm sorry,' Merry stammered. 'You took me by surprise. I didn't know what was going on.'

Felix gazed at him for a long moment, then he put his arms round him and held him close. 'Oh, Merry! What am I going to do with you? What do I have to do to prove that you can trust me?'

'I do trust you!' Merry mumbled into his neck. 'It's just that I know how honest you are. I was afraid you'd decided you couldn't live a double life.'

Felix drew back a little. 'But we've been through all that. I told you, as far as I'm concerned, the only people who matter are you and me and Harriet, and we all know what's going on and agree to it. The rest is just window dressing.' He frowned, his eyes clouded. 'I've made a mess of this, haven't I. I wanted it to be a very special moment for us. Instead, all I've done is frighten you half to death.'

'No!' Merry shook his head vehemently. 'It was a wonderful idea. I'm the one who's spoilt it.'

'Well, let's not let it be spoilt,' Felix said. 'Come and have some champagne.'

Merry held back. 'No, wait a minute.' He raised his hand and looked at the ring on his finger. 'Thank you, Felix. I'll treasure this for the rest of my life. I just wish I'd accepted it a bit more graciously. And I wish I'd thought of the same thing. I'd like to give you a ring in return.'

'Funny you should say that,' Felix said, smiling. He reached into his pocket again and produced a second, identical box. 'Grandfather must have brought two back and given one to Anthony. I found it among his things when we turned out his room. If you'd like, I'll wear this one for you.'

Merry opened the box and revealed a ring that was almost the twin of the one on his own finger, except that the symbol engraved on the jade was slightly different. 'It ought to be one I bought for you,' he said doubtfully.

'I don't see why,' Felix replied. 'I didn't buy the one you're wearing. And I like the idea of them both being the same.'

'Yes, you're right,' Merry said. Now that he had recovered from the shock he was buoyed up on a sudden wave of relief and joy. He took Felix's left hand and slid the ring on to his little finger. 'Till death us do part, my dearest. And may we all live happily ever after!'

They kissed, and then Felix turned away and opened the champagne. As they settled on the sofa side by side Merry remarked, 'What do we say if people ask how we come to be wearing identical rings?'

'Tell them they're the insignia of some frightfully secret Chinese sect,' suggested Felix.

'Perhaps Italian would be more credible,' Merry mused. 'Since we've both served there.'

'Oh, yes! A branch of the Mafia. And we'll get our throats cut if we breathe a word about them.' Felix chuckled happily. 'Have some caviar.'

They ate for a while in silence and then Felix said, 'Do you want any more of this?'

'Not really. But it would be a shame to waste the bubbly.'

'Quite,' Felix agreed. 'We'll take it to bed with us, shall we?'

Richard arrived at the church early, hoping to find the organist and have a brief rehearsal of his solo before the guests assembled. In the event, the only people present were an elderly verger and a woman putting finishing touches to the flowers. Before long, three men in RAF uniform joined him and introduced themselves as old friends of Felix's who had been pressed into service as ushers. Felix and Merry appeared soon afterwards, immaculate in dress uniforms, and while Felix chatted to the others Merry drew Richard to one side.

'Look, I thought I ought to warn you . . . well, not warn, prepare you. It's a bit last minute, I'm afraid . . .'

'Prepare me for what?' Richard asked, with a prickle of misgiving.

'Rose is going to be one of the guests.'

'*Rose!*' The word exploded into the echoing silence of the church and the woman doing the flowers looked round enquiringly then hastily turned back to her task.

'Yes, and all her family. Felix particularly wanted them to be here because they have been very good to him – well, to both of us – over the last few years. I would have mentioned it sooner, but we only heard yesterday that Rose was going to be able to make it.'

Rose and all her family! The words rang in Richard's head. 'For God's sake, Merry . . .' he began furiously, but at that moment a short, plump man came bustling up to them and introduced himself as the church organist.

'You're singing the solo, I gather. Sorry I wasn't able to get here sooner. Have you got your music?'

'Yes, of course.' Richard fumbled in his music case and produced the sheets.

' "I'll walk beside you". Oh yes, lovely piece, very appropriate. Do you want to come up to the organ loft, so we can have a quick run-through – make sure we're on the same wavelength with regard to tempo, et cetera?'

'Yes, yes. Fine,' Richard responded automatically, and followed the little man towards the stairs, casting a look of mingled fury and despair at Merry.

He stumbled through a brief rehearsal on autopilot and by the time he came down to the nave the first guests were arriving. To his immense relief there was no sign of Rose as he made his way to his allotted place in the pew immediately behind Felix and Merry. Out of habit ingrained in him since boyhood he dropped to his knees on the hassock in front of him and buried his face in his hands, but prayer was far from his mind. All he could think of were Merry's words. *Rose and all her family. That must mean Matthew Armitage and whatever children they had produced. How many? They would have been married for – what? – four and a half years? Not more than two children, then, presumably. Boys or girls?* His brain chattered on, like an irritating acquaintance, when all he really wanted to think of was how to escape. He would have to sing, of course. He couldn't let Felix down. But the reception was definitely out. There was no way he could get through that without coming face to face with Rose – and look what had occurred last time that happened. If he hung around after the service, perhaps he could slip out by a side door without being noticed. He would make his apologies to Felix later. Anyway, it was his fault, his and Merry's. Why on earth hadn't they warned him sooner?

There were footsteps and a rustle of silk close by and he looked up to see a tall, fair woman, elegantly dressed. As he scrambled to his feet she extended her hand. 'You must be Major Stephens. I'm Edward's mother. How do you do? Edward has spoken of you often. We're so glad you were able to be here.'

Edward? Who the hell is Edward? Oh, Felix, of course! Aloud he said, 'How do you do, Lady Malpas?'

She shook his hand and then turned away and sank to her knees. Richard glanced at the pew in front and saw Felix bend his head to listen to a murmured remark from Merry and respond with a broad grin. He looked at his watch. Only four minutes to go before the bride was due to arrive. He risked a look behind him but could see no sign of Rose among the congregation. Perhaps she was not coming after all. He drew a deep breath and flexed his shoulders, beginning to relax.

There was a small disturbance at the back of the church and a child cried and was quickly hushed. Richard looked round again, and there she was, looking extremely smart in a sapphire blue coat and skirt, with a perfectly outrageous hat. At some level of consciousness he registered that this was surprising for a farmer's wife, but the forefront of his mind was taken up by the child in her arms. A baby of perhaps six months – he was no expert on such matters. And there was the tall figure of Armitage beside her, taking the child from her. That plump woman following must be her sister, Bet, and there was Mrs Taylor, red in the face and looking breathless. Who were those two boys? Too old to belong to Rose and Matthew. No, those must be Bet's children. No sign of Bet's husband. Probably bought it during the war, poor blighter.

The thoughts ran through his mind in the few seconds it took for the little party to slip into a pew at the rear of the church, so that he could see nothing of Rose except the feather in her hat. He turned away and a moment later the organ struck up Haydn's Trumpet Voluntary and the congregation rose to greet the bride.

Harriet had eschewed the traditional white dress and wore instead a suit of pale green silk and a small hat trimmed with iridescent plumes. Richard looked at Felix's face as he turned to greet her and saw genuine affection and appreciation there. The service proceeded and Richard stood and sat and murmured the responses with half his mind, nerving himself for the moment when he must stand up and face the congregation and somehow find the courage to sing. When it came, his long training carried him through. He had sung naked and shivering in that cellar at Beaulieu, under mock interrogation. He had sung for Massimo Parigi, in front of an audience of German and Italian officers. He had sung on the stage of the opera house in Bologna as the Allied armies advanced on the city. But he had never had to call on deeper reserves of courage and technique than in that quiet church. He fixed his eyes on the rose window at the end of the nave, so that they could not stray to the face under the feathered hat, and put all his heart into the song.

There was no applause, of course. It would not have been fitting in church. But as he sat down he heard a murmur of appreciation from the congregation and knew he had done himself justice. Seconds later, the organ struck up the fanfare at the beginning of Mendlessohn's Wedding March and Felix and Harriet appeared, beaming, from the vestry, followed by the rest of the wedding party. As soon as they had passed him Richard sank to his knees again and hid his face. People might think what they liked, but no one would interrupt a man at prayer. He stayed that way as the sounds of shuffling feet and murmured greetings faded and the organ fell silent. Then, when he was fairly sure the church was empty, he got up and looked round in search of a side door.

That was when he saw her, standing quietly beside the font at the rear of the church. She was alone and there was no sign of the child. Unable to avoid the encounter, he went towards her, feeling that he was wading through air suddenly as thick as water. She made no move to meet him, and her face, dominated by eyes bigger and a deeper blue even than he remembered, was calm. But he saw that her hands were clasped in front of her, holding her bag and gloves, and the gloves were shaking.

In spite of that, her voice was quite steady. 'Hello, Richard. It's good to see you.'

'You, too.' His own voice was thick and he had to clear his throat. 'You're looking very well.'

'So are you. Merry said you were wounded. Are you quite recovered?'

'Oh, yes, thank you. I'm fine.'

'That's good. And you're a major! Congratulations. Last time I saw you, you were just a private.'

'Yes, well, I was offered a commission. It seemed silly not to take it.'

'Yes, of course.' They looked at each other in silence. He took in the changes in her. The old diffidence had been replaced by a composure and an authority that took him by surprise. But she was still beautiful, more beautiful than ever, her skin smooth and her make-up perfect. Again, not what you might expect in a farmer's wife. She had kept her figure, too.

She said, 'I enjoyed your solo. You still have a beautiful voice.'

'Thank you.' He paused, forcing himself to confront the unspoken barrier that stood between them. 'By the way, congratulations to you, too.'

'What on?'

'The baby. Is he – she – the first?'

'What baby? Oh!' She laughed and blushed. 'She's not mine. She's Bet's. Bet's and Matthew's. You didn't think . . . ?'

His lips felt numb and it was a moment before he could get the words out. 'Bet and Matthew? I don't understand. You're married to Matthew.'

'Me?' She stared at him. 'But surely you don't think . . . I wrote to you. Twice!'

'Wrote to me?'

'After you turned up on that New Year's Eve, when Matthew announced our engagement, I knew I'd only agreed to marry him because I thought you had forgotten me. When I realised you hadn't I couldn't go ahead with the engagement. But you disappeared before I had a chance to tell you.' The mask of composure had slipped now. He saw her colour come and go and her words tumbled over each other. 'So I wrote to you, but I didn't have your address. I knew Merry did, and he was staying in our flat in Lambeth, so I sent the letter there for him to forward. Only he moved out before it arrived and I didn't realise until I went back and found it, months later. But by then I had got your mother's address, so I wrote again and enclosed my original letter. You didn't get it?'

'When was this?'

'Oh, let me think. August, September, 1941.'

''41? I was . . . abroad. Oh, just a minute! My parents were bombed out that November. Everything in the house was destroyed.'

'So you never got the letter? You never knew?'

'No.'

They were silent again, gazing at each other. Richard swallowed. 'So, what have you been doing, then? I imagined you settled on the farm in Dorset.'

'Me? I've been working with ENSA.'

'Dancing?'

'Yes, and other things. I've been doing the choreography and looking after the girls.'

'Like Madame back in the old days in Fairbourne.'

'The same sort of thing, but a bit more ambitious.' He saw a flicker of pride in her expression. 'I've done some quite big shows. I had twelve girls under me at one time.'

'Well done you!'

'You've been doing some exciting things too. Merry said you've been blowing up bridges behind enemy lines in Italy.'

'Well, strictly speaking he's not supposed to know about that. When did he tell you?'

'When I met him in Naples.'

'You were in Italy?'

'Yes, at the same time as you. I know you sang in Merry's big Christmas production. I'd have been there to hear you if the Jerries hadn't blown up a bridge, too.'

'You mean we only just missed each other?'

'Yes.' There was another pause. Then she said, 'How's Priscilla?'

'Priscilla?'

'Isn't she with you?'

He felt as though someone had hit him with a sandbag. 'Priscilla's dead.'

'Dead!'

'Killed in an air raid last year.'

'Oh, Richard! I am sorry!'

'No, no! It doesn't matter.' He pulled himself up. 'I mean, of course it matters, to her and her family. But we were divorced long before that. We hadn't actually lived together for months – years really. It was all a terrible mistake, for both of us.'

'Oh.'

He felt as if he were drowning in the depths of her eyes. After a moment she said, 'So, we're both free, then.'

Something was rising up within him, like a sea eagle shaking itself free of the waves. 'Free, yes!' He laughed uncertainly. 'Free as a bird – a pair of birds.'

The church door opened and Bet appeared. 'Rose? Are you coming? The car's waiting for us.'

'Yes!' Rose tossed the word over her shoulder without looking round. 'I'll be with you in a minute.' She took half a step away from him. 'You'll be at the reception?'

'Yes. Yes, of course.'

'We can talk some more then.'

'Yes.'

Bet's voice came more faintly from outside. 'Rose! Come along!'

'Coming!' She moved to the door and looked round at him. 'See you in a bit, then.'

'Yes, I'll see you there.'

When she had gone Richard sank down on the nearest pew. He was not sure whether what he felt was elation or bitter regret. All these years he had imagined she was out of his reach. All these years he had tried to forget her, but without success. Even when he was making love to Chantal, even when he proposed to Priscilla, it had been there at the back of his mind, the sense that if he couldn't have Rose he might as well take what he could get. How different might life have been if only he had not run away, in that bitter winter dawn of 1941?

He pulled himself back to the present. Rose was waiting for him at the reception. Perhaps, after all, it was not too late. He went out into the street and hailed a taxi.

30

By the time Richard arrived at the Dorchester most of the guests had passed the receiving line and gone on into the dining room. He shook hands with Felix and kissed Harriet on the cheek, murmuring words of congratulation with his mind already going ahead of him, searching the room for Rose.

Merry was standing in line, next to the chief bridesmaid, a pink-faced girl whose complexion was not flattered by the shade of lime green that Harriet had chosen for her attendants' dresses. 'Where the hell have you been?' he hissed as Richard shook hands. 'I was beginning to think you'd done another of your disappearing acts.'

Richard mumbled something about traffic and Merry leaned closer. 'I'm relying on you to preserve me from a fate worse than death!'

He rolled his eyes sideways, to the girl, who was engaged in animated conversation with a young officer. Richard grinned briefly. 'I'll do my best.'

He moved on into the dining room, scanning the guests, who were assembling at round tables. He found Rose, on the far side of the room, and was about to cross to her when he heard a squeal of delight from behind him.

'Richard! Richard Stevens! It really is you! I can't believe it!'

Sally Castle, pin thin and vividly made up, wearing an

unseasonal fox fur draped round her shoulders, threw her arms round his neck.

'Darling! It's so lovely to see you. We all thought you'd perished, really we did.'

As he detached himself, feeling the colour burning in his cheeks, she turned to a large man in a civilian suit whose wide shoulders immediately evoked in Richard's mind the newly coined epithet 'spiv'.

'This is my husband, Tommy. Tommy, this is Richard Stevens, an old flame from my days as a dancer.'

'Not exactly an old flame,' Richard protested, shaking hands.

'Not for want of trying, eh?' Sally giggled, leaving her husband to determine who it was who had been making the effort.

As he shook hands Richard saw behind the pair a plumpish young woman, conservatively dressed and leading a small girl by the hand. At her side was a florid-faced man in army uniform bearing the badges of rank of a lieutenant colonel. For a moment the mousy brown hair and demure manner confused Richard. Then he recognised Sally's sister, Lucy. As he was introduced to her husband he found himself looking from one sister to the other and remembering the two flighty blondes who had vied with each other for the attention of any eligible male during that summer at Fairbourne. The contrast now was so striking that he found himself wondering what sort of family reunions would take place over the ensuing years.

Behind them came another familiar figure – squat, frog faced, instantly recognisable. But who was the plump, grey-haired woman at Monty Prince's side? Surely not Dolores da Ponte, the autocrat who had so intimidated them all during their time with the Follies.

Monty seized Richard by the hand. 'Richard, my boy! Delighted to see you! We thought we'd lost touch with you for good.'

'How do you do, sir?' Richard said politely. He had never felt able to be as informal with his one-time employer as some of the others.

'Monty! Monty!' the little man protested. 'You remember my wife, of course.'

Richard took the outstretched hand and bent his head slightly. 'Madame.'

'Oh, call me Dolly, for heaven's sake!' came the response, in a voice that had lost all trace of the pseudo-Italian accent she had once affected. 'I haven't set foot on a stage for six years.'

Richard was about to excuse himself and head for Rose's table when the master of ceremonies banged his gavel and invited them all to be seated. Richard felt a hand on his arm.

'Come along, you're next to me on the top table.' It was the chief bridesmaid, fluttering her eyelashes as she looked up at him. 'By the way, I'm Edward's cousin, Melinda. We haven't been properly introduced but I've heard a lot about you. I loved your solo in the church.'

For a second he was tempted to argue and insist on moving to Rose's table but he realised that it would be bad manners to cause a disruption over the seating arrangements. He cast a look of mingled frustration and apology in Rose's direction as Melinda led him towards the top table and thought he caught a fleeting smile in return.

The meal seemed interminable. During the early courses, Melinda devoted her attention to Merry, who was seated on her other side, keeping up a stream of chatter and receiving more and more monosyllabic responses. Richard tried to make conversation with the bridesmaid on his other side. She was a pale, shy girl with bloodshot eyes and a sniffle, and all he was able to get out of her was that she was a cousin of Harriet's and the flowers in her bouquet had brought on her hay fever. By the time the sweet course arrived, Melinda had clearly given up on Merry and turned her attention to Richard, employing the full battery of giggles and coy innuendoes and flirtatious looks. Meanwhile, across the room he could see Rose chatting amiably with a young man in RAF uniform and an elderly gent with a red moustache and a face to match.

It was a relief when the moment arrived for the speeches. Lord Pembury, Harriet's father, spoke with the confidence of one used to addressing his fellow peers in the House of Lords, and made the expected remarks about the groom's heroic war record and his daughter's prowess as a photographer. He told everyone that they had been childhood sweethearts and opined that, had the war not intervened, they would have been married years ago. All was now well, however, and he was convinced that they were ideally suited to tackle whatever the future held.

The toast having been drunk, Felix rose to reply. At once Richard was aware of a change in the response of the guests as Felix began to exercise the charm that had held audiences enthralled during his performances with the Follies. He thanked Lord Pembury for his good wishes, and for allowing him to marry his daughter, and then added, 'You referred to us as childhood sweethearts. I'm afraid that's not quite accurate. We were chums, that's true, but I never thought of Harry as a girl. She was always one of the lads, and as such not only a pal but a rival. Who was it who always beat me in the pony club races at the local gymkhana? Harry! Who was it who dared me to climb to the top of a particularly tall tree and then had to come up after me when I got stuck?' His look invited the audience to join in. 'Harry!' they duly offered. 'Who was it who always tried to jump the biggest fences when we were out hunting and almost invariably fell off?' The audience, now well primed, shouted, '*Harry!*' 'No,' said Felix, grinning, 'that was me actually. But then,' he went on more soberly, 'one day I walked into the local hop at the village hall and there was this stunning young lady – and at that point I realised Harry wasn't one of the lads at all.' He glossed over their pre-war relationship and passed on to speak of his great good fortune in finding a wife who was the ideal person to help him restore Malpas and the estate after the disruption of recent years. Then he went on, 'There are a great many people I need to thank, at this point, not least all of you for being here today and for your generous wedding presents. We shall, of course, be writing to everyone as soon as we have time. But there are one or two special people I should like to single out for my particular thanks. The first one is the man who gave me back my face after I was shot down. And more importantly, helped to put me back together again mentally as well as physically. A service he performed not only for me but for many others as well.' At this point he was interrupted by cries of 'hear, hear', and table-thumping from the little group of disabled and scarred men. 'Ladies and gentlemen,' Felix continued, 'I should like you to raise your glasses to Archibald McIndoe, skilled surgeon and guide, comforter and friend.' He lifted his own glass. 'Here's to you, Boss, with my heartfelt thanks.'

When the toast had been drunk Felix resumed. 'There is one other name I should like to mention in the same context. Someone else who helped me through those dark days – and they were dark – someone without whose companionship and loyalty I should have found life very hard indeed. He's here now and no one ever deserved the title of best man more than he does.' He raised his glass again. 'Here's to you, Merry, and again, my thanks.'

Richard saw Merry cast one fleeting glance upwards at his lover's face and then drop his eyes to his plate. He could not be sure, but he imagined that he saw a sparkle of moisture on the downcast lashes.

'There is one more thing I want to say,' Felix went on. 'I want to pay tribute to my mother, who has borne up so nobly under two cruel blows. Not only that, but all through these difficult years she has taken on herself the entire burden of running the estate, and done it magnificently. And coupled with my tribute to her, I should like to drink to the memory of my father and brother, both lost to enemy action within six months of each other. I know that many of you will have lost fathers and brothers and sons and friends, so I think it would be appropriate at this moment if we stood and drank to absent friends.'

As Richard rose to drink the toast he felt the tug of tears at his own throat. So many faces rose in his memory. Chantal's first and foremost, but also the noble Dr Rodocanachi, dead in one of Hitler's concentration camps, and Antonia's fiancé, Gianni, who had perished so terribly, and other young men of the partisans, many of them hardly more than boys – and lastly Priscilla, a bright flame snuffed out so near the end of the war.

There was a brief silence as they all sat down again, and then Felix lifted the mood by proposing the health of the bridesmaids. 'They have graced our wedding today and, looking at them, I am quite sure it will not be very long before they find themselves playing the leading roles in another wedding.'

Merry rose to reply and Richard was immediately reminded of the lugubrious-looking pianist he had first met in that dank little theatre at the end of the pier. By contrast with his earlier relaxed cheerfulness, Merry had on what Felix always called his 'Eeyore face' – an expression of world-weary acceptance of the sheer unfairness of life.

'Ladies and gentlemen,' he began, 'it is my duty to thank the bridegroom on behalf of the bridesmaids. At least, that is what the books of etiquette say. But it is my impression that the function of the best man's speech is to pass on embarrassing revelations about the groom's disreputable past.' Here there were encouraging cheers from Felix's old RAF friends. 'I have to tell you,' Merry continued, 'that I have some extremely grave disclosures to make.' The encouraging laughter became slightly less confident. There was something in Merry's expression that worried people. Richard felt a twinge of apprehension. Was it possible that, underneath his apparently happy acceptance of Felix's marriage, he had all this time been plotting a grim revenge? He scanned Felix's face. He was looking up at Merry with an expression of amused anticipation, but the scars on his face had become slightly more visible than before.

Merry continued. 'I have to tell you that the man sitting here on my right is not at all what he seems. In fact he is an impostor.' It occurred to Richard that he should create a diversion of some sort. Faint, overturn the table, shout 'Fire!'. But already it was too late.

'The world knows him as Lord Malpas,' Merry was saying. 'To you, most of you, he is Ned Mountjoy, squadron leader and ace pilot. But a few of us here know his true identity.'

At this point the ex-members of the Follies realised where this was leading and began to laugh and bang the tables. Richard sank back into his seat and felt the sweat break out along his hairline.

'Ladies and gentlemen,' Merry went on, permitting himself

the ghost of a smile, 'you are attending the wedding of one Felix Lamont, also known as Mr Mysterioso, magician and *illusioniste extraordinaire*. Before the war, this man was the best conjuror and magician to be seen on any stage.' (Loud cries of 'hear, hear' from the Follies group. Murmurs of amazement and disbelief from some of the other guests.) 'I recall that one of his most popular illusions was called 'The Lady Vanishes', in which an unsuspecting young lady from the audience was invited to step into his magic cabinet. Harry, if I can give you a word of advice. If he asks you to enter a wardrobe or a cupboard of some sort, don't do it. He wasn't always as good at making them reappear as he was at making them vanish.' There was general laughter now, and knowing nods from those who were already aware of Felix's past career. *You devil!* Richard thought. *You knew you were going to frighten some of us shitless!* Merry went on, 'However, he has surpassed himself today. Not only has he magically metamorphosed into a peer of the realm, but even more remarkably he has reversed his most famous trick and conjured up this beautiful and elegant lady at his side and actually persuaded her to marry him. And this time it is not an illusion.' The applause was enthusiastic and Felix half rose to take a mocking bow. Merry went on to read telegrams, which had come in from all corners of the war zone, and finally to propose once again the health of the bride and groom.

His duty done, instead of sitting down again Merry moved along the table and bent to murmur something in Felix's ear, then left the room. Caught short, Richard assumed. He looked across at Rose again and wondered whether he dared move round to sit with her, but at that moment the master of ceremonies announced that, if the guests would care to move through to the next room, there would be music for dancing.

Felix led Harriet through the communicating doors and as the rest of the guests followed Richard thought his chance had come at last, only to find a hand tucked into his arm.

'Oh, goody! I adore dancing,' said Melinda. 'I hope you do too. I seem to have lost my proper partner.'

Reluctantly, Richard allowed himself to be propelled into the next room, where a band was playing 'Bless You for Being an Angel'. Richard caught his breath and then laughed out loud. On the dais at the far end was a group of musicians, every one of whom might have been found playing solos with the dance bands of the most exclusive clubs and hotels. Directing them from the piano was Merry and on the front of the bass drum was emblazoned the slogan GUY MERRY-WEATHER AND THE MERRYMAKERS.

From the look on Felix's face, Richard guessed that this was as much of a surprise to him, but after a momentary pause he led Harriet down the room and stopped in front of the piano. The band fell silent and Merry announced into the microphone, 'Ladies and gentlemen, Lord and Lady Malpas will now lead the first dance.'

He saw Harriet cast a bewildered glance towards Felix's mother, then comprehension dawned as, laughing, Felix led her to the middle of the dance floor. Instead of the conventional waltz, the band struck up a quickstep. Watching the pair, Richard was reminded of those afternoon tea dances at the Palace Hotel, where he had first danced with Rose. He could hear her voice, uncharacteristically waspish, remarking, 'Well, that dress may be worth a month's wages, but she can't dance. Poor old Felix is practically having to carry her round the floor.' Well, nothing had changed there. It was unkind of Merry to choose that tempo, he thought. Then he recognised the tune and grinned.

Button up your overcoat, when the wind is free
Take good care of yourself, you belong to me!

Other couples were filtering on to the floor now and Melinda smiled up at him.

'I simply adore this tune. Shall we?'

With an inward groan Richard realised that she had taken it for granted that they were partners for the afternoon. He had no option but to lead her on to the floor and, as he did so, he saw Rose on the arm of the young airman, whom he now recognised as the boy who had lost all his fingers. She caught his eye and once again they exchanged rueful, helpless shrugs.

As soon as the first set of dances was finished, Richard excused himself and headed for the Gents. He could not see Rose in the ballroom and hoped that he might find her lurking in the corridor, but there was no sign of her. Returning, he saw her on the far side of the room, talking to Monty and Dolores, but once again, as he started in her direction, his arm was seized, this time rather more forcefully.

'Not too grand to dance with an ex-Windmill girl, are you?' said Sally.

'No, of course not,' he murmured, 'but . . .' Even as he spoke he saw Rose accepting the invitation of another of McIndoe's patients. What was it, he wondered irritably, that made them all gravitate to her? But he knew the answer. It was the softness in those violet eyes which had drawn him to her in the first place.

The next dance was a Paul Jones, where partners moved on after each sequence, but frustratingly the music came to an end when Rose was two pairs away from him. They started towards each other and then Merry's voice came over the loudspeakers.

'Ladies and gentlemen, I'm sure you could do with a breather. If you would like to take your seats for a few minutes, we have some further entertainment for you. You all heard him sing in church, but you are about to discover that he is an extremely versatile performer. Ladies and gentlemen, Major Richard Stevens!'

They had planned it in advance but Richard had temporarily forgotten. Now there was nothing he could do except raise his hands in a gesture of apology to Rose and make his way to the dais. Merry was already playing the opening bars of 'A Nightingale Sang in Berkeley Square'. Richard took possession of the microphone and began to sing in the intimate cabaret style he had learned from Chantal. Letting his eyes rove over the assembled guests, he found Rose's face. Her hands were pressed to her lips as if to suppress a cry of surprise, but as he caught her eye she lowered them and smiled.

He followed on with the song from *Casablanca* that was still on everyone's lips, and which seemed poignantly appropriate, 'As Time Goes By', and then ended the set with another tune that everyone had been humming and whistling ever since they learned it from the German troops – 'Lily Marlene'.

As the applause broke out he turned and murmured a few words in Merry's ear. Merry nodded and smiled and ran through a few chords, finding the right key, then launched into the introduction to an old song that had been popular during the first war. Abandoning the microphone, Richard began to sing.

Roses are shining in Picardy
In the hush of the silver dew.
Roses are flowering in Picardy
But there's never a Rose like you.

He let Merry take the next few bars solo, then, as he approached the last verse, he stepped down off the dais, his eyes on Rose.

And the roses will die with the summertime
And our roads may be far apart
But there's one Rose that dies not in Picardy
'Tis the Rose that I wear in my heart.

She was already on her feet and as he sang the last words he held out his arms to her and she walked into his embrace. Then, as Merry segued smoothly into foxtrot rhythm and the rest of the band joined in, they glided away across the floor, as if they were still in the ballroom of the Palace Hotel, Fairbourne. In that moment it seemed that the six years of conflict and separation had been wiped out, like a child's sandcastle vanishing under the rising tide.

HISTORICAL NOTE

As usual, the main characters in this book are fictional but many of the peripheral ones are real and many of the events actually happened. 'Pat O'Leary' was the *nom de guerre* of Albert-Marie Guérisse, a Belgian doctor who offered his services to the British after the fall of his own country. He was eventually arrested by the Germans and sent to Dachau where he was tortured but survived until the camp was liberated. He received the George Cross and the DSO for his services and died in 1989. Ian Garrow was a captain in the Seaforth Highlanders who chose to stay in France to assist the escape line. He was arrested but later escaped and survived. Dr and Mrs Rodocanachi were Greeks who had taken French nationality. They sheltered many escaping servicemen in their flat in Marseilles, at great risk to themselves. Dr Rodocanachi was arrested and died in Buchenwald in February 1944. Jimmy Langley and Airey Neave were the officers in charge of MI9, whose brief it was to help in the rescue of Allied servicemen. Neave, who was a lawyer by profession, went on to be one of the prosecutors at the Nuremberg trials. He entered Parliament and died when his car was blown up by the INLA outside the Houses of Parliament in 1979. Captain George Black commanded the army's entertainments unit, Stars In Battledress, and Basil Dean was in charge of ENSA.

Those wishing to learn more may like to consult the following:

Stars in Battledress – Pertwee, Bill. Charnwood Library 1993
The Greasepaint War – Hughes, John Craven. New English Library 1976
Showbiz Goes to War – Taylor, Eric. Robert Hale 1992
From Cloak to Dagger – Macintosh, Charles. William Kimber & Co 1982
Special Operations Executed – Lees, Michael. William Kimber & Co 1986
Saturday at MI9 – Neave, Airey. Hodder and Stoughton 1969
Spitfire Against the Odds – Ashman, R.V. Wellingborough 1989